THE START OF A DÉTENTE

Something tilted within him, and Geoffrey gave in to the need that had been building for days.

He kissed her.

It was no sweet suitor's kiss, begun with a slow lean and fraught with anticipation. No, it was a hungry kiss, initiated first by his hands, which cupped Liliana's face in a firm grip, followed by his mouth, which enveloped hers with ravenous desire.

She moaned low in her throat, a velvety sound that shot fire through him. He half expected her to pull away, but instead, she leaned up on her toes, relaxing into his hold and pressing herself against him. She opened to his exploration, allowing his tongue access to her mouth. Her skin was soft beneath his hands, like satin as his finger brushed the tender underside of her earlobe. She shivered in reaction, sending a tremor through him as well.

Sweet Enemy

A VEILED SEDUCTION NOVEL

HEATHER SNOW

A SIGNET ECLIPSE BOOK

SIGNET ECLIPSE
Published by New American Library, a division of
Penguin Group (USA) Inc., 375 Hudson Street,
New York, New York 10014, USA
Penguin Group (Canada), 90 Eglinton Avenue East, Suite 700, Toronto,
Ontario M4P 2Y3, Canada (a division of Pearson Penguin Canada Inc.)
Penguin Books Ltd., 80 Strand, London WC2R 0RL, England
Penguin Ireland, 25 St. Stephen's Green, Dublin 2,
Ireland (a division of Penguin Books Ltd.)
Penguin Group (Australia), 250 Camberwell Road, Camberwell, Victoria 3124,
Australia (a division of Pearson Australia Group Pty. Ltd.)
Penguin Books India Pvt. Ltd., 11 Community Centre, Panchsheel Park,
New Delhi - 110 017, India
Penguin Group (NZ), 67 Apollo Drive, Rosedale, Auckland 0632,
New Zealand (a division of Pearson New Zealand Ltd.)
Penguin Books (South Africa) (Pty.) Ltd., 24 Sturdee Avenue,
Rosebank, Johannesburg 2196, South Africa

Penguin Books Ltd., Registered Offices:
80 Strand, London WC2R 0RL, England

First published by Signet Eclipse, an imprint of New American Library,
a division of Penguin Group (USA) Inc.

First Printing, February 2012
10 9 8 7 6 5 4 3 2 1

This book is dedicated to the loves of my life:

My first love—my mother, Sarah Fry—who taught me what unconditional love is and who always told me I could do anything I set my heart to . . .

My lost love—my grandmother, Gretchen Shepherd—who inadvertently began my love of romance novels when I found hers stashed on the very bottom shelf of her bookcase, hidden behind her recliner. I miss you, Nana, and I hope you would have loved *Sweet Enemy*—even if I would have blushed to know you were reading my love scenes . . .

My lifetime love—my husband, Jason—without whom I would be utterly incomplete . . .

And my special thanks go to:

Mona Snow, Gretchen Jones, Fran Abram and Stacey Long, who waded through so many beginning drafts of this story as I found my way that it bordered on the cruel and unusual . . .

And to:

Katy Madison, Elisabeth Burke and Keri Smith, who helped take my writing to the next level. I couldn't have done it without you . . .

Prologue

Rejected. *Again.* Blasted men—they were so short-sighted. Could they just not see what she truly had to offer?

Liliana Claremont entered the cottage through the kitchen, muffling the click of the latch with her wool scarf. She had no wish to wake Carsons, her butler and all-around manservant. She'd given the rest of the staff holiday since she wasn't expected back for a fortnight yet. But after the Royal Society rejected her paper on the possible isolation of chemicals from plant life, she couldn't stomach staying in London another moment.

She removed her hooded cloak with a frustrated tug. She would have swallowed her pride and remained in Town if the Fellows would have allowed her to attend their upcoming lecture. But the only woman ever to make it past the hallowed doors of the Royal Society had been the Duchess of Newcastle, and she only once. Liliana huffed. She was no duchess, but one would think that being the daughter of an esteemed chemist, she would at least be able to attend a meeting as a silent guest. Particularly since she had the support of his colleague, who'd taken up her scientific education after

Papa's death. *Alas, no.* How would she ever become the first woman admitted to their ranks if she couldn't even get past the threshold?

A loud thump jerked her attention to the hallway.

A frown creased her face. What could Carsons possibly be doing at well past midnight?

A rumbling crash came next, followed by a series of bumps. Almost like books hitting the floor ...

Liliana dropped her cloak and dashed down the darkened hall. Light spilled from the library doorway. Foolish man. Carsons was five and sixty if he was a day. He needn't be moving things, and especially not when there was no one around should he fall.

She flew through the door, scanning the room for the servant. "Are you all ri—" The words died on her lips and shock stilled her feet. She felt her eyes go wide. Books lay everywhere, pulled from their shelves haphazardly like so many feathers plucked from a stew hen. Drawers had been torn from the desk and upended onto the flagged stone floor. The cushions of the settee had been sliced, vases smashed, even plants yanked from their pots, soil scattered around—

A hand clamped over Liliana's mouth and she was jerked back against a solid chest. A sinewy arm snaked just below her clavicle, pinning her upper arms against her body, and her against the intruder. Her heartbeat spiked with her fear and she drew a sharp breath through her nose. *Who? What?* She struggled, fighting to wrench free.

A calloused thumb moved down to pinch her nose, cutting off her breath. "Be still," a rough voice growled against her ear. She immediately complied. As a scientist, she knew precisely what would happen to her body if she didn't start breathing again—and soon. Her lungs screamed and her blood pulsed urgently through her veins in a futile attempt to deliver air to her starving system. Yet he didn't relent.

Finally, as black spots danced before her eyes, the man

released her nose and Liliana greedily sucked air back into her lungs.

"Where does your mistress hide her valuables?" the voice demanded.

Mistress? Liliana's head still spun. Ah, the man must think her a maid. Disheveled and dressed as she was for travel, and given that *she* wasn't supposed to even be in Chelmsford, it was a logical assumption.

He removed his hand just enough to allow her to croak, "Valuables?"

"Jewels and the like."

Liliana scrambled for an answer that might win her freedom. But she had nothing of the sort the thief seemed to be looking for. What would he do to her when he realized? He'd already proven himself a vandal and showed no reluctance to do her harm—and God only knew what he'd done to poor Carsons. Her only hope was escape. "I dunno, sir," she said, mimicking the lower speech of the villagers. "I only just started here round Christmas."

The man made a disgusted sound and started to pull her backward, to God knew where. Liliana tried to remain calm, but she couldn't catch her breath, as the clamoring of her heart seemed to take up all of the space in her chest. Her upper arms were still pinned, but she could move her forearms just a bit. She surreptitiously slipped a hand into the deep pocket of her dress, her fingers curling around the tiny decorative tinderbox she carried with her always, as a means to light candles or lamps or spirit burners in the lab. She flicked the catch with her thumb. Its contents were an experimental mixture of her own creation and weren't caustic to the touch—but if introduced to the tender tissue of the eyes might do damage enough for him to release her. Though it went against everything in Liliana to harm another person, she would do what she must to escape and run for help.

His grip loosened as he tried to maneuver her through

the doorway. It was now or never. Liliana dug a sharp elbow into her captor's ribs, taking advantage of his surprise to pull away. She spun, her other arm coming round as she raised the tinderbox to her lips and blew the powder into the man's face.

"Ah! Christ!" he yelled, his hands immediately flying to his eyes.

Liliana didn't waste her chance. She ran—down the hall, through the kitchens and into the night, not stopping for more than a quarter mile, until she reached a neighboring estate.

Three days later, the cottage was nearly back to rights. By the time Liliana had returned with help, the intruder had fled. They'd found Carsons trussed up, with a wicked knock to the head but otherwise unharmed. He'd been recovering nicely with the tincture she'd concocted in her father's old laboratory, which was now hers.

Liliana ran a dust rag gently over a volume on eudiometry before placing it back in the shelves of the library. As most of the books had been tossed during the ransacking, she'd decided to recatalogue her collection. But the entire episode still troubled her. While she'd heard crime had surged in England since the end of the war, hearing and experiencing were two vastly different concepts. The local magistrate had concluded that her cottage must have been targeted because she'd been out of town for several weeks and credited her with chasing the villain off before he could burgle others, too.

She climbed down the rolling ladder and retrieved another volume—this one on Dalton's atomic theory—dusted it on the way back up and slid it into the stacks. It caught on something, not quite fitting against the back of the shelf. Liliana pulled it out again, looking to see what blocked it, but saw nothing there. She shoved with more force and heard a *click*.

Odd. When she tugged the book out once more, she

saw a crack in the wall behind the shelf. No, not a crack, but an intentional division—a *door*. She must have tripped some sort of lock. Her natural curiosity bubbling, Liliana shoved the books aside until she was able to open the door fully. The space couldn't be wider than two hands square. And there was something in it.

She reached inside and pulled out a wrapped bundle, testing its weight. What could it be? It was light, no heavier certainly than one of her thinner books. Papers, maybe?

She scrambled down the ladder, excitement pushing aside her earlier concerns. Given that Claremont Cottage had been in her family for eight generations, there was no telling what the find might be. *But oh, if it were something of Papa's* . . . Just the thought that it could be sped her feet. She had precious little of him. Only his scientific papers and a few scraps of silly coded messages he'd given her to solve as a game they'd played in the last few months of his life. He'd been taken so young, so unexpectedly—the victim of a vicious attack by footpads. Long before a man in his prime might have thought to preserve his legacy.

She cleared the desk and seated herself, laying the bundle out before her. The plain linen had yellowed slightly with age, but it didn't appear too old—no more than a generation. Her father certainly could have been the one to secret the bundle. It took great restraint to unwrap the cloth gently as anticipation buzzed through her. When the material fell away, two packets of letters appeared, tied neatly with red ribbons. Love letters, perhaps? Maybe even between her parents. Wouldn't that be excellent? She'd cherish a glimpse of her mother, whom she couldn't remember at all.

Liliana picked up one of the packets and untied the ribbon. Silk shushed against silk as the knot gave way. Eager, she plucked the first letter from the stack and began to read:

26 May, 1803.
Spring is glorious this year. None of winter's
gloom dare cling to the air. We were fortunate to
sell many sheep at the Shropshire festival, more
so than in years past.

Drat. Her breath whooshed from her nose as she slumped back into the chair. Not love letters at all, at least not between her parents. Her mother had been dead seven years by then, having died when Liliana was just three.

She skipped to the last page of the letter and found it unsigned. She scanned the others. They were all in the same handwriting, dated between May and December 1803, but with nothing to indicate the author. They weren't even interesting. Full of words but with no real content — just babble about the weather and farm husbandry and such. How disappointing.

She picked up the other packet and tugged the ribbon free. Masculine French scrawl covered the pages. Liliana read, her brow knotting in confusion. These letters had about as much substance as their English counterparts and were also unsigned. Who would have kept such drivel?

She checked the linen and found one loose paper still within its folds. She lifted the vellum. This letter was marked by a broken red wax seal. She flicked open the page, expecting something thrilling — like a treatise on horse manure as fertilizer.

19 Dec, 1803.
We have been compromised. Meet me two days
hence. Same time and location.

Liliana sucked in a breath, choking on her harsh inhalation. December nineteenth? Two days before her father had been killed?

Meet me two days hence.

Her father had *met* someone on the night that he'd been attacked?

Memories of that night flooded Liliana's mind.

Papa was going to love his Christmas present this year. Maybe even so much that he wouldn't take her to task for playing in his laboratory while he was out. Really, she didn't see why she shouldn't be allowed in the lab without him. She was ten now—not a baby.

Liliana pinched the dropper, squeezing fat drips of cobalt chloride into the chemicals she'd already mixed. Her own invisible inks. She didn't know what had Papa so distracted lately. It certainly wasn't any experiment he was working on. He hadn't been focused in weeks. But he still took time to play with her, and for months now, his favorite game had been to leave her coded messages to solve. So she'd decided to create different inks to take their game to a new height. With these mixtures, she could leave him invisible messages and he would have to figure out what chemical revealed them. She couldn't wait to try it.

Footsteps scrabbled across the floor above her. Liliana looked up. A loud voice shouted something, but she couldn't understand the words, muffled as they were by the layers of carpet and wood and stone that separated her from the upstairs parlor. She hastily stored the precious chemicals and then went straight up.

When she came around the corner, her heart squeezed into her throat. Papa had returned? She was caught for sure. But . . . he was on the floor. Carsons was bent over him, calling for a doctor. "Why does Papa need a doctor?" she asked, but no one paid her any mind. She rushed to his side, but when she saw him, she shrieked, recoiling. "Papa?" she asked in a trembling voice, dropping to her knees beside her father. His skin was purple in places, swollen, mottled with bruises, and blood trickled from his nose, his mouth, even an ear.

"—*street thugs, sir?*" Carsons was asking.

Papa's head jerked in a diagonal motion. "Be." He gasped for breath, a rattling sound that sent chills down her spine. "Trade," he mumbled.

"*Papa?*" *she cried, not knowing what else to say, what to do, how to help.*

His hand snaked out, grabbing her wrist. He squeezed hard and she moaned, a hot tear slipping down her cheek. The one eye he was still able to open bored into her. "Find them. At summer."

Summer? *Terrified and confused, all she could say was* "W-what?

"*At . . . summer.*" *His grip slackened, and he slipped into a coma from which he never woke.*

"Be. Trade," she murmured. It had sounded so nonsensical at the time. But . . . she looked down at the letter she still held in her hand. *We have been compromised. Meet me two days hence.* Liliana tested the words on her tongue again. "Be-*trayed*." Tears sprang to her eyes. Her father's death hadn't been a random tragedy. He'd been lured to it. By this note.

She stared at the offensive paper, grabbing the English packet of letters. The handwriting was the same. While they weren't signed, this last had been closed with a seal. A noble seal.

She rushed to her shelves, searching . . . searching. There! She found a dusty old copy of *Debrett's*. Its spine likely hadn't been cracked in fifteen years or more, but it should still contain what she needed. She laid the heavy volume on the desktop and flipped it open, scanning the histories of the noble families of England, looking for the seal that matched the one she held in her hand.

Tonight she'd learn *who* betrayed her father. Then she'd find a way to make sure they paid.

Chapter One

Shropshire, April 1817

He'd never wanted to be the earl, but the one thing Geoffrey Wentworth had learned since becoming such was that an earl could get away with practically anything.

He sincerely hoped that included matricide.

"Let me understand you plainly, Mother," he growled, resisting the urge to brush the road dust from his coat onto the pristine drawing room floor. "You called me away from Parliament claiming dire emergency . . ." He swallowed, his throat aching with the need to shout. By God, he'd nearly run his horse into the ground to get here, aggravating an old war injury in his haste. His lower back burned almost as badly as it had when he'd been run through. He breathed in, striving to keep the irritation from his voice. "Because you would like to host a house party?"

Genevieve Wentworth, Lady Stratford, sat serenely on a floral chaise near the fireplace, as if he'd politely dropped in for tea instead of racing at breakneck speed to answer her urgent summons. Geoffrey eyed her suspiciously. His mother was typically a calm woman, but he'd been known to send seasoned soldiers scurrying with no more than his glare. She hadn't so much as flinched in the face of his anger. No, in fact, she looked strangely triumphant. His stomach clenched. Mother was up to something, which rarely boded well for the men in her life.

"Geoffrey, darling, do sit down," she began, indicating the antique caramel settee across from her. "It strains my neck to look up at you so."

"I should like to do more than strain your meddlesome neck," he muttered, choosing to remain standing despite the ache that now screamed down his leg. He turned his gaze to the older gentleman standing behind her. *"Et tu, Brute?"*

His uncle, at least, had the grace to look chagrined. Geoffrey shook his head. Uncle Joss always had been easily led. Geoffrey knew his mother played Cassius. This conspiracy had been instigated by her.

Joss squared his shoulders. "Now, m'boy, I must agree with your mother. It's high time you accepted your responsibilities to this family and provided an heir."

Hell. So that was what this was about. Well, he wasn't going to fall in with their scheme. He'd nip this and, after a hot meal and a night's rest, be on his way back to London. The Poor Employment Act wasn't going to finish writing itself, and Liverpool wanted it ready to present next month. What was more, Geoffrey had received a disturbing letter that needed to be dealt with. He itched to return to Town to investigate whether the blackmailer's claims held any credence. The note implied that his late brother had been paying the scoundrel for his silence to protect the family, but Geoffrey couldn't believe a Wentworth had done anything treasonous. Still, the threat needed to be neutralized.

"Host all of the parties you want, Mother. I've never tied your purse strings." He pivoted toward the door, determined to escape yet another lengthy discussion about duty. Pain flared through his back and leg. Christ, he'd very nearly given his life for duty. Yet his mother didn't understand that. No, in her mind, duty was defined by one word—*heirs*. "I shall be quite tied up in Parliament for the foreseeable future, so you needn't worry about inconveniencing me with your entertainments."

He'd barely stepped one booted toe into the rose-marbled hallway when her words stopped him cold.

"It is not I, dearest, who is hosting our guests, but you."

Me? He scoffed for a moment before the rest hit him. *Is?* As in right this moment?

The fist in his stomach tightened. The ride to Somerton Park had quite jarred his teeth loose. He'd blamed it on spring rains, but it could have been . . . Hell, it would have taken a *legion* of carriages to rut the road so deeply. He scanned the hallway.

Where were the servants? He'd yet to see one, not even Barnes. Sure, Geoffrey had bounded up the front steps straightaway, but there were always a few maids milling about in the entryway or the main rooms, unless . . .

Unless they were all busy seeing to the settlement of guests.

He turned slowly, his only family rotating back into view. Uncle Joss' easy smile faltered at whatever he saw in Geoffrey's expression, but Mother's widened with a familiar gleam that struck fear into every wealthy titled bachelor in Christendom.

Geoffrey advanced, his boots clicking an irregular rhythm against the drawing room's walnut floors. He prayed his suspicions were incorrect. "What have you done?"

"Taken matters into my own hands," his mother confirmed in a satisfied clip. She stood, her skirts swishing smartly as she retrieved a handwritten list from atop her escritoire. "I have been observing ladies of suitable age, station and character for quite some time now." She waved the list for emphasis. "Since before you returned, even. In fact, wartime is an excellent time to judge one's integrity, at home as well as on the battlefields. It is imperative that the future Countess of Stratford be above reproach." She sniffed, probably expecting him to argue, as his older brother would have done were he still alive. Since Geoffrey wholeheartedly agreed with his mother on that one point, he remained silent.

"Though I'm sad to say we've lost some wonderful candidates to marriage recently, there remains an excellent list from which to choose," she finished, tapping the vellum she held with one perfectly manicured finger.

"Absolutely." Uncle Joss nodded, his head bobbing several times in quick succession. "I've even added a few names m'self. And they are all here on display, just for you." He winked.

Winked! As if they fully expected that Geoffrey would just fall into line, peruse their list of names and pick a wife at their whim. He imagined they intended him to court said wife during their little house party and propose by the end of the week.

Bloody well not.

Geoffrey straightened his shoulders and raised his chin, slipping into the stance that had become so natural during his military life. "I hope you have better entertainments planned for your guests than Catch an Earl by His Nose or I fear they will be sorely disappointed." He again turned to the door, lamenting for only a moment the hot meal and good night's rest he would have to forgo. "As *I* shan't be here."

He strode toward the hallway, contemplating the wisdom of pushing his horse another two hours back to the nearest coaching inn. It couldn't be helped. A man had to stand on principle, after all. He would not have a bride foisted upon him. The earldom, yes. The responsibility of bringing his family back from the brink of financial ruin after more than a decade of his brother's negligence and reckless spending, certainly. But a bride?

Never. Whom he married would be his choice alone. And he had very specific requirements that his mother wouldn't possibly understand.

"Before you leave," his mother called out, her voice still too smug for his liking, "you should know that when I sent the invitations—marked with *your* seal, of course—I made sure to include the Earls of Northumb and Manchester. Oh, and Viscount Holbrooke, I believe, as well as Lord Goddard. They were thrilled to accept."

For the second time in as many minutes, Geoffrey halted with one foot out the door. *She sent invitations using my name, my seal.* By God. Were she anyone else, he'd have her thrown in Newgate. Hell, the idea sounded rather appealing at the moment. How she'd gotten her hands upon the seal when it was kept under lock and key in his study, he didn't know. He'd have to see it moved. But now he had a more pressing problem. She'd invited powerful political allies he couldn't afford to offend. Had she known he was actively courting the support of these particular men?

She must have.

He closed his eyes—embarrassed, really, at having been so outmaneuvered. His mother had managed to arrange this entire farce without even a whisper reaching him. Had he underestimated the French this badly, he'd never have survived twelve long years of war.

As he faced her once again, Geoffrey eyed his mother with grudging respect. Her smile held, but her knuckles whitened as she gripped her list. At least she wasn't completely sure of his capitulation. Geoffrey took some small satisfaction in that.

Still, she'd left him no immediate choice. He knew when to admit defeat.

"It seems, Mother, that you have won the day," he conceded with as much grace as he could muster. He gave his relatives a curt nod and, on his third attempt, quit the room.

Geoffrey slapped his leather gloves against his aching thigh as he climbed the grand staircase to his rooms, one thought reverberating through his mind in time with his echoing footfalls.

But I am going to win the war.

*   *   *

Miss Liliana Claremont fixed what she hoped was an appreciative smile on her face as she viewed Somerton Park for the first time. She found the Earl of Stratford's country home rather attractive, for a lion's den. But then, so was the Colosseum, she imagined.

As her aunt and cousin bustled out of the carriage, Liliana studied the imposing redbrick home. A columned templelike portico dominated the front, forceful and proud. Like the rest of the house, it annunciated the wealth and power of the Wentworth family.

Liliana swallowed. Had she really considered what she was up against?

"Do hurry, girls!" Her aunt Eliza's anxious voice interrupted Liliana's contemplations. "That infernal carriage wheel has made us terribly late. We'll be fortunate if we have time to make you presentable before dinner." She eyed Liliana and her own daughter, Penelope, shrewdly. "The competition for Stratford shall be fierce. It's not often young ladies have a chance to engage him in a social setting, and you can bet those other chits have spent all afternoon turning themselves out just so." She clucked her tongue, reminding Liliana even more than usual of a fretful hen. "We are so far behind already. First impressions, my dears, can be the difference between becoming a Lady or settling for just plain *Mrs.*"

Penelope turned and gave Liliana a conspiratorial smile. Liliana tried not to squirm. Contrary to what she'd led her aunt to believe, she had only one objective in mind here at Somerton Park, and it *wasn't* to lure the Earl of Stratford into marriage.

No. She wanted to uncover the truth about her father's murder.

Liliana reached into the pocket of her pelisse, fingering the red wax seal of the letter that had led her here. An unfamiliar chill slithered down her spine, causing her to scan the many windows of the facade. She had the oddest feeling, as if the house itself knew why she had come and was keeping its eye on her. She gave her head a quick shake at the ridiculous thought.

Liliana hardly noticed the elegant front hall with its Roman pillars and prominent dentil moldings, or the grand staircase, as she rushed to follow her aunt and cousin. Their excited chatter rang off the gleaming marble, but she barely heard. Instead, she struggled for breath as the band around her chest tightened with every step she took into the lair of her enemy.

Still, a surge of excited determination shot through her. This was where she would finally unlock the mystery of her father's death. It hadn't taken her long to realize that those letters she'd found had been in code, but none of them had been in her father's handwriting. She could only assume his side of the conversation was hidden somewhere else.

An unexpected jolt of anguish stole her breath. For a moment she missed her father fiercely, pain slicing through her heart as if he'd been taken from her only yesterday. She remembered his gentle smile, his infinite patience as she'd asked him hundreds of questions about his work, about the world...about her mother. How she'd loved to listen to him talk.

Find them at summer. His last confusing words had often plagued her thoughts. But when she'd learned the seal belonged to the house of Stratford, she'd understood what her father had been trying to tell her. *Find them at summer.* He hadn't said *summer*, as she'd thought, but *Somer.* Yes, the letters she needed to crack his code were here at Somerton Park, and she had just less than two short weeks in the Wentworth house to find them.

Maids fluttered about the airy guest room she'd share with Penelope, unpacking dresses and accoutrements to be aired and pressed. Penelope got right to work on her main contribution to the scheme. Sifting through various evening gowns of muted silk, satin and sheer muslin, she began making selections.

Useless in matters of fashion, Liliana instead unpacked the sketch pad and pencils she planned to use to map out the house. Hers would be an organized search, one she would begin as soon as she could feasibly slip away.

"It wasn't easy creating the perfect ensemble for you on such short notice. Thank goodness Madame Trompeur values our business." Pen let out an exaggerated sigh. "Mother was so excited at the prospect of your being willing to consider marriage, she didn't bat an eye at the added cost for such quick work. It really is a shame to get her hopes up so." She contradicted her words of censure with a grin.

Liliana winced as her eyes traveled over the array of lustrous fabrics and winking jewels. "She really should have known better, given how vehemently I've eschewed every suitor she's presented over the years. I do feel guilty about the expense, however. I intend to pay it back." *Somehow.* The inheritance from her father was enough to allow her to live independently, but only if she scrimped.

Penelope, whose back had been turned while digging through a trunk for matching slippers and gloves, straightened and looked over her shoulder. "Bah, we're rich enough. The entertainment value Mother will get from trying to tempt you to marry will be ample repayment, I'm sure. I don't think I'll ever forget the rapturous look on her face when you begged her to secure you an invitation to Somerton Park. She views this as her last chance to see you properly settled. You know it galls her that your father's will didn't stipulate you finding a husband. I don't think you comprehend what you've let yourself in for."

Liliana groaned.

Pen held a gown away from herself and eyed Liliana as though she were one of the paper dolls they'd played with as young girls, waiting to be dressed and accessorized at Penelope's whim. "Pastels just don't do you justice. A deep blue or a lovely aubergine would suit

your darker coloring so much better." Penelope *tsk*ed,
her blond curls bouncing as she shook her head. "However, as delicate colors are all the rage this season, at
least the lavender will bring out the violet in your eyes."

Liliana waited until the maids moved out of earshot.
"I have no desire to be all the rage. I leave that to you. I
just want to appear as if I'm here to catch an earl, like
everyone else. I'm counting on the machinations of the
other women to keep Lord Stratford adequately distracted, leaving me free to investigate."

Penelope laid the ensemble out upon the counterpane
and turned to Liliana. "And I will do my part, as I promised, out of love for you—even though I'm not entirely
convinced the Wentworths are complicit in Uncle Charles'
death."

"It's the most reasonable explanation, Pen. It was a
letter from someone in *this* family that lured him to his
death. It had to have been a Wentworth who betrayed
him." Liliana swallowed her frustration. She couldn't
blame Penelope for her doubts, since she'd been unable
to bring herself to tell Pen the rest of her suspicions.

Once Liliana had realized that the letters had been in
some sort of code, a hypothesis naturally formed. Though
she had been only ten at the time, Liliana remembered
her father acting oddly in the weeks before his death.
Hurried. Distant. Secretive. The timing was suspect, also.
The Treaty of Amiens had broken down by the time the
first letter was written, and hostilities between Britain
and France had recommenced in May of that year. So
why would her father have coded letters in French *and*
from the late Earl of Stratford, dated well after war was
declared? Given her father's claims of betrayal and his
violent death, the most logical conclusion was that he
and a member of the Wentworth family had been involved in some sort of espionage gone wrong.

But she would never voice such an accusation. Not
without proof. Proof she intended to find before she left
Somerton Park.

"Well, if that truly is the case," Pen said, her voice softening in a rare moment of gravity, "the Wentworths will surely not want their involvement known, so please ... be careful." Penelope turned to select her own wardrobe for the evening.

Liliana clutched a sketch pad to her chest, mulling over her cousin's warning.

"La!" Aunt Eliza sailed into the room, dressed for the evening in a turquoise organza gown, a matching turban covering her hair—a concession to the rush to get her charges downstairs, no doubt. "Why are you trifling with that now?" She snatched the pad from Liliana's hands and tossed it aside, shaking her head as if she'd never understood her niece and never would. Catching Liliana by the elbow, Aunt pulled her to the dressing screen. "You both must get washed and dressed at once."

A maid came around the screen bearing the lavender evening gown Pen had selected. Liliana gave herself over to the hurried ablutions, turning her mind to the meeting ahead.

Penelope had reason to worry. With the current earl's connections to Wellington, he was fast becoming a powerful political figure. He would not want any complicity in her father's death made public. She'd have to school her features well, not betray any emotion or thought. If he suspected what she was about, he'd banish her from Somerton Park without delay.

Or worse. She mustn't forget that. Not for one moment.

"It is as I feared. We've missed the reception line," Aunt Eliza grumbled as the trio pushed their way into the crowded salon. Guests milled about in stylish clusters. The assembly, more female than male in number, certainly seemed energized. Bright faces and even wider smiles abounded. And why not? One of London's most eligible bachelors stood on the marriage block.

Aunt raised her voice over the din. "Some other girl

has probably already caught the earl's eye," she groused, stopping just inside the door. She craned her neck in a frustrated half circle. "I can't see Stratford, but judging by the collection of women near the back corner, I'd say he's holding court somewhere in that vicinity." She nodded her head in the direction where, indeed, a small crowd had gathered. "Come."

Liliana followed her aunt and cousin, turning this way and that as they squeezed between rustling skirts of taffeta and silk. Cloying perfumes—a hodgepodge of orange blossom, tuberose, jasmine and plumeria to name but a few—assaulted her nose. The diverse scents proved quite unappetizing when mingled in the same room. The overly sweet haze wafting from dozens of husband hunters only increased the churning in Liliana's stomach, and she quickened her step, anxious to get her first meeting with the Wentworth family over with.

Though taller than most, Liliana struggled to see over elaborate coiffures and plumed headwear. The slow trudge reminded her of one of her earliest experiments. When she was seven, she'd decided to find out how quickly snails could move. She'd meticulously observed and recorded the progress of six different specimens. They'd averaged four inches every seven minutes. Liliana shook her head as her party inched forward. Those snails would have reached the Earl of Stratford before she would.

She strained to get a glimpse of her adversary amongst the glittering masses.

"—more handsome than his brother, don't you think?" an older woman in the crush was saying to her daughter. Liliana turned her head, drawn to any snippet of information she could collect.

"Wellington himself has said Stratford exemplifies the best of English courage—"

"—almost died saving another man's life," came a whisper.

"How heroic," said another woman with a dramatic sigh.

Heroic. Liliana frowned. The word contradicted her expectations of the man—though she had, of course, heard tales of his bravery.

"Sure, he ruffled a few feathers with that poverty relief bill he championed last season, but all great men have their crusades. He'll step in line, with the right woman's influen—"

Aunt Eliza tugged Liliana forward before she could hear any more.

These women talked about Stratford like he was some sort of paragon.

Liliana firmed her jaw. Well, maybe he was. But hero, saint or crusader for the masses—it mattered not. She would discover what had really happened to her father, even if she had to ruin Stratford to do it.

"At last," Aunt Eliza said as they came to the pastel-clad barricade surrounding the earl. Not to be denied, she dug a discreet elbow in here and there until she broke through, Penelope and Liliana in tow. Liliana drew in a lungful of air and braced herself.

"Lady Belsham, you've arrived." A woman, presumably the countess, stepped forward to greet them. Her smile was that of an accomplished hostess, though not a particularly warm one. The countess was flanked by two men of remarkably similar appearance. As one of the men looked obviously older, Liliana assumed the gentleman to be an uncle.

Her eyes fixed upon Stratford. He stood mere feet away, tall, rigid and oddly detached, as if his mind were elsewhere. Black hair complemented winged brows of the same hue. An aquiline nose lay above long, full lips that Lothario himself would envy.

Stratford devastated her senses—she, who was normally very much inured to the physicality of men. The realization shook Liliana. Air expanded in her lungs, relieving the tightness but doing little to calm the unusual tension that thrummed through her limbs.

She lowered her lashes. It wouldn't do to be caught

staring, though the desire to observe the Wentworths' faces nearly overwhelmed her. Could you see guilt in someone's eyes? And if so, how did you quantify it?

Liliana kept her head politely bowed through the tale of their broken carriage wheel. But her breath shortened and her nerves tingled. Gooseflesh prickled her arms as an urge to flee swept over her like a frigid breeze. She curled her toes to keep them firmly planted.

When she looked up again, Stratford's attention was on Penelope's introduction, giving Liliana an opportunity to settle herself. She couldn't say what she'd expected upon finally meeting the earl, but certainly not this riot of indefinable awareness. She drew another deep breath. All she had to do was get through the moment and she'd feel normal again.

"And may I present my niece, Miss Claremont?" Aunt Eliza said, touching Liliana's elbow.

Stratford's gaze moved to her, and he stiffened. She'd never seen eyes so sharp, so blue. His eyes narrowed and focused intently upon her.

Liliana's heart thumped—hard—then skipped a beat. Claremont was a common enough name. So why was he looking at her so? Unless her arrival alarmed him because he knew whose daughter she was and guessed why she'd come . . . Unease rolled like waves through her.

She affected a small curtsy, as much to compose herself as because his rank dictated. But as her eyes dipped, she noticed the signet ring on Stratford's pinky and her resolve solidified. The Stratford seal was emblazoned on the ring, only inches from her. She was this close to learning the truth. She straightened, snapping her gaze back to the earl.

The man's expression smoothed to one she could not fathom. "Miss Claremont," he acknowledged with a slight bow, his voice deeper, rougher than it had been when he'd conversed with Aunt or Penelope.

Lady Stratford's mouth creased into a frown. And didn't the uncle's eyes widen, just slightly?

A hot flush spread over Liliana's face and neck. Stratford and his family had reacted to her name . . . she was sure of it.

The dinner gong sounded, the reverberating clang startling Liliana. She automatically looked toward the noise. When she turned back, all three Wentworths wore polite, benign smiles. And then they were gone, leading the assembly into the dining room.

Liliana stood still, immobilized by a surreal uncertainty quite unlike her. Had she imagined their responses because she'd expected to see something?

She stared after their retreating forms. Lady Stratford whispered something to her son. Liliana noticed his frown in profile, and her suspicion deepened.

No. If her hosts had nothing to hide, then she would find nothing. If they were guilty, however, she owed it to her father to bring the truth to light.

The question was, if she discovered something of an incriminating nature, to what lengths would the powerful Earl of Stratford go to silence her?

Chapter Two

"Are you sure this is a good idea, Mother?" a feminine voice Liliana did not recognize whispered in the darkness. A ring of glowing candlelight advanced upon her in the hallway.

She flattened herself against the wall, squeezing between an ornately carved Chippendale chair and a massive wall cabinet containing shadowy sculptures and decorative vases within. She silently prayed the navy walking dress she'd donned would be dark enough to conceal her as she shut her eyes and forced herself to hold still.

"Of course, gel," a voice answered, closer now. "Just pretend that you're lost, and being a gentleman he won't be able to refuse..." The voice faded as the women passed round the corner.

Liliana let out a breath at the near miss. She hadn't anticipated that she wouldn't be the only person sneaking around Somerton Park tonight. She shook her head. Whatever—*whomever*—other people hunted was none of her concern.

An image of black hair and arresting cobalt eyes flashed through her mind. An unwelcome rush of feminine appreciation rolled over her as she recalled her introduction to Stratford. He'd been a head taller than any other gentleman in the room, and even with his sleek muscles fully covered by black evening clothes, Liliana recognized that he would be a specimen worth hunting.

If, of course, he didn't turn out to be a traitor. After she'd learned whose family crest had marked the seal, she'd done some research. Stratford's father had been earl in 1803, so the letters had most likely come from him. But if he and her father had been passing—or receiving—sensitive information, who had more opportunity to carry that information across enemy lines than the *current* earl, who was then a soldier moving throughout the continent with his regiment?

Sure that the other women were far past, Liliana slowly felt her way in the shadows toward the central staircase, in search of the library. She was grateful she'd thought to leave her slippers behind. Even in her stockings, she imagined she could hear her every footfall on the cold marble. Her heart sped faster with each step.

After a frustrating half hour of wrong turns and missteps, Liliana came upon a set of double doors. They stood open, revealing only several bookshelves and shadowed furnishings. At least none of the husband hunters thought to lay in wait in the library. Of course, she couldn't picture the ladies she'd seen tonight reading much beyond gossip rags or fashion plates.

Praying for solitude, she slipped into the room and closed the doors. In the oppressive darkness, Liliana made out the lines of a fireplace, cold and dark. Drat it all. Was it really too much to hope some fire remained for light?

No matter. She reached into a pocket of her navy dress, one of several she'd designed herself. While in London, she wore only fashionable pastels. But in the country, her darker dresses were more practical while working in her laboratory and out gathering the specimens she used in her efforts to isolate chemicals from plants to create more effective medicines. Not only could she carry several items in the oversized pockets, but the fabric stained less easily. The added benefit of keeping her hidden in shadow while sneaking around strangers' homes was a bonus she'd never needed or appreciated before.

Liliana withdrew her tinderbox, a taper candle and a holder. She felt her way to the mantel, where she found a jar of spills. Opening the little drawer, she tugged a bit of char cloth into the open and snapped the drawer shut with her thumb. The flint sparked and the cloth began to smolder on the first attempt. Pride swelled as her experimental accelerant flared. She lit first the spill, then the taper.

She looked about. The high-ceilinged space swallowed the golden flicker of her candle after mere feet. The distant corners of the room disappeared into inky blackness. She would have to risk more light. Liliana made her way to the outer wall, where shutters covered the windows, and flicked a latch, willing the wood not to creak.

Moonlight flooded in, illuminating shelves and wall sconces.

Her stomach fell. The main room dwarfed her own study-cum-library many times over. Hers was more the size of *one* of the two nooks that flanked Somerton Park's main collection. She counted the number of shelves around her and swiftly extrapolated. *My God.* She could spend her entire two weeks in here and barely scratch the surface. How would she ever find her father's letters in this enormous manse—much less other evidence to link Charles Claremont to the Wentworths?

Impatience flared, sparked by the burning need to understand why her father had been struck down. She'd always had it—this compulsion to break things down to their elements. To discover the *why* and the *how*. It was what drove her to continue to pursue science, even though she'd been harshly discouraged by her aunt and rejected by the male establishment. And in a sense, it was what drove her now. She *would* discover the truth.

Liliana picked up her candle and started across the room, dodging shadowy sofas, settees, tables and ottomans. The most logical place to look first would be Stratford's desk. Lighting her way with her taper, she found only a rosewood writing desk, with nothing inside but writing implements. Unlike Claremont Cottage, Somerton Park must have a separate study.

Two locked doors cleverly tucked between bookshelves seemed the most promising locations, but she saw no locking mechanisms she might manipulate. She ran her fingers over their seams and tugged on the wall sconces that flanked them, hoping to find a trick lock. She gave up after a time. There had to be another entrance to Stratford's study elsewhere.

She chafed at the probability of leaving empty-handed and returned her gaze to the library. Could Somerton Park's shelves house a secret compartment as her father's did?

She rushed to the first set of shelves, using her taper to light a wall sconce. As leather-bound volumes came into sharper view, she abstained from reading the multicolored spines and instead methodically checked each shelf as high as she could reach. She ran her hands behind the books, feeling for anything unusual—a raised section, a changed texture. Finding nothing, she hurried to the fireplace, where a rolling ladder rested. She braced it in front of a bookcase and climbed, her stocking feet smarting at the hardness of the rounded rungs.

By the time she'd reached the third case, the muscles in her thighs and calves trembled slightly and her left arm ached from anchoring herself to the ladder. By the fourth case, small beads of sweat broke out on her brow from her exertions. If she were wise, she'd give in for the night and start fresh tomorrow.

Then something caught her eye. Excitement charged her blood with a crackling energy. In the very top right corner of the highest shelf, a black leather volume stood out like a crow amongst colorful songbirds. The unmarked binding gave no hint of its contents. Of course, it could be nothing. But it resembled a journal or a ledger book, either of which would surely have a sample of handwriting she could compare to the killer's letter.

A tingle danced up Liliana's spine. She gripped the ladder and scrambled to the top.

The black volume loomed just out of reach. Liliana stretched out her arm in an effort to grasp it. She strained, fingers trembling for a long moment. She gripped a bookshelf with both hands and tried to inch the ladder farther by shimmying her hips in a rather undignified manner, but it wouldn't budge.

Liliana clenched her teeth and looked longingly at the book. She had to know what was in it. Aunt Eliza always said her unladylike curiosity would be her downfall, and perhaps tonight that would prove to be true. Regardless, finding something of interest in that black book was Liliana's only hope to salvage this entire day.

Blowing a wayward curl from her face, she straightened. She raised her left foot and stepped up another awkward rung. She eased her other foot from the ladder, extending her stance wide to rest her toes on a lower shelf. Liliana's heart galloped, spurred by her precarious position. Holding on with her left hand, she reached with her right. Her middle finger brushed the spine of the book, the leather soft and supple. She stretched harder, triumph bubbling into a smile as her fingers slipped between the book's cover and the wood. She wiggled it loose.

A sharp *click* echoed from below.

The ladder shuddered beneath Liliana just as the book came free. She wobbled and let the book drop, clutching the bookcase with both hands. She shifted some of her weight to her right foot, no longer trusting the ladder.

The book hit the floor with a resounding thud.

Liliana strained to look down over her shoulder. Suddenly a bookcase shifted as if trying to open as a door would, but the ladder blocked its path.

"What the hell?" came a muffled voice. The bookcase

moved again, slamming into the ladder this time. A jarring crash rent the air, and the ladder shot from under Liliana.

She shrieked, panicking in an effort to hold on. Without the ladder for support, gravity ripped her from her hold and she fell.

Flailing, Liliana grasped at thin air. She wrenched herself around, trying to catch at anything. She squeezed her eyes shut, preparing for impact.

"Ooomph." A masculine groan of pain followed.

Liliana squeaked as she was jerked upright against something solid and warm, smelling of soap and spice and . . . mint?

Her eyes flew open to meet an equally shocked gaze of indigo blue, framed by thick black lashes. She failed to catch her breath, either from fear or from the fact that the Earl of Stratford's muscled arms held her crushed against him.

It hardly mattered. Breathing was the last thing on Liliana's mind.

In the dim light she watched, fascinated, as those eyes lost their surprise and narrowed in confusion. Then they softened and sharpened all at once. Was that possible? Indigo melted into warm cobalt, a blue fire that heated Liliana from within. She felt his gaze all the way to her toes, which she realized had yet to touch the ground.

She noticed other things, too. Like the fact that she held on to him for dear life, grasping his shoulders, his silky jacket crushed between her curled fingers. That her chest moved in unison with his, her breathing having sped up to the same rhythm. That her breasts felt heavy and soft crushed against his harder, muscled pectorals, yet her nipples had tightened and sent tiny bursts of sensation through her as they brushed against her clothing with each breath.

Her gaze raked his face, long and sculptured, with dark brows that slashed over hooded eyes. The veriest hint of evening stubble darkened his jaw.

Stratford's gaze dropped to her lips. Liliana nervously wetted them, and his eyes flared. For an endless moment he stood there with her suspended in his arms, the lengths of their bodies pressed tight against each other.

Eventually, Stratford released an uneven breath and lowered her to the floor. The intimate glide stole Liliana's breath, the friction tantalizing her, confusing and exhilarating. Her feet touched the cold wood, startling her out of her sensual haze.

But not as much as his words did.

"If you think getting yourself 'discovered' alone with me will win you a husband, Miss Claremont," the earl said, ice in his voice, "you are sadly mistaken."

Chapter Three

Liliana Claremont's gasp of outrage sent her flying from his arms. The sight might have amused Geoffrey ... if he weren't so damned irritatingly aroused. Her shocked expression, the delicate hand spread across her chest in a "how dare you accuse me" gesture. Oh, she was good. No doubt about that. Geoffrey ruthlessly shoved aside the part of him that wondered, given their recent embrace, what else Miss Claremont would be good at.

He exhaled as the burning pain that speared through his lower back eased a bit. He shouldn't have held her so long. Geoffrey willed his discomfort into the background and instead focused on the fiery woman standing before him.

Her eyes sparked, sending embers sizzling through his chest. The flame she'd roused when he'd met her earlier this evening flared back to life. He squelched it.

Geoffrey raised a brow, waiting to see what excuse she would give.

Miss Claremont took a deep breath and stiffly lowered her hand to her side. Her pouty lips opened, then snapped closed and firmed. Geoffrey thought he could actually see her mind working through the accusation he'd leveled at her.

He watched this transformation from accused innocent to affronted angel with fascination. God, she was exquisite—for a conniving little actress.

"I beg your pardon?" Her husky voice sounded purposefully controlled.

"As well you should," Geoffrey snapped. "I thought the chit who tried to corner me on the terrace tonight had nerve." He shook his head. "Not as much as the industrious mother-daughter pair who staked out the hallway to my chambers, however." He glared at Miss Claremont, taking in her dark attire. "But at least *they* didn't skulk around in shadow waiting to pounce."

"I am not skulking," she retorted, her voice high.

"No?" Determined to shed more light on this absurd situation, he snatched a spill from the jar above the mantel, lit it from a sconce, then lit the fire. Satisfied, he faced her.

Her violet eyes still glared at him from her flushed face. Heat streaked through him once more. She was even lovelier in the increased light. The wisps of chestnut hair near her brow had dampened into clinging curls. He remembered how she'd looked a moment ago, when he'd held her close. It was easy to imagine how she'd look in the throes of passion. Too damned easy.

Geoffrey snorted. Probably what the little minx was counting on. "It is common knowledge amongst the staff that I frequent the library at night." He suppressed the need to rub his lower back and instead waved his hand in an irritated swipe. "It would be nothing for an enterprising young miss to ferret out that information and use it to her advantage."

And nothing for me to fall for it, as his quickening blood would attest.

Damn his mother for inviting all of these title-chasing vixens here.

Ever since he'd inherited the bloody title, women threw themselves at him shamelessly. While some men might relish the attention, Geoffrey couldn't. He knew it wasn't *him* they wanted. For once, he'd like to meet a girl who wanted Geoffrey, not the Earl of Stratford.

Instead, he was always on guard. He'd already thwarted two husband hunters tonight. *Third time's a charm* . . . His eyes widened as a sick dread grabbed him.

"I presume your aunt is 'conveniently' posted outside?" He stalked to the entrance, ignoring Miss Claremont's gasp, and wrenched the doors open, determined to set Lady Belsham straight before sending her and her intrepid charges packing, lateness of the hour be damned.

Relief washed through him at the empty hallway, mingled with an odd sense of deflation. He closed his eyes briefly, then turned on his heel and marched back into the library, careful to leave the doors open.

"You couldn't be more mistaken." Miss Claremont's chest rose and fell rapidly. "I did not come here tonight hoping to find you, and my aunt is most definitely *not* lurking in the hallway. Contrary to what you *and* she might think, not every woman's world revolves around catching a man."

Her words hung between them. Geoffrey furrowed his brow. What was her game? "Then why are you here?"

Her eyes darted around. "I . . . I couldn't sleep, so I thought to borrow a book."

"I don't mean tonight," Geoffrey clarified. "I meant, if you didn't come to this party in hopes of snagging a suitor like every other female in this house, why are you here?"

Miss Claremont looked discomfited by his direct question. Geoffrey didn't care. He believed in getting to the point. Life was too short to prevaricate.

He let the silence draw out—a tactic he'd always found useful. He'd learned long ago that most people were uncomfortable with silence. To fill it, they'd blurt out the most revealing things without thinking.

It surprised him how much he wanted to hear what she'd say.

Her pearl white teeth tugged at her lower lip as she scrambled for an explanation. That she didn't have one cemented his suspicions. Naive girl. Any good husband hunter would know to at least bring a witness.

"My cousin desired a companion," she offered finally, with a shrug. "As I thought a jaunt to the country would be ideal, I decided to join her. I understand Somerton Park's gardens are lovely."

He smiled. "They are," he acceded, all politeness, as if her excuses weren't a desperate attempt to salvage the situation. "The woodland and lakes are also spectacular. I do hope you find time to explore whilst you are here."

Her smile faded. "I will."

Geoffrey shook his head. She had to realize he didn't believe a word.

Not want a husband, indeed. What woman didn't? His eyes traveled over her burnished curls, which glinted in the dim firelight, taking in her pixielike face. He held her gaze for a moment before moving to her lush lips, her slender neck. He imagined he could see her pulse beating strongly in its delicate hollow. The dark dress she wore concealed ample curves, but his body tingled as he remembered the feel of her. Miss Claremont should have no trouble finding a husband, beautiful as she was. No man in his right mind would turn her out of his bed.

Just the thought of her in *his* bed made Geoffrey's loins tighten.

"Surely you can understand my *mistake*," he said, hoping his emphasis conveyed his doubt. "I wasn't expecting to encounter anyone here."

On the contrary, he'd wanted to escape the snares of the determined ladies who already hounded him. He'd also planned to go over Somerton Park's accounts again. Frustration had been gnawing at him for weeks. He knew he was missing something in the complicated mess that was the Wentworth finances, and he was anxious to get it sorted. Particularly if the discrepancies he'd noticed might be related to the blackmail threat he'd received last week.

Yet a different frustration swirled around him now, growing with each moment in Miss Claremont's presence.

"Nor was I, my lord," Miss Claremont said, bringing his attention back to her. A delicate pink stained her cheeks, though it could as easily be from irritation as from embarrassment. "And while I suspect it was you who knocked me from my perch," she said, glancing pointedly at the bookshelf, which now stood open to reveal the hidden passageway from which he'd entered, "I suppose I must thank you for your timely rescue, nonetheless." She raised a chestnut brow.

He'd be damned if for a brief moment he didn't feel badly for deigning to enter his own library. Geoffrey tilted his head and narrowed his eyes. She wouldn't turn this around on him so easily. He'd had enough of being manipulated for one day and more than enough of calculating women. Left unchecked, Miss Claremont would likely grow as devious as his mother. Unless someone dissuaded her from that path, showed her she could not play games without consequence.

"I wouldn't offer thanks yet," he murmured. Miss Claremont's haughty expression slipped as he moved to the open doors of the library. Yes. Enlightening Miss Claremont would be a service to unsuspecting men everywhere, and besides, something about the woman tempted him fiercely. He couldn't deny that he wanted to taste her.

And since he was certain no one else was near, he could think of nothing he'd rather do than show the scheming Miss Claremont what happened to young ladies who placed themselves alone with men in darkened rooms.

"What are you doing?" she asked, her voice rising. "Surely there's no need to call attention . . ."

Her voice trailed off as Geoffrey drew the double doors closed. The audible *click* of the lock echoed in the now silent room.

Geoffrey turned to face her. Her eyes shone bright in the low light, and she glanced toward the opening in the bookshelves as if it offered escape. She visibly tensed and shifted on her feet. Good. She should be wary. He smiled as he advanced upon her.

"Why would I wish to call attention to us, Miss Claremont?" he asked lightly, stepping closer as she backed herself against a bookcase. "As I've made clear, I have no intention of being found in a compromising position." He stopped directly in front of her and rested his hands on the shelves on either side of her waist.

Her amethyst eyes widened. With a directness that both surprised and inflamed him, she searched his face. Her gaze dropped to his mouth, and her pink tongue darted out to wet her own lips. By God, the little minx was curious. Geoffrey sucked in a breath, curiosity tingling through him as well.

He suspected if he kissed her, she wouldn't protest. She was nervous, yes, but he could see desire on her face, hear it in her breathing, smell it on her skin—a heady ambrosia that drew him. He leaned in closer and inhaled her scent. Apples and . . . lemon verbena? Unfamiliar with women's fragrance, he could be sure only that she smelled clean and crisp.

Miss Claremont's voice snagged as she asked, "A-and this is not compromising, my lord?"

"Ah," he drawled, "that is the rub." He brought one hand up to her nape, using his thumb to caress her cheek and jaw, steeling himself against the jolt of pleasure he received just from touching her. She would be the one learning a lesson here tonight, not him. "To be well and truly compromised in society's eyes, my dear, one has to have a witness."

Her eyes flew to his, uncertainty lightening them a shade to the most alluring lilac.

"As there is no one here but you and I," he whispered, "I could taste you." He brushed his lips against hers in a light caress. She trembled but did not jerk away. "Touch you," he murmured, trailing a finger down her neck to nearly graze the swell of her bosom before detouring to her delicate collarbone. Her chest hitched beneath his touch. "Anywhere," he purred as he took her lips in a kiss meant to scandalize.

Geoffrey swallowed her surprised gasp, coaxing her lips open with little effort. Apples and lemons enveloped him. Christ, he'd never get the scent of her out of his memory.

She accepted his tongue with a hesitation that told him she'd never been kissed. His instincts whispered to hold back, but then she returned the kiss with a fervor that fired his blood.

He couldn't stop his hand from sliding into her silken hair, tugging it from its pins as he luxuriated in the feel of her tresses. His other hand held her still so he could explore her mouth fully. He couldn't get enough, couldn't get . . .

Only when he heard his own moan did Geoffrey recall where he was, and with whom. He sucked a deep breath through his nose and gentled the kiss.

He wasn't a cad, after all. He just wanted to teach her a lesson in managing men, particularly him: *Don't even try it.* He indulged himself with one last lingering taste, then stepped back from Miss Claremont, shaken at how ragged his breathing still was. He couldn't let her see how she affected him. He waited until she opened her dazed eyes and smiled grimly.

"I can do all that and still not have to marry you in the morning," he stated flatly.

Her gasp felt like a slap, so much so that Geoffrey grimaced.

She raised a trembling hand to her lips, her eyes accusing. The confusion and hurt Geoffrey saw in her expression stilled him, taking the edge off of his righteous anger. Damn, but she looked so innocent. Could he have been wrong about her intentions?

She lowered her arm, eyes narrowing as her hands fisted at her sides. "You scoundrel," she uttered, low.

Geoffrey stood up straighter and gave her a curt nod. An apology formed on his lips just as a sharp spasm clinched his back, turning his words into an involuntary grunt of pain.

Miss Claremont's eyes widened and her head tilted slightly to the side. Her gaze took on an assessing look he didn't care for.

Now that his mind had once again seized upon the pain from his war injury, it sharpened. Geoffrey gritted his teeth, struggling to give no other outward sign of his discomfort. He needed to get off of his feet. He needed a drink. He needed Miss Claremont to leave.

"Just so," he clipped. "Now, I suggest you return to your room. Un—" Another spasm seized him, stealing his breath. "Uncompromised."

The euphoria that had coursed through Geoffrey while he'd kissed her quickly lost its hold as pain overrode his senses. He tried to relax the knotted muscles around his lower back, praying she quit the room before he disgraced himself by groaning aloud.

But she didn't. Rather, she opened her mouth, seemed to think better of it and closed it again. Did she plan to give him a much deserved set down? Well, he bloody well wished she would get on with it and leave.

Instead, she uttered a disgusted sigh. "I hurt you when I fell from the ladder, didn't I?"

Surprise lanced through him as surely as the burn speared through angry muscle. Whatever he'd expected her to say, it wasn't that. Still, the last thing he needed was a rush of female pity right now. "I assure you, I am well—," he said, only to be cut off as she stepped near and raised her hand to his brow. Her cool fingers barely skimmed his skin, bringing gooseflesh followed by a rush of heat.

"I recognize the signs of pain," she murmured, her eyes on his briefly before sweeping him. "Your pupils are dilated more than the dim light accounts for and your skin is slightly clammy and cool to the touch despite your proximity to the fire."

Her hand trailed down his neck, where she pressed gently. He swallowed, hard.

"Your heartbeat is still accelerated. Intoxication would cause such symptoms," she said, removing her hand from him. "Yet judging from your reflexes as you caught me and the fact that I—" Her face turned nearly crimson in the firelight. "I ... tasted no liquor on your lips, you aren't the least bit intoxicated."

He glanced at the decanter of brandy on the mantel, relief so tantalizingly close, yet so far away. "Not yet," he grumbled.

Miss Claremont cleared her throat. "Well, while you don't deserve it after behaving like such a ... such a ... *bounder*," she said, finally settling on an insult, "I can't, in good conscience, let you continue to suffer when you injured yourself catching me. Not when I can help."

Geoffrey snorted. Why wouldn't the woman just leave, so he *could* get intoxicated? It was the only thing he knew that would dull the agony. "*You* can help? What are you? Some kind of debutante doctor?"

Miss Claremont's violet eyes flashed and her lips pursed. "Something like that."

"I appreciate your concern, but it is nothing that won't be fine by morning. Now, go back to your room."

She stared at him a long moment, a frown pulling at the corners of her lips. And yet she also looked vaguely ... relieved. "If you insist, my lord."

Geoffrey relaxed his stance as he watched her walk away, grateful he'd soon be alone.

Miss Claremont paused beside the bookcase nearest the passageway opening and bent to retrieve something.

His gaze followed her movement. He saw a book, lying open, cover up, on the floor. Oh yes. He'd thought he'd heard a thud right before she'd landed in his arms. As she picked it up, he squinted his eyes to see which volume had so interested Miss Claremont that she'd risked climbing a rolling ladder in the dark to reach it.

He blanched when he realized what she'd chosen. Had she known what she was pulling from the shelf? Alarm clenched his gut. Had she looked inside it yet? God, he hoped not. He should have removed that book years ago. "Miss Claremont," he barked.

She ignored him, quickening her step.

His lower back throbbed as he limped after her. She reached out to unlock the double doors as if she hadn't heard him. "Miss Claremont," he bellowed. "Halt!"

She jerked to a stop, her shoulders stiff. Geoffrey grimaced, regretting his authoritative tone. He stopped beside her. Moonlight washed her face pale and she kept her expression blank and controlled. He *was* a cad, an ogre even, not to let her escape the library with what dignity she had left after he'd trapped her, kissed her and then so harshly rebuffed her offer of help, but he couldn't allow her to take his brother's private volume. She had no business seeing anything it contained.

"I'm sorry," he said as he held out his hand. Miss Claremont surrendered the book easily, much to Geoffrey's relief. She wouldn't look at him, but her hand trembled minutely as she withdrew it. His remaining anger deflated. "Might I assist you in choosing another book?"

She turned her head to him then. Her face was as cool as the sea off Cornwall, yet her eyes blazed purple fire. "No, thank you, my lord," she said bitingly. "I find I no longer care for your *library*, or anything in it." She took a deep breath and swung open the doors. "You shan't find me here again." She marched off in the direction of the central hallway.

Geoffrey scowled at her retreating form for a moment, then pulled the doors closed. He limped back to the fireplace, stopping at the tray that held the brandy.

He laid his brother's book on the mantel, grasped the decanter and poured.

He knew from experience that he'd need more than a couple of drinks to dull the pain before he could stretch out his gnarled muscles enough to sleep. He threw back another glass and settled into the wingback chair near the crackling fire.

"You ass," he said aloud, shaking his head. His behavior had been deplorable. This damned house party had him on edge. Yet he couldn't deny the thrill he'd felt with her in his arms and at the awareness he'd seen form in her eyes. He breathed in her scent, which still clung to him. What a pleasure it would be to awaken Liliana Claremont's passion.

Geoffrey caught himself. "Watch out, old boy," he said, taking another swallow of brandy. *That* was the pleasure of a husband.

He pictured his mother's smug face earlier this afternoon when she'd sprung this ordeal upon him, and his fingers tightened around his glass.

What the hell had he been thinking, taking such a chance with Miss Claremont? The countess would have invited women cut from the same cloth as herself. Miss Claremont might have shown compassion because she thought she'd caused his injury, but no doubt on the morrow she would find a way to use his foolish actions to her advantage. Damn.

After several drinks, his pain and guilt receded on a brandied cloud and his mind returned to her. He'd have to apologize, of course. And then he'd determine what the delectable chit's real intentions were toward him and nip them if he must.

Because he'd hang before he married *anyone* attending his mother's bloody little house party.

Chapter Four

Liliana peeked around the corner of the upstairs family wing, looking to see if any servants still hung about. She saw nothing but the late-morning sun streaming in through the massive mullioned windows.

She'd spent most of her morning looking for another way into Stratford's study while maids had tidied the family suites and the private parlors. Now she intended to try her luck searching them.

She stifled a yawn. *Curse Stratford,* she thought for the umpteenth time this morning. Her fatigue could be laid squarely at his arrogant, self-righteous feet. After their little encounter, she'd hardly slept a wink. She tried the first door handle but found it locked.

What a blasted fool she was. How could she blurt her true feelings about not wanting a husband? Stratford had given her the perfect excuse for her presence, both in his library and at Somerton Park, when he'd accused her of setting out to trap him. Why hadn't she leapt on it?

Liliana released a tight breath as she tried the next door handle to no avail. *Because I don't think well on my feet.* She preferred things to go as planned, and when they did not, she needed time to process.

And then she'd gone and drawn more attention to herself because she couldn't bear to see the man suffering on her account. Yet an entire sleepless night spent evaluating her actions—and his—left her more troubled than resolved. He'd seemed awfully sincere in his belief that she was just one of the many females out to land him. Perhaps he hadn't connected her to her father. Perhaps he didn't suspect her true motives at all.

Liliana groaned. If he hadn't before, he very well might now. Considering their disastrous encounter it had become imperative to avoid him at all costs.

A scuffling sound drew Liliana's attention. Her muscles tensed and she held her breath, listening. A rhythmic scraping, like slippers on wood, raced up the stairs at a hurried pace. A loud creak sounded from one of the upper steps. Drat—if she were caught again, she'd certainly be exposed!

Liliana shot down the hall, hoping to make it around the corner before a maid or housekeeper emerged. She jerked left into a tiny nook and jiggled the door handles on either side, but neither would give.

Blast. But she wasn't caught yet. She tucked herself as tightly into the corner as she could manage, praying the servant had no reason to venture this far.

The footsteps persisted, getting closer, and Liliana stopped breathing.

"Psssst." The harsh whisper sounded familiar. "Lily, are you up here?"

Relief poured through Liliana. "Penelope?" The stricture in her throat eased. She stepped around the corner to see her cousin looking quite out of sorts. A blond ringlet had slipped from Penelope's normally perfect coiffure, and she struggled to catch her breath from the quick upward flight.

"There you are!" Penelope gasped. "I've been searching for you everywhere." She rushed forward, grasped Liliana's hand and started tugging her back toward the stairs.

"Why?" Liliana asked, allowing herself to be pulled along. "And where are we going in such a hurry?"

"Back to our room," Penelope answered over her shoulder. "I just hope we're not too late. I know I promised to cover for you should you be missed, but even I can't help you now."

Had Stratford told Aunt Eliza about last night? That was the only reason for Penelope to be so upset.

"Too late for what?" Liliana demanded, her chest tight.

"Mother is on her way up to our room right now to fetch you."

"Fetch me?"

"Yes. Now that Mother knows Stratford is interested in you, she won't let you alone for a moment," Penelope said. "And if you're not in your bed, sick, *like I told her you were*, there will be a lot of explaining to do."

"What?" Liliana asked, confused. She jerked to a stop, her grip on Penelope's hand pulling Pen up short as well. "What are you talking about?"

"Stratford," Penelope snapped, as if it were Liliana's fault she didn't understand. "He came up to Mother and me after the morning festivities. He asked about you. He seemed particularly concerned with your *whereabouts*."

Thank goodness. He hadn't told after all. Liliana smiled and released a breath before the real worry grabbed her. "Why would he do that?" She grimaced, berating herself. She'd been a fool last night, too careless, too loose with her tongue. *In more ways than one.*

"I don't know." Penelope tilted her head, her heart-shaped face etched with concern. "Do you think he's onto you?"

Probably. "No," Liliana assured her. "Of course not. I've given him no reason to look twice at me."

Penelope stared hard for a moment, and Liliana did her best not to squirm. She never could get one past Pen. "Well, whatever the reason, Mother's convinced Stratford is smitten with you," Penelope tossed over her shoulder as she resumed their pace.

"That's absurd," Liliana exclaimed as they exited the

stairs and made their way to their door. Despite her words, something that could only be described as excitement ran through her, pooling in unfamiliar places that left her feeling unsettled and . . . unsatisfied. She frowned.

"Nevertheless," Penelope said as she bustled Liliana inside the still empty room, "she's determined to take advantage." She finally let loose of Liliana's hand and skirted around behind her. "I warned you that by not telling Mother your true reasons for accepting this invitation, you were giving her tacit approval to matchmake," Penelope scolded, quickly unbuttoning the back of Liliana's dress. "I told you that you didn't comprehend what you were letting yourself in for."

Liliana stepped out of the garment, which Penelope snatched up and draped over a cream armchair.

"You know I couldn't tell her the truth," Liliana defended, the familiar anger simmering through her. Aunt would prefer to pretend that her brother and his unorthodox wife never existed. Aunt had always considered it an embarrassment that Liliana's mother had flouted convention and practiced as a healer . . . and that her father had allowed it. Maybe that's why the woman had always tried so hard to change her, to erase her parents' influence—causing Liliana, in turn, to fight harder still to carry on their work, to not let her parents' memories die.

Her fingers fumbled as she undid her garters and rolled her stockings off. "Besides, Aunt never would have agreed to fund this trip if she didn't think I was serious about finally finding a husband." She reached for the thin nightgown Penelope held and yanked it over her head. "I didn't think she'd aim so high. I'm virtually on the shelf, for goodness' sake. I'd rather hoped she would focus her efforts on snagging Stratford for you." *And ignore me.*

Penelope huffed. "Oh, wonderful. Throw me to the wolves."

"You know that's not what I meant," Liliana replied as she climbed into bed, settling herself under the covers.

Penelope waved a hand. "Of course. Poor Mother ... when she learns that I've set my cap for a mere baron, she'll likely have an apoplexy. With all of these hasty preparations, I don't think I've had the chance to tell you, but I met Michael in the park the afternoon before last and he—"

The doorknob turned sharply, and Pen's mouth snapped shut. She dropped into a chair just as Aunt Eliza pushed into the room.

"Good afternoon, Mother," Penelope chirped, a little too enthusiastically.

"Good afternoon, Aunt," Liliana parroted, quite feebly.

"It is precisely that ... *afternoon*." Aunt Eliza's green gaze pinned Liliana. "An entire morning wasted. Gentlemen have been arriving in a steady stream whilst you lie about and let the other girls have the advantage. Of course"—her voice dropped in tone and volume—"so far I have been less than impressed with the quality of prospects. Only a handful of titles amongst them, and very little in the way of fortune." She *tsk*ed, staring thoughtfully at a point behind Liliana and Penelope both. "Several are quite old," she remarked, "and there is at least one or two who I am certain are not even persuaded toward ..." She blinked, catching herself before saying something Liliana was sure would have been quite interesting.

Aunt Eliza clapped her hands sharply and crossed toward the bed, looking down on Liliana. "Never mind that, as it appears *you* have already caught Stratford's attention, my dear—and he, the best catch here!" Aunt's pinched face broke into a rare smile of approval.

Liliana returned the smile weakly.

"I see you are still flushed," Aunt Eliza observed. Her expression softened as she reached out a hand to touch

Liliana's face. She motioned for the family's longtime servant, Mrs. Means, to enter the room.

Liliana relaxed and blew out a wan breath. Perhaps she could play on Aunt Eliza's sympathy and buy herself more time. "I'm afraid I'm not up to going out this afternoon," Liliana said. She touched her own hand to her forehead. "I'm still not quite well."

Aunt Eliza snapped her fingers. Mrs. Means scurried over and handed Aunt a silver cup. "Pish. This is a campaign, my dear, and our adversaries will not rest on their laurels. You haven't the time to be unwell." Aunt swirled the cup, agitating a sluggish brown liquid. A foul smell wafted and Liliana's nose twitched. "Mrs. Means has prepared a tonic that will have you feeling up to snuff in no time."

Liliana shook her head, turning away from the offensive offering. Even she, with all of her experience with healing herbs and tinctures, was unable to discern what made up that sludge. She slid off of the bed to escape Aunt Eliza's ministrations but didn't make it far.

Aunt grasped Liliana's shoulder, pressing her down onto the embroidered stool of the vanity. "We shall have to place you in Stratford's path at every opportunity," she said as she plopped the tonic in front of Liliana, the silver cup clicking against the wood.

Liliana's stomach clenched. That was the *worst* thing they could do. She opened her mouth to protest. "I—"

"First, we must ensure Stratford stays entirely focused on you." Aunt Eliza took in Liliana's appearance as if evaluating which slice of beef to serve Prinny himself. She snapped her fingers again, and Mrs. Means stepped behind Liliana, vigorously taking a brush to her hair. "We shall turn you out beautifully. Penelope?"

"Yes, Mama?"

"Fetch the light blue striped muslin," Aunt said, "and the sapphires, I should think. Oh, and the matching parasol and gloves. We shall be out of doors this afternoon."

Liliana could hear Penelope rummaging through the armoire. "Surely tomorrow will be soon enough for me to join the group," she argued, swiping at the brush. She'd worry about how to get out of tomorrow's activity tomorrow.

"Stratford inquired about you *today*," Aunt Eliza said, her lips firming. "That means you are on his mind, but you won't be for long if we don't get you down there. By tomorrow, this afternoon even, another could have taken your place. Particularly Emily Morton," Aunt Eliza murmured thoughtfully, tapping a finger to her lip. "Yes, she is quite persistent and rather lovely."

Liliana caught Penelope trying to contain a sympathetic smile and failing miserably.

Mrs. Means swept Liliana's curls into an artful coiffure, efficiently pinning it into place.

Liliana tried one last tack. "I'm sure you make too much of Stratford's interest, Aunt. I'd wager he was only showing a host's concern over the welfare of an ill guest."

"Young ladies don't wager," Aunt scolded automatically, then flashed a triumphant smile. "Yet you would lose. The Northumb girl did not show this morning, either, and I heard nothing of Stratford asking after her." Aunt Eliza reached out and pinched Liliana's cheeks. "I don't know how you did it, but you've definitely caught his interest, gel," she said slyly.

Liliana's fake illness quickly became real. This was not going at all how she'd planned.

In short time, she was stuffed into the full-skirted round dress. Aunt Eliza slapped a blue parasol into Liliana's hands as she was pushed toward the door. She could see no way out.

Fine. She'd give in—for now. She needed to determine exactly why Stratford was suddenly interested in her. And when Aunt Eliza wasn't watching, she'd do everything she could to ensure she *lost* the earl's attentions.

Only then could she resume her search.

*   *   *

Aunt Eliza hurried Liliana and Penelope down wide stone stairs and through a small courtyard surrounded by a living wall of hawthorn. A break in the tiny lace-work flowers opened to an expanse of parkland just east of the house, where the tinkle of laughter and glassware rang on the air.

As they breached the hedgerow, Aunt slowed their pace to a leisurely stroll. Liliana scanned the assembly. It seemed the entire household had turned out for the al fresco event, along with several new faces. Everyone smiled easily into the pleasant sunshine. Round tables covered with flowing linens and fresh flowers were scattered beneath a grove of trees.

Chaises had been brought out as well, and several matrons had taken their spots in the shade, but the majority of guests milled around an open field to Liliana's right. Ladies in their lavender and pink and pale yellow dresses stood out on the green lawn like so many Easter eggs collected in a giant's basket. They gathered in small groups, twirling their matching lacy parasols, gossiping. They flirted coyly with passing gentlemen while angling for position to watch what appeared to be a sporting exhibition.

Liliana's steps faltered, overwhelmed as she was by the conviction that she didn't belong in this world. She'd never wanted to be part of these impractical pursuits, this superficial society that Aunt Eliza forever pushed upon her. Her father had understood that, had encouraged her to follow where her mind would lead. Whereas Aunt Eliza had always maintained that Liliana would outgrow her silly love of medicinal science and settle into a life more appropriate for a young lady. A fierce ache pierced her for all that she'd lost.

"Come along," Aunt said, reaching back to capture Liliana's elbow. "We're just in time." Aunt wove them through the crowd with the expertise of one long accustomed to navigating a crush. When they emerged from the pastel swarm, Liliana caught her first glimpse of Stratford since his shocking "lesson" in propriety.

Discomfiting ripples of heat flowed from her middle straight through to the tips of her fingers and toes. Odd, but it was as if she could feel him against her even now. She hadn't been surprised by the curiosity that had gripped her when she'd given in to his kisses—after all, she was nothing if not inquisitive. Any good scientist worth her sodium chloride was.

But what still heightened her every nerve until she thought she'd go mad with wanting? What elemental force made her physically desire a man whom she not only did not know but could never trust?

Chemistry. That's what they called it, but chemistry unlike any *she'd* ever studied. As blood rushed to her cheeks, she drew a calming breath, trying to force the infernal blush to subside. Stratford didn't deserve the satisfaction of knowing he unnerved her.

He stood with several gentlemen, conversing casually, a half smile playing about his lips. Like a handful of other men, Stratford wore no coat and was instead dressed to compete in sport. He'd donned tawny breeches and a plain cotton shirt that opened at the throat to reveal the strong column of his neck. Liliana swallowed in time with him, her eyes fixed upon the bob of his Adam's apple.

She flushed, feeling foolish. *Ninny*. One couldn't expect men to battle one another frilled up in cravats, now, could one?

The bright of day did little to diminish Stratford's darkly sensuous appeal. Why should *he*, of all men, draw her so? Whatever the reason, she couldn't deny that Stratford affected her as no other had. Although she longed to scorn him after last night's humiliation, a part of her yearned to explore this appalling attraction, and that was as impossible as it was shameful.

Aunt Eliza stopped as she, Liliana and Penelope neared the marked field—directly in Stratford's line of sight. Very craftily done, indeed. Aunt was rewarded when Stratford pulled away from his companions and started toward them.

Liliana tamped down her anxiety. He hadn't informed Aunt Eliza that he'd caught Liliana out of her room last night, but would he now? Was he only waiting to dress her down in public to complete her lesson? Her gaze latched onto his face, searching for any indication of his thoughts, but his chiseled features revealed nothing.

"Good afternoon, Lady Belsham, Miss Belsham," Stratford greeted as he joined them. He insinuated himself right next to Liliana.

She shifted uncomfortably, his presence overwhelming and subtly charged. Liliana caught a hint of mint—wintergreen, and stronger than it had been last night.

"Miss Claremont," he said, turning his vivid blue eyes to her. "I am relieved to see you looking so well." He gave her a practiced smile. "My compliments on your fetching ensemble." He lowered his head, his voice rumbling against her ear. "Much better suited for catching a husband than your dress of last night," he murmured.

His warm breath brushed against Liliana's neck. Her ears turned hot with a mixture of confusion and rising ire. Did he mean he *knew* she wasn't hunting a husband last night in her drab, dark attire? Or did he mean he still thought her a husband hunter, only much improved by a wardrobe change? Either way, she should be offended. She opened her mouth to set him down, but Aunt Eliza's encouraging smile stopped her. "Why, thank you, my lord," Liliana said sweetly, loud enough for Aunt to hear. "It's so kind of you to notice." She turned to Stratford and muttered low, "Too bad your manners don't extend to private company."

His facile smile slipped. "We need to talk," he whispered. He turned back to Aunt Eliza. "Lady Belsham, might I steal your niece away for a stroll?"

Aunt beamed. "Of course." She nodded at Liliana. "If you feel up to it, my dear?" All three pairs of eyes turned to look at her expectantly.

Liliana dearly wished to say she most certainly did *not* feel up to it—that she'd rather walk with the devil. As he stood there with his dark good looks, she decided he might very well *be* Lucifer. Was that jab about catching a husband designed to put her at ease, lull her into thinking he didn't know why she was here? Why did he *really* wish to talk with her?

He raised an impatient black brow in challenge, and Liliana narrowed her eyes. He *knew* she didn't want to go anywhere near him, blast him. He also knew she couldn't risk him opening his mouth about last night.

He offered his arm.

Aunt Eliza discreetly cleared her throat.

Liliana cursed under her breath. "A stroll would be lovely."

Chapter Five

Geoffrey clasped Miss Claremont's slender hand and tucked it securely in the crook of his arm. For a moment, it seemed she might snatch it back, but after a brief hesitation she settled her gloved fingers on his forearm. Yet her annoyance broke over him in waves.

He swam in dangerous waters. He'd behaved despicably last night, and she had every right to be angry with him. Geoffrey glanced over at Miss Claremont — Liliana. He'd kissed the woman. He might as well make free with her name. She looked straight ahead, tension creasing the corners of her pursed lips. If she pressed them much harder, they would quickly turn as blue as the muslin caressing her bosom.

In his experience, a piqued woman was a volatile one. He had no wish to face his mother should Liliana work herself up to accusing him of ungentlemanly conduct, witness or no.

He was half surprised she hadn't already. Now he intended to find out if she meant to.

Geoffrey placed his hand over hers where it rested on his forearm. "We both know ill health is not what kept you from breakfast this morning. You look far too becoming to be indisposed," he said, glancing over at her. And she did. Her skin glowed a creamy gold in the afternoon sunlight, and her hair glinted like copper coins when she turned her head. He wasn't the only man to notice, he saw with no little disgruntlement. "Which makes me wonder ... what reason would you have for not joining us this morning?"

Liliana's face paled. Then bright flags of color splotched her cheeks and, if possible, she pressed her lips even more tightly together. Behind her stony expression, Geoffrey glimpsed a flicker. Guilt. No doubt about it.

Liliana maintained her silence, yet she could not hold his gaze. She looked away.

Geoffrey sighed. She *had* been plotting something this morning, some way to use his behavior last night to her advantage.

He'd lost control of their kiss. Even an innocent like her would recognize that he desired her. No doubt she'd spent the hours dressing just so, turning herself out perfectly to entice him. By absenting herself, perhaps she'd thought to whet his appetite a bit further.

His gaze raked her and desire coiled through him, twisting his gut with sharp longing.

Smart girl. Bloody hell.

And still she said nothing.

"Come, now, Liliana. Don't say it's maidenly distress that's got your tongue." He lowered his voice, partially to keep from being overheard but also to disguise the huskiness that entered his own tenor. "I know from the way you responded to my kiss last night, distress is far from what you feel."

That got a reaction. The amethyst glare she leveled on him burned a path straight to his groin. Geoffrey sucked in a breath. Yet behind her outrage, he recognized awareness in Liliana's eyes. And confusion. Grim satisfaction settled over him.

"You are quite correct, my lord," Liliana bit out around a tight smile.

Geoffrey gave her a quick nod. Good of her to admit

she'd been affected by their interlude and was equally unsettled by it.

"Distress is not what I feel," she continued, "so much as"—she tilted her head and raised a chestnut brow—"indifference."

Geoffrey stopped abruptly, bringing Liliana awkwardly to a halt beside him. *Indifference?* He stared at her.

Her lips twisted, her other brow rising to join its sister.

Geoffrey narrowed his eyes. Indifference his arse. While he might not be sure exactly what *else* she wanted, he knew when a woman wanted him. And by God, Liliana Claremont wanted him.

"And, yes," Liliana continued, slipping her arm from his and stepping ahead. "I admit I did prevaricate slightly about being ill this morning, but not for whatever reasons *you* think." She continued walking, not even bothering to see if he followed. "I simply wished to avoid an awkward situation," she said. She waved a hand backward in his direction. "For you."

"For me?" Geoffrey snorted, disliking the way his voice ended on a high note. He trailed behind in an effort to hear her, like a damned lovesick boy.

She turned to him then, her violet eyes squinting slightly in the afternoon sun as she once again stopped. "Why, yes. To save you the embarrassment of having to apologize, of course. I know how men detest admitting they are wrong. However, since you've forced the issue, I suppose the only polite thing to do is to listen to your offer of contrition."

Geoffrey choked.

Liliana tilted her head, giving him a smile that was both irritation and condescension yet fell short of actually being rude. Just.

Firming his jaw, he took a sharp breath through his nostrils. Had he lost his brass? Twice in two days he'd let a woman turn the tables on him.

He eyed Liliana for a moment, noticing the stiffness

with which she held herself, the rapid rise and fall of her breasts with each breath, the flurried irregular blinking of her eyes. The vision calmed him. He recognized bravado when he saw it.

She actually wanted to retreat. His every instinct told him so. Could she have been telling the truth when she'd insisted she had no designs on him? She wasn't acting like a woman who wanted his attentions. Not like ...

He glanced around the park, eyeing the legions of women and their mothers who were also eyeing him—and all but salivating and licking their lips. Geoffrey made a decision.

"Quite so, Miss Claremont," he said, smoothly recapturing her arm and settling it again on his as they resumed walking. "I do owe you my deepest regrets. That is precisely why I requested this stroll. In fact, as an olive branch of sorts, I insist you accompany me for the rest of the afternoon activities."

She blanched. "Accompany you?" Liliana gave a quick shake of her head. "Thank you, my lord, but that's quite unnecessary. Your apology will suffice."

Geoffrey gave her his best smile. "Oh, but I insist. It will give us a chance to start our friendship anew." He patted her hand where it rested on his arm, gratified to elicit another shiver, to see her curtain of insouciance slip a bit. "Come," he said as he led her toward the open field where the afternoon games were ready to commence.

He looked out over the grassy green field, which had been staked out in a rather large rectangle. He shook his head at the festooned ribbons looped through the posts. His mother had coined the afternoon festivities "A Return to Chivalry." Each contestant was to choose a lady to champion, whom he would later escort to dinner and a supper ball. He knew she expected him to squire either Lady Emily Morton or Lady Jane Northumb, two of the most eligible debutantes in attendance. Geoffrey had been furious at first. But now he smiled to himself.

Mother would be the furious one when she saw his selected companion.

He cut his eyes to Liliana. She was tugging her lower
lip between her teeth, likely trying to think of a way out
of his company.

Why? Spending the afternoon with him wouldn't hurt
her. Besides, she'd pricked his pride, and the strictly
male part of him couldn't let that stand.

Geoffrey knew he would acquit himself well on the
field. His years spent in the military gave him a distinct
advantage over the country gentlemen he'd be compet-
ing against. In his experience, women were drawn to
that prowess, and he was fairly certain he could remember how to turn on the charm.

He'd be damned if by the end of this night Liliana Claremont would still be claiming indifference to him.

"Newton's apple," Liliana muttered, the curse falling
from her lips as naturally as said fruit fell to the earth
when dropped. She considered it almost blasphemous to
use Newton's name as a curse, but she couldn't quite
bring herself to take the Lord's name in vain, and to her,
Sir Isaac was the next best thing.

Stratford led her to the front of the crowd and depos-
ited her on a chair nearest the field of play. Brows around
them rose, and envious glares speared her when he lifted
her hand to his lips, making the tips of her ears burn.

Or perhaps it was the way Stratford wickedly caressed
the underside of her wrist beneath her glove as he
bowed.

"I do hope you enjoy the exhibition," he murmured
low, so only she could hear. A benign statement, but the
way he said it sent a hot shiver through her.

Liliana could manage only a nod.

Stratford flashed her a devilish smile and departed to
join a gathering group of gentlemen.

Feeling eyes upon her, Liliana shifted, smoothing her

skirts and tucking one foot behind the other. Her fists balled in her lap. She hated being under scrutiny.

She clenched her teeth. She also hated being delayed. She *should* be searching for her father's letters this very moment.

Liliana watched Stratford from beneath her lids. She'd done her best to put him off, but instead it was as if he'd dug in his heels.

Her stomach fluttered as she released a shaky breath. She raised two fingers to her temple. Never could she remember feeling such confusion, such a jumble of nerves and unknowns circling her brain, causing a nauseous churning in her middle.

She'd thought for sure that she'd been caught when he asked the reason for her absence this morning. Liliana wrinkled her nose. Insulting him probably hadn't been the appropriate reaction to his charges, but it was the only thing she could think of to distract him from his interrogation. And now she still didn't know whether he suspected her or whether he was just—

"Your ribbons, miss."

Liliana turned her head in surprise toward the maid who'd appeared on her right. The girl stood looking at Liliana expectantly, brandishing a silver tray. Three lavender ribbons lay pooled on the shiny surface.

"*My* ribbons?" Liliana asked.

"Yes, well, I know they're not the same color as your dress, but we didn't have any ribbons that shade of blue." The maid sniffed, then gave a little shrug. "His lordship picked these out for you special. Said they reminded him of your eyes." The maid pushed the tray toward Liliana, who picked up the ribbons, still unsure what she was to do with them. But the girl flounced off before Liliana could question her further.

"Stratford is certainly taking this chivalry business a bit far," came the pinched voice of the young lady sitting to Liliana's left. Liliana glanced over at the pretty blonde, attired in a pale pink gown. She held three ribbons of a similar shade between her fingers.

What did she mean, this chivalry business? Not having attended the morning activities or nuncheon, Liliana felt at a distinct disadvantage.

"Yes," answered a brunette dressed in yellow, holding three yellow ribbons. "Choosing the least acceptable woman here is too much."

A sinking feeling overcame Liliana as her eyes traveled down the row. There were twelve women, including herself, each holding three ribbons. The other eleven were staring right back at her, some curiously, some disdainfully, and a couple downright angrily.

She turned her gaze back to the field. Bright red and blue and green pennants flapped in the wind, surrounding a field that was absurdly marked with streamers. A multicolored tent was staked beneath a large oak. Stratford and the other gentlemen had disappeared into it, presumably to ready themselves for the games.

Liliana looked behind her. Amongst the gathering crowd, several young ladies—Penelope included—stood near, ready to watch the sport. Yet they had no ribbons. An elderly matron not so discreetly pointed toward Liliana while others openly stared, appraising her before whispering behind their fans or open hands.

The clues clicked into place.

Drat Stratford! He'd made her the center of attention, choosing her to champion in some ridiculous farce of a tournament. And for what reason? To keep his eye on her or . . .

A strange melting sensation drizzled down Liliana's middle.

Could he actually *be* interested in her? An improbable likelihood, but—

Several trumpets blared, signaling the start of the event. Liliana turned in her seat, her back straightening, trying to ignore the stares of the crowd. Drat, drat, drat Stratford!

As if curses called him to her, he emerged from the tent flap, his black hair shining almost blue in the sun. Liliana's breath caught. She hadn't noticed before how tightly the buckskin breeches molded to Stratford's hips, clinging to his legs and accentuating his muscled movements. His chest was now covered in a scrap of leather, but her mind easily filled in what her eyes could no longer see, what her hands had felt beneath them last night in the library.

Though the other competitors looked somewhat plain out of their formal dress, this casual guise seemed to fit Stratford. Liliana shook her head. *Fit* was perhaps not the right word so much as . . . *suit*. As he strode across the expanse toward her, with the hint of a roguish smile tugging at one side of his mouth, he looked strangely . . . unburdened. Like he was truly comfortable for the first time in a long time.

Liliana huffed. How would she know that?

What she did know was that he eclipsed the other men, blotting them out with his sheer presence.

Some long-dormant female nerve shivered as he stopped before her, bowing low.

"M'lady," he said, his voice swirling over her. He extended his hand, helping her to rise. His eyes caught hers, staring into them for a prolonged moment before giving a cluck of his tongue. He nodded at the ribbons she still held in her hand. "I had hoped the lavender would suit, but I can see now that no man-made shade of purple could ever compare to your eyes."

Liliana felt a ridiculous urge to smile, but then firmed her jaw. What was he up to? "The ribbons are fine. Thank you, but—"

"I shall have to scour the garden for a natural shade to match them," he interrupted. "Violets? No, too dark. Freesia, perhaps? Or sweet peas." His eyes glinted. "I have it. Globe thistle." He smiled, his teeth white behind the slow spread of his lips. "Prickly, yet passionately purple."

Liliana stared at him, openmouthed, she feared. He was playing with her, but to what purpose? Her toes felt warm. In fact, heat was seeping into all kinds of unusual places.

"I—" Liliana swallowed around a dry throat. "Thank you . . . I think. But I must insist—"

A trumpet blare cut off her rebuttal.

Stratford removed his sword from its scabbard. "While I find my mother's entertainments frivolous"—he gave Liliana a long-suffering look—"I am ever the dutiful son. Therefore, would you do me the honor of allowing me to wear your colors into battle, m'lady?" He held an oddly decorated sword out to her, hilt first, with an exaggerated flourish.

The other women in her row were dutifully tying their ribbons around the swords of the other competitors. Liliana looked behind her. Aunt Eliza raised her eyebrows in encouragement.

Liliana sighed, then took one of her ribbons and tied a neat clove hitch around the hilt.

He looked up at her in surprise.

Perhaps she should have tied a bow.

She met his questioning gaze blandly. One corner of his mouth turned up in a half smile as he spun away, strode out onto the field and took his spot across from an opponent.

Liliana cast a glance over her shoulder. Sneaking away was out of the question—nor realistically possible given her highly visible position. She dropped onto the chair. She could still feel more than one glare coming from her left.

Irritation burned. How had she ended up here? Not only were these foolish games keeping her from her search, but she'd now attracted the attention of a pack of jealous harpies.

She took a steadying breath, willing her feet to stop fidgeting. She couldn't change that now, at least not where this afternoon was concerned. If she were fortunate enough that Stratford did not suspect her, she needed to make the most of this debacle.

She would do her level best to annoy him so badly that he would run the next time he caught even a glimpse of her. But how to do that? Liliana thought about all of the things she detested most about her own sex. Simpering? Crying? Batting of the eyelashes while acting weak and helpless?

She snorted. No. While she did hate those things, she'd never be able to carry it off. She wasn't an actress, after all.

She'd be herself—well, sort of. She'd share her mind. She'd be opinionated and flaunt her intelligence. And, of course, she'd criticize his every move, and then tell him how he could have done it better.

Men hated that.

Stratford would be begging to see the last of her by the time this afternoon was through.

Chapter Six

Geoffrey flicked his wrist, testing the weight of his sword.

His *wooden* sword.

"Hell's bells," he muttered.

"What's that?" asked the man across from him. The newly belted Viscount Holbrook stood eyeing his own "sword" dubiously.

"Only a woman would organize this foolishness," Geoffrey grumbled, looking over the assembly. It looked like a damned medieval fair. Guests sat on one side of the marked field looking jovial and relaxed, while servants crowded the opposite end, like the nobles and peasants of old. Twelve women sat apart in places of honor, ready to cheer on their champions. All that was missing were juggling jesters. Ridiculous.

Thank God Holbrook was the only political sort who'd come up so far. The rest weren't due to arrive until week's end.

Geoffrey tugged at the leather breastplate that served as armor. So much for dazzling Liliana Claremont with this display. By God, he felt like a bloody stage actor. "Why the devil are you playing in this farce?" Geoffrey asked the younger man.

"For sport, of course. Besides, I've need of a bride,

same as you," Holbrook said as he shifted on his feet, limbering up for the competition. "You've certainly invited the crème to this little party. Thought I'd try my hand at impressing one or two." Holbrook flexed his shoulders. "Rotten luck drawing you as challenger. While the bragging rights of having bested Wellington's darling would be well worth it, you're sure to give me quite a drubbing." Holbrook smiled good-naturedly. "S'pose I'll just have to count on finding m'self a sympathetic young chit to tend my wounded pride."

Geoffrey laughed, twisting to loosen his knotted left hip. "Even newly returned from the continent, I've heard of your reputation with a blade," he said. Indeed, which was why Geoffrey had switched his opponent to the very skilled Holbrook.

Mother had originally paired Geoffrey against some poor milksop, no doubt to make him look better by comparison. Geoffrey scanned the field, shaking his head. She must really think he needed help. A man in the pair nearest them had no idea how to even hold a sword properly, and his partner looked to be in his dotage, swallowed by the armor, with his balding pate sticking up like the head of a wizened old tortoise.

At least Holbrook would be fair competition. "I expect we shall make a good show of it," Geoffrey stated as he squared himself to Holbrook.

"Ah, Stratford, that is what the ladies want, is it not?"

Geoffrey snorted. His gaze immediately flew to Liliana Claremont. He'd intended to throw the match, just to thwart his mother, but no more. Liliana sat coolly in the warm afternoon sun, not laughing and smiling like the other girls around her, but with a regal air. She reminded him of a master's painting of a dark-haired queen.

Only her rapidly tapping foot belied her sense of calm. Clearly, she wished to be anywhere but here.

That made two of them.

"En garde."

Geoffrey turned his attention back to Holbrook,

whose easy smile had vanished. At the blast of a trumpet, the matches commenced.

Thwack.

The sound jarred Geoffrey. Wood certainly differed from the clanging of metal upon metal, but after only a couple of passes he fell easily into the familiar moves of combat. In his periphery he noted the clumsy attempts of those around them.

Holbrook's were anything but.

Geoffrey dodged Holbrook's thrust, which shot pain through his lower back. He sucked in a breath. Damn. The last time he'd done any hand-to-hand fighting, he'd taken a bayonet through his side. He was considerably slower on his feet these days.

He adjusted his stance to accommodate and swung his stick in a swift upward arc, catching Holbrook's side.

"Point," Holbrook acknowledged with a nod. The game was to ten. The men faced each other again and Geoffrey led with a thrust toward Holbrook's middle.

Fifteen minutes and several points later, only the two of them remained. Geoffrey led nine points to eight, but his back burned and he struggled to hide his limp. He didn't want to show Holbrook his weakness so close to the finish.

The air rang with the clacking of wood and with the cheers and enthusiastic groans of the spectators. Geoffrey drew a deep breath—he could almost smell the victory to come as blood pulsed through his veins. He hadn't felt this alive in more than a year. He'd been a fool to think he could have thrown the match any more than he could just roll over and marry whomever his mother wanted him to.

His eyes darted once again to Liliana, sure that now he'd see at least appreciation on her face.

He couldn't see her face at all. In fact, she wasn't even watching! Instead, she focused on her lap ... What was she doing? It looked as though she was scribbling something—

Pain exploded through his left side.

The crowd roared.

Geoffrey hobbled backward, catching himself before his weak side crumpled.

"Point!" Holbrook shouted, exuberant.

Damn it. He'd let himself be distracted by a woman who by all appearances could not care less about him.

Geoffrey glanced back at Liliana. She hadn't looked up from her doodling even to see what the roar was about.

He shook his head. Well, appearances *could* be wrong.

The two men squared off for the final sparring. As Geoffrey circled Holbrook, he couldn't help but wonder if maybe Liliana wasn't like the other women here. Ever since she'd been dragged across the lawn by her aunt this afternoon, he'd noticed her discomfort. He'd swear it was the social situation that made her so. And when he'd called his mother's games frivolous, Liliana didn't prettily demure. Though she hadn't said as much, he was certain she'd agreed with him. In fact—

Crack. Geoffrey barely blocked Holbrook's thrust. Holbrook grunted, then danced away from him.

Geoffrey's thigh throbbed and his lower back knotted. He thrust Liliana Claremont from his thoughts. He needed to end this. He planted his feet, knowing that moving was beyond him at this point. He shifted as much weight to his right as he could and tightened both hands around the hilt of his sword as he waited for Holbrook to come to him. If Geoffrey were to win now, it would have to be with strength and cunning rather than agility.

Holbrook advanced, his face alight—he, too, anticipating victory. Geoffrey brought his stick down, blocking Holbrook's quick swipe. Holbrook shifted to his own left, quickly striking again. Geoffrey had to twist hard to his right to fend off Holbrook's blow.

He saw the moment Holbrook realized his advantage. The blond man's eyes narrowed and one corner of his mouth rose in a triumphant smile. He moved even farther to Geoffrey's right and raised his sword high to deliver the final strike.

Geoffrey crouched, his lower body screaming as he moved into the unnatural position. He shifted his sword into his right hand, then passed it behind his back to his left, a move he'd never have been able to make with the weight of a true sword.

Holbrook's swing missed high.

Geoffrey arced his sword up and around with his left arm, catching Holbrook in the side. As the crowd erupted around them, Geoffrey's leg crumpled and he dropped to his knees.

"Damnation, Stratford," Holbrook exclaimed, grinning as he reached down to help Geoffrey up. "Thought for certain I had you there."

"As did I," Geoffrey grunted, regaining his feet and nodding thanks. He straightened, ignoring the agony, and turned toward the spectators. His eyes sought only one.

Liliana had risen along with the rest of the crowd, and while she didn't clap like the others, she did at least have a smile on her face—albeit a cool one.

A servant came running onto the field from Geoffrey's left, bearing a bouquet. Mother had intended the victor to present his lady with roses. Geoffrey hoped his valet had had time to fulfill his earlier request.

Geoffrey straightened, dusting himself off a bit as he anticipated presenting Liliana with her flowers. It hadn't been pretty, but he had won the contest and he was absurdly proud of the accomplishment. Now he would be rewarded with the praise of a beautiful woman. He accepted the wrapped bouquet from the servant and smiled. Perfect.

He turned toward Liliana, his eyes drawn to her shimmering hair, which was swept up in a loose chignon. Stray curls escaped as though they couldn't bear to be away from her captivating face for even a moment. He couldn't blame them—she was enchanting.

As he advanced toward her, she shifted. It was a slight movement—she caught herself and stilled quickly—but he noticed. Her eyes darted to either side. He sensed that she didn't like everyone watching her, that she was out of her element.

Empathy swelled within him—along with confidence that he'd chosen the safest debutante to champion. If she were trying to win him, he'd expect her to be beaming as he approached. Proud of her position as his "fair maiden," at least for the day, smiling coquettishly, ready to gush and coo over him.

Instead, she straightened her spine and pasted a false smile on her face.

He stopped before her. As foolish as he'd felt when the games began, he now found himself tight with anticipation.

"For you, m'lady," he said, presenting her with the bouquet.

Liliana accepted the flowers and looked down. Her smile changed for a moment, softening. He felt it deep in his gut.

Her violet eyes rose to him. "Prickly, yet passionately purple," she murmured, her voice low. Her tone rolled over him with waves of sensuality that drifted low, causing a slow burn. He'd have to reward his valet for finding globe thistle on short notice. Her pleasure at the gesture had been well worth it.

His breath caught at her loveliness. She *was* a queen, he thought, with high cheekbones and a narrow chin. Her full mouth entranced him and her skin fairly shimmered, though her complexion was darker than your average English rose. A knight of old could have done far worse in a maiden.

Then she seemed to remember herself. She dropped the bouquet onto the seat behind her and the fake smile returned. "Congratulations, my lord," she said, her sensual tone turning imperious. "'Twas quite a spectacle, though I must own to being surprised by your victory."

Any heat he'd felt moved swiftly to his head. "Surprised?" he choked.

She nodded. "Shocked, actually. Your form is quite deplorable," she remarked. She glanced down, pointedly. "Were I you, I would focus on my footwork. You can't just stand there all day and expect to overpower your opponent with brute force. You must be fleet of foot."

"Fleet of foot . . . ," Geoffrey repeated. His lower back howled.

"Precisely," she returned, looking earnest. "Lord Holbrook is a much more graceful swordsman. Had it not been for that bit of trickery at the end, you surely would have been defeated."

Trickery? *Trickery?* Did he say "queen"? More like "fishwife." Why, if they weren't surrounded by a crowd of people, he'd— "How would you know?" Geoffrey sputtered, remembering her scribblings. "You hardly observed the match." Her hands were empty, so he looked behind her. On the chair, peeking out from beneath the discarded bouquet, he saw a corner of paper. He reached around her and snatched it up. What *had* she been writing?

She gasped, grasping for the paper but missing. "That's private!"

He ignored her, opened the page and looked. Then looked again. It resembled the mathematical equations he'd suffered over as a boy at Harrow, with long and short lines and addition, subtraction and equals symbols. Yet there were also little arrows and letters instead of numbers.

"What is this?" he asked, intrigued.

"It's none of your business," she said and held her hand out.

He didn't give it back. She firmed her lips and narrowed her eyes. In answer, he raised a brow.

She sighed. "I was working out a reaction," she said.

"A reaction?" He looked again at the paper, then back at her.

She glared, and the most darling little V appeared between her chestnut brows. "I was trying to combine a biological reaction with a chemical one to prove a theory of mine," she said. She snapped her fingers and opened her hand again in a demand that he return her paper. "You wouldn't understand."

This time, Geoffrey firmed his lips. No, he wouldn't understand, but he most decidedly didn't care for being told that by a slip of a woman. Any more than he liked her criticizing his footwork when she had no idea of the pain he was in. Besides, he'd wager she'd never even lifted a sword in her life.

He handed the paper back to her. "Probably trying to concoct some sort of love potion to snare unwilling suitors," he grumbled, turning his back on her.

Geoffrey heard her gasp as he stalked away and smiled.

Point, him.

Geoffrey had calmed considerably by the time he rode out for the second competition. Having a horse beneath him always had that effect, though it felt odd being seated on a mount other than Grin.

Geoffrey's ire started to rise as he turned toward Liliana, however. Damned woman. Ever since she'd dropped into his arms last night, he'd been tied in knots. On one hand, desire gripped him. On the other, the need to turn her over his knee until she admitted it was the same for her rode him. On the third hand, if he had a third hand, lay the question of who she was. Why had he never seen her out in society? But more important, why was he so conflicted over this rude, irritating girl? Hell, that was like five hands. He'd have to be Kali to decipher his response to Liliana Claremont.

For her part, she stood politely but without enthusiasm, a lavender ribbon in her hand. She looked bored. No wonder he'd never seen her out in society. The woman had the manners of a horse. She probably bit, too.

He halted his mount in front of her and bowed his head. "M'lady?"

She stepped forward, and he was struck by how tall she stood compared to the women around her. Liliana didn't look to be intimidated by his horse, either. While some women approached their champions' mounts warily, Liliana held her hand out beneath his mount's nose and cooed something to him. The horse whinnied and nuzzled her. She smiled, delighted. Geoffrey was sure the damned horse smiled back.

Well, of course the horse would like her. She smelled of apples. *And lemon verbena,* he remembered, and with that sensual memory came every detail of her innocent, passionate kisses. He remembered how perfectly she'd fit in his arms, how natural it had been to lower his lips to hers. How right. Geoffrey's groin tightened painfully.

Oblivious, she stroked the horse's nose, then tied a frilly bow around its bridle. "Good luck," she said in a way that made Geoffrey think she was wishing the horse luck rather than him.

Brilliant. Now he was jealous of a nag.

He whipped the reins and turned toward the field. The green grass lay dotted with rounded barrels and semi-treacherous wooden jumps. The course included tight turns and tricky maneuvers. Geoffrey could only imagine the blunt it would take to repair the lawn after a dozen horses tore through it. Perhaps he *should* cut Mother off.

His horse nickered as they lined up at the start. Geoffrey reviewed the course, mentally strategizing. The design had skewed the race once again toward Geoffrey's skill, which was why he'd refused to ride Grin. A seasoned battle horse, Grin would have ridden rings around these civilian mounts. Besides, Grin would have been mortified to have ribbons braided into his tail.

Holbrook sidled up next to him on his own mount. "Victory not all it's purported to be?" he asked, laughter edging his voice.

Geoffrey grunted. Damn. He'd hoped his and Liliana's interchange hadn't been overheard. "Women."

Holbrook did laugh then. Geoffrey smiled as well. He liked the young viscount and hoped to convince Holbrook to work with him on presenting some measures to Parliament.

"Perhaps she'll be more impressed with your horsemanship," Holbrook offered.

Geoffrey glanced at Liliana, who was again scribbling on her paper.

Somehow, he doubted it.

The trumpet blared and they were off.

Geoffrey's horse got off to a slow start, but he didn't worry over it. They'd make it up when it came to the turning obstacles. Geoffrey's lower back twinged as he flew over the jumps, landing hard, but he hardly cared. On the back of a horse was the only place he felt at home.

Coming out of the jumps, he turned his horse sharply, heading straight for the barrels. He was still a bit behind, but as he deftly skirted them, first left, then right, then left, left, right, he whipped his mount around well ahead of the pack.

Exhilaration rushed through Geoffrey and he gave the horse his head, leaning forward. They flew back to the finish, several strides before any other pair.

The crowd cheered.

Most of the crowd, anyway. Geoffrey sought out Liliana, who again stood docile but at least smiling.

A servant ran out and handed Geoffrey a bouquet. The pretty purple flowers mocked him. Perhaps he should have sent for straight thistles this time.

Still, he was determined to present the bouquet with all politeness and head back to the tent.

He rode over to Liliana, who immediately stepped up and stroked his horse's face. "Well done," she murmured to the animal. Her husky voice floated up to Geoffrey, and for a moment he wished it were he she stroked.

She looked up at him then. "And well done to you, my lord," she said. "You are a superb horseman."

Geoffrey waited for the insult, but it didn't come. He smiled, the pleasure of her compliment warming him. He handed down the bouquet with much more grace than he'd intended to moments before. "Thank you, Miss Claremont."

"You're welcome." She smiled, taking the flowers. She discarded them on her chair without even glancing at them. "Of course, I fully expected you to win this competition. Don't you think it's rather unsportsmanlike to expect other men to compete with a decorated cavalryman?" Her smile stayed in place, wide violet eyes blinking up at him in seeming innocence.

Geoffrey's ears burned. She must be more angry with him over last night than he'd thought. By God, he'd been a fool to attach himself to this contrary chit for the rest of the day and evening.

"I daresay none of the other men want to win," he answered down his nose. "They fear their maidens will be as solicitous as you." He wheeled his horse around and headed back toward the tent.

As rejoinders went, it was pretty weak. But what he truly wanted to say to Miss Claremont wasn't fit for public consumption.

Geoffrey gritted his teeth.

Point, her.

Chapter Seven

Liliana congratulated herself as Stratford trotted away. It was all she could do not to laugh aloud. Her plan was working brilliantly! She'd seen murder in Stratford's eyes. Even if he *had* planned to keep her under surveillance, he certainly wouldn't willingly put himself in her company after today.

"Are you mad, gel?" Aunt Eliza's harsh whisper came from behind. "What on earth did you say to put Stratford in such a foul disposition?"

Liliana turned in surprise. Aunt had made her way through the crowd and now stood before her. Though Aunt Eliza's face appeared calm on the surface, her eyes flashed.

Liliana thought fast. She didn't want to completely alienate her aunt, who could, after all, make the rest of her stay quite difficult.

"A new stratagem, Aunt," Liliana whispered. "A theory."

Her aunt blinked, lips firming. "Not one of your theories."

"Think about it," Liliana coaxed, making things up as she went. "I have nothing in the way of fortune or connection—"

"You're niece to a marquess," Aunt Eliza huffed.

"By marriage," Liliana acceded, her tone hushed and conspiratorial. "But other women here are much more highly born. Once Stratford thinks upon it, he'll see we're not well matched."

"So you plan to prove that to him quickly to save him the trouble?" Aunt asked, incredulous.

Amongst other things, yes. "Of course not," Liliana assured her. "My plan is to prick him a bit, make certain that I'm the girl he can't forget." Liliana hoped she sounded reasonable to Aunt. To herself she sounded like a twit. "It's the only chance I've got to distinguish myself from the rest."

"Foolishness." Aunt shook her head in disgust. "Only my brother could sire such a headstrong, imprudent girl," she muttered. She raised herself to her full height, well beneath Liliana's nose. "I command you to stop this nonsensical behavior and apologize to the earl."

Anger rose in Liliana's chest. She'd listened to Aunt Eliza criticize her father most of her life. Besides, she would not apologize for being herself. Well, certainly she'd overplayed it. She wasn't typically rude, but she did, nearly always, speak her mind. Stratford's footwork *had* been deplorable, and holding a horse race when one is clearly more experienced than others was quite unfair. She'd said nothing that wasn't true.

"I shall not," Liliana said. "A gentleman such as Stratford has dozens of girls bowing and scraping to him, trying to win his hand. I believe he's the sort of man who likes a challenge."

The moment the words left her mouth, Liliana frowned. They made more sense than she'd expected, and she had the strangest feeling they might be true. Heavens. What if her incendiary words had done the equivalent of throwing down a gauntlet? No! That would be disastrous.

Aunt opened her mouth in rebuttal, but Liliana stayed her. "Nevertheless, Aunt, I shall take some bit of your advice," she appeased. After all, the damage had surely been done. "I shall treat Stratford with the utmost respect and solicitude for the rest of the afternoon."

Aunt gave her a disgusted look, then retreated into the crowd.

Liliana removed the bouquet from her chair and dropped it atop the other one on the grass beside her. She sat, troubled. Perhaps Stratford did like a challenge, but he couldn't possibly want her and her sharp tongue anymore, if he ever did.

Her eyes sought Stratford. The third event had been set up. Targets were affixed to old barrels several yards out. Archery perhaps?

She spotted Stratford off to her right, standing with the other gentlemen. They looked to be checking pistols. A shooting competition, then.

Well, at least she wouldn't be subjected to another display of masculine grace and form. Goodness, it had been near impossible to keep her eyes from Stratford all afternoon. Yes, his footwork had not been up to snuff for a swordsman, but as a man—he was quite the specimen. He exuded strength and purpose. Even now, she noted the concentrated intensity with which he cleaned his weapon. If he turned that intensity upon a woman in the bedroom ...

Liliana felt herself blush and snatched up her equation. She couldn't explain this awful attraction, so she did what she always did. Focused her mind on cold science. Yet this time, it didn't suffice. After scratching through three mistakes in her formula, she set the paper down.

Stratford was such a contradiction. At first, she'd been certain he was on to her. Yet then he'd surprised her with the thoughtful bouquet of globe thistle. When he'd presented her with it, he'd seemed like a true suitor, anxious for her praise. And he'd deserved it. Not only had he fought well, but she'd seen the pain in his eyes. He'd struggled through and come out the victor. She'd felt rotten insulting him so.

Had he truly just been trying to impress her? A warm sensation flowed through her before she squelched it. It hardly mattered if he had.

Still, it wouldn't hurt to act the proper lady for the rest of the afternoon. If Aunt had noticed her slights, others had as well. That wouldn't do. Should Stratford win the last event, she'd compliment him. Not effusively, mind you. Just more . . . nicely. She'd draw no more attention to herself. And then, if it turned out he wasn't onto her after all, she could slip back into obscurity and complete her search.

The murmuring of the crowd quieted as the men lined up. Liliana sat up straight and fixed her eyes on the field. She would watch this match with interest.

Several feet separated each contestant from his neighbors. Servants stood behind with horns of gunpowder and extra ammunition. Stratford stood nearest to the crowd, giving Liliana a perfect view.

The trumpets sounded and each man raised an arm. Balls shot from twelve pistols with a deafening boom. The yellow-dressed girl gave a little shriek. Liliana rolled her eyes.

She watched Stratford as he meticulously reloaded, pouring his powder precisely. He was close enough that she could see the ripple of muscle on his forearm below his rolled-up sleeve as he took careful aim and pulled the trigger. Another shot exploded from the muzzle.

Again she watched his precision, a trait that she, as a chemist, truly appreciated. Oh yes, concentrated intensity. Her blush returned and she looked away.

After five shots, the men lay down their arms, and servants darted out to retrieve the targets. The targets were taken to a table near the tent, where a panel of judges pored over them before once again declaring Stratford the winner.

This time, Liliana stood and clapped with everyone else. She smiled prettily, waiting to congratulate him.

But the man who stalked toward her with a bouquet

held haphazardly upside down in one hand and a target in the other was no sweet suitor. He was fourteen stone of cross male, and he looked to be spoiling for a fight.

"Congratulations—," Liliana began, but Stratford tossed the bouquet toward her. Not hard, but clearly without care. She caught the lovely bunch of yellow roses and tucked them in the crook of her arm, as if he'd handed them to her gently.

She took a quick step back when the target was thrust into her face.

Five shots clustered very near the bull's-eye.

Liliana cleared her throat. "Well done, my lord."

Stratford lowered the target and glared. "Is that all you have to say?"

"Well, yes, I—"

"Because I can assure you, Miss Claremont, most of my shooting experience has been from the back of a moving horse," Stratford claimed. "With a rifle, *not* a pistol."

Liliana didn't know what to say, so she nodded.

"So my victory meets your ideals of sportsmanship?"

Liliana nodded again, astounded. Her plan had worked better than she'd thought.

"Did my stance meet your approval?" he challenged. "Not leaning too far forward or back?"

"Your stance was perfect," she said slowly.

He raised himself to his full height and looked down on her, cocking a raven brow. "So even you, with your uninformed petty little standards, could find nothing wrong with my performance?"

Liliana narrowed her eyes. Uninformed? Petty? She'd had quite enough of his display. Yes, she'd been rude, but he was being a boor.

She stepped toward him, raising herself as well—she was no shrinking violet. "Since you asked," she said, simply because she couldn't help herself, "you didn't hit the center, not even once."

She could actually see the blood rising up Stratford's neck to his face before he exploded.

"No one hits the center with a flintlock!" he exclaimed, throwing his hands up in the air. "It takes so long for the powder to ignite, it throws off one's aim!"

Liliana shrugged.

Stratford's fist clenched and he gave her such a fierce stare, Liliana feared to take so much as a breath. Not that she sensed he'd do violence to her person, but she'd never seen someone so angry.

Then he collected himself, a mask of indifference slipping over his features. When he spoke, his voice was nonchalant. "But then, what would a woman know of a man's pursuits?" He capped his mocking words with a shrug of his own and turned away.

Liliana sucked in a breath. Laughter tittered around her, but it hardly registered through the swiftly rising haze of fury. "A man's pursuits?" she asked, her voice sounding low and dangerous to her ears. Her entire life she'd been told to keep her nose out of *men's pursuits*. As if men alone had a brain worth educating. As if only men were capable of understanding complex scientific theory or making any worthy contribution to the world besides babies.

Well, not today. Liliana took a bold step forward. "I'd wager, *my lord*," she scoffed, "that this *woman* can not only make that weapon fire faster, but increase its accuracy measurably."

Stratford stopped and turned back to face her, both brows raised. People around them hushed in expectation. Liliana heard Aunt Eliza's groan from the crowd.

"And how do you propose to do that?" Stratford asked, sounding more surprised than scornful.

"That is none of your concern," she snapped. "Do you take my wager or not?"

Stratford's cobalt eyes narrowed slightly, thoughtful. "That depends, Miss Claremont," he said after a moment. "How would you propose we test your claims? Will you shoot against me?"

Liliana's stomach clenched. She'd never fired a

weapon in her life. She had little chance at hitting a target.

"Because while we can verify accuracy easily enough, the only way to test whether a gun fires more quickly than another is to shoot them at the same time," he pointed out reasonably, with a smile that said he knew very well she couldn't shoot.

Liliana clenched her jaw. "I have no experience," she admitted.

Stratford nodded. "Well then, unless someone steps forward as your proxy, I don't see how I could take your wager, tempting though it may be."

Liliana's heart fell as the silence dragged on. Of course no one would challenge Stratford on her behalf. She closed her eyes. Not only had she made a fool of herself, but she'd made sure there was plenty of attention on her now. Her only consolation was that after this embarrassment, people would expect her to stay away in shame. That would clear up her time so she could search the house.

She only hoped she'd be allowed to stay.

"I will shoot on the lady's behalf," came a rich baritone. Liliana's eyes flew open and she turned. The crowd parted, and a dashing man stepped forward and came to her side. "As I've missed the afternoon games, I'd enjoy getting in a bit of sport."

Relief flooded Liliana, though she couldn't place her rescuer. She didn't think she'd ever seen him before. Definitely not since she'd been at Somerton Park.

Like Stratford's, his hair was as dark as night, but that's where the similarities ended. His glittering green eyes were framed by long black lashes and had an exotic slant that reminded Liliana of a gypsy.

He was taller than Stratford as well—taller and leaner, with a smile that flashed quickly, unlike Stratford's slower, warmer one. Yet he didn't make Liliana's breath catch in her chest as Stratford did—a fact that deeply annoyed her.

"If that meets your approval, mademoiselle?" the stranger asked, giving Liliana a slight bow.

Liliana swallowed. "I'd be delighted, sir . . . ?"

The man straightened and laughed. "Stratford, don't you think you should introduce the lady to her new champion?"

Stratford's face had gone stormy. "Miss Liliana Claremont, Lord Derick Aveline, heir to Viscount Scarsdale."

"A pleasure, Miss Claremont," Aveline said. Liliana gave him a quick curtsy. "Now, shall we begin?" Aveline held his arm out to Liliana and, after securing her hand, took a step toward the field.

"Not quite," Stratford said, drawing Liliana's gaze back to him. She and Aveline stopped walking. "We've yet to agree on the terms of the wager. What have you in mind, Miss Claremont?"

Oh, dash it all. This had become enough of a scene. She couldn't very well ask him to hand over any information he had about her father's death, and she wanted nothing else from him.

"I had nothing particular in mind," she answered. *Other than to prove your chauvinistic views as nonsense.*

Stratford gave her a look that said wagers were a man's pursuit as well. Drat him.

"I've an idea," Aveline interrupted. "It is my understanding that Stratford chose to champion you for the day, yes, Miss Claremont?"

Liliana nodded.

"And that you were to spend the rest of the evening and supper ball with him as escort?"

She hadn't known that part. Still, she nodded.

"Well, as I am your champion now, should we win the wager, I propose that you spend the evening with me instead."

The wager sounded innocuous enough and would get her out from beneath Stratford's watchful eye. "That would be preferable," she said, knowing it insulted Stratford, but she was beyond caring. "If we should lose?"

She looked over at Stratford, who stood rigid, the tic of a muscle evident in his jaw.

"Then Miss Claremont spends the rest of the house party with me."

A gasp came from somewhere behind them.

"Every breakfast, every luncheon, every supper and every activity."

What? Good heavens, this couldn't be happening. "I don't really think—"

"That's hardly equitable," Aveline spoke over her, which annoyed her, yet he voiced the truth.

"Be that as it may, that is my demand," Stratford said, his voice hard.

Aveline patted her hand where she gripped his forearm. "Then I must insist the same. Should we win, *I* shall escort Miss Claremont for the duration."

Absolutely not. She'd never be able to search, then. She must put a stop to this.

"Done," Stratford said, holding out his palm.

Aveline reached out and shook Stratford's outstretched hand.

This was *her* wager, blast them! "Gentlem—"

Aveline squeezed her arm and lowered his head. "Don't make this worse than it is," he whispered.

Liliana slumped. He was right.

"I don't know what lies between you, but if you don't wish to spend the next two weeks with Stratford, I suggest you make certain we win," Aveline said, and turned her toward the shooting line.

The crowd followed, silent and rapt, as if watching a carriage wreck. Servants rushed to set up two new targets.

Liliana's stomach turned over. There was more than her feminine pride on the line now.

Dear God, she absolutely had to win this wager.

Chapter Eight

"**D**o you agree, gentlemen, that these weapons are of similar make and quality?" A blond gentleman, who had been introduced to Liliana as Viscount Holbrook, stood between Stratford and Aveline as each man weighed two matched pistols. After examining one, Stratford traded it to Aveline for the other.

Liliana fidgeted, shifting her weight from foot to foot as both men nodded and handed the weapons back to Holbrook.

"In the interest of fairness, Aveline, I must inquire as to your shooting ability," Viscount Holbrook stated. Being met with silence, he clarified. "What I mean is, do you feel you are on par with Stratford?"

Liliana looked to Aveline, who had elected to remove his jacket but retained his waistcoat and neck cloth. In his buff-colored leggings and burgundy-striped vest, Aveline radiated sheer elegance, even while rolling up his puffed sleeves. Dear Lord, how could a town gentleman have a chance against a military veteran like Stratford?

Aveline regarded Holbrook with hooded eyes.

"I am a decent shot," he answered vaguely.

A decent shot? Liliana nearly groaned. Her chances could be up in smoke before the hammer was even cocked. Aveline's bland smile did nothing to reassure her. She prayed his relaxed attitude was the benefit of confidence and not a product of his lack of stake in the game.

"I will admit that I have yet to hit the center with a flintlock pistol, m'self," he added, sounding unconcerned.

Holbrook nodded. "Stratford, as you will be firing the unaltered weapon, first choice is yours." He flipped the guns in his hands and held both curved burl-wood handles toward Stratford.

Debating only a moment, Stratford chose the pistol on the left. He walked over to the firing line without saying a word, determination lining his features.

He hadn't once looked at her since making his ridiculous demands, while she'd caught herself staring at him numerous times. She hated to admit it, but it rankled.

Holbrook drew her attention.

"Miss Claremont, do you require time and, or, er"— Holbrook flushed, likely not sure how to phrase the question—"tools to make your modifications?"

Her chest tightened as seemingly every other eye on the estate turned to her as well. There were some, like her aunt, with faces pinched in disapproval, but many showed rampant curiosity.

It took all of her willpower not to pull a silly face at the lot of them. Did they think she'd file off half of the barrel or something? An irrational smile threatened as she visualized herself manically sawing through metal as all and sundry looked on.

"Just a few moments," she answered, motioning a passing maid. How she wished she wore one of her own dresses. She always carried her tinderbox in the oversized pockets. Liliana sighed. Regardless, she could still win. She'd just have to substitute.

Liliana whispered to the girl, then started over to where Aveline stood, checking his munitions. He held the gun out as she approached. "How do you intend to alter this weapon?" he asked.

Liliana waved it away. "I won't touch the gun," she said, "just the powder. Be sure to clean the pan, flint and frizzen very well. Leave no residue—wipe it with a moist cloth, then a dry one if you have to—and load the ball as you normally would. I'll put in the powder."

Aveline contemplated her, his sharp green gaze assessing. Then he started brushing out the pan with quick, efficient flicks.

Liliana cut her eyes to Stratford, who methodically cleaned his own weapon.

What had prompted his rash terms? He couldn't truly want to spend time with her . . . could he? Was it wounded pride that demanded her presence, or had he known what she was about all along? He could see winning this wager as the perfect way to keep her underfoot and unable to investigate.

His wooden expression gave no inkling.

The maid appeared and handed Liliana a wrapped handkerchief. Thin lines of confusion marred the girl's face. Liliana didn't blame her. All she had time for was a parlor trick at best. She wasn't even sure it would work.

Liliana unwrapped the contents, then laid the handkerchief out on the judging table and removed her gloves. She measured a portion, crumbling a bit of the gritty crystalline substance with her thumbnail, and began crushing it with a spoon the maid had provided. What she wouldn't give for a mortar and pestle—the finer the grain, the faster it would burn. Still, this should do.

"What's that?" Aveline asked.

Liliana smiled. "Magic." She finished grinding, then scooped the handkerchief up with the powder inside. She walked over to Aveline. "All right, now, fill the pan not quite a third full with the priming powder," she instructed. The spoiled-egg odor of sulfur tickled her nose. "Be careful not to add too much."

Aveline quirked a black brow at her but followed her command wordlessly.

"Perfect," she whispered as he finished. "If you

wouldn't mind?" she prompted, indicating the prying eyes of the crowd around them. Aveline understood and shielded their actions from the others with a turn of his body.

"Thank you," Liliana murmured, then took a pinch from the handkerchief and sprinkled it into the pan. She cocked her head and debated, then added half a pinch more. She plucked a pin from her hair and gently stirred the powder mix. "That should do it," she said.

Please, please, please, this had to work.

Aveline furrowed his brow but took his place at the firing line, where Stratford already waited.

Stratford turned and looked at her then. The gaze he fixed her with melted her to the spot. She knew he intended to win, and his look promised retribution when he did.

Liliana drew in a thready breath as he turned his attention back to his target.

"Shooters ready?" Holbrook's voice queried. The crowd quieted.

Stratford and Aveline both squared themselves to their targets.

Liliana's heart thumped hard.

"Aim . . ."

She firmed her jaw. This was the moment. The moment where she'd be made a fool or be proven right. *And likely still be considered a fool, by male and female alike.* She frowned. Well, better a vindicated fool. "Aim true," she whispered, her eyes fixed on Aveline's back.

"Fire!"

Two distinct shots rang out, one just before the other. Liliana resisted the urge to whoop. Though it was impossible to gauge with the naked eye, in her heart she knew Aveline's weapon had fired quicker. If his aim was good, they should win out.

Servants ran out to retrieve the targets. Liliana stepped up to Aveline's side, squinting as she watched the boys. She held her breath.

"Nicked it, 'e did!" came one of the boys' shouts. "Lord Aveline. Near dead center."

The boy looking at Stratford's target just shrugged.

Liliana felt her face spread in a relieved smile. She closed her eyes, ridiculously proud of herself.

The results were quickly verified, and an appreciative cheer went up. Choruses of "Nice shot, Aveline" were heard mostly, but an occasional "Well done, Miss Claremont" peppered the murmurings as the majority of the crowd dispersed.

Liliana looked to Stratford. She found him staring right at her, his eyes narrowed. Not with anger, she thought, but something altogether more dangerous to her—

"Yes, well done, Miss Claremont." Lord Aveline's smiling face appeared before her, blocking her view. He handed the spent weapon over to Holbrook. "Usually, I aim a little low, but I put my faith in you and aimed right for the center. She fired so fast!" He grinned. "Now, you must tell me how you did it."

"Chemistry," Liliana answered, moving her head to look around Aveline at Stratford, but he'd disappeared. Where had he gone? She returned her attention to her champion. "I simply sped up the reaction, which propelled the ball out of the barrel at a faster rate."

Aveline squinted his eyes and pulled his head back a touch, giving her the male version of Penelope's "drop the scholarly tone and speak plain English, please" look. "Yes, but how? What did you add to the powder?"

Liliana laughed. "Sugar."

"Sugar? As in tea and milk and all that?"

She nodded. "Yes. Gunpowder is generally a mix of charcoal, sulfur and saltpeter or niter, in very precise mixtures. Charcoal is the fuel, and saltpeter the oxidizing agent."

Aveline nodded. "Yes, I know that, but where does the sugar come in?"

Liliana glanced around once more. Where was Stratford? Winning didn't seem nearly as satisfying if one couldn't flaunt one's victory a little.

Still, several people had gathered around them, listening. A mixture of pride and unexpected stage fright swirled around in Liliana's middle.

"Sugar is a carbon, much like charcoal. I simply altered the mixture a smidge, giving the powder more fuel. Since the fire caught quicker and burned hotter, the gases expanded more rapidly, increasing the speed and force with which the ball left the gun."

"Ah," said someone.

"Brilliant," said another.

Liliana's chest swelled.

Aveline chuckled. "Splendid. I shall have to add a lump or two to my powder from here on."

A chorus of gentlemen's laughter went round.

Liliana's smile froze. "Ah," she drew out. "I wouldn't recommend that, my lord."

Aveline's brows drew down in confusion. "Whyever not?"

"There are too many variants that can affect the stability of the ratio," Liliana explained. "Take moisture, for example. I knew the humidity was right today for a positive outcome, but if it had been damp, it may not have worked as intended. There are many other such things you'd need to take into consideration if you wanted to try it again."

"Ah," Aveline said, lifting one shoulder. "There goes my advantage. Nevertheless, it was my honor to be your champion."

Liliana returned his smile. "My savior, more like." Of her pride and, what's more, from the fate of two weeks stuck by Stratford's side.

She glanced around for Stratford one last time and caught a flash of his tall frame slipping through the hedgerow. It seemed she'd annoyed him so greatly he couldn't even bring himself to congratulate her. Liliana let out a puff of breath. At least she'd seen the last of him, but . . . She blinked. Was that disappointment she felt? Oh my, it was! What had gotten into her?

Aveline pulled a watch from his vest pocket and glanced at it, drawing her attention back to him. "As much as I hate to leave, Miss Claremont, I must get back home if I'm to have time to dress and return as your escort tonight."

"Home?" If Aveline was leaving, she'd have the rest of the afternoon free. "You're not a guest at Somerton Park?"

Aveline shook his head. "My family estate borders Stratford's land to the east. I can enjoy the festivities here by day and still sleep in my own bed at night."

Liliana smiled. If Aveline wasn't staying at the house, he'd likely have to return home *every* afternoon to dress for dinner, giving her at least some time to search. If she used it efficiently, she could still find what she came for.

Aveline tucked the timepiece back into his waistcoat. "You realize, of course, that I have no intention of holding you to the wager."

"You don't?"

Her elation must have shown on her face, because he said, "You needn't look so happy about it." But he grinned, so Liliana didn't feel too guilty. "They were ridiculous terms anyway, made in the heat of masculine bartering. I have no desire to bind a woman to me who would rather be elsewhere."

Brilliant! That had been almost too easy. Still, if she didn't at least protest, Aveline might take it as insult. "My lord, that's not—"

"You needn't flatter me, Miss Claremont." Aveline laughed. "We've only just met. However, I reserve the right to try to convince you that I have more to offer than just my steady aim."

Was Aveline flirting? The wink he tossed her way certainly suggested so. How novel. Nonetheless, she wasn't interested. The only thing she wanted was to discover who killed her father and why so that she could see justice done.

And fortune smiled upon her. Not only had she won the wager, but she'd been freed of the terms. No doubt she'd find what she was looking for in no time.

Geoffrey trailed his mother's quick gait through the family hall, with Uncle Joss shuffling close behind. The countess threw open the door to her private parlor. Like most of the house, the room had been completely redone after Geoffrey's father's death. What he remembered as a warm, if somewhat plain room now boasted a screen of Corinthian columns and red flocked paper on the walls. The plasterwork had been picked with gilt and a bold pattern of reds and blacks wove through the Axminster carpet. It was an aggressive room, much like his mother.

Right now, she reminded him of an angry terrier—compact, bristling with pent-up energy and ready to snap at unsuspecting passersby. Which was why he'd agreed to follow her off the tournament field rather than stay to congratulate Liliana and Aveline as a gentleman should have. He didn't need Mother's fuming tirade to add to the gossip that would inevitably result from his and Liliana's ill-conceived wager. It would be bad enough as it was.

The countess whirled on him as soon as Uncle Joss snicked the door closed.

"I demand you send that little upstart packing." Mother's voice pitched high, and her eyes glittered with hostility in her thin face.

"Miss Claremont, you mean?" Geoffrey put as much nonchalance into his voice as he could. He crossed his arms and leaned a negligent shoulder against the doorjamb. "Whyever would I do that? I quite like her." A bit of a stretch, perhaps. An odd mixture of irritation, interest and now admiration—in ever-changing order—seemed to characterize his feelings for Liliana.

But he wouldn't have Mother dictating to him. She may have run roughshod over his father and brother, but the military had taught Geoffrey much about command. Using your opponent's worst fear against them had always worked well, and he couldn't imagine anything disturbing his mother more than the prospect of a daughter-in-law that she deemed unacceptable.

"*Like* her?" His mother sputtered, bringing a grim smile to his lips. He felt little remorse for upsetting her. Served her right for springing this affair upon him.

"Quite," Geoffrey confirmed.

The countess rose to her full height, which would be nearly a foot beneath his eyes were she standing next to him instead of across the room. She set her jaw. "Well, you can *un*like her. She's entirely unsuitable." Mother's pale skin splotched red as she balled her fists.

"I disagree," Geoffrey stated, though he suspected the countess was right, at least where he was concerned. He accepted he would have to wed. He had a responsibility to produce an heir, of course. But even more, a year spent in Parliament had shown him that politics required finesse. A savvy and well-connected political hostess would go a long way in persuading other peers—and their wives—to move in the direction he wanted them to go. If he wanted to change living conditions for ex-soldiers, he'd need to find a partner who brought very specific feminine social skills to the altar.

But that didn't stop him from tormenting Mother with the idea of Liliana Claremont for the time being.

"She's beautiful, well-spoken and, as she proved this afternoon, quite clever." Indeed. Geoffrey had very much wanted to stay and hear Liliana's explanation as to how she'd accomplished his defeat.

His mother made a moue of distaste. "She's unnatural," she countered. "She hasn't been out in society for the past three seasons. The stupid girl turned down the only offer of marriage she ever received, and I understand that she spends most of her time ensconced in the country doing God knows what," the countess spat, as if a lady who didn't regularly dance attendance at society soirees was an abomination. "Lady Turnberry claims Miss Claremont only comes to Town to attend *chemical* lectures and to pester the Royal Society to accept her as a member. Can you imagine? A woman who thinks herself a scientist?"

Geoffrey digested this new information. Her wager made much more sense to him, knowing this. What had he said to her? Oh yes, he'd asked her what a woman would know of a man's pursuits. He inwardly winced. No wonder she'd challenged him.

He envisioned the determined look on Liliana's face, and admiration moved to the forefront of the emotional jumble.

Mother, taking his silence as agreement, he supposed, moved toward him, shaking a finger as she closed the distance between them. "I went to considerable trouble arranging this party. How dare you squire around the only inappropriate miss here." Her lip jutted out in a pout. "You're doing this deliberately, aren't you? Just to provoke me."

Outrage burst in his chest, past hurts exploding into remembrance. The countess had always been a virago, doing her best to manipulate and control everyone in her sphere. But he was no longer a little boy, trying to please a mother who thought only of herself. It was high time she realized he had no intention of being ruled by her ever again.

He glared down at his mother and said in his most authoritative voice, "I dare what I will. Should I choose to march right back out to that field, drop to my knees and beg Miss Claremont to be my bride, you *will* abide by my decision."

The countess' eyes widened as she took a step back. He'd succeeded in shocking her, at least. She looked at him as if she'd just realized she didn't know him at all. Which, if he thought about it, was true. She'd paid him little attention growing up, preferring instead to focus her energies on his older brother, Henry, who took after her in both looks and personality. And now that Geoffrey was back from the continent, he was a different man altogether.

Geoffrey noticed Uncle Joss' wary look and let out a short breath. Estranging himself from his family was not his intent. He forced calm into his voice. "If she were so unsuitable, why on earth did you invite her?"

Mother's chin shot up. "I didn't. I invited her cousin, Lady Penelope. But then her aunt, the marchioness, demanded to bring the chit along."

Geoffrey nodded. He didn't really care, and for his part, he was glad Miss Claremont had been included. He felt a wry grin slide over his face. The party certainly hadn't been a bore.

A discreet scratching came from the door. His mother's face lit and she pushed past him, probably glad for the distraction.

The door opened as Geoffrey moved into the room and went to stand near the bank of windows. He heard an urgent whisper. The countess nodded and slipped out, sucking the enmity right out of the room.

Geoffrey turned back to the oversized windows and stepped between two columns to look outside. He peered down at the tournament field through watery glass. Even three stories above her, he spotted Liliana immediately. She was still on the field, a small group of women surrounding her. Liliana glowed like a beacon in blue, the other girls seeming pale in comparison. She looked so lovely, so confident as she gestured animatedly. He wished he could hear—

"Geoffrey?" The raspy voice so startled him that he nearly jumped. Good God, for the briefest of seconds he'd thought his father spoke to him from beyond the grave. When Geoffrey turned, only Uncle Joss stood there.

It was uncanny, the resemblance sometimes, but now

that Geoffrey focused upon the older man, it faded. Joss was slighter than his father had been, more soft-spoken ... though he carried the trademark Wentworth eyes and black hair, which was now shot with gray. Geoffrey wondered if Father's would be, too, were he alive.

Joss stood with his hands folded in front of him, looking at Geoffrey as he always did—as though uncertain of his reception. Geoffrey sighed. Uncle Joss' reticence was Geoffrey's own fault, and he was sorry for it. But since his father's death Geoffrey had found it difficult to spend much time in the company of the man who so reminded him of Edmund Wentworth in appearance. It was too painful.

Uncle Joss cleared his throat, and Geoffrey smiled to put him at ease. Aside from Mother, Joss was his only family.

"Forgive me," Joss began, his voice now the tenor Geoffrey knew. "I don't want to overstep my bounds, but I ... I'm sure you know how proud your father was of you. He would have been pleased to see you as earl ... not, of course, that he would have wished Henry ill," Joss was quick to say, "but he told me many times he thought you'd make the better earl."

Geoffrey opened his mouth, but Joss halted him with a raised palm.

"And now that you are, with no brothers behind you, your father's greatest wish would be for you to marry and produce an heir to carry on his line. You certainly don't want to leave the estate up to me should you pass without issue," he said with a laugh.

"You did fine," Geoffrey assured. When news of his brother's death had reached him, Geoffrey had been clinging to life after taking a bayonet through the back at Waterloo. Uncle Joss had had to act as proxy until Geoffrey's health stabilized enough to make the trip from Belgium.

"Well, I didn't run it into the ground, at least," Joss admitted with a self-deprecating smile. Then his ex-

pression turned sober. "But we're not discussing me.
We're discussing your duty to this family. Why do you
fight it so?"

Geoffrey debated how to answer the man, suspecting
that every word he said would be relayed to Mother to
be used in further attempts to "influence" him. Yet Joss
wore such an earnest expression. Geoffrey regarded him
closely. Uncle Joss was a man with no sons, and he a man
with no father. Perhaps confiding in Joss might start
them on the path of a renewed relationship, which,
Geoffrey realized with some surprise, he wanted.

He took a deep breath. "I don't fight my duty, Uncle. I
know what's expected of me." He crossed his arms and
sat lightly on the ledge of the window. "It's just that I
know how fragile life is . . ." He swallowed as the faces of
friends snuffed out on countless battlefields assailed
him. "And I understand the value of it. I intend to make
the most of my life, both as an earl and as a man."

Even as he spoke the words, emptiness yawned inside
him like an endless black gullet, yet nothing seemed to
fill the gorge. He knew he had to embrace his future if he
were ever to make a difference, to learn to be at peace
despite all he'd seen and knew of life's injustices—
friends lost in ugly, senseless death, and his men returning home to poverty and suffering while he returned to
this privileged world where he no longer fit. Where he
was all alone.

Joss' black brows formed a V. "Your mother is only
trying to—"

"The countess will have to cede to my wishes on this
matter." Geoffrey's tone rang with finality. No matter
how lonely he felt, he would not attach himself to some
"nice" girl who tolerated him because she wanted to be
a countess. Neither would he settle for the miserable excuse his parents' union had been. He would find a bride
he respected and who respected him—not for his title,
but for his passions. One who would work side by side
with him to change their country, who wouldn't balk at

diverting their personal wealth to help the common Englishman.

Liliana's face blossomed in his mind's eye, but Geoffrey banished her before the thought could even take shape. Even if she were someone who might suit, she didn't possess the connections he'd need to push through his reforms.

"I will find the right bride when I'm meant to. What's more, choosing a wife is not my first priority," Geoffrey said. The lives of returning soldiers—the lives he'd vowed to better—were more important than his own.

Joss regarded him for a moment, though he clearly wanted to say more on the subject. He finally settled on, "What are your priorities, then?"

Geoffrey considered how much to divulge. He'd shared little of himself with anyone since his return. He knew Uncle Joss had been his father's confidante. Why shouldn't Joss be his, as well?

Geoffrey leaned forward, shifting on the window ledge. "I'm sure you heard something of the uproar last year after I presented my Poverty Relief Bill to Parliament." He snorted. "You'd have thought I was committing treason by some of the remarks directed my way in the guise of 'healthy debate.'"

"I remember," Joss said, nodding. "Plenty of talk went round the clubs at the time, about how you'd been a peer for less than a year and there you were, spouting off about the poor. Aren't there more pressing problems you could champion?"

Geoffrey shook his head. "There is no problem dearer to me than this. Not when nearly four hundred thousand of the so-called poor are soldiers returning home from the wars." He could see Joss didn't understand. Perhaps if he made it more personal, more real.

Geoffrey flexed and stretched his left leg in front of him, shifting on the window seat. "Let me tell you what started me on this path. One day, walking along Bond Street, I ran into an old friend from my regiment—a good, honest man who'd served his country for ten dangerous years. I'd personally seen him show leadership, character and courage, like so many other valiant Britons I served with from *all* classes."

Geoffrey paused for emphasis. "He was starving, Uncle. Absolutely destitute. When he returned home, it was to nothing. Like so many other soldiers, he was released from the military once he was no longer needed, with no money and no prospects. He left his family and fought for his country, only to have her turn her back on him." Even now, Geoffrey felt anger swelling inside his chest. He gritted his teeth against it. Anger by itself never did any good.

"I had no idea," Joss said, not without sympathy.

"Yes, well, neither had I. I'd been so wrapped up in my own responsibilities. I did what I could for his situation, but it naturally led me to look into the plight of other soldiers. There are hundreds of thousands of them on the street who can't find employment, housing or food. And what poor relief does exist is a top-up system, based on the price of a loaf of bread and the number of children in a household. These men were off fighting, not having families, so they are the last on the list for aid that runs out long before it gets to them. Therefore, they are being forced to steal just to survive," Geoffrey said fiercely. "It's appalling after what they've given, and something must be done about it."

Joss crossed his arms over this chest and regarded Geoffrey with a worried expression. "You're not likely to change the views of the moneyed peers. Didn't how soundly your bill got trounced show you that?"

Geoffrey pushed himself off of the window ledge. "You're right, of course. I won't change their minds, not the way I went about it last time. I must retreat and leave the overt rumblings to come from the House of Commons. Then, as my social and political influence grows, I'll use it to slowly turn the tide, with Liverpool's and Wellington's help."

Joss raised his brows. "Well, my boy, if you plan to accomplish all that before you take a bride, I suppose I'd better start looking these girls over myself. As heir presumptive, it would seem up to me to carry on the family name."

Geoffrey laughed. "Look if you will, Uncle, but I doubt it will come to that. Next month, Liverpool will be presenting the Poor Employment Act, which will make significant loans to companies who agree to do public works projects by employing day laborers. That will go a long way to getting soldiers off the streets."

Joss let out a low whistle.

"Yes, and his liberal Tories will be pushing for more of that kind of change in the future, quietly, of course. Liverpool has asked me to lead that charge, behind the scenes. To do that, I must be a respected member of society and maintain an impeccable reputation."

The blackmailer's threat that loomed over him caused Geoffrey to frown, but he pushed worry away. There couldn't be any substance to it. Once this infernal party was over, he would go back to London and put it to rest. "And I will need to take a wife, as expected of a man in my position, which I intend to do."

Joss opened his mouth to reply, but at that moment, Mother sailed back through the door, a victorious smirk riding her face.

"It seems we shan't have to toss Miss Claremont out after all. Lady Belsham is as mortified by her niece's behavior as I. She and her charges shall be departing within the hour."

Chapter Nine

Liliana floated down the guest hallway on a happy balloon of self-satisfaction. By the time she'd left the field, several persons had come up to praise her for her ingenuity. Even some of the ladies had expressed their congratulations, though Liliana suspected they did so only out of relief that she obviously no longer posed competition for Stratford's affections.

She turned the knob and slid into the room. "Pen, where did you run off t—"

Liliana nearly stumbled in her shock, saved only by her grasp on the cool bronze door handle.

The room buzzed with activity as maids in their black dresses and streamered caps flitted around, shaking out garments. Only had their ruffled aprons been yellow would they look more like worker bees in the hive.

Leather trunks splayed open on every available surface, covering the celadon counterpanes, the rich mahogany tables, even the expansive window seat that looked out over an Italianate garden fountain.

Penelope, however, was nowhere to be seen. Aunt Eliza's harried voice filtered through the adjoining sitting room that separated Penelope and Liliana's chamber from her own. Liliana's breath strangled in her throat as she picked her way through both rooms to Aunt's door.

". . . never been so humiliated in my life. Did she think Stratford would overlook such an insult?" Aunt shrieked.

Dear God. They were being evicted from Somerton Park.

Panic fisted in her chest, mingled with outrage. He'd been the one who'd insulted *her*. Well, all right, she'd nettled him first, but only to dissuade his attentions. What kind of gentleman loses a wager and then tosses the victor out on the street in a fit of temper?

Liliana released a pent-up breath and tried to apply some logic to the situation. Stratford undoubtedly employed strategy here. *If* he had been involved in her father's death, or knew someone in his family had been, he might suspect she'd come to discover the truth. And if, as rumor had it, he had political aspirations, he'd want to banish her from his home as soon as possible, before she could find any proof.

Fool that she was, she'd given him the perfect excuse. And for what? Her pride? Moisture stung her eyes. Deep inside she knew that if she left Somerton Park today, she'd never uncover the truth.

Liliana blinked, keeping her frustrated tears at bay. Could she fix this somehow? If she were mistaken about his intentions, if he were removing her just to assuage *his* pride, would an apology buy her a reprieve? It would gall her to do so, to apologize for being herself, but she would do it.

However, first she'd need to determine how severe the situation was. She pushed open the heavy wooden door to Aunt's room.

Penelope sat, leaned forward on an armchair, an anxious, pursed expression on her normally cheery face. Pen's usual pink cheeks were more the color of the cream stripes splitting the cornflower fabric of the chair. Aunt Eliza paced at the foot of the ornately carved bed, the massive piece dwarfing the woman in size, if not ostentation. Her plump face snapped up at the intrusion.

Aunt's matronly features, already mottled, colored a

deeper shade of red. Liliana could see the gathering storm in Aunt Eliza's eyes. The room fairly crackled with it.

"You," Aunt muttered, and the wealth of distaste, disapproval and worse—disappointment—packed into that one little word pierced Liliana with a sharpness that stole her breath. God help her, she'd thought herself beyond being hurt at Aunt's inability to understand and accept her.

Not that Aunt hadn't tried, in her way, to care for and nurture her brother's orphan. But every time Liliana's actions had been contrary to what Aunt Eliza expected, Aunt took it as a personal failure. Even the subsequent tongue lashings had never completely removed Liliana's own sense of guilt for letting down the only "mother" she'd known.

"This! This is the thanks I get for securing you the most sought-after invitation in a decade?" Aunt cried, flailing her arms in Liliana's direction. "I wash my hands of you. You and your *theories* . . ." Her lips flattened, as did her voice. "You're an embarrassment. I don't know why I ever thought you'd change."

Liliana's throat constricted as she swallowed the defensive words that shot up. A tendril of unease snaked up her spine. Aunt had been angry in the past, but she'd never threatened to be done with Liliana completely, and in such calm tones.

"I convinced myself that three years on your own had brought you to your senses," Aunt said. "That after living in that drafty, bare cottage on the meager funds your father left, you'd be eager for a husband and act accordingly." Aunt turned her face away. "I had such high hopes for this party." She huffed. "I'd never dreamed you might interest Stratford, but I'd thought you might catch the eye of a nice country squire. But now . . ."

"I'm sure it's not as bad as all that."

"Ha!" Aunt stepped nearer to Penelope, waving a hand. "Have you considered how your distressing behavior taints your cousin?"

Liliana's heart twisted, and she glanced at Pen, who subtly shook her head as if to say "Don't worry about me." Liliana truly regretted any embarrassment to Penelope. She, too, was being asked to leave. That wouldn't do. "I will apologize to Lord Stratford," Liliana offered. "Try to convince him to let us stay. I do not wish for you or Pen to be punished for my actions."

Aunt turned back to face Liliana squarely. "Stratford did not demand our departure—which is a credit to him. Credit me, however, with knowing when we've overstayed our welcome."

"Then you've initiated our departure?" Hope leapt in her chest. Perhaps Aunt might be made to see reason and they wouldn't have to leave after all. "Please. Don't draw more attention than the situation deserves. Any gossip should blow over quickly and not touch Penelope at all. Besides, I actually received several kind compliments . . ."

Aunt narrowed her eyes, but Liliana rushed on.

"And Lord Aveline praised me effusively. I don't think he was just being kind. I think he quite liked me." Rather desperate—to throw another potential suitor in the mix—but she'd use anything at her disposal. "I promise, I shall be on my best behavior if you change your mind. Please." Liliana crossed her mental fingers. She couldn't remain here alone without Aunt's support and chaperonage. "Please let us stay."

Aunt Eliza's face contorted. "No. You have no 'best behavior.' Never have. I can't risk you making us more of a laughingstock. And I must seriously consider the wisdom of allowing Penelope in your company in future. You're a bad influence."

Liliana felt her blood drain to her toes.

"Penelope?" Aunt directed her daughter with a flick of the wrist. "I suggest you oversee the packing of your things." Aunt turned her back on Liliana.

That was it, then. Liliana gritted her teeth and closed her stinging eyes. The desire to rail at the injustice fairly burst out of her. Were she a man, the wager would have

been seen as friendly sport. She would be congratulated
for her cunning, not threatened with losing her family.
And most of all, she wouldn't be forced to leave because
of her aunt's ridiculous sensibilities.

Liliana knew very well that if she did ever marry, it
would be worse, even, than this. A husband would virtually own her. Her mother had been fortunate to find a
kindred spirit in her father, a man who had seen her
value and her talents and had encouraged them, society
be damned.

Yet times had changed even in a generation. Young
ladies were expected, more than ever, to act like shel-
tered possessions rather than people, a beautiful trinket
to adorn a man's side—unable to think and reason like a
man, and lost without one. Three seasons amongst the
beaus of the ton had shown her that. Well, they and the
one suitor Aunt Eliza had pressed upon her. Sir Aberna-
thy Colton-Smith. Liliana shuddered at the memory of
the odious man and his boorish attitudes. He'd even forbid her to continue with her work as a contingency of his
suit, a condition Aunt Eliza had encouraged. Thankfully,
she'd had the meager living Papa had settled on her, so
she'd been able to refuse. Liliana longed for the day she
was firmly on the shelf. At least then she'd have some
semblance of freedom.

A knock sounded in the distance, perhaps from the
door that separated the sitting room from the guest hallway. A few moments later, a maid popped a hesitant
head into Aunt's chamber.

"Beggin' yer pardon, my lady." The maid bobbed. "Er,
'is lordship requests to speak with you and the young
misses."

"What?" Aunt snapped, her graying blond head tip-
ping to the side. "Now?"

The maid's lips pressed together, as if she were out of
her element and trying valiantly to brazen through. "Yes,
my lady. He wonders if you might join him in your sitting room."

Aunt turned her head to glare at Liliana, as if to say "See what you've done?"

"Of course," Aunt murmured, pointing at Liliana and Penelope to precede her.

Stratford paced near the hearth, his hands clasped behind his back, an uncomfortable grimace on his face that somehow didn't detract from his stark handsomeness. He turned at their entrance, his bearing erect and tense, as if preparing himself for an unpleasant task. Liliana closed her eyes. He'd come to demand their departure after all, it seemed. There would be no saving the situation.

Stratford cleared his throat. "Forgive the irregular nature of my call, Lady Belsham," he said, "but it has come to my understanding you plan to leave us."

Liliana opened her eyes. Those weren't words of expulsion.

Aunt gave a brisk nod. "Yes, my lord. Please forgive my *niece's* awful behavior this afternoon," she said, emphasizing their relationship as if trying to distance herself and her own daughter as much as possible. "I regret the scene she caused. You shall be rid of us, posthaste, and most discreetly."

Liliana trembled as mortification flooded her. She felt Stratford's eyes on her and she looked up, struck again by his intense blue gaze.

"No," he said.

No?

Aunt blinked, seemingly as taken aback at his short utterance as Liliana was.

"I do not wish you to leave," he said, amazingly. "And it is I who owes Miss Claremont an apology, as well as my congratulations." He crossed the room in an elegant stride to stand before Liliana. Her heart catapulted into her throat as he stared down at her, his smell of musk and mint subtly surrounding her. "I thoughtlessly provoked you this afternoon, and for that, I am sorry. Please don't feel as if you must leave on my account. In fact, I would prefer you to stay. Besides"—his lips turned up in a wry smile—"I don't think I could live without knowing exactly how you gave Aveline the up on me."

Liliana stared so long at him that her eyes turned drier than sodium sulfate. Why was he being kind? And why, if he suspected her intentions, would he ask her to remain in his home? "I—" She couldn't think of anything to say.

He took advantage of her flummox and smiled, which, oddly enough, flummoxed her all the more. "It's settled, then? I'm so glad." He turned to Aunt Eliza, who stared at him as if he'd sprouted another nose. "I do hope the three of you"—he glanced back and nodded at Liliana—"and Lord Aveline, of course, will join me at the head of the table. It's only fitting your niece be given the place of honor for her brilliant performance this afternoon."

"Of course," Aunt said automatically. Aunt would never willingly offend Stratford.

"Good," he said, turning back to Liliana. Something in his eyes made her go all hot inside. "Until this evening." He nodded and left the room.

Aunt turned to Liliana, pinning her with a speculative gaze. "It seems we shall be staying."

Penelope skirted out of the room with a bright smile, and Liliana could hear her directing maids to unpack and rehang their clothing.

Liliana nearly slumped with relief. Stratford had saved her, provided her another chance to find her answers. Her relief quickly turned to an uncomfortable bewilderment. Why had he done it?

And what did it say about her if she used his kindness against him?

Geoffrey sat at the head of the imposing sixteenth-century dining table, where generations of Wentworths had held lavish suppers much like this one. Several leaves had been removed, as only forty or so guests joined him this evening, but the table could accommodate as many as eighty diners with room to spare.

Glassware tinkled and ornate silver cutlery dinged against china in melodic counterpoint to the lively conversation.

Geoffrey set down his heavy spoon, the lobster bisque barely touched. He knew several—at least seven—more courses were to follow. During his years in the army, there had been many days when he and his men had been grateful to have one sparse meal. Perhaps broth. Maybe bread or cheese. His stomach turned at the knowledge that many of his fellow soldiers were likely not eating any better than that even today. How he wished his table was filled with them right now, rather than this privileged class that he was both part of and apart from.

His eyes strayed to Liliana, seated next to him on his right. In appearance, at least, she'd fit in at his imaginary table. How lovely she was, even with her hair swept up in a plain chignon and her long neck unadorned by flashy jewels. In her simple satin dancing dress trimmed with shiny gold piping around the sheer sleeves, hemline and bust, she stood out in stark contrast to the wasteful opulence that surrounded her. He remembered how ill at ease she'd seemed this afternoon surrounded by some of the more frivolous members of society. Nothing in her mannerisms gave her away tonight, but he got the distinct feeling that she, like him, would be more comfortable with soldiers and commoners than with this lot.

She laughed at something Aveline said, and the husky timbre of her voice vibrated through Geoffrey, his body hardening in reaction. Just being in her presence affected him, had from the moment he'd broken her fall in the library. It was as if his very skin hummed with energy, every nerve on edge. The closest feeling he could compare it to was the invigorating moments just before battle, when he felt more alert and alive than at any other time in his life, ready to take on the world.

How inconvenient that Liliana seemed the sole woman to do that to him. If only he could find a bride just like her, who made him feel the way she did but who was better connected and moved more easily in society.

The countess, seated directly across from Liliana on Geoffrey's left, snatched a wineglass from the table. His mother had nearly had an apoplexy when he'd announced the amended seating arrangements for tonight's dinner. Thankfully, she'd stayed mutinously silent, except for the occasional snort as the tale of Liliana's sugared gunpowder had been retold.

But he could tell by the way Mother gripped her stemware coupled with the calculating gaze she aimed at Liliana that the silence would not last much longer.

"Tell me, Miss Claremont," Mother asked with deceptive idleness, "was it your father who encouraged your *unconventional* education?"

A distinct lull in the conversation around them became noticeable as eager ears tilted in their direction.

Liliana's golden skin went white. Geoffrey clenched his hand into a tight fist.

Liliana's aunt, Lady Belsham, raised a finger in defense. "Oh, I can assure you that Liliana received an entirely proper education for a young lady." The woman smiled at Lord Aveline when making her statement, a fact Geoffrey noted with irritation.

Mother slanted a glance at the marchioness and gave a slight twist of the lips. The countess would not be overtly rude to a woman who outranked her. But Lady Belsham had been a baron's daughter before marrying a marquess. Geoffrey knew Mother considered her own superior bloodline enough of a buffer to excuse a touch of spite.

"I'm certain you made sure of that, as best you could, Lady Belsham," the countess conceded, but her tone conveyed her doubt that the lessons took. "It must have been a challenge, taking on a girl practically grown and untutored. But who could expect her to be properly trained when she was raised by a bachelor father?"

Damn his mother. Geoffrey had insisted Liliana stay at Somerton Park largely because he knew her reputation would suffer if it appeared she'd been asked to leave. Not her moral reputation, of course, but the gossips would have enjoyed spreading how she'd earned the disapproval of the house of Stratford. Now Mother was making sure the scandalmongers would still have their fodder.

He tossed his napkin aside, ready to put a stop to this.

"Widowed," Liliana clarified, forestalling him. She eyed his mother with a steely gaze, her jaw firm.

Mother's feral smile widened, threatening to rip the girl to shreds.

"Ah yes," Mother said, steepling her fingers and tapping the indexes together. "Your mother passed when you were quite young. A gentleman's daughter, was she not?"

The pitying glances being tossed Liliana's way proved that his mother couldn't have done more damage to the girl had she stood up and screamed, "Unfit to be at this table!"

"Yes, and a gifted healer, one who gave her life helping others," Liliana countered, "which in my view is the *true* definition of being a lady."

The countess laughed, a trill that grated Geoffrey's nerves. Others within earshot joined in with their own nervous titters. "How very *progressive* of you, my dear."

Liliana's eyes narrowed, but Lady Belsham cringed, looking as if she wished to melt from her chair into a puddle and drip through the floorboards. This had gone far enough.

"I, for one, agree with Miss Claremont," Geoffrey stated. Several pairs of shocked eyes turned in his direction as he countermanded his mother. He'd hoped to avoid a scene, but he would not allow any more damage to be done. He reached for a cut-crystal wineglass, then stood. "As am I quite impressed with her resourcefulness and quick thinking, two traits I hold in the highest esteem." He angled his body toward her and raised his glass, looking out over the assemblage with a raised brow until all, save the countess, had followed suit. "To Miss Claremont."

"To Miss Claremont," came the response, not heartily, but well enough. He'd done what he could, short of starting a very public war with the countess. Diners returned to their conversations, and he resumed his seat.

Liliana stared at him, her eyes seeming to take his measure. He glimpsed uncertainty in her gaze, as if she wasn't quite sure how to view him. She gave him a slight nod before turning away to respond to something Aveline said.

Geoffrey took another sip of his wine, aware that others continued to watch him. His words might be seen as defense of a guest, but some would guess at his true feelings. How he detested the pervasive attitude that the more highborn one was, the better class of person. He'd been raised to believe that, as well, but his years in the military had turned his values on end. He'd seen highborn men cut and run while the lowliest common soldier stood bravely until the end, and knew damned well that birth had little to do with one's character.

Still, something else the military had taught him was to choose one's battles. Geoffrey regarded his mother from beneath his lids. She fairly seethed. Toying with Mother by squiring Liliana around today had been enjoyable, but since he couldn't offer for a girl like her, the best thing he could do for Miss Claremont would be to steer clear for the remainder of the party and thus spare her from the countess' wrath.

Chapter Ten

Satin slid around Liliana's calf as she rolled out of a twirl. A sigh escaped her as the rousing cotillion came to an end and her skirts settled back around her ankles. She immediately smiled, hoping Aveline perceived her exhalation to mean she'd enjoyed the dance instead of what it truly meant—that she wished he had stayed home tonight.

After all, it wasn't his fault the two days since "the Major's Wager," as people had taken to calling the shooting match, had left her ready to weep in frustration.

She still hadn't found a way into the study. Nor was she closer to discovering a link between her father and the late earl. Two days of searching hadn't even produced so much as a handwriting sample to compare with the killer's note.

Worse, she still didn't know what to think about Stratford himself. He'd had his chance to be rid of her, to ensure she found nothing. A guilty man would have taken it. Maybe.

She nearly groaned aloud. It did her no good to speculate about Stratford's motives, but there was one way she could be sure, once and for all, whether or not *he* was the author of the letters that lured her father to his death.

She scanned the room, catching Stratford out of the

corner of her eye as he escorted Lady Emily Morton from the floor. Hmm. That meant he'd danced with Lady Emily, Jane Northumb, and Ann Manchester so far this evening.

That gave her one-in-three odds.

This would have been much easier had Stratford asked *her* to dance just once in the past three nights. But he hadn't hadn't spoken a word to her since dinner the night of the tournament.

Aveline took her by the elbow. "Shall we stroll for a bit?" he asked, leading her from the parquet dance floor.

She turned to him. "I'd prefer a bit of a rest, actually," she answered, touching a hand to her face. "Might you fetch me a lemonade?"

She couldn't very well carry out her aim with him tagging along.

"As you wish." He nodded and strode away.

Liliana blew out a breath, relieved to be rid of him.

Which was quite unfair. Aveline had proven to be a most ideal and fortuitous escort. Though he'd released her from their wager, he'd arrived every morning and breakfasted with her, a situation Aunt Eliza found very encouraging. He'd partnered her in a morning game of bowls. He made light, pleasant conversation and had even charmed Aunt Eliza on several occasions, which did much to relax the strain between aunt and niece.

Best of all, Aveline departed after lunch, claiming estate business, not to return until dinner—leaving Liliana to her own devices all afternoon without making anyone suspicious.

A perfect arrangement, given her circumstance. And she'd been most grateful to have missed Lady Stratford's more ridiculous frivolities, which tended to happen after lunch—though she might have paid to see the line of women wrangling to have their hooks baited by Stratford in yesterday's female fishing derby.

But her time at Somerton Park was dwindling.

She turned on her heel and made her way to the la-

dies' retiring room. She slipped in quietly, letting her
eyes adjust to the dimmer light. The hum of feminine
murmurings disconcerted her, as always, bringing back
unpleasant memories of the three seasons she'd been
forced to endure before Aunt finally gave up on her.

Liliana scanned the parlor, spotting her quarry. Emily
Morton's sage skirts blended into the green satin striped
chaise on which she half reclined, one arm thrown over
the back of the lounge.

Liliana looked at the girl's other hand, which rested
splayed across her stomach. Only a shimmering emerald
bracelet adorned her wrist.

Moving into the room past two primping ladies, Liliana casually skirted the headrest of the chaise. She
slanted her eyes downward. A pretty green ribbon tied
the dance card to Miss Morton. She had to get a look at
Stratford's signature.

She bent at the knees, squatting as she pretended to
fiddle with her slipper. She turned her head toward the
dangling card. Blast. It faced the wrong direction.

She reached out and gripped the paper, tilting it.

Holbrook ... strong masculine scratching. *Banbury* ...
rather loopy on the *B*.

A rustling sound came from above.

Thornton ... horrible penmanship. Ah, here was
Wentworth ... but that would be Josslyn Wentworth,
Stratford's uncle, as Stratford himself would use his title.
Still, it was not even close, the writing much too effemi-
nate to match. Next was *Str*—

The card slid from her grasp. She instinctively clamped
her fingers together, giving it an inadvertent tug.

Emily Morton shrieked and sat up, yanking her arm
and the card completely out of Liliana's reach. The sudden movement startled Liliana so, she jerked backward
and toppled, landing solidly on her rear.

"What ... ?" came Emily's bewildered voice. Liliana
glanced up as a blond head appeared over the back of
the chaise.

Liliana's cheeks heated. "I'm sorry. I . . ." She clamped her lips. She could hardly say "I just need your dance card for one more moment, please."

The girl frowned and narrowed her eyes. Liliana braved it out with a tight smile. Better to be thought clumsy than to be caught red-fingered, as it were.

Emily turned her back with a *humph* and hurried out of the room.

Muffled sniggers came from behind her. Liliana's shoulders slumped. How she wished she could vaporize like mercury over a hot flame. She shuddered to think what story Miss Morton would be spreading about the ballroom this very moment.

The door clicked open as someone else entered the room. Wonderful.

"Dare I ask?" Penelope stepped around the chaise and reached down to her.

The two primpers edged past them and left the room, probably off to add their accounts to the tale. She could only hope Aunt Eliza didn't hear of it.

Liliana accepted the hand up and dropped onto the chaise. "I'm stymied, Pen," she sighed.

"Mmm," Penelope murmured over the swish of her skirts as she lowered herself to sit beside Liliana.

"I just tried to lift a cursed dance card simply to get a look at Stratford's handwriting." Liliana slapped her palm sharply against her thigh, but the thick satin muffled the sound—leaving her quite unsatisfied.

"Whyever would you want to see Stratford's handwriting?" Penelope asked, bemused.

"Because I'm utterly desperate," Liliana admitted. "Presumably it was the late earl who corresponded with my father and who drew him out on the night he was murdered, as the letters were marked with his seal, but without a handwriting sample, I can't be absolutely certain of that. I haven't found a journal, correspondence, household accounts—anything that I can compare those letters to." She dropped her head. "It's as if everything of a personal nature has been stripped from this house with military precision."

"Oh," Penelope said, her winged blond brows pulling slightly together. She patted Liliana's hand. "But if you're looking for the dead earl's handwriting, why do you need to see Stratford's? Wasn't he already off to war when Uncle Charles was killed?"

"I'm not sure, precisely, when he left England. And besides . . ." Liliana sighed. Pen had done everything she'd asked of her in this charade, asking very little. It was only right to share her suspicions that her father had been involved in some sort of espionage and what logical implications sprang from that. Pen's eyes widened with the telling. "So you see?" Liliana finished. "I need to rule Stratford out as the author of the letters. I also need to learn where both he and his father were during the months they were written, and particularly in December of 1803, but I'm coming up empty."

Her feelings of defeat must have shown in her face, because Penelope put a consoling arm around her shoulder. They sat together in silence a moment before Pen said, "Servants! They know everything that goes on in a house, particularly when you wish they didn't."

"I thought of that," Liliana said, "but Stratford's brother turned the staff over completely during his tenure." As she'd learned from the current housekeeper.

"I see," Penelope said, touching a pink-gloved finger to her lip. "Perhaps some of those older servants still live in the village and would remember that winter."

Liliana nodded, hope stirring to life. Improbable, maybe, that she would develop a lead from such a visit, but one thing her father taught her—keep experimenting until you find an answer. "But the village is not within walking distance, and I am at the mercy of Stratford's stable." How she hated this helpless feeling. "How would I get there?"

"Hmm . . ." Penelope seemed to deflate, echoing Liliana's feelings. Then she brightened. "Well, if anyone can find a way, you will. You have always been one who works doggedly for what you want. I remember how many nights you stayed awake until your candles were nubs to study your sciences. All because Mother thought she could force you to forget the idea if she insisted you complete her approved course work first."

Liliana smiled reluctantly at the memory. Aunt Eliza had tried ceaselessly to mold her into the perfect English lady. She'd been adamant that Liliana study the typical feminine pursuits—French, literature, music, deportment. Even though Papa's will had provided for her to study the natural sciences with a colleague of his, she was allowed to only *after* she finished her other studies. Liliana had slept very little. But she'd refused to give in, to lose what part of her father she still had by wasting her life on frivolity. To not use her intelligence to carry on his work would have been like him dying all over again. Like his life had meant nothing.

Some days, it had seemed an impossible task, but it had deepened her determination, a trait that served her well later in life as she struggled to become recognized in the scientific world even though a woman. And it would serve her well now. She would do whatever it took to find the answers she was looking for. Tomorrow she'd find a way to escape to the village. Her likelihood of success might be slim, but scientists dealt in seeming impossibilities every day.

The one thing she knew was that the only true failure was to quit trying.

And she would not give up today.

Chapter Eleven

Puffs of white gusted from man and beast in the crisp morning air. The thundering of hooves and the harsh exhalations of his own breath were all Geoffrey heard, all he could focus on as he pushed Gringolet faster and faster.

The day had dawned in brilliant hues. Pinks and deep yellows were just starting to chase away myriad colors of indigo and blue that hovered in the mist. It blanketed the ground, rising like smoke on the battlefield. Geoffrey squeezed his eyes shut and pushed Grin harder.

After ten years together in the 12th Light Dragoons, Geoffrey couldn't have parted with the charger. The horse was a tie to his past, a bloody past he desperately wanted to let go of but never could. Grin was just as vital to his present. Without their daily ride, without the avenue to pound out the frustrations of this new life, Geoffrey didn't know how he'd survive. He needed the escape, this morning in particular.

He drove the horse until Grin's chest heaved beneath him. Geoffrey eased back on the reins, bringing Gringolet to a halt on the low rise overlooking the lake. He reached forward to stroke Grin's sleek gray neck. The stallion's heartbeat pulsed vigorously, as did his own. Grin blew a long breath that fluttered his horsey lips.

"I'm sorry, old boy. We're not as young as we used to be," Geoffrey lamented, a frown creasing his face. Why was he taking such chances? Only a fool would ride that dangerously fast without a host of enemies chasing him.

Geoffrey led his horse nearer to the water. The sunrise reflected in the still, glassy lake, and as Geoffrey looked out over the expanse, he envied its peace and serenity. God knew his life since inheriting the earldom had been severely lacking in those qualities.

As if taking on the enormous responsibilities of the earldom's vast holdings and business dealings while wading through Parliament weren't challenge enough, the blackmail threat had arrived earlier this week at his town house. No, his reign as earl had not been peaceful, and he had no expectation it would become so anytime soon.

Yet he suspected something else drove him to recklessness this morning.

Or rather some*one* else.

For the third night in a row, he'd been kept awake by thoughts and dreams of Liliana Claremont. Damn, but she'd gotten under his skin.

He'd done his best to ignore her since dinner three nights past, but his body hummed with awareness anytime they were in the same room. His eyes were drawn to her every efficient yet graceful move, his ears attuned to her husky voice. Even his nose smelled apples and lemons where there were none.

Like now. Geoffrey drew in a deep breath of crisp morning air to clear his senses.

This had to stop. But ignoring Liliana wasn't working . . . The harder he tried, the more she haunted his dreams. Last night, his "fantasy Liliana" had come to him in the library clad only in a filmy ivory dressing gown. Her creamy golden skin had glowed against the lighter fabric, the hints of red in her hair glinting in the firelight. She'd said nothing, simply beckoned him with her violet gaze. She'd knelt before him and—

Dear God. His entire body hardened at the memory. He couldn't go around like this for the remainder of the house party. What was it about that woman that attracted him so, against his better judgment?

Gringolet's ears perked and the stallion raised his head, alert. Geoffrey looked in the same direction but saw nothing. Nor did he hear a sound out of place amidst nature's morning cacophony. He'd learned years ago to trust Grin's instincts, however. Geoffrey sat motionless, tense in the saddle, ready for whatever came.

The horse burst through the woodland into the meadow like a covey of grouse at first shot. Geoffrey could hear the echo of the nonexistent gunshot, so real was the impression. Then he realized it was simply his own heart pounding in his ears.

Liliana.

He wasn't sure how he knew it was she, for the rider was in breeches and sitting astride. A cap covered her hair and she was at least fifty yards to the other side of the lake, but there was still no doubt. He prickled with that singular awareness he'd come to associate only with her.

She bent forward, leaning over the horse's neck as she said something to the mount. Encouragement, most likely, if the burst of speed was any indication. Only a few of his stock could fly like that . . .

By God, she rode Amira. She must have convinced Griggs she was a capable rider, or the stable master would never have saddled Geoffrey's favorite mare for her. Still, he'd have to have a word with the man. Amira was too valuable for guests to take out.

His concern eased as horse and rider raced closer. Amira was in capable hands, and Liliana's obvious skill told him she rode astride often.

Yet another trait that supported Geoffrey's growing opinion that Liliana Claremont was no ordinary miss.

He accepted that he'd been wrong about her. She'd proven she had no interest in winning him. Rather demonstrably. She'd insulted him, ridiculed him, challenged him and bested him. After his anger had abated, he'd realized she also intrigued him.

Liliana slowed the mare to a canter, then a trot. She'd been coming from the east ... Something squeezed within him. Aveline's holdings lay just over the park. Geoffrey's fists clenched. While he'd been overly aware of Liliana these past three days, she'd had eyes only for Aveline, rot him. Did she return now from a night in his arms?

No. Geoffrey gave his head a shake. Amira had been in the stable when he'd saddled Grin, and he'd been riding only an hour. And while one could certainly do the deed in less time, Geoffrey had never known Aveline to seduce innocent young maidens.

The urge to throttle the other man eased, and Geoffrey relaxed his shoulders. He'd forgotten how easily jealousy could make one think like a fool.

Jealousy? Of course not. He straightened in his saddle, unease creeping in. Jealousy was a precursor to love, and he adamantly refused to succumb to *that* debilitating emotion. Just because he'd been intrigued by the chit didn't mean his feelings had been moved. Admittedly she provoked a powerful attraction, but that had nothing to do with finer emotions. He wouldn't allow himself to fall victim to his father's fate. Look what love had gotten him.

Still, his curiosity roused. Why was Liliana out riding unaccompanied and so very early, not to mention scandalously dressed? Well, he wouldn't know unless he asked.

Geoffrey knew the exact moment Liliana became aware of his presence as he and Grin emerged from the greenery. Her face went blank and her eyelids fluttered down. She glanced toward the house, probably judging whether she could pretend she hadn't seen him and flee to the stables.

Instead she waited in the meadow.

Amira tipped her head and nickered a welcome that

Grin returned. Liliana greeted Geoffrey with a tight smile and a nod. She looked prepared to bolt.

"A lady who rises before noon," Geoffrey marveled. "I thought surely this would be the last place I would encounter one of my female guests."

Liliana's brow creased, then smoothed as she tilted her head. "An eligible lord who is wealthy, handsome and not well into his dotage?" She shrugged. "I'm surprised you're not being stalked from hill to dale, regardless of the hour," she said, her tone full of irony.

And she smiled.

And that smile lit him, drawing one in return. "Is that what you are doing, Miss Claremont? Stalking me?" he teased. "First the library and now on my morning ride . . . I do believe that's a pattern."

She huffed. "Since I arrived in the library well before you, I couldn't possibly have followed you there. This morning, however, I shall admit to nothing." She looked up at him in her direct way but gave him a decidedly mysterious smile that told him he'd been forgiven for his erroneous assumption in the library that first night. "I shall leave you to wonder."

Geoffrey grinned. He couldn't help it. "Then my ego shall, of course, believe you are stalking me most shamelessly."

Liliana ducked her head on a smile. How unexpected.

Satisfaction spread through Geoffrey like a warm salve. Liliana might not want marriage, as she claimed, even to the Earl of Stratford. But she did want him—Geoffrey.

And he was happier about that than he should be.

Still, she hadn't satisfied his curiosity.

"You're quite a horsewoman," he remarked. His eyes roamed over her tawny pants, which showcased long, slim thighs and shapely calves. The flowing white shirt gave cover to her derrière, but Geoffrey could easily imagine the fabric clinging tightly to her.

She followed his eyes, then seemed to remember her

unorthodox attire. She clearly wanted to groan, but good manners won out.

"Thank you," she said, choosing not to address her apparel or saddle choice.

He smiled at her aplomb and tried a different tack. "Amira fits you well. How did you get Griggs to part with her?" Geoffrey asked, though he had his suspicions. If Liliana had smiled at Griggs the way she did at him, he couldn't possibly take the stable master to task with good conscience.

Her face flushed. "Is that her name? It means *princess*, does it not?"

"In Arabic, yes," he replied. "I thought it fitting, as her sire's name is Sultan."

"Ah." Liliana nodded to Grin. "And who is this handsome gentleman? Arabian as well?"

"Close," Geoffrey answered, tapping his ring finger impatiently upon his thigh. Was she avoiding his question? "Gringolet's a Barb, a breed similar to Arabian but originally from North Africa."

"Gringolet?" she inquired, raising an eyebrow. She leaned toward Geoffrey, just slightly, which brought to mind his fantasy of last night. "Fancy yourself Sir Gawain, then?"

Now *he* felt himself flush. "Not quite. The other soldiers in my regiment gave me that moniker, though Gringolet's name did spring from it."

Liliana raised both eyebrows this time. "Sir Gawain is portrayed as the consummate ladies' man. Is that how you earned your name?" she asked boldly, but her ears turned pinkish.

"King Arthur's nephew was also known as the friend to young knights," he defended. "I took it upon myself to look after the new recruits. I like to think *that* is what inspired the name." He wasn't about to tell her it was likely a bit of both. And how had they come to be discussing him? "Griggs didn't give her name when he saddled Amira for you?"

Liliana's lovely features pulled into a grimace. She shifted in her saddle.

"Ah ... well. As to that. I—" She wrung her hands, her leather gloves creaking as they twisted together. She took a deep breath before meeting his gaze. "I horsenapped her."

Geoffrey blinked once, wondering if he'd heard her correctly. Then he blinked again. He couldn't have been more shocked had she told him she was the illegitimate daughter of Maria Fitzherbert and Prince George himself.

Liliana swallowed, the sound audible only to her ear, she hoped.

Stratford's head dropped slowly as he fixed her with his intense stare. "You horsenapped my prize mare ... ?" he repeated.

At least he sounded more confused than angry.

Perhaps she could yet brazen her way out of this situation.

She'd nearly lost her breakfast when Stratford had appeared like a wraith out of the mist. Of all persons to encounter when she'd been so close to returning unnoticed.

But as he'd approached, the oddest thing had happened. Her fear had dissipated, to be replaced by something warmer. Something that prickled her skin and caused her to shiver as fear would, but then settled pleasantly in her middle.

Now, however, nervousness returned. She thought she'd managed the conversation well so far, but what could she say to that?

"Y-yes," she admitted. "Though I didn't know she was your prize horse. She was most beautiful, of course," Liliana praised, knowing men liked to be flattered. "And the most ... convenient," she finished lamely, but didn't look away.

Stratford sat upon his steed, mouth agape, regarding her as if she'd just escaped Bedlam. She didn't know if she'd ever seen such a befuddled look on a man before, unless, of course, she were trying to explain John Dalton's theory of chemical atomism to them.

An absurd urge to laugh overtook her. She knew it was only her mind's physiological response to the strain, because truly, this wasn't the least bit comical.

Stratford closed his mouth, then opened it again. Then closed it like a sturgeon out of water.

All right, perhaps it was a bit funny.

"But why on earth would you feel the need to steal my horse?" he finally asked.

Why indeed. Liliana glanced to her right. She couldn't possibly tell the truth. Yet Penelope had accused her time and again of being a terrible liar. She should be as honest as she could and pray for the best.

Why *would* she feel the need to steal his horse if not to sneak to the village to ask questions about him and his family?

"I am accustomed to riding every morning," she explained, able to make eye contact again. That was true, at least. "I did not wish to ask your permission, given we are so much at odds." She bowed her head and tried to sound contrite. "I do apologize."

There. She peeped at him from beneath her lashes. A gentleman would accept her apology and send her on her way, perhaps with an admonishment.

Stratford leaned back slightly in his saddle, his eyes narrowing thoughtfully. "And you hadn't time to pilfer a sidesaddle, I gather," he remarked drily.

Liliana's head came up as she fought off a scowl. She composed herself. She'd stick to as-honest-as-possible answers.

"It is my habit to ride astride," she stated. "I find it more practical when out collecting specimens and data for my experiments. It is much easier and safer amidst the brambles and bogs I frequent."

"Your experiments?" he asked, drawing his brows together.

"Yes," she said. "I am a chemist. And a healer." Liliana felt her chin rise, expecting him to ridicule her as he had that night in the library when she'd offered him her help.

But he didn't scoff today. "I should like to hear more about your experiments," he said, quite shocking her to her toes. "However, before we get to that, I must admit to a different curiosity. I've known some first-rate horsemen in my life, many of whom looked no better in the saddle than you. This isn't the first time you've raced through the countryside at breakneck speed," he guessed.

A laugh escaped her, neither rich nor brittle. It sounded something in between, something bittersweet that she feared revealed more than she'd wanted to.

Blast. She should leave, should whirl Amira around and race back to the stables. But Stratford leaned toward her, his face awash with interest. A genuine interest no man, save her father, had ever shown her, and she couldn't help answering, "No. Nor do I consider myself a great horsewoman, though I rarely miss a morning. Riding for me is simply . . ." She searched for the right word.

"An escape," they both said at the very same moment.

Silence hung between them. What could a rich lord like him possibly feel the need to escape from?

"Escape from what?" Geoffrey voiced her question, but to her.

"From the strictures of my life. From the frustrations of being born a woman with a scientific mind in a man's world. From being pressed by my aunt to always—" She clapped her mouth shut, shaking her head. She'd shared quite enough; and she wasn't even certain why. "You wouldn't understand," she demurred.

"You might be surprised," he answered, his voice quiet and solemn and just a touch rough. Her breath caught as well, and she couldn't look away from him. His eyes held a haunted quality she'd never noticed before—something lurked in their depths that called to her.

And discomfited her, greatly.

She turned her face from him. "That might be true. However, as both of us will be expected at breakfast, we haven't the time," she said, grateful her tone sounded brisk. She sat up straight, pulling Amira around. "I am sorry I took your horse without permission, my lord. It won't happen again."

"No, it won't," he answered as he, too, brought his horse around. "As you now *have* my permission to ride any morning you like whilst here at Somerton Park. I shall have Griggs leave a saddle in Amira's stall, to make it easier for you to nab her."

She must have looked stunned, because he smiled.

"I can't have you shocking my stable boys with your unusual attire." He hitched his leg, bringing Gringolet even with Amira as they ambled back toward the house. "Nor can I deny such an able rider her morning pleasure." His voice dipped low, sending thrills of sensation rioting through Liliana.

"Th-thank you," Liliana stammered. She felt rather off center. Stratford unsettled her. He hadn't taken her to task for stealing his horse. He hadn't berated her for embarrassing him in public. He hadn't judged her for her unconventionalities and was now, in fact, conspiring to enable her. "You are very kind," she said, and realized she spoke the truth.

How awful. She didn't want to think of him as kind. She didn't want to think of him at all, except as a suspect or a relation thereof. Yet increasingly she was viewing him as something more than an adversary, which only complicated matters.

"Miss Claremont?"

"Yes?" She turned her head to look at him. His gaze was fixed out over the lake, his lips pressed together and his brow dipped, as if he contemplated something of great import.

"I, too, ride alone every morning, just shy of sunrise." He shifted his eyes, and his gaze captured her. "Would you care to join me tomorrow?"

"I ..." *Couldn't,* she almost said. But she'd accomplished little during her foray into the village. Due to the earliness of the hour, only the baker's shop had been open. She'd thought her search had finally borne fruit when she discovered the other customer in the shop was the maid of all work to Geoffrey's father's former valet. He could have been a wealth of information.

Her hopes were quickly dashed, however, when she'd learned that the man, Mr. Witherspoon, was gravely ill and had been unable to receive visitors for many months. Liliana had asked several questions of the girl about his condition on the walk back to the man's cottage. Then she'd quickly jotted down the recipe for a concoction she thought might help him. The maid had taken it dubiously but promised to pass it along to her mistress.

Liliana held out little hope, however. Maybe she could sneak away one afternoon later in the week to check on him, or to interview other people in the town, but it would be risky.

Liliana chewed her lip. What could it hurt to spend more time in Stratford's company? He might let something slip. It was more of a prospect than anything else at the moment.

"I would like that," she answered.

The hint of a smile appeared on Stratford's face.

This could work, she rationalized. Still, she had the feeling she'd just combined two unknown substances and started a reaction she couldn't control.

Well, if she were going to give herself up to it ... "I should also like it if you would call me Liliana," she murmured.

Stratford's smile spread. "Liliana" rolled off his tongue, and he closed his mouth on her name as if savoring a treat. "And I am Geoffrey."

That feeling that wasn't quite fear caused goose pimples to prickle her arm.

Enemy, thy name is Geoffrey.

Chapter Twelve

Liliana slid her barely touched plate toward the center of the table. Not that the light fare of turbot served with lobster sauce and roasted root vegetables wasn't appetizing—the appreciative sighs of the assembled luncheon crowd assured her it was. She simply couldn't countenance food right now.

And I am Geoffrey.

It had been a mistake to give him leave of her name this morning. His natural response had been expected, yet those four little words had shifted something within her.

Geoffrey.

Not Stratford. Not even Wentworth. But Geoffrey, a man.

The first man to have ever kissed her. She flushed warm with the memory.

It had been easy not to think of that kiss when she'd held no consideration for him as a person. But now . . .

Liliana splayed her hand across her chest, just below her neck.

"Are you all right?" Aveline inquired, drawing her attention. She turned to the right, where her escort patted a linen napkin to his lips as he glanced at her discarded plate, then at her. Aveline's green eyes darkened with concern. "You look a tad overheated." He handed her a glass of iced champagne. "Take this."

Liliana accepted it and sipped. The liquid slid down her throat in a chilled burn as frosty bubbles tickled her nose.

"Thank you," she said, taking another sip and forcing a smile. But she was not all right. She was confused. And confusion was not a state she handled well.

Why had Geoffrey— *No! Stratford.* She blew out an exasperated sigh. She might as well accept that her mind had made the switch.

Why had Geoffrey invited her to ride with him tomorrow? What was it she'd seen in his eyes? Why hadn't he tossed her off his estate? No one would have protested, not even Aunt Eliza. What could he want of her?

The unanswered questions balled within her. Liliana detested the unknown. The desire to act vibrated through her. She had to do something—*anything.*

She'd take Amira to the village this afternoon. Yes, it bent the spirit of what Geoffrey had intended, but he *had* given her permission to ride. She wouldn't wait. If only this infernal meal would come to an end so Aveline would depart.

"So what talent shall you be displaying this afternoon, my dear?"

Liliana quirked her brow as Aveline's question registered. "Pardon?"

He chuckled, amusement dancing across his lean features. "Have you been listening to a word I've said?"

Liliana relaxed into a chagrined smile. "I'm sorry, my lord. Woolgathering. Forgive me."

"No, forgive me," he said. "I shall endeavor to be a more entertaining companion."

"Oh no," Liliana rushed to reassure him. "You've been perfect. I've just something on my mind."

Speculation glimmered in Aveline's expression for just a moment before his easy smile supplanted it. "Your upcoming performance, perhaps?"

Liliana shook her head. "I'm afraid I don't understand."

"This afternoon's affair?" Aveline prompted. At her shrug, he explained. "The countess has arranged for several of the young ladies to demonstrate their most accomplished of the feminine arts, with Stratford as judge."

"Oh my," Liliana said. Poor Geoffrey. He'd been less than excited about the tournament. She wondered how he felt about this display.

"Yes." Aveline nodded. "I take it you weren't invited to perform?"

"I'm not exactly the favored guest around here." Liliana gave a smiling wince. "Thank goodness."

Aveline laughed, a rich sound that drew a few looks. "No, though I can't see any reason why not," he murmured. "That is a shame, however. I'd rather looked forward to discovering how you would top your skills as a gunsmith." Aveline tossed his napkin onto the table. "I expect it will be entertaining nonetheless, don't you think?"

She'd rather do a qualitative analysis of what made paint peel. Politeness dictated she answer otherwise. "Yes. I'm only sorry you shall miss it, what with your afternoon business affairs."

"Actually, I'd made plans to spend the afternoon with you today." He stood, extending a friendly hand. "If you'll have me?" Aveline smiled, and the look he gave her was one of . . . anticipation?

Oh no. Liliana tried not to show her dismay. She couldn't very well turn him down. He had, after all, been her savior and had done quite a bit to ease the tension between her and Aunt Eliza. Yet neither did she wish to encourage him. She'd enjoyed his escort simply because he'd been so undemanding of her time.

"I'd be honored," she said, pushing the words past the disappointed lump in her throat. Her foray to the village would have to wait. She took his proffered arm and accepted her fate. "Shall we?"

She pasted a smile on her face as Aveline joined them to the line of guests making their way toward the music room.

She prayed she was mistaken about Aveline's interest and that his decision to spend the afternoon at Somerton Park would be a onetime occurrence.

Somerton Park's sizable music room rang with conversation as Liliana and Aveline took their seats very near the back.

"In case some of the ladies' feminine accomplishments are not quite so accomplished," Aveline explained with a wink as he placed a finger in one ear.

Liliana laughed, but her eyes sought out Geoffrey, who stood at the front nearest the bank of tall windows. The expanse of glass admitted generous sunlight into the room. Brightness prevented her from seeing Geoffrey's expression, but his posture was stiff and formal, much different than his relaxed, easy manner of this morning. This was a man not pleased to be here. She could certainly sympathize.

Standing next to him was his uncle, Josslyn Wentworth. The man was smiling, yet something in his expression seemed off . . . disingenuous. Not in the same way as the countess, but— Liliana scoffed. Who was she to judge? She knew she, of all people, would be inclined to see ugliness in any Wentworth. But then why did she not feel that way about Geoffrey anymore?

Joss Wentworth caught her staring and frowned. Liliana flushed and turned her gaze back to the room.

Streaking rays illuminated three magnificent instruments, which anchored the décor. A Taskin harpsichord of giltwood with a japanned case was the centerpiece, flanked by a stunning mahogany square piano in the neoclassical style. It boasted gilt bronze mounts and medallions of cut horn against a blue paper background.

The most interesting piece was a lavishly carved pedal harp with painted scenes of pyramids, birds and clouds on the pine sound box. The crown featured a wooden figure in Egyptian headdress. The harp looked much older than one designed to complement the current rage for Egyptian décor. Perhaps someone in Geoffrey's family had been a lover of Egypt before Napoleon had so popularized it.

"Quite a way to choose a wife, eh?" Aveline commented, leaning close so as not to be overheard. "I must say, when it comes my time to be shackled, the music room is not precisely the one I would wish my viscountess be accomplished in."

Liliana snapped her head around to see Aveline's half-cocked smile.

"What?" he asked, giving a shrug. "I would rather she excel at watercolors, sculptures, things of that sort. Do pull your mind up out of the cellar, Miss Claremont." The roguish gleam sparkling in his green eyes spoiled his innocent expression.

She lifted a pert eyebrow. "I had thought you quite tame, but perhaps I should reevaluate my opinion," she said. "I do believe you might be rather wicked."

Aveline flashed a lopsided grin. "All part of my attempt to be a more engaging escort." He winked. "And I had thought you imperturbable. It seems I was correct."

She shrugged. "Practical, analytical and unimaginably factual, too," she said in her most dry voice, but she couldn't repress a smile.

"Hmm." Aveline shifted in his seat as Lady Stratford welcomed everyone to the room and introduced the afternoon's first performer. Lady Jane Northumb sat prettily at the harpsichord, her face serene and not a blond curl out of place. Lady Stratford beamed at the girl, as if bestowing her blessing upon the perfect daughter-in-law. Liliana frowned.

The unmistakable notes of Mozart filled the room.

Liliana sat up straight, looking to see how Geoffrey was enjoying the performance. Did he gaze upon Jane Northumb as the perfect epitome of womanhood? Not that she cared, of course. But she couldn't spot him. Perhaps he sat behind the matron with the turquoise organza hat, somewhere on the other side of the peacock-plumaged adornment.

As the allegro flared, Liliana gave thanks that she hadn't been expected to participate. As much as Aunt had tried to force music upon her, Liliana hadn't the patience for endless hours of practice. She'd preferred to spend her time poring through as many writings on organic chemistry as she could get her hands on, searching for ways to apply those principles to the healing arts she was learning. So while she loved listening, she played abysmally, unlike Jane's proficient recital. Lady Stratford would be appalled.

The tiny hairs on the back of Liliana's nape rose, and she stiffened in her seat.

"Perhaps this isn't such a bad way to choose a wife," Aveline commented, drawing her attention away from the odd sensation. "Take Lady Jane, for example." He gestured idly with his right hand. "By choosing Mozart, she tells us much about herself. Mozart is beautiful and harmonic but also technically perfect. Every note fits neatly into its little box. That leads me to the conclusion that Lady Jane needs everything to be in order, that she's a 'no mess' type of female. Wonderful for running a household and raising well-adjusted children. Stratford could do well selecting her."

An image of Geoffrey smiling at Jane over the breakfast table, of the two of them standing arm in arm as they watched their children playing at the hearth, pierced Liliana. She shook her head to clear the vision.

Moderate applause signaled the end of the performance. Lady Stratford introduced Lady Ann Manchester, another blond beauty, who took her place at the square piano.

Beethoven sang from the instrument as Lady Ann deftly fingered the keys.

A subtle scent tickled Liliana's nose. Spice and mint.

Geoffrey. Warmth flooded her. Was he somewhere near? Liliana shifted in her seat to search for him, but Aveline touched her arm and she turned back toward him.

"Lady Ann, however, has chosen Herr Ludwig," he remarked, seemingly oblivious to her sudden tension. "Where Mozart is neat, Beethoven is elemental. Powerful, emotional, very messy . . . but also very exciting. Having Lady Ann for wife might not promise a smoothly run life, but it would be worth it in other areas."

Liliana shot Aveline a quelling look, but his gaze was fixed on the apparently very messy Lady Ann. An image of Geoffrey grabbing Lady Ann, pressing her against the bookshelves in the library and kissing her with unreserved passion flashed through Liliana's mind. She swallowed, perturbed by the rush of sensual memory that crashed over her as she remembered Geoffrey's taste upon her own lips. How his hands had roamed over her—

Lady Ann finished to applause. Liliana turned her hands to touch her heated face. Geoffrey's scent lingered in her nose, very real and not just a figment of her memory. She glanced to the other side of Aveline, but of course Geoffrey wasn't there. He must be behind her somewhere. Could he have heard Aveline's indelicate commentary? Mortification heated her face another degree. What Geoffrey must think if he did.

Lady Emily Morton was next to perform. Given that Liliana knew the countess to be parading potential brides in front of her son, Geoffrey must prefer blondes. The thought disgruntled her. She wondered if Lady Emily—tall, graceful, nearly flaxen haired and so very different from herself—was what Geoffrey looked for in a woman.

Lady Emily tipped the harp back and cradled it between her knees.

"Now, that one is pure trouble," Aveline pointed out. "See how she uses the harp as an excuse to show a bit of her slim ankle?" He *tsk*ed. "A flashy one, her. I'll bet—"

"Do stop," Liliana hissed, closing her eyes against a vision of Lady Emily flashing Geoffrey her— "I am attempting to enjoy the music." And she didn't want Geoffrey to think any worse, as she was now quite certain he sat directly behind her. Her entire back tingled with awareness.

Aveline raised his brows. "Not imperturbable, then," he murmured and remained blessedly quiet for the remainder of the performance as well as through a rather shaky flutist and one frightful vocal performance. Liliana could hardly focus. Her body was alive with sensation. It was as if her very core responded to Geoffrey's perceived nearness.

She tapped her slippered foot briskly, warmth making her uncomfortably fidgety. And what was this twinge of dreadful envy? Why should the idea of Geoffrey with any of these women bother her? He was nothing to her, for goodness' sake, save for the means to discovering the truth about her father's death.

After the sad aria, Lady Stratford called for an intermission.

"Still flushed, I see," Aveline noted. "Shall I fetch you another glass of champagne?"

"Yes, please," Liliana answered, the smile feeling brittle on her face. As he departed, she gripped her hands tightly together, hoping she'd been mistaken and that Geoffrey was nowhere near.

"Which composer's piece would you play, then, Liliana?" came Geoffrey's rich voice. He was behind her, as she'd known he would be.

Liliana startled anyway, gasping as she turned. His lips pressed into something not quite a grin, but he was clearly amused. Blast. He had heard all.

"How long have you been sitting there?" she asked, afraid of—yet knowing—the answer.

"Since the performances began."

Wonderful. Embarrassment bloomed, even though it was not she who'd made the provocative comments.

"But . . . I thought you were the judge of this contest."

"I am," he grumbled, his tone clearly put out. "I escaped the front row by telling Mother my presence distracted the performers."

Liliana nodded. She could certainly understand that.

"But you didn't answer my question," Geoffrey pressed. "Which composer would you have chosen?"

"I don't play." She gripped the back of Aveline's chair, where her arm rested in her twisted position.

"But if you did? Humor me."

"Truly, I have no idea," she said. "Music never was my forte."

"Come now, Liliana," Geoffrey cajoled. "Surely there is a composer you favor over all others."

She hated answering when she was unsure of the subject matter. But she could see he would pester her until she responded. "Handel, I should think." She blurted out the first composer to come to mind.

"I see," Geoffrey said in a way that left Liliana wondering what exactly it was he thought he did see. "Interesting choice." Geoffrey brought one long-fingered hand to his mouth and rested his first two digits just below his bottom lip. He cocked a raven brow. "Handel never married, did he?"

"I have no idea," she answered. What an odd observation. Geoffrey must have marriage on the mind—well, how could he not, considering his guest list and how doggedly he was being pursued?

"Perhaps Aveline's interpretations have merit after all," he said.

Liliana tilted her head. "Pardon?"

Geoffrey leaned forward, resting elbows on knees. "You chose Handel, a composer whose life mirrors your own."

"I don't see—"

"Handel's family insisted he forget music and pursue law, a more practical gentleman's pursuit. His mother alone encouraged his musical aspirations, yet he went on to arguably create one of the most memorable contributions to musical history with his *Messiah*. And," he pointed out, "Handel paved the way for composers after him. In fact, Beethoven himself has said Handel was the greatest composer to ever live."

Liliana's breath stilled in her chest. She hadn't known any of that.

"You told me this morning you were a chemist. I am certain people in your life have discouraged you from it. Yet someone, like Handel's mother, encouraged you, yes? Not your aunt . . ."

Liliana shook her head, her gaze riveted to his blue one. "My father," she said softly.

Geoffrey nodded. "I expect you hope to make some lasting contribution to the world in that regard. My mother mentioned you've applied for acceptance into the Royal Society and have been turned down."

"Seven times in the past three years," she found herself saying. "But I refuse to give up. Someday, men will recognize that women and science are not incompatible. If I am not the first woman member of the Royal Society, then I can at least hope my efforts will help pave the way for whoever is."

"My point exactly." He watched her, assessing, with no hint of mockery or disdain.

Liliana took a shallow breath and pulled her head back slowly, feeling exposed and vulnerable. She had the most uncomfortable feeling he was looking right into her very heart.

Dear God, she was the one who was supposed to be getting answers from him—and yet he'd gotten her to unknowingly reveal intimate parts of her soul just by uttering a name.

She was in over her head.

"Forgive me," Geoffrey murmured and sat back against his chair. "I've upset you."

She hazarded a glance at him. His eyes were hooded, his brows drawn together with puzzlement.

"No, I . . ." She cleared her throat and called forth a polite smile. "I am just a bit taken aback. I . . ." She probably sounded the idiot. Now she would look like one, too, for she couldn't stay here with him a moment longer. She stood abruptly, knocking her chair with the back of her knees. "Please convey my apologies to Lord Aveline," she said, backing out of the row. "Tell him I am a bit flushed, after all, and that I will join him later this evening."

Liliana didn't wait for Geoffrey's response, didn't want him to see any more in her face than he already had. She fled the music room.

Her equilibrium returned in bits as her long-legged stride carried her farther from Geoffrey, as she pondered their conversation. He'd shown no flicker of response when she'd mentioned her father. No remorse, no acknowledgment that he'd ever heard of Charles Claremont. Was it possible he knew nothing about her father's death?

Perhaps. But scientists didn't make assumptions. They proved or disproved premises. Tomorrow, when they went riding, she'd risk asking him a few pointed questions and gauge his responses.

Still, she mustn't forget that even if he knew nothing, she could not count on him to help her find justice. She'd run her finger over the raised seal of Stratford hundreds of times since she'd discovered her father's cache.

Fidelitas ut prosapia. Loyalty to family. Liliana hadn't needed a translation of the family motto—Latin was the language of science, after all.

Someone in Geoffrey's family was responsible for her father's death, and she fully expected that when the time came, Geoffrey would protect his own.

Movement caught her eye as she passed by the hallway that led to the library. Was that—? She turned quietly, inched back to the opening and peered around the corner.

Someone exited the library, and not in the way one

would had he been there just perusing. The hallway was shadowed, so she couldn't make out a face. The man turned away from her and walked at a fast clip in the opposite direction.

She couldn't be certain, but the tall, lean frame brought to mind Lord Aveline.

Why on earth would Aveline be sneaking from the library when he'd been supposedly fetching champagne?

Chapter Thirteen

The brisk morning breeze sent a shiver down Liliana's spine as she made her way through dew-laden grass to the stables. The air was quiet in the dark moments before sunrise, the absence of noise making it seem as if even the birds had yet to rise from their comfy nests. Perhaps they were the wise ones.

As Liliana slipped inside the stable door, a glow of soft light shone from the far stall. The rumble of quiet male voices echoed back to her and Liliana instinctively stilled, keeping to the shadows. There'd been no one about yesterday when she'd appropriated Geoffrey's mare, and though he'd given her permission to ride Amira this morning, she had little desire to explain herself to a stranger, particularly dressed as she was in breeches. Funny, it didn't seem to bother her that Geoffrey saw her thus.

"—very 'appy, Major. Can't thank you enough," a man said.

"The war is over, Tom. You needn't address me so anymore."

Geoffrey's familiar tones flowed through Liliana like a good glass of sherry, leaving her relaxed and rather warm. She shook off the effect and continued toward Amira's stall.

"M'lord, then."

Geoffrey's low laugh struck Liliana as rather self-deprecating for a man of the nobility. "Certainly not that, my friend. Not after all we've seen together. I'd prefer you call me Geoffrey, but I can see from the look of horror on your face that you won't do that. Shall we settle on Stratford?"

"Don't seem proper, sir, given you're an earl now," the man answered, his voice dubious. "But if you insist."

"I do."

Liliana stopped short of the stall, taken aback by the men's odd conversation. Geoffrey was apparently encouraging someone below his station to call him by his given name, and clearly considered the man a friend. She'd never known a peer who held to such ideas. The thought intrigued her, but it also disturbed. She didn't like to admit she might be wrong about him. Perhaps she'd need to reevaluate how she perceived Geoffrey. Perhaps, at heart, he was as unconventional as she.

She cleared her throat in way of announcement, still curious, but loath to eavesdrop further when the conversation clearly had nothing to do with her. She dropped her head and tugged her cap low so as to hide her features from Geoffrey's companion.

Geoffrey stepped out into the open. His eyes crinkled with genuine pleasure, and his smile of greeting sent warmth sliding through her. Was he glad that she'd joined him?

"Liliana," he said, surprising her by his use of her name and again when he reached for her hand, bringing it to his lips for a brush of a kiss as he led her into the stall.

Liliana's eyes darted to the stranger and she squinted, perplexed. The man Geoffrey insisted address him so casually was a stable servant? It certainly seemed so from his rough trousers, coarse linen shirt embedded with bits of straw and dusty vest. A bud of unease sprouted in her middle. Servants notoriously gossiped, and the last thing she wanted was Aunt to hear of her unorthodox morning activities through the servant grapevine.

"Allow me to introduce Tom Richards. Tom, Miss Claremont." Geoffrey must have sensed her reticence, as he gave her hand a quick squeeze. "Tom and I served together for many years. He's as loyal a friend as they come. I trust him with my life, as can you with your reputation."

Mr. Richards nodded. "Miss."

Liliana smiled in return, assessing the other man. Geoffrey had called him a friend and fellow soldier. Might the stable hand be a source of information, should Geoffrey prove difficult to crack?

"Tom here will have Amira saddled for you each morning, and any other time you wish to ride," Geoffrey said. "Just send him a message with your intentions and he'll see to it you have everything you need."

Liliana kept her smile in place, but she inwardly cringed. Either Geoffrey was being considerate or Tom was his way of keeping abreast of her activities. Regardless, it would certainly be harder to sneak off to the village again.

"Shall we?" Geoffrey led her to Amira and assisted her onto the already saddled mare. Heat emanated from his hand, even through Liliana's buttery soft gloves. She glanced up, startled, and was certain she saw that same heat flash in his eyes. But then she was up, and he was mounting his Gringolet.

As Geoffrey straightened in the saddle, Liliana's breath hitched and she was forced to draw air through her nose to calm her rioting senses. His chin lifted, his shoulders settled back and his gaze looked out through the stable entrance as if anticipating the day's adventure. He exuded such easy confidence that it made her want to follow him anywhere. Foolish, yet she saw for a moment why his fellow soldiers had nicknamed him Sir Gawain. Geoffrey carried himself like she imagined the knight of old would. Gawain was purported not only to be noble, but also to be the very spirit of chivalry and loyalty. Was it possible Geoffrey was equally honorable?

That was the question of the day, wasn't it? From what she'd observed of him over the past week, he didn't seem the sort to be able to commit murder—well, other than when she'd taunted him during the tournament. He'd looked quite capable of strangling her then. But to rule him out completely, she must find out where Geoffrey had been when her father was killed.

"I thought we might ride some of the estate today," Geoffrey said as she brought Amira up beside him. "I do try to survey as much as I can on my trips home."

Liliana nodded. "Lead on." She briefly closed her eyes as he pulled just slightly ahead. Now was the time to take control of the conversation . . . he'd given her the perfect opening. "You must enjoy being back in England. How long were you away?"

His shoulders rose a tad, as if he'd tightened at her question. She watched him closely. She realized, of course, he might not tell her the truth, but she had to try and hope she'd be able to tell if he were lying.

"I left home the nineteenth of May 1803," he said, his voice light and steady, giving Liliana no reason to suspect he spoke anything but the truth. "The day after we declared war on France."

The rhythmic clop of hooves rose from the earth as they skirted the lake. Liliana waited, giving Geoffrey time to elaborate, but it seemed all he would say on the subject.

Just knowing he'd left England seven months before her father was killed made her breathe easier for some odd reason.

With a start, Liliana realized she didn't want Geoffrey to have been involved. Nor, in fact, to have any knowledge of it . . . which was silly, really, because she needed answers, and how could he reveal what he didn't know?

Pushing her contrary thoughts aside, she pulled even

to him and pressed on. She had to establish his where-abouts on and around the twenty-first of December of that year. "It must have been difficult," she ventured, "leaving home so young. Were you able to visit much that first year? Maybe around Christmastime?"

He slanted his eyes to her and gave her a bemused smile. "I was not much younger than you are now, I imagine," he said, sidestepping her question entirely. "How many years have you? Two and twenty?"

"Four," she replied.

He swept her with his eyes, lingering for a moment in the vicinity of her hips, which she knew the boys' togs accentuated rather than hid. The appraising nature of his look set off a twittering in her stomach. But then he turned his focus on the park ahead.

"Yes, well, I was just a week past twenty and anxious to prove my mettle fighting for my country." A wry note crept into his voice, and his gaze took on a faraway qual-ity. Something in his manner—in the contemplative, troubled look that crossed his face—told Liliana that he was a man living with regrets. She had an absurd urge to reach out to him, to . . . do what? Offer him comfort? She frowned and tried to focus on his meaning.

What, exactly, did he regret? Things he'd done for his country? Or something altogether worse?

Liliana tapped her fingers against her thigh. He'd yet to answer her. She thought a moment on how to re-phrase her inquiry. "I'd like to hear more of your early days in the service," she tried.

Geoffrey laughed, the cloud lifting from his features. He looked over at her. "'Twas nothing exciting, I assure you. Besides, enough about me. I should like to hear more about your experiments."

Any other time, she would have loved to expound on her work, but not when he was so effectively evading her questions. She narrowed her eyes before she caught herself. "They're nothing exciting, either."

"Oh, I doubt that," he said. "You stated yesterday that

riding astride was more practical in the 'brambles and bogs' you frequent. That sounds quite stimulating."

Did he intend the entendre she heard in his tone?

She flushed, either way.

"I've an idea. Grin, here, is used to a more invigorating pace of a morning," Geoffrey said, patting the horse's neck. "And Shropshire is known for its lush marshlands. What say we race to the western edge of my property, where I can promise you any number of bogs that might interest you? Then you can give me a firsthand introduction to your passion."

Liliana felt the ensuing blush heat more than just her cheeks. Truly—he must see how her face had pinkened. Thankfully, her clothes covered other places that had warmed at his words. Yet his innocent expression gave no hint of innuendo.

His charger's ears had perked at the word *race*, however. Gringolet's energy seemed to have transferred to Amira, as well. Liliana could feel a new tension in her mare, a current that seemed to run through her own body, too. The sun had risen behind them, illuminating the park for a safe run. What harm could there be? A brisk breeze might cool her, while a hard ride might relieve some of her frustration at being thus far thwarted.

"How can we race when I've no idea where we're going?" she asked.

Geoffrey grinned, and her heart tripped.

"What makes you think you would ever be in the lead?" he asked, digging his heels into Gringolet's side.

Cresting a flat-topped summit, Geoffrey bent low over Gringolet's neck, exhilaration singing in his veins. In a few hundred yards, the pasture would give way to a heavily wooded valley and then finally to the marshlands below. Geoffrey gave the horse his head.

He was ten kinds of fool to be out with Liliana unescorted, yet it seemed as if he had no sense of self-preservation when it came to her. In fact, as embarrassing as it was to admit, he'd raced to the stable well before dawn, buzzing with anticipation. When Liliana had arrived, he'd felt like a damned lad of fifteen, keen to impress a pretty young maiden. Ridiculous for a man of his age and experience, and more so given how fundamentally wrong for him a woman like Liliana would be, not only in the political realm but also in his personal one. She made him feel things, and that was perilous to a man who had decided never to love.

Pounding hoofbeats echoed just behind and to the left. Amira's occasional snorts let Geoffrey know Liliana was in lockstep with him still. Damn, she was a magnificent rider. He'd given no quarter, and she'd matched him the entire way. In fact, if she'd known the area, he'd lay odds she might even have been able to outride him.

In his mind's eye, Geoffrey pictured Liliana leaned over her mare's neck, her thighs tight as she rose in the stirrups, her derrière elevated from the saddle. In her boys' pants, he would have an excellent view of her bottom—the shape of it, at any rate. He had half a mind to let her pull ahead, just so he could see his imaginings in real life.

Perhaps tomorrow he would let *her* lead.

Geoffrey sucked in a breath. Was he actually contemplating a tomorrow with Liliana Claremont?

Impossible. Yet, a mixture of longing and excitement tightened his chest. What was it about Liliana that put such dangerous thoughts in his head?

Desire pulsed through him in blaring answer to his question. Yes, that could be the reason. After all, he'd dreamed of her again last night, had awoken clutching his pillow in a desperate attempt to drag her from his dreamworld to his reality.

But that could never be. Aside from the madness that had gripped him in the library, he wasn't the type to dally with an innocent young lady without being prepared to offer for her. As drawn as he was to Liliana—

nay, *because* of how drawn he was to her—he could see no future with the woman. He never should have even suggested—

A flash of brown streaked past him. Liliana released an unladylike whoop as she and Amira deftly cut him off. How in the blazes? Geoffrey tried for some competitive indignation, but the rise and fall of Liliana's delectable backside as she galloped past more than made up for any wounded pride.

Her laughter reached him as they slowed their horses near the edge of the valley. Burnished curls had slipped from beneath her cap, and her eyes sparkled an almost unnatural violet in the morning's haze, as if she were some woodland nymph sent to entice him. Her vivacity swirled around him like the mist that rose off of the moist grass, touching a place inside of him that hadn't smiled in long years . . . a young, innocent place, unspoiled by war and death, responsibilities and regrets.

"I'm sorry, my lord. You took off so quickly, I didn't hear what you said about leading," Liliana teased.

Geoffrey shook his head but couldn't contain the half smile that spread his lips. "You have outdone me once again," he said, giving her a nod. "And unlike last time, allow me to extend my sincerest congratulations."

She shrugged nonchalantly, but the effect was ruined by her delighted smile. "Thank you."

Good God. He would let her win at anything and everything to see that self-satisfied grin upon her face. Of course, he'd prefer to see satisfaction of a different kind overtake her features.

"This is becoming a rather annoying habit," he added, knowing she'd take it to mean her besting him. But the truth of the matter was that she kept him in a constant state of arousal.

Her grin slid into a throaty chuckle that shot straight to his groin.

He was in serious trouble. Without even trying, she was luring him in like a fat trout.

He cleared his throat, striving to keep his voice normal. "As promised, the bogs lie just below. Shall we?"

He motioned her to follow down an ancient winding path, past two-hundred-year-old gnarled holly trees interspersed with rowan, birch, oak and crab apple.

Perhaps mucking around in the swampy undergrowth would get his mind out of places it shouldn't be.

They rode companionably through the landscape, the rich flora proving a needed distraction from the disturbing undercurrents of desire. Geoffrey had forgotten how much he loved this part of Somerton Park . . . the sounds, the smells. The bluntly toothed petals of mountain pansy and the flowering stalks of heath speedwell that grew on the grassy verge looked exactly as he remembered. These pastures and the woods that surrounded them had been a favorite stomping ground of his as a boy— and a good place to avoid the countess. He wondered if Liliana had been drawn to similar places in an effort to avoid her interfering aunt.

He veered right as they reached the floor of the valley and dismounted. "The ground becomes quite spongy here," he said. "We'll need to go the rest of the way by foot."

"Of course." Liliana climbed down from Amira without his aid, and he couldn't help but notice her long, long legs as she swung from her mount. His throat went dry and he stepped back.

He found a spot to rest the horses away from the crab apple trees. Grin nudged him in protest. "Much too much temptation over there," Geoffrey mumbled, as much to himself as to the horse. "You, my friend, have an appalling lack of self-control." *As does your master.* "And I have no desire"—*to find myself married to a woman completely wrong for me*—"to nurse a sick horse all the way home," he said, patting Grin on the rump. Grin whinnied and flicked his tail, slapping Geoffrey with coarse, stinging hair.

Liliana did a poor job stifling her amusement. But as

her laughter died, she regarded him with an evaluating look that made him wish he could see her thoughts. "You have great affection for him," Liliana said after a moment. "And he, you. Did your love of horses lead you to the cavalry? Or the other way around?"

"My years in the regiment deepened my respect for horses," he said as they secured their mounts to an ancient oak, "but I learned to love them here at Somerton Park."

"Did you ride with your father then?" she asked as they picked their way down the path toward the marsh.

"No. Alone." More hovered on his tongue, but he wouldn't share that, even then, riding had been his escape—only he'd been running from his mother or his parents' vicious fighting rather than his demons. A change of subject was in order. "Ah, here we are," he said, gesturing to the largest of the valley's bogs. "What think you? Is it all that I promised?"

Liliana pressed her lips together, and her brows dipped into a slight frown, but as she turned, her expression changed. Her head tilted ever so slightly to the side and her gaze fixed on the area, as if she were examining the landscape. Gauging it somehow, giving Geoffrey an intriguing glimpse of the chemist in her.

"It's incredible," she said, walking forward. She hesitated at the edge of the water only a moment before wading in with no missish qualms. She reached for a bunch of bright yellow starlike flowers with leafless stems and snapped a few. She held them up to the light, inspecting them, turning them in her hands. "You've a hearty patch of moor-golds," she said.

"Moor-golds?"

"Narthecium ossifragum," she murmured, her mind clearly on evaluating another stalk of the rather ordinary plant. A wry smile crossed her face and she looked up at him. "Bog asphodel," she clarified. "I wish I'd brought my satchel. I'd love to collect some."

"Pick whatever you wish. I'll carry them back to the

manor for you." Geoffrey stepped into the marsh, venturing the few feet to join her. "But you must tell me why you want it." He reached out and brushed his finger over the spiky petal. "It seems a rather ugly flower, as flowers go."

She laughed and selected a large, healthy-looking stem. "If you were cursed with the King's Evil, you might find this ugly little flower quite beautiful."

"King's Evil?"

"Yes, scrofula," she said, snapping more stalks. "It's a form of consumption that attacks the skin, causing great ugly growths, mainly around the neck. It sometimes accompanies traditional consumption, but more times than not, it is curable." She chose several more flowers, and rather than break them, she tugged them gently from the peat, holding up the clumped root-ball. "Bruised asphodel root can be used to dissolve scrofulous swellings," she explained, "and the rest of the flower is used as an antispasmodic as well as"—she blinked in her recitation and a light blush stole over her face—"to assist with feminine concerns." She ducked her head and went back to tugging flowers with a vengeance.

"I see," he said, and he did. Saw yet another reason Liliana could never be for him. At four and twenty, she was dressed like a man, standing knee-deep in muck, when by all rights she should be in a parlor somewhere, children tugging at her skirts. He certainly couldn't see the woman before him, plucking herbal remedies from a swamp, hosting Peers of the Realm and their wives at political dinners. So why did his traitorous body—and he feared something more tender—seem to hope otherwise?

"So your experiments have something to do with plants, then?"

She looked up at him, her eyes gauging the intent behind his question, no doubt. By her wary look, Geoffrey imagined she'd experienced much ridicule over the years—indeed, even from him when she'd offered to help him that first night in the library. He kept his gaze open and nonthreatening, as despite his better judgment, he wanted to know more about her. How had a gently bred young woman escaped marriage and pursued science and healing instead? What did she hope to accomplish?

"Partially," she said, the word drawing out slowly from her lips. Her gaze shifted over his shoulder, her attention drawn to something behind him.

Geoffrey turned. Liliana brushed past him and stopped before the strangest-looking plant he'd ever seen.

"Sundews," she said, reaching out but not touching. Petals burst from the stems in bright colors—some red, some green, some pink—reminding Geoffrey of Chinese fireworks when they spread through the sky. Each bloom had tiny tentacles with glistening drops of moisture beaded on the tips. "It's a carnivorous plant, much like a Venus flytrap," she explained. "But this little beauty has superb medicinal properties." Liliana looked the plants over, then selected one and reverently plucked it. "Sundews are invaluable in the treatment of lung diseases, severe coughs and breathing difficulty." She picked three more, cradling them protectively as she waded out of the bog.

Geoffrey followed, carrying his armful of asphodel, his curiosity riding higher. "So your experiments are partially concerning plants . . . and?"

She looked over at him, as if debating how to answer. He remembered her gibberish scribblings. More likely, she was debating how much he'd understand, which irked, true though it probably was. He sensed her mental shrug. "And water and air and living organisms, human and otherwise." She paused, thinking. Melodic chirps and the crunching of leaves under their boots filled the silence. Liliana pursed her lips and her brow furrowed, as if struggling to express herself.

Geoffrey found the effect endearing, which only increased his attraction to her. He shook his head. He was beginning to think that anything Liliana did would arouse him, which was all the more reason he *should* steer clear of her after this morning.

"I believe chemistry and physiology are interrelated," she said. "Inside each living body, chemical processes are occurring all of the time. Much of what we understand of experimental chemistry has changed in the last few decades, yet great debate exists as to whether the chemical substances found in living things are fundamentally different in character from the inorganic."

Enthusiasm bubbled in her voice, and her eyes had taken on a zeal reminiscent of passion. Geoffrey glanced away, his body reacting to her excitement, even though his mind knew it had nothing to do with him.

"I also believe the processes are more similar than we think, and if I can prove the correlation, just think what we could learn about precisely how our bodies work and how to prevent, or at least better treat, disease."

He couldn't keep his eyes from her for long.

"There has to be a way to isolate the chemicals within living things," she continued, holding up one of the strikingly beautiful sundews, "like plants, and synthesize and reproduce them to create even more potent medicines."

How fascinating she was, and how wholly different from any woman he'd ever known.

"So you're trying to . . ."

"Ease people's suffering," she said, raising her chin. She stared at him, as if debating her next words. "Like yours."

Shame heated his face, remembering how she'd offered to help him that first night and how curtly he'd dismissed her. "I owe you an apology—"

She raised a hand to stop him. "There is no need. You were in pain, which can make even a saint snappy. I had thought it was due to your catching my fall. But now . . ."

He stared at her, uneasy and yet fascinated with the

turn the conversation was taking. He couldn't stop himself from asking, "Now?"

"It's clear to me that you are in pain almost constantly." She watched him avidly, and he did his best not to squirm. Her eyes were so large, so very expressive. "And not from any recent injury."

Geoffrey regarded her with admiration. She was incredibly perceptive. Hiding the constant pain he'd been living with the past two years had become second nature. He hardly even noticed anymore, it being always in the background . . . a part of him now, more a constant tension of the muscles around his injury, strained from trying to compensate.

Still, he didn't care for the vulnerability Liliana's words and looks made him feel.

"Perhaps," he allowed.

"Your war wound?" she asked, not mincing words.

He nodded, not surprised she knew of it. It was no secret, after all, though he never spoke of it.

"Can you tell me the nature of your injury?" she asked. "I really may be able to help."

He regarded her, the desire to open himself both alarming and relieving. "I took a bayonet through the side," he said. "Actually, it went in my back but came out the side," he said, remembering the hot white agony, the spill and stench of his own blood. "But I was lucky. It missed my vitals."

"But it tore through your muscles," she said, nodding, "which would have stitched themselves back together however they could. I notice you often smell of mint. Is that a liniment you apply?"

Again Geoffrey was struck by her perceptiveness. "Yes, an old stable hand suggested I use a salve he'd made for horses." He shrugged. "It helps."

Liliana tugged at her lower lip. "Would you be willing to try a few of my suggestions? They might help as well."

"I would," he found himself saying.

She smiled, and he was absurdly pleased to have been

the one to have caused such a radiant expression. "First, I suggest we add some meadowsweet to your liniment. If we boil the root, it will help with the pain. How do you sleep at night?"

Geoffrey grinned at her rapid-fire responses. His intoxication with her grew, but this time not because of any physical stirrings, but because of her passion. "Not well. I'm usually so knotted, I require several drinks to relax. And then my bed is so uncomfortable, I end up sleeping on the floor." He couldn't believe he was admitting such delicate information.

"Hmm . . ." Her mouth twisted to the left. "I suggest less alcohol because it can actually inhibit sleep. We should try a few drops of willow bark beneath your tongue at night and before you do anything vigorous."

Geoffrey felt himself flush hot, picturing vigorous things he'd like to do with her.

Oblivious to his randy thoughts, Liliana went on. She made suggestions such as a heel implant inside his boot on the injured side to compensate while he was walking or standing, and hardwood slats beneath his bed to make it firmer. Simple things that made common sense, something so many young ladies were lacking. But Liliana proved herself every day to be more than just a typical young lady.

Still, why did she affect him so? He took in her open, easy expression, her simple, free hairstyle, the rough, practical nature of her attire, boys' togs though they were. She reminded him less of a society debutante and more of . . .

Of the women he'd become friends with during the war. That must be why he felt so comfortable with her. Several women had accompanied his regiment throughout the years—wives, mistresses and camp followers alike. Many a night was spent around the fire talking with this woman and that. He was always fascinated by their strength amidst the horror, by their courage, by their natural acceptance of life as it was—sometimes painful, sometimes beautiful, often fleeting. How frivolous those women would find the lives of the ladies of the ton, how impractical. How wasteful. Much like Liliana seemed to.

He actually smiled. That must be it. No mystery, no stirrings of dreaded love, just comfort breeding familiarity and all that.

"How did you know I suffer with chronic pain?" he asked, curious. "Most people cannot tell. Or at the very least, they never mention it."

She blushed at his reference to her boldness. But she answered. "My father was a scientist—a chemist, actually, but after he met my mother, a local healer, his passion turned to more medicinal science. He had many great theories, was working on several projects that would have helped mankind, but . . ." She looked away. "He was killed suddenly."

Geoffrey blanched at the raw pain in her voice. "Killed? How?"

She turned her gaze to him and stared into his eyes, as if searching for something. "By street thugs," she said finally, "when I was ten. My mother died when I was three. She contracted smallpox while caring for a local family." Liliana lifted her shoulders in a vulnerable shrug that caught at his heart. "I suppose I am an amalgam of my parents. My life's work, an extension of theirs. I want to use my knowledge and skills to make people's lives better."

Her life's work.

Odd to hear the term from a woman. Utterly captivating and provocative and completely misplaced for her gender, as well. Yet he understood, having an overriding passion of his own. But how did she think to carry on such an endeavor with the responsibilities of home and famil— "You really don't intend to marry at *all*, do you?"

She stopped walking, her eyes wide. With a slow shake of her head she said simply, "No."

And at once several things about her made sense.

"You're only here because your aunt forced you to come," he said, remembering now how it always seemed Lady Belsham was dragging Liliana around, indeed even that very first night when they'd been introduced.

A slight frown marred Liliana's face, but she gave a short nod.

She'd told him she had no desire to marry, of course, but he realized now that he just hadn't believed her, hadn't understood.

His chin lowered and he felt his shoulders loosen, as an unexpected mixture of disappointment, regret and relief flowed from his chest through his limbs, muddling his thoughts.

He should be thrilled, feel quite relieved, as it were. Knowing he could indulge his increasing desire to spend time with Liliana without fear of expectations, that he could enjoy the company of a female who wanted nothing from him but possibly friendship, should fill him with pleasure.

So why didn't it?

Chapter Fourteen

"Mother wants to know what you've done to run off Lord Aveline," Penelope inquired as she and Liliana trailed behind a dozen other girls through the high street of the village. The caravan of young misses drew curious glances as they passed, while shopkeepers threw open their doors, rushing out to display hats and ribbons or trays of divine-smelling cinnamon buns in an effort to entice the group inside. "She insists you must have tried another one of your *theories* on the poor man."

"Of course not," Liliana said absently. She glanced behind her. Unfortunately, another half dozen girls followed, making it impossible to slip away.

She detested shopping. She'd already been dragged through the milliner and a glove shop, yet not one of the group wanted to meander through the apothecary or the bookstore, and their chaperones—who were ensconced at the tea shop—insisted the girls stay together. Liliana had agreed to join this impromptu excursion only because it might give her the chance to check on Edmund Wentworth's former valet. Though it had been only one day since she'd left her remedy for the man, she hoped he would feel up to visiting with her this afternoon.

Accepting that escape was impossible at this moment,

she turned back to Penelope. "Aveline has many business concerns," she said. Still, she wondered at his sudden disappearance. Aveline hadn't been at breakfast, though it had been his habit every morning this week. Nor had he shown for dinner and dancing last night. Had she offended him by abandoning him in the music room yesterday? Though she had no interest in Aveline, she had no wish to injure his feelings after the kindness he'd done her.

Yet doubt niggled. Aveline's absence could be due to a completely different reason. She was quite certain it had been him she'd seen sneaking out of the library yesterday. An absurd protective instinct welled up in her chest for Geoffrey. She couldn't fathom why Aveline would feel the need to sneak about their hosts' home. Perhaps she should ask Geoffrey how well he knew his neighbor.

A short huff escaped her. She was one to call the kettle black.

"What?" Penelope asked, turning her head.

"Nothing."

"Hmm," Penelope said, eyeing Liliana. "Men and their business. Strange, isn't it, the way the countess marched into the breakfast room and announced that Stratford, too, had some business come up and would not be attending any festivities today? What, do you suppose, is so important?"

"I've no idea, but whatever it is, it must be imperative enough to make it worth incurring the countess' wrath." Lady Stratford had been seething as she'd announced that her son wouldn't rejoin the group until supper before abruptly calling off all planned activities for the morning and afternoon.

Unease fluttered in Liliana's middle. What had prompted Geoffrey to cancel out on the party after being such a good sport this past week?

"My maid overheard that the countess and Stratford had a great row about it," Lady Ann Manchester piped up from behind them, her eyes shining brightly. Several heads turned, and as if by unspoken agreement, the women came to a halt to hear the latest bit of news. "The countess apparently had quite a tizzy when Stratford told her he'd be otherwise engaged for the day. She was heard shouting that there wasn't anything more important than securing a proper wife."

Liliana's eyes were drawn to Lady Jane Northumb, standing two people to her right, listening avidly. Blond, fresh faced and from a prominent family, Lady Jane would be the kind of wife the countess would expect for her son.

Wouldn't Lady Stratford be appalled to know Geoffrey had spent his morning with another, wholly unsuitable woman? Liliana had been reckless, staying out so long with him. They'd returned long after sunrise and had had to sneak in through a little-used servants' entrance behind the back gardens. But, oh my, had it been exhilarating. Even though Geoffrey had frustrated her efforts to glean information, she couldn't remember the last time she'd passed a more pleasant morning. She generally spent her early hours alone, working, so perhaps it was just the novelty of being with another person. But the moment the thought entered her mind, it rang false. She'd enjoyed herself so much because she'd been with Geoffrey.

And he'd asked her to ride with him again on the morrow.

A giddy anxiety swept over her, and she shoved it aside, frowning.

"I'm beginning to suspect Stratford was not in on the planning of this party at all," said Lady Emily Morton. "He certainly hasn't singled one of us out to court, as expected." Her tone clearly implied she'd fully expected that one to be her. She waved an arm to indicate the town around them, her lips dropping in a frown of distaste. She sniffed. "Had I known that wasn't his intention, I'd never have agreed to journey to this dreary place."

"Me, either," chimed in a girl whose name Liliana didn't know. "It's so deadly dull. I'd much rather be in London, but when the chance to align with the Stratford family presented itself, Papa all but booted me out the door."

Liliana shook her head. Somerton Park and its surrounds were anything but dull. If situations were different, she could envision herself riding the countryside every sunrise, exploring her way through the vast marshlands collecting samples and specimens, perhaps even turning that abandoned folly she'd spied at the far side of the lake into her own laboratory. And the library . . . she could spend years in there. Why—

"I suppose you disagree, Miss Claremont?" Lady Emily asked.

Liliana blinked and stared back at all of the inquiring faces turned toward her. Newton's apple. What had she done to give away her thoughts? She cleared her throat. "I find Somerton Park quite lovely."

Lady Emily gave her a speculative look. Then her face cleared. "You would. You never were much of a success in London."

Titters of laughter sounded as the women turned back around and resumed their stroll up the street.

Liliana bit her tongue. It wouldn't serve her purposes to blister Lady Emily's ears. In fact, she'd use this opportunity to hang back, let everyone think she was upset by Emily's callous comment, then slip away to the valet's.

Penelope turned around, her eyes asking if Liliana was all right. Liliana winked and gave her a slight shooing motion. Pen nodded and turned back with the group.

Liliana let the girls walk on, stepping backward slowly until they had disappeared into the dry-goods shop. Now she just had to retreat three blocks, turn west, then follow that lane to the valet's home.

She turned on her heel and ran straight into Lady Jane Northumb.

"Oh!" the girl exclaimed.

Liliana stepped back, her heart beating wildly from the startle. "I'm so sorry. I didn't realize you were behind me."

Lady Jane placed a delicate hand on her chest. "It's quite all right. I should have made myself known."

The two women faced each other. Lady Jane seemed to Liliana as so many other debutantes fresh out of the schoolroom, somewhat shallow but with a sense of security Liliana had to acknowledge made her a little envious.

At barely nineteen, Lady Jane knew her place, accepted it and didn't think beyond that. She wasn't constantly fighting against society's expectations of her. She didn't have to make the choice between having a family of her own and doing what she was born to do, because no man would have a wife who bucked custom and was determined to excel in a traditionally male discipline.

Liliana pushed that depressing thought from her mind. She'd long ago made peace with her choices. What now had her thinking such nonsense?

"You shouldn't let what Emily said bother you, you know," Lady Jane said with a gentle smile. "She just has a bee in her bonnet because Stratford hasn't fallen at her feet."

"That's very kind of you," Liliana answered, trying to think how she would rid herself of Lady Jane and still be able to sneak off. "You mustn't worry about me. I'm made of sterner stuff than that."

Lady Jane ducked her chin. "Yes, you are. In fact, I've been meaning to ask you . . ."

Liliana tapped her foot, waiting for the girl to continue.

Lady Jane looked up and took a deep breath. "How did you ever find the nerve to challenge Stratford on the field? I could never be that brave."

Liliana blinked, surprised. Despite their differences, she had never disliked the fresh-faced young miss who was the gossiped forerunner in the hunt for Stratford's affections. Lady Jane had never before actually sought out or spoken to her, but neither had she been unkind.

"I'm not certain," Liliana answered, "though I can tell you bravery it was not. Pride, I suppose."

Lady Jane tittered, eyes wide. "My father would have starved me for a week had I done something so foolish. He's ever so hopeful of an alliance between Stratford and myself."

Something in her tone struck Liliana as off, and for the first time Liliana considered that perhaps other women felt as hemmed in as she. Not in the same way, certainly, but confined all the same. "But you are not?"

The younger girl bit her lip. "I'm not opposed, I guess. It's just that he's so . . ."

Striking? Intense? Yet good-humored and dashing?

"Old." Lady Jane made a moue. "And dark. Not like Lord Holbrooke."

Liliana held in a scoff. Old? Dark? How could Jane not find Geoffrey the most attractive specimen she'd ever laid eyes on? And to prefer Holbrooke? Why, the younger man, all slight and blond, literally paled in comparison. Geoffrey would—

Jane let out a sigh that sent the ribbon from her bonnet fluttering through the air. "Still, I shall marry Stratford should he ask. It's what Papa wishes."

Liliana strove for a bland smile. Where was her head? First, she had no reason to be thinking of Geoffrey in such a light. Second, an alliance with someone like Lady Jane would be precisely what Geoffrey would want. The Earl of Northumb was purportedly a lion in the House of Lords—a family connection that would open many a political door for Geoffrey. A tight ball that smacked of jealousy lodged in her throat, nonetheless. She couldn't stop herself from asking, "Has Stratford given you any reason to hope?"

Confusion stole over Jane's face. "Not particularly—a situation I, too, find odd given the nature of this party.

None of the other girls can claim any more attention than I, which is why Lady Emily is in such a foul temper. In fact, the only person it seems he's singled out in any way is"—an expression befitting a much more experienced society miss gleamed in Lady Jane's eyes—"you."

Liliana flushed, dropping her gaze to the cobbled path at their feet. She ran a slippered toe along the crevices of the stone and managed a wry laugh. "Stratford feels nothing more for me than an intense relief that after next week, we shall never see each other again." The ball that had been in her throat moved down to her stomach, turning it suddenly sour.

Lady Jane laughed and the moment passed, but Liliana's feeling of sickness lingered. She took a deep breath.

"If you'll excuse me, I've decided I do want that pair of gloves I saw in the last shop after all," Liliana said, bowing her head before sidestepping the girl.

"Shall I come with you?" Jane asked.

Liliana waved a hand behind her. "No, thank you. I'll only be a moment. Join the others and I'll meet you all at the tea shop soon enough."

She didn't look to see if Jane followed, only strode down the street with brisk steps. She welcomed the bracing breeze on her hot face. Her feelings regarding Geoffrey were becoming more and more of a muddle. The foolish emotions that had overcome her while talking to Lady Jane proved that.

The sooner she got this puzzle solved and left Somerton Park *and* Geoffrey behind her, the better. She hoped her next stop would finally provide her with some answers.

Geoffrey was finally getting some answers, much as he didn't want to hear them.

"Someone's been systematically siphoning money from my family for at least ten years?" Geoffrey shoved a hand through his hair, which was a more civilized alternative to slamming his fist into the desk, as he really wished to do. Damn it all. He'd tasked his man of affairs with poring through the estate accounts in hopes of *disproving* that his brother had been being extorted. Not the other way around.

Clive Bartlesby—another ex-soldier and trusted friend Geoffrey had taken on—flattened his lips, his eyes crinkling as his head moved in something between a nod and a shake. "It seems so, sir."

"Henry, what did you do?" Geoffrey muttered aloud, as if his dead brother could hear.

"Do you think it could have something to do with that letter you asked me to look into?" Bartlesby asked. "That your brother may have been paying the blackmailer all these years, and now that he'd dead, the bloke's trying to collect from you?"

"I'm not sure." Henry had been a profligate, utterly and shamelessly dissolute. A wastrel of the first order. And yet ... "As earl, Henry would have had control over the money. He wouldn't have had to steal from himself to hush anything up. You and I both know he spent indiscriminately," Geoffrey said, referring to the past months he and Bartlesby had labored to clean up his brother's financial messes.

"Unless he didn't want anyone else in your family to find out what he was paying for."

Geoffrey ran his fingers down the row of columns again, tapping at one entry in particular. He then flipped the pages back and repeated the motion, one page after another after another. Not so close as to be immediately noticeable, but when taken together ...

"Bloody hell."

"Exactly. And it's not just in the rents." Bartlesby grabbed another book, flipping it open. "See here, in the records of annual wool sales from your northern estate. The price received from each buyer, while never exact, is fairly consistent. Yet right here, the income is recorded as approximately two hundred pounds less than usual. I checked with this particular buyer, and he insists he paid the same as the others." He looked up at Geoffrey, his face cringing slightly, as if Geoffrey were a lord of old and he the poor messenger about to get his head lopped off for bearing bad news.

Geoffrey let out a long breath. "It's the same with produce, grain, household accounts and so on. But there's no pattern to it. Taken so sporadically over all of my family's vast properties, it's no wonder none of my stewards caught on." He walked to the shelf behind him, grabbed a glass and decanter and poured a drink—to hell with the fact that it was barely ten in the morning. His back, already stiff from his morning ride, tightened further, as it often did during times of stress. He offered a snifter to Bartlesby, but the man declined.

"Yet, I'm hard-pressed to figure how it was done," Geoffrey said. He placed his finger on a column, pointing to one of the suspect entries. "Look at this. There's nothing to differentiate it from the entry above or below it, aside from the number. Nothing crossed out, no change in handwriting even. Nothing to indicate at a glance there's aught amiss."

He pulled out a register from the estate in Northumberland, then another from here at Somerton Park and yet another from his estate on the coast. "Each of these books is kept by a different steward, yet the same problem exists."

Bartlesby remained silent, standing with his hands behind his back.

"Yet you say this has been going on clear back to a couple of years after my father's death?"

Bartlesby nodded.

Damn. "Several of those estates have had more than one steward over the years. We'll need to track down each man and interview him."

Geoffrey closed his eyes, pinching the bridge of his nose. His day had started out so well. He'd returned from his morning with Liliana refreshed, rejuvenated and more than a bit aroused by her—not only physically, though there was indeed that, but intellectually. Deeply. Curiously.

But when he'd arrived back at the manor, he'd been informed that Bartlesby had arrived from London and awaited him in his study. Geoffrey opened his eyes and looked at his man of affairs. "I've seen no out-of-place entries since my brother's death. Have you?"

Bartlesby shook his head. "Not one." The man looked road weary and exhausted.

"Go. Get yourself a meal and have Barnes settle you belowstairs. After you've rested, there will be plenty of time to put our heads together and sort this new development."

"Thank you, sir." The man nodded and left the room.

Geoffrey resumed his seat and picked up the account books. The first suspect entry he'd noted was in the fall of 1805. He grabbed a fresh quill and vellum and began tallying his figures with the ones Bartlesby had uncovered. The amounts were small, almost unnoticeable at first, growing ever larger like cresting waves as the years went on. When he reached the last book and scratched the final mark, the number astounded him.

Energy prowled through his limbs, bringing him to his feet. His instinct was to leave today, to visit each of his four estates and interview every last steward who had ever worked for the house of Stratford. He supposed he could send Bartleby in his stead, but that had never been Geoffrey's style. He wanted to get to the bottom of this right now, himself.

Instead, he refilled his drink. He couldn't leave Somerton Park now, not when influential men like the Earls of Northumb and Manchester and others would be arriving in two days. He may be new to Parliament, but Geoffrey understood that much political maneuvering was done outside of London, over drinks and friendly games of billiards in country homes much like his. He needed to win support for the Poor Employment Act, and if he could get Manchester and especially Northumb behind it, the bill would certainly pass.

Besides, he'd sent for the surveyors to mark out the mine he planned to sink at the edge of his property, and he needed to oversee the placement. A smile crossed his lips when he thought of how outraged his mother would be when she learned he planned to convert acreage to a thriving lead mine and village.

This matter of missing money and blackmail would have to wait at least another week.

Setting his snifter on the corner of his desk, Geoffrey once again sat and opened the books from 1805. He'd been away from England two years by then. He tried to remember if he even knew the steward who'd been overseeing Somerton Park then. He searched his mind but came up blank.

Wait. He might not remember who the steward was at the time, but Witherspoon might. His father's valet had stayed on at least a couple of years after the old earl died. The man might have some insight that could help Geoffrey solve this mystery.

He'd heard Witherspoon and his wife still lived in the village, and he had been meaning to get by and pay his respects. Bartlesby would be sleeping for at least a couple of hours.

Geoffrey swept up all of the account books and stowed them away in his desk. He knew he had only this afternoon before he'd have to rejoin the party and play the gracious host for a few more days.

He'd saddle Grin and head to town right now.

Chapter Fifteen

After a brisk walk to the far side of the village, Liliana was feeling much more in control. The narrow lane leading to the Witherspoon cottage was a bit overgrown, the pickets of the weathered fence a bit askew, but the overall effect was pleasant. The tiny cottage her father had left her in Chelmsford possessed a similar quaint charm, and standing here on the Witherspoons' shabby stoop brought a pang of homesickness.

Well, there was no time for that. Liliana rapped her knuckles against the hardwood door of the cottage. She bounced on the balls of her feet with nervous energy. Mr. Witherspoon just had to be well enough to see her today—there was no telling when she might be able to check on him again.

Muffled voices came from within. Liliana worked her thumb in circles against her index finger as she waited.

The rumble of hooves registered behind her and she turned to look over her shoulder. A rider slowed his mount as he came down the lane.

Liliana's breath caught as disbelief sent her stomach plummeting to the vicinity of her toes. *Geoffrey*. What could he possibly be doing here? Had he found her out and come to prevent her from speaking to Witherspoon?

Her heart tripped in her chest, stumbling and skipping

like an exuberant toddler chasing after a rabbit. She fought the urge to hide, knowing he'd already seen her.

As he dismounted, Liliana tried to imagine what might have given her away. This morning she'd thought for certain she had nothing to worry about. She'd watched him carefully when she'd mentioned her father and his death. Geoffrey had shown only compassion, no guilt. He'd shown no shred of suspicion or caution where she was concerned, and given that he'd been far from England when her father was killed, she'd decided he really knew nothing.

Liliana shifted on her feet, her hands clenching even as she pasted a smile on her face.

Geoffrey tied Gringolet to a fence post and turned in her direction. Gravel crunched beneath his boots as he moved to join her. A hesitant smile touched his lips, one of surprise and puzzlement. The tight knot in Liliana's chest dissolved to be replaced by sharp relief. He hadn't expected to see her here any more than she had him. The feeling lasted only momentarily, however, as she realized he'd want an explanation as to her presence here.

Newton's apple. Not only would he want an explanation, but there'd be no way she could interview Witherspoon now, even if the man *were* feeling up to it.

"Liliana," Geoffrey said as he stepped onto the tiny stoop with her. Had she noticed before how wide his shoulders were? She caught his scent of mint and man, could feel the heat from his body. She felt an answering heat rise in her and she stepped back, moving closer to the door. His presence overwhelmed her but didn't frighten her. Instead, a hot anxiety filled her, one she seemed to experience more and more in his presence.

His tone was genial, his smile gentlemanly, but there was something in his eyes that stirred her as his gaze dropped to her lips. A melting heat drizzled down Liliana's middle, and her lips tingled as she recalled how he'd looked at her just so this morning before he'd bid her good day in the gardens.

Then he blinked several times and stepped back from her as well. He tilted his head to the side and his eyes narrowed slightly, though his voice remained friendly when he asked, "Whatever are you doing here?"

Unease came roaring back. "Well, I—"

A sharp click sounded and the scarred oak door creaked inward. An older woman poked her head through the door, blinking against the bright sun. The smell of stale urine, sickness, and overboiled cabbage wafted through the door and Liliana tried not to wrinkle her nose. The odors combined with the tired lines on the woman's face to dim Liliana's hopes of Mr. Witherspoon's recovery.

The woman glanced briefly at Liliana before dismissing her as a stranger and turning her gaze to Geoffrey. Brown eyes widened with shock and recognition before one hand pushed back a lock of stringy grayish brown hair. The other hand began dusting off her well-worn skirts.

"M-my lord!" she exclaimed, flustered. "Whatever are you doing here?"

The question of the day, it seemed. Liliana turned toward Geoffrey to hear his answer, grateful to have been given a reprieve in answering it herself.

Geoffrey bowed to the woman. "Forgive me, Mrs. Witherspoon, for not coming to visit you earlier." He rose to his full height, and again Liliana felt almost crowded by him, even though she had ample room on the stoop. "I was wondering if I might speak to Mr. Witherspoon."

Liliana looked back at the woman, curious to see if Mr. Witherspoon was, indeed, up for visitors. There was, of course, the chance that the maid of all work hadn't given the tonic recipe to her mistress at all. And even if she had, the woman very well may have tossed it, being that it came from a stranger who'd not even examined her husband.

Mrs. Witherspoon didn't answer, but instead fixed her curious gaze on Liliana, who felt heat stain her cheeks.

Geoffrey gazed at her, too, likely still wondering why

she was here when Mrs. Witherspoon obviously didn't know her. Yet he smoothly said, "Forgive me again. May I present Miss Claremont?"

Liliana opened her mouth to make an explanation when Mrs. Witherspoon gasped.

"Miss Claremont? You're the young miss what come by yesterday and left the directions to make that concoction for m'poor Harold!" she exclaimed, pushing the door wide. Her expression changed, her crooked smile beaming. "Glory be." She threw her arms around Liliana. "I don't know how to thank you."

Liliana staggered back at the unexpected embrace, then awkwardly patted the shorter woman's shoulders. "Is Mr. Witherspoon improving, then?"

Mrs. Witherspoon released her, nodding vigorously as she wiped moisture from the corner of her eye. "Ever so much. I haven't seen him this well in ten years or more." She laughed, and a sense of pride swelled in Liliana at the relief in the older woman's voice. Liliana couldn't stifle a wide smile. This was why she spent so many hours poring over her tonics, why she worked so hard to find the link between sickness and chemistry, biology and environment.

Still, she had to remember why she'd come. "Is he well enough that I might pay him a short visit?" She glanced over at Geoffrey, who was watching her with a mixture of bemusement and something more intense. Curiosity? Admiration? Pleasant prickles bubbled through her chest. She abruptly returned her gaze to Mrs. Witherspoon and tried to sound proficient while she made up an excuse for her presence. "To check on his condition, of course." Perhaps she could sneak in a question or two, though how she'd manage to ask anything substantial escaped her.

"I think so," his wife replied. "Please, come in," she offered, grabbing Liliana's arm. As she pulled Liliana in through the door, she seemed to suddenly remember she'd left Geoffrey on the stoop. "You, too, of course, my lord." She let out an embarrassed chuckle as she motioned him in. "I'll just check and see if Harold feels up to visitors."

Mrs. Witherspoon bade Liliana and Geoffrey wait in a darkened parlor. Liliana shot Geoffrey a bland smile, trying to act as if nothing about their situation was unusual. He still watched her with an expression she couldn't fathom, yet sent tiny tremors off in her middle. She glanced at the floor, then all around the room, looking everywhere but at him. But she couldn't ignore his presence, and though he stood a respectable distance from her, it was almost as if he were pressed up against her, so alert and attuned was her body to his. It seemed as if whatever attraction was between them grew exponentially stronger each time he was near, like a reaction that burned hotter and hotter the more substance one introduced.

"I wasn't aware you were acquainted with anyone in the village," Geoffrey said.

Even uttering the most mundane of words, his voice moved over her like a warm velvet caress. Closeted with him in this dim parlor as she was, that feeling of having her space pleasantly invaded returned. A delicious shiver snaked through her.

"Not acquainted, exactly," she said, slanting a glance his way. Had he moved closer to her? Her heart sped up. "I ventured into the village during my morning ride yesterday. I . . . I had an overwhelming urge for a hot cross bun," she said, hating the lie even as it passed her lips. Allowing Geoffrey to think she'd come to Somerton Park only at her aunt's insistence had been bad enough, but at least then it hadn't been necessary to actually lie to the man. She'd just nodded at his erroneous conclusion. But now she was actively deceiving him, and it didn't sit well.

"The Witherspoons' maid was picking up the morning bread at the bakery and we began talking. She told me of her master's condition, one I recognized the symptoms of, so I gave her the recipe for a tonic that might help." She shrugged.

That look of concentrated intensity she'd seen on his face before, as when he'd precisely loaded his pistol during their wager, was turned upon her. She squirmed beneath it.

"I see," he said after a moment. "Just part of your life's work." There was no doubt of the admiration in his voice and his expression.

She shrugged again, embarrassed and more than a little uncomfortable. How odd. She'd spent her life chasing recognition, yet the look she saw in Geoffrey's eyes shamed her. Here he was thinking lovely things about her while she lied to him.

Liliana tried to focus her attention on the parlor as distraction. The windows were covered with heavy fabric, the air musty and filled with dust. The house had probably been shut up while Mr. Witherspoon convalesced, a common enough practice, but one she wholly disagreed with.

A few moments passed in silence, but Liliana could feel Geoffrey's occasional stare. Finally, a shuffling sound drew their attention.

An older man, rawboned and gaunt, ambled down the hall with the help of his wife and the maid Liliana had met yesterday. As Mr. Witherspoon passed into the light, Liliana blanched at how pale he looked, his ghostly skin blotched with spots. Yet when he smiled at her, Liliana glimpsed what he must have been like in his younger years—a rascal, no doubt.

As was proper, Witherspoon greeted Geoffrey first, but he almost immediately turned to her. A perplexed look crossed his wizened old face as he glanced between her and Geoffrey.

"So you're my angel," he said finally, coming to stand before her.

Liliana felt her cheeks pinken. "How are you feeling?"

"Chipper as can be, thanks to you," he answered.

"I'm glad I could be of help. I wasn't sure you would try my suggestions, given I'm a complete stranger who appeared out of nowhere on your doorstep."

Mr. Witherspoon barked a laugh that sounded quite hearty to her. "Believe me, miss, when you've been feeling as rotten as I have these past months, you're willing to try anything . . . even if old Scratch brought it to your door hisself."

Liliana felt the corners of her lips rise. But as she took in his pallid tone, she glanced around the dark room once more. She remembered seeing a fence around the side of the thatched cottage. Perhaps there was a courtyard in the rear. She decided to take a chance.

"Well, perhaps you'd be willing to try another piece of advice?"

A wooly white brow rose in expectation.

"Might we sit out in the sunshine while we visit?"

Mrs. Witherspoon gasped, clutching protectively at her husband's elbow. "Out of doors? Are you mad?"

Liliana held firm. "I know it goes against common wisdom, but there is something about sunlight that is very reviving to a body." She waved her arm in the direction of the windows. "Fresh air, too. In fact, my suggestion would be to take down these drapes and throw open the windows. Not only here, but in Mr. Witherspoon's rooms as well. Unless there is worry of contagion, there's no reason to be confined when the weather is fair. It will do you a world of good, sir," she said, keeping her eyes on Mr. Witherspoon, not daring to look at Geoffrey to see if he, too, thought she was mad.

"Now, see here," Mrs. Witherspoon sputtered. "I thank you for what you've done, but—"

"Calm yourself, Martha," Mr. Witherspoon said, laying a skeletal hand on his wife's plump shoulder. "For years now we've listened to that old quack, yet after only a day under this young lady's care, I feel better than I have in remembrance. Why, I even feel up to some of your wonderful cabbage soup." Mr. Witherspoon gave his wife a reassuring pat. "I think we should take her advice."

Liliana waited in the silence, keeping her gaze on the couple. Their obvious love and concern for each other touched an empty place inside of her.

"I agree," came Geoffrey's voice, quite startling Liliana. "I've known Miss Claremont to be most capable. I would trust her with my own well-being."

Liliana turned to look at him, pleasure at his words and guilt at their sentiment warring within her. She'd never once considered his well-being in her machinations, and yet the conviction in his voice indicated he meant his words. Despite the pangs of remorse that twinged within her, gratification overrode all. It lightened the emptiness and at the same time agitated her. Since when did one person's opinion, other than her father's when he was alive, have the power to move her emotions? Nothing about this could be good.

"See, my dear," Mr. Witherspoon soothed. "Even the earl trusts Miss Claremont." He looked between Geoffrey and Liliana again, eyes squinted slightly. "We can do no less."

A dubious look crossed Mrs. Witherspoon's face, but she gave a stilted nod. "Let's get you situated, Harold, dear. Then I'll see to taking down the drapes."

"Nonsense," Geoffrey said, stepping forward. "You'll feel better if you stay with your husband. With the assistance of your maid, I can see to opening up the cottage."

Both Witherspoons turned, looks of horror on their faces and denials spewing from their lips.

Geoffrey cut them off with a raised hand. "I insist." He turned his commanding look upon Liliana. "Will you see them settled outside, Miss Claremont?"

"Of course," she said slowly, nearly in as much shock as the Witherspoons. No man of quality she knew would deign to do manual labor in service to a servant. A retired servant at that. Liliana felt a softening sensation, somewhere in her chest, that she attempted to ignore. She moved to Mr. Witherspoon's side and assisted Mrs. Witherspoon in maneuvering him to the courtyard.

After he was seated comfortably, Liliana asked, "Are you chilled? I could fetch a blanket for your lap."

Mrs. Witherspoon waved her offer aside. "I shall fetch one," she said, bustling into the house and leaving Liliana at last alone with the former valet. Now was her chance.

But Mr. Witherspoon closed his eyes, lifting his face to the sun and resting the back of his head on the chair. He inhaled a deep breath, and a rickety smile crossed his face. Liliana found she couldn't interrupt his obvious pleasure. Goodness knows when he was last allowed outside.

Instead, she turned her gaze to the rustling drapes through the parlor window. The fabric shifted, tightened and then disappeared altogether, leaving Liliana with a clear view of the Earl of Stratford shaking out drapery and chatting amiably with a blushing maid of all work. Who could blame the girl? It must be surreal for her to be working hand in hand with a Lord of the Realm.

Liliana watched as Geoffrey deftly folded the drape and moved on to another. Who was this man? He certainly wasn't at all who she'd expected him to be, and if that were the case, would he even—

"He's chosen well," came Mr. Witherspoon's weathered voice.

Liliana jumped in her seat, snapping around to look at the old man. He was still resting his head against the back of the chair, but his eyes were open and he regarded her closely.

"We'd all heard that a bunch of fine ladies had descended upon the manor. Everyone speculated the earl had finally decided to take a bride," Mr. Witherspoon continued. "I'm only glad to see he's chosen a bride of such quality. Not like his father did, poor man."

Of course he would make such an assumption, considering that as far as they knew, she and Geoffrey had appeared on their doorstep together. Why else would Geoffrey bring her to pay a call if they weren't affianced? Liliana opened her mouth to correct the man, heat touching her cheeks. But she stopped just short of issuing the denial. Something in Witherspoon's tone made her hold her tongue. She might as well take this conversation as far as it would go. There would be enough time to correct his misassumption.

"The late earl was not happy in his marriage?" she asked.

"Ha!" the old man huffed, which sent him into a fit of coughs. When he regained control, he sat up straight and leaned toward Liliana, who sat directly across from him.

"The earl and countess detested each other," he said. "Spent as much time apart as physically possible. She ran off to London every chance she got, while the old earl enjoyed the peace and solitude of the country. Only went up to Town for meetings of that Society of his."

"Society?" Liliana asked. Certainly Edmund Wentworth had never been a member of the Royal Society of London for Improving Natural Knowledge, as her father had been. She'd memorized every bit of the Royal Society's history in her so far unsuccessful bid to be the first woman admitted.

"Oh," Mr. Witherspoon raised a hand and gestured side to side. "Antiqui-something. My lord loved anything to do with history, particularly history of far-off places."

"The Royal Society of Antiquaries," Liliana murmured. She couldn't remember her father ever having any dealings with that group.

"That's the one," Mr. Witherspoon confirmed.

Well, that explained the Egyptian influence in the music room. Still, it brought her no closer to establishing a link between the late earl and her father.

"Anyway, the countess thought the earl was an old fool. Couldn't understand his interest in anything but her. Course, it wasn't like she was the least bit interested in him. Only thing that woman loved, if you could call it that, was that firstborn son of hers. Don't mean to speak ill of the dead, but that boy was nothing but trouble. As for the current earl, I won't go into how the countess treated him. Only one that cared a whit for that boy was his father."

"Harold!" Mrs. Witherspoon whispered in a harsh voice as she came into the courtyard bearing a lap blanket.

"Now, Martha, dear," Mr. Witherspoon said, slowly sitting back in his chair. "I've got one foot in the grave, and we both know it. What can that old witch do to me now? Besides, if my healing angel here is going to marry Stratford, she deserves to know what she's getting for a mother-in-law."

Liliana couldn't bring herself to correct him yet. Tiny hairs rose on the back of her neck. There was something else he wanted to tell her—she was sure of it.

Mrs. Witherspoon frowned, settling the blanket around her husband's legs. "It's none of our business," she muttered, glancing over her shoulder to where Geoffrey was still working in the parlor, but didn't gainsay her husband further.

When she had him all tucked in, Mr. Witherspoon gave his wife an affectionate smile. "I think my appetite is returning, dearest. Might you fetch me some of your soup and a piece of bread?"

Mrs. Witherspoon gave him a wary look but obeyed, going back into the house.

Gooseflesh popped up on Liliana's skin, so certain was she that she was about to hear something very important.

"After what you've done for me, I couldn't let you join that family without warning you." He reached forward and grabbed Liliana's hand.

She shivered as his dry, papery skin slid over hers.

"Never trust the countess," he said, giving her hand a squeeze. "Don't ever turn your back on her."

Liliana frowned. Having been the recipient of the

woman's dislike and calculating glares, she understood the sentiment. "But why?"

Mr. Witherspoon grimaced, releasing her hand and sitting back into his chair. He seemed to think about the question for a long moment, then let out a rusty sigh. "I've never spoken of this before. Not to anyone. But staring my own death in the eye has made me wonder if keeping silent all these years was the right thing to do." He regarded her. "I'll leave it up to you whether you share this with Stratford once you're married. I've never had the courage to tell the boy myself."

Liliana flushed but scooted forward in her seat.

"I think the countess murdered her husband."

Liliana gasped. Whatever she'd expected to hear, it wasn't that. "Whyever would you think that?" she asked once she could speak properly.

Mr. Witherspoon bobbed his head, as if he'd been expecting that reaction. "A few weeks before he died, the earl was in a state like I'd never seen him. Secretive, jumpy, excitable . . . yet agitated, too."

A chill slithered its way down Liliana's spine. Her father had been just the same.

"The countess, of course, was off to London. But she came home one night unexpectedly, all in a fury. Seemed she'd caught wind of something the earl had done. Had a terrible row about it. I couldn't gather what about exactly—the earl sent me away, which was unusual, given I'd witnessed countless arguments between those two before." He shook his head sadly, then looked Liliana directly in the eyes. "But the very next morning, the earl was dead."

Liliana sat back in her seat, a hundred scenarios flying through her mind at once. She wanted to ask why he thought that, but she needed another question answered first. *Debrett's* had told her that the earl passed in 1804, the year after her father, but not exactly when. "When was that?"

"Around Epiphany, I'd say."

Liliana gasped again. She couldn't help it. "You're certain?"

Mr. Witherspoon nodded.

The late earl had died around January 6, 1804, only a couple of weeks after her father's death in December of 1803. Why hadn't she thought of that before? She'd assumed there was more time between their deaths given the dates. What a fool she'd been, allowing herself to focus on the years of their passing instead of the actual days. Her head spun. What did this mean?

She swallowed, asking the next question she must. "But what makes you think the countess was involved?"

Witherspoon grimaced, his yellowed eyes growing moist. His voice cracked as he answered. "I'm the one that found my lord. When I went into his chamber the following morning, he was cold and stiff in his bed. I raised the alarm, of course. The doctor came and, after examining him, said he passed of natural causes. But I don't think so."

"Why not?" Liliana asked again, impatient and listening for any clues that might tell her what truly happened to the earl.

"Well, I've seen people pass before, and when they go of natural causes, they tend to look all peaceful when they're gone. My lord, he didn't look peaceful at all." He closed his eyes, as if he were seeing it all over again. When he opened them again he said, "And here's the other thing. He smelled of almonds . . . his skin, I mean."

Almonds. A sick dread sprang up in Liliana.

"Which was very odd to me," Mr. Witherspoon said, his voice hushed. "My lord detested almonds, so much so that he wouldn't touch amaretto or even nibble a bite of marzipan. So why would he smell of almonds?"

Bile rose in Liliana's throat. Cyanide was tasteless, fast acting and easy to administer. Death by poisoning would account for the late earl's harsh visage. And cyanide smelled of almonds . . .

"All finished," Geoffrey said, a smile riding his face as

he entered the courtyard. Liliana started, her eyes snapping to him. His black hair was tousled, a light sheen of sweat glistened on his forehead and his normally pristine jacket was covered in dust.

As Liliana looked at Geoffrey, something cracked within her. Never had she thought to have anything in common with him, much less something she would never wish upon another person. A piercing empathy filled her.

Someone had murdered his father, too.

Chapter Sixteen

Geoffrey straightened his cravat as he made his way to the ballroom. Mother was likely incensed, given that he'd skipped supper, but he'd spent the late afternoon and early evening going over strategy with Bartlesby, setting the man several objectives to be met before Geoffrey could take up the investigation himself.

His trip to see Witherspoon had been rather enlightening, only not in the way he'd expected. Geoffrey hadn't had the chance to ask Witherspoon any questions. By the time he'd finished up in the cottage and joined the former valet and Liliana in the courtyard, Witherspoon had tired. If possible, the man had looked twice as old as he had less than an hour before.

No, the revelation had been Liliana. Every day, perhaps every hour, his regard for her grew. What was it that compelled a young woman to risk her reputation to visit a stranger, simply to make him feel better? What kindness of heart made one go out of one's way, wanting nothing in return? Indeed, Mrs. Witherspoon had insisted upon paying Liliana, but she'd refused even though Geoffrey knew she was a woman of little means.

More and more, he realized he wanted to delve into the enigma that was Liliana Claremont, to uncover more of what drove her. And that set him on dangerous ground.

But he wouldn't have to worry about that tonight. The strains of violins and a cacophony of voices floated down the hallway. Tonight, he'd have to "do the pretty," as it were. More guests had arrived this afternoon, and the numbers were expected to climb until the house party was in full swing in two nights' time.

The moment he stepped into the ballroom, Geoffrey knew he was in for it. It seemed his mother intended to ratchet up her campaign to see him married, for she was waiting for him. And that was never a good thing.

"Your business is finished, I trust?"

Even her tone set his teeth on edge.

"As much as can be done for the moment," he said, tugging first one cuff, then the other. He scanned the ballroom, not certain what he was looking for, only certain he had no intention of being caught in a discussion with the countess. To give her eye contact would simply encourage her.

He alighted upon Lady Emily Morton. With her nearly flaxen hair and luminescent silvery gray eyes set off by a low-cut gown of white silk, she was quite stunning. His gaze grazed over pale skin so delicate he could see traces of blue veins. She reminded him of a mute swan, all light and grace and fragility.

Until he met her eyes as she boldly stared him down. Then he imagined how a carcass might feel under the beady gaze of a buzzard.

He turned back to the countess, who suddenly seemed the safer of the two.

"The Morton girl *is* a bit forward," his mother acknowledged with a slow nod of her head. "I can see why you've largely ignored her. You wouldn't want an"—she seemed to search for a word—"aggressive wife, I'm sure. I may have miscalculated, thinking she might tempt you."

Geoffrey nearly snorted. His mother, of all people, should know that he'd choose someone as different from herself as he could find.

Lady Stratford squeezed her arm through the crook of his, pulling him into what likely appeared to onlookers as a casual mother-son stroll around the ballroom.

"But I didn't make a mistake with Lady Jane," she said. "She's sweet and biddable. She's also young, which should make her easy to mold. Not to mention she's the daughter of a man without whose support your little bill won't see the light of day."

Geoffrey stiffened. Damned Joss. He'd really hoped he could have trusted his uncle with the sensitive information, but it seemed Joss had proven to be as weak an ally as he'd feared. It seemed he could count on no one.

Except Liliana. Geoffrey started at the unexpected thought, and yet he didn't refute it.

"Come, Geoffrey. We both know there's little love lost between us. But can you not admit that I want what's best for this family?"

Geoffrey did snort then. "Since when did you want anything other than what's best for you?" He shook his head, irritated that he'd even allowed himself to be drawn into this conversation. He made his tone as formal as he could. "I fail to see what you could possibly want out of my marriage, madame."

"You wound me, Geoffrey," his mother said, a slight tremble in her voice.

Geoffrey glanced over, surprised by the uncharacteristic weakness. He raised a brow, trying to decide if this vulnerability she showed was just another ploy to sway him.

The countess took a shaky breath. She kept her gaze straight ahead but lowered her voice. "You and I are all that's left," she said. One shoulder lifted in an absent shrug. "Well, there's Joss, much good as he is." She sighed. "I suppose he does have his uses."

Yes. As your spy. Geoffrey held his tongue. How like his mother to regard one's value as only what one could do for her.

"I never expected to outlive your brother," the countess

said after a few steps, and for a moment Geoffrey actually believed the stricken look upon her face. If she'd had any tender feelings in her life, they would have been for Henry. "Or you, for that matter," she added, slanting her eyes to him, "even though you were at war for so long."

She immediately looked forward again. "When your brother was killed, and then you were so grievously wounded, I realized that I could very well lose you both. And with you gone, I'd be at the mercy of your spineless uncle and whatever greedy little fool he could convince to marry him."

Ah. There it was. Geoffrey almost smiled. That was the mother he knew.

"I'm no fool," she said as they made the turn at the east end of the ballroom. She smiled and nodded at a member of the local gentry but did not stop. "I know I lack the power over you that I commanded over your brother. He was weak. You are not. I also know that you are ambitious, where he was not. I think you will find that I know you better than you think."

She stopped walking and disengaged her arm, turning to face him. "I truly did give the invitees my sincerest consideration. With the exception of one or two . . ." A frown crossed her face before her expression returned to its customary coolness. "Any number of the others would be a very good match for you, politically and personally. I know what you want, son. Don't let your dislike of me blind you to the possibilities," she implored.

Geoffrey clenched his jaw, the truth in her words irritating. Not that she knew his personal desires . . . although the realization that maybe she did disturbed him. After all, wasn't he, in trying so hard not to replicate his father's role in a marriage, trying to imitate his mother's instead? The thought made Geoffrey nauseous. While he would never treat a spouse the way his mother had treated his father, wasn't his refusal to give his love so as not to be the vulnerable one in a marriage in the same league?

No. It couldn't be. He would never do what his mother had done. She'd been horribly, horribly wrong.

However, she was right in that she'd made stellar choices in her prospective-brides list. More likely than not, he would find the woman who would fulfill all of his needs amongst this group . . . He'd briefly considered more than one of them when he'd seen them in London. She was also correct in that he'd refused to consider a single one of them while they were under his roof by her invitation.

Perhaps he was letting his relationship with the countess interfere with his own good. Perhaps he should engage one or two of the ladies to see if there was any potential.

His mother smiled suddenly, causing Geoffrey to narrow his eyes. "Ah, Lady Northumb," she said, reaching an arm out in greeting. Geoffrey turned his head to see the woman and her daughter standing right behind them. At the other matron's conspiratorial nod, he felt his blood heat. By damn, his mother had expertly maneuvered him around the ballroom and right into the clutches of another matchmaking mama.

"Geoffrey, you remember Lady Northumb and Lady Jane, of course."

"Of course," he said, bowing.

"Lord Stratford," Lady Northumb greeted. "May I say how much we are enjoying your hospitality? Indeed, my husband will be most gratified to discover how excellent a time we've had when he arrives on Saturday," she said. "As will my brother, Christopher Wakefield, who shall be traveling with Lord Northumb. I believe you know my brother, from the Commons?"

Geoffrey kept his easy smile in place. Mother had certainly coached Lady Northumb on how to get his attention. If Lord Northumb was one of the most influential men in the House of Lords, Wakefield was his counterpart in the House of Commons. An alliance with Lady Jane would be very beneficial to Geoffrey, and everyone standing in this little circle knew it.

"I do," Geoffrey said, "and I am very much looking forward to discussing issues with them both."

The strains of a waltz filled the room, no doubt perfectly orchestrated, again by his mother. Three pairs of feminine eyes watched him with expectation.

Geoffrey managed to hold in his sigh. "Lady Jane, might you join me in the waltz?"

The diminutive blonde smiled and held out her hand. Geoffrey led her to the floor.

As they took their places amongst the dancers, Geoffrey reasoned with himself. Lady Jane might very well be the perfect bride for him. It was no secret her father desired an alliance, one that might be very good for all involved. She was pretty enough. Geoffrey determined to swallow his resentment at the machinations of their mothers and assess Lady Jane on her own qualities. Of course, if he settled on her, he wouldn't approach her until a few weeks after the house party ended. He wouldn't give his mother the satisfaction.

He rested one hand on Lady Jane's waist and raised his other to clasp hers in preparation for the first steps. While her waist was tiny and flawlessly formed, he felt not even a shiver of desire. He frowned. Not exactly what one hoped for in a potential spouse, but perhaps desire would come as he got to know her.

He led Lady Jane into the first twirl. She followed his lead well, but Geoffrey found himself disappointed. Still, there were more important considerations in a wife than a well-matched dance partner.

"Tell me, Lady Jane," he said, "what sort of activities do you enjoy?"

"Well," she said, a perplexed smile gracing lips that reminded him of blushing rosebuds. "I enjoy helping Mama host dinner parties for my father's friends."

Geoffrey nodded. Good. Northumb held many a fete with political undertones. She would no doubt be well qualified in that realm. Her voice was pleasant, too. That might be a small thing, but if he were going to listen to someone for forty years, he'd rather it not be torture on the ears.

"I play the harpsichord passably well," she said.

Ah yes. Geoffrey's mind rushed back to the afternoon in the music room. She'd been Mozart. What had Aveline called her? Beautiful and harmonic, a "no mess" kind of female. As Geoffrey led Lady Jane around the dance floor, he reflected that Aveline was very likely correct in his observation, unorthodox as it was.

Without thinking, Geoffrey caught himself humming the *Messiah* chorus. He cut himself off, smiling apologetically to the startled Lady Jane. Heat rose up his neck to his face for the first time in years. But he knew immediately where the song had come from.

Liliana. His Handel. Just the thought of her brought the scent of apples and lemons to his nose. The desire that had been so noticeably lacking upon touching Lady Jane came roaring to life with the mere memory of Liliana, making his body tighten.

"You play very well," Geoffrey said around the knot in his throat. He needed to refocus his attention on Lady Jane. "But what is it you truly like to do? What is your life's work?"

Even as he said the words, an image of Liliana in her boys' pants, wading through the bog, rose to greet him. It was followed by the smile of satisfaction he'd witnessed light her face this afternoon when Mr. Witherspoon had professed his improvement.

Lady Jane blinked her eyes several times. "My life's work?"

"Yes," Geoffrey said, thinking it telling that he'd used Liliana's terminology. "What do you hope to accomplish once you leave your father's home? What mark do you hope to leave on the world?"

"Well, I—" Lady Jane closed her mouth, her brow furrowing in obvious confusion. "I suppose I want to be a good wife, a good mother. I want to help my husband in whatever he chooses to do."

Geoffrey barely heard her answer as awareness stole through him. His head automatically turned toward the entrance.

Liliana.

A vision in blue, she plucked his attention from his partner as surely as she'd plucked the yellow bog asphodel from the marsh this morning. His eyes were immediately drawn to her bosom. Good God, he'd never seen her wear such a low-cut gown. She was every bit as perfect as he'd imagined. Half of him longed to look his fill while the other fought the urge to rush over and cover her with his jacket.

Liliana couldn't be any more different from the girl he held in his arms. Liliana's dark hair with its unruly curls and glints of red glistened in the candlelight, whereas Lady Jane's perfect blond coiffure seemed flat in comparison. Liliana's olive skin glowed golden against the rich blue of her dress, whereas Lady Jane's seemed to blend into her lighter gown. Liliana gave off waves of sensuality, intelligence and tranquility in equal measure, whereas Lady Jane gave an impression of social poise and the confidence of noble birth, but little else.

And Liliana made Geoffrey want to sweep her away and do unspeakable things with her in private places, whereas Lady Jane inspired only a desire to return her to her mother.

Geoffrey tore his gaze from Liliana and focused his polite attentions back on his dance partner. He owed that to Lady Jane until the conclusion of the waltz, yet he found that simple act more difficult than sitting still on the battlefield while the surgeon cauterized his wounds.

Lady Jane was still looking at him oddly. Geoffrey smiled to put her at ease. But in truth he wanted to laugh, one thing becoming perfectly clear to him. "Lady Jane," he said, "I'm certain you will make someone an excellent wife."

But not him.

When the interminable dance ended, he politely escorted Lady Jane toward Lady Northumb. His ire rose as he observed the woman and his mother whispering back and forth, confident smiles wreathing their faces. Discussing wedding gowns and cakes, no doubt. Well, it wouldn't bother him one bit to disappoint them.

He presented Lady Jane to her mother. "Not only are you an accomplished musician," he said, refraining from kissing Jane's hand, "but a superb dancer, as well. Thank you for the pleasure."

He nodded, then turned on his heel and departed, making straightaway for Liliana. He didn't need to look back to see his mother's face. He knew she'd be furious.

He cared not. On the surface, Liliana Claremont was absolutely wrong for him. But underneath, he was beginning to think she might be absolutely right. No, she'd never be the political hostess he'd need, but she could be a partner. A real partner. She and her passions made him feel alive. Her life's work, as she put it, complemented his own and was inspiring in and of itself. They could accomplish much together. At least he knew that he could trust her. And if love did develop with a woman like that, would it be so awful? He didn't know.

But there was only one way to find out, and as the strategy formed in his mind, it seemed the perfect way to thwart his mother's plans while advancing his own.

He'd have to phrase things delicately. Liliana had made it clear she had no plans to marry, but what he had in mind could hurt her chances should she change her mind. Nor did she seem to be fond of others' scrutiny, which his attentions to her would quite guarantee. On the other hand, Liliana was rather unconventional and most decidedly had her own mind. She may very well be open to his idea.

He certainly hoped so, as he wanted to get to know her a whole lot better, starting right this moment.

*　　　*　　　*

"Might I tempt you to join me in the Allemande, Liliana?" Geoffrey asked, bowing before her.

Liliana took a deep breath and gave him her most welcoming smile, though inside she was all aflutter. He'd noticed her the moment she'd entered the ballroom. She'd felt his gaze like a living thing, and whatever heat had caused his cobalt eyes to burn had warmed her blood until it tingled in her veins.

"The Allemande?" She placed her hand over her chest. If memory served, that particular dance wasn't too vigorous. She shouldn't have to worry about coming out of the top of her very *fashionable* bodice. "I think that should be safe," she muttered.

Geoffrey's lips curved up in smile.

He led her across the ballroom with its damask-covered walls and high ceilings. The multiple arched windows were open and covered in a gauzy material that floated with the light breeze. Liliana gave silent thanks for the cool night air, for it seemed that when she put her arm on Geoffrey's, the temperature in the room spiked.

As they passed by the countess, a chill broke through Liliana's flush and skittered down her back. Liliana nodded a greeting. Lady Stratford's face remained cool, as usual, but her eyes flashed hostility. Liliana couldn't contain the involuntary shiver.

As she and Geoffrey took their places facing each other at the end of the row of dancers, Geoffrey said, "I'm sorry about Mother. I'm afraid she's not happy that I've chosen you to partner over her selection."

"Is that why she's taken a dislike to me?" Liliana asked, as casually as she could manage. Lady Stratford would certainly prefer that Geoffrey spend his time with Lady Jane rather than with her, but was that the true reason she'd been so cold to Liliana from the moment they'd first met?

Witherspoon's story had shaken Liliana, throwing her thoughts into a jumble. Could the countess have been the cause of her husband's death? And if so, what, if anything, could that have to do with Papa's murder?

Geoffrey stepped toward her, to the center of the aisle. Liliana started, remembering she was supposed to be dancing. She met him, touching her right hand to his as they bowed to each other. Even through her glove, the touch seemed intimate, and for a moment all of her attention focused squarely on Geoffrey.

"You look dashing tonight," she blurted, then nearly clapped a hand over her mouth. She was such a ninny when she was distracted, too used to speaking her mind to remember to hold her tongue.

Geoffrey's slow smile made the slip almost worth it. "Do I?" He leaned in close, and she caught a hint of mint. His voice deepened as they circled each other in the first steps of the dance. "Surely you know how ravishing you look tonight."

Liliana was glad the dance called for her to turn away from him at that moment so he couldn't see her blush. She'd never call herself *ravishing*, but she knew the blue of her dress accentuated her coloring well. She'd been mortified when the modiste had suggested it. The bodice was cut extremely low, and the high waist showcased her bosom. She'd almost refused it after the final fitting, but now, given the pleasure she got from the way Geoffrey looked at her, Liliana was fiercely glad Pen had made her order the little satin slip dress.

"You flatter me overmuch, Geoffrey," she said as she turned a graceful figure eight around first him, then the woman next to her in the procession. Geoffrey followed suit with the gentleman next to him.

"I believe that is the first time you've used my name," Geoffrey said, taking her hand as they twirled. He gave it a slight squeeze, drawing her gaze to his intense one. "The first of many times, I pray."

Their hands touched and her forehead nearly grazed his. She could almost feel the vibration of his voice.

"I've come to like you very much, Liliana," Geoffrey

murmured. "We have a great deal more in common than I'd imagined. And as to that, I have a proposition for you."

Liliana was loath to move away from him into the figure eight that would once again advance them down the line. What could Geoffrey possibly mean, a proposition?

Finally, a gliding step brought her face-to-face with him. "A proposition?" she asked, but before he could answer, he had to turn away.

Blast this dance! Always moving one away from her partner. Liliana joined arms with the woman next to her perfunctorily, yet inside she bristled, anxious to return to her conversation with Geoffrey.

They met in the center, Geoffrey taking her hand for the twirl. "Well, as I see it, you and I have been done the same wrong," he said, his voice dropping lower.

Liliana's stomach clenched, the pressure so powerful it cut off her breath. All the while, the figure eight forced her away once again. He couldn't mean their fathers. He couldn't. Yes, he'd spoken to Witherspoon alone, but only for a moment. Surely not long enough for the man to relay his tale. Nor had Geoffrey seemed upset when he'd escorted her to the tea shop so she might return with the other ladies.

Liliana and Geoffrey met face-to-face, touching hands before turning away. Another loop with the neighbor woman, and Liliana again joined Geoffrey in the center. Best to act ignorant, not give away anything until she knew more. "I don't understand."

"My mother," he said, shaking his head. As close as their foreheads were throughout the twirl, Liliana felt the air move counterpoint against her skin. "She's put me in a regrettable position, I fear."

"Yes," Liliana murmured. She could certainly see where learning his mother may have killed his father would be regrettable. But why would Geoffrey say they had been done the same wrong?

Liliana sucked in a breath. Could he mean Lady Stratford had also been responsible for her father's death?

"Just as your aunt has put you," Geoffrey continued.

What? Liliana missed a step in the intricate dance and trod upon the foot of the woman next to her, who yelped in surprised outrage.

Liliana mumbled an apology and tried to recover. What had her aunt to do with anything?

"Your aunt brought you here hoping you might attract a husband," he explained when next he moved close enough to keep their conversation private. "My mother has invited all of these women here in hopes that I might choose a bride. Neither of us wishes to comply. Therefore, I propose we band together."

A hysterical giggle bubbled from Liliana's lips, earning her more than one glance.

My goodness. What had she been thinking? It was just that after what she'd learned from Witherspoon, Geoffrey had surprised her with that "done the same wrong" statement, and then—

"Is something amiss?" Geoffrey asked, tilting his head with concern.

"No, no," Liliana assured him. "Just embarrassed over my footing. Please, go on."

"Well, I'd like you to agree to allow me to squire you exclusively for the remainder of the house party," he said.

"You would . . . ?" she said slowly.

"I would. It should sufficiently annoy my mother and perhaps satisfy your aunt into letting you alone. Unless . . ." Geoffrey narrowed his eyes, a frown setting like the sun over the horizon of his lips. "You don't have hopes where Aveline is concerned, do you? I wouldn't wish to interfere if you have an understanding with him."

"What? No," Liliana answered, marveling at the change in Geoffrey. His clenched jaw and rigid posture suggested he most certainly did wish to interfere with such a thing. A feminine thrill uncoiled in Liliana, even though she had no business feeling it. "No. In fact, I received a note from Aveline just this afternoon explaining he'd been called to Town and wouldn't return to Shropshire for some time. I don't expect to see him again."

Something about that still bothered Liliana, but she had far too many other mysteries to solve at the moment.

Geoffrey cleared his throat. "Good."

Still, she should at least ask . . . "How well do you know Aveline?"

Geoffrey shot her an odd look but answered. "Well enough, I suppose. We've been neighbors for years, though I've been gone for well over a decade."

That didn't help much. "But would you consider yourselves friends?"

Geoffrey shrugged, though he seemed to be bristling from the line of questioning. "He's a good enough man, as far as I remember. His mother was French, came over well before the Terror, but certainly because her family sensed what was coming. Aveline took a bit of ribbing over being half French after war broke out. It grew worse when he was detained in France for several years, along with other British tourists. Some questioned his loyalty," he said, taking her hand once more as they entered the last movement. "But I don't want to talk about Aveline. I'd rather discuss my proposal."

The ending strains of the violins echoed through the air. Geoffrey turned Liliana in the final twirl.

"What do you think?" Geoffrey asked, settling her arm on his.

"I must consider for a moment," Liliana said, mulling over his suggestion. Part of her found it difficult not to rub her hands together with satisfaction. Her chances of finally uncovering the truth behind her father's death increased a hundredfold if she attached herself to Geoffrey. And yet, his exclusive attentions would be considered by some to be tantamount to declaring himself. He'd been away for more than a decade and had probably not spent many years in the ballrooms. He might not understand that when they eventually parted, she would be the one looked at as tainted, as though something must have been wrong with her to lose Geoffrey's regard. It would be her reputation ruined, if not actually, then practically.

Was learning the truth worth her future?

"I think it's an excellent idea," she answered.

"Splendid," Geoffrey said, his slow smile lighting his face. Once again, Liliana's breath caught, but this time for an entirely different reason.

A thought occurred to her. "Since we shall be spending so much time together, would you prefer me to give you your solitude on your morning ride?"

Geoffrey's hand tightened over her forearm, almost as an involuntary response to keep her with him. "Of course not. In fact, I have plans for us at dawn," he said.

The pleasure that had uncoiled in Liliana earlier now spread through her, pushing out the unease. She couldn't stop it if she tried. She told herself what she felt was due to him falling so easily in with her own scheme. Liliana let out a little breath. She wasn't even good at lying to herself.

"If you still wish to join me, that is," Geoffrey amended, looking anxious for her answer.

Liliana gave him her most brilliant smile, surprised to realize she didn't have to fake it at all.

"I wouldn't miss it."

Chapter Seventeen

She was late.

Geoffrey strode another circuit around Amira's stall. Of course Liliana wasn't late. They hadn't set a time to meet, after all, and the sun had barely pinkened the farthest horizon. It was only that he'd been dressed and at the stables since well before dawn, driven out of his bed by lustful dreams of the very woman he suddenly couldn't seem to wait a moment longer to see.

Whoever would have thought the Allemande could be so bloody sensual? Why the patronesses of Almack's thought they should dictate which young debutantes possessed strong enough moral convictions to waltz while blithely allowing anyone and everyone to dance the Allemande, he couldn't say. The waltz was tame when compared to the slow glide of the Allemande — the touching of hands, the leaning so close one seemed enveloped by one's partner's scent . . .

Geoffrey cleared his throat. Indeed, an Allemande with Liliana had proven much more dangerous than a hundred waltzes with the likes of Lady Jane or Lady Emily. He supposed with the right person —

"Where is Mr. Richards?"

Geoffrey turned at Liliana's soft question. Her hair was pulled back from her face, and her olive skin glowed against the white shirt she wore. She looked young, natural, yet more beautiful than any woman he'd seen. He drew in a deep breath, as if she were fresh air and he a man who'd been trapped indoors for an age. All of the nervous tension left his body, to be replaced by a low thrum of a different kind. Even covered completely in her scruffy boys' togs, she had the power to arouse and titillate him.

"I told him to enjoy his bed," Geoffrey said. Truth be told, he'd come down to the stables last night after the ball to inform Tom his services wouldn't be needed this morning. Geoffrey had felt ridiculous as he'd tromped through the dewy grass in his evening finery, but he'd wanted Liliana completely to himself. "I am perfectly capable of saddling a lady's horse."

"As am I," she murmured. "But thank you."

Geoffrey imagined that Liliana was perfectly capable of many things. Unfortunately for his rioting senses, each of those imaginings revolved around her luscious body and how she might use it to please him. He wondered if she even understood just what she *was* capable of.

More and more, he wanted to show her.

"What do you wish to show me today?" she asked, walking over to softly stroke Amira's nose.

Geoffrey started. Had he said that aloud? "I'm sorry?" he said, feeling as if he should apologize for the lurid turn his thoughts had taken, even if she was oblivious to it.

"You said last night you had plans for us. Did you wish to show me another bog?"

"Oh," Geoffrey said with a relieved laugh. He really must get control of his wretched libido. "No, something altogether different. Do you feel up to a longer ride this morning?"

"I feel up to anything," she said, and though he knew her words were uttered in complete innocence, he had to turn away lest she see the evidence of desire they evoked.

Geoffrey set the pace as he led Liliana toward the easternmost edge of the Wentworth lands. While the pace was far from the vigorous race of yesterday morn, he still kept up a brisk trot. There was much he wanted her to see and the sun was already edging the sky. They'd nearly been caught out yesterday, since they'd returned to the house later than was wise. Liliana would have certainly been compromised, leaving him no choice but to marry her.

And would that have been so bad?

Geoffrey mulled the question his mind tossed at him. His body tightened painfully and he rolled his eyes. It seemed at least *that* part of him was ready to admit he desired a union with Liliana.

Geoffrey tried to push the idea out of his mind. He was just gently exploring the possibilities. He didn't have the time or attention to devote to securing a bride, what with the vote on the Poor Employment Act coming up, a blackmailer to be uncovered and the Wentworth finances still to be sorted.

But he slowed his horse a bit all the same.

As the ground became hillier, a new excitement rose in him. It was as if he were a lad again, anticipating a visit from Saint Nick. He wasn't certain when he'd decided Liliana would be the first to see his plans for employing ex-soldiers right here at Somerton Park, but as they neared the mine site, he knew he'd chosen well. He certainly had no desire to share this moment with his mother, and Joss had proven not to be a good confidant, either. Nor could he imagine someone like the perfectly biddable Lady Jane by his side.

He looked over at Liliana, riding beside him in companionable silence, the breeze blowing through her loosely tied-back hair. She'd dispensed with the cap after that first morning, a fact he very much appreciated.

An ache pierced his throat. He also appreciated her presence. It was a sad thing, to have no one to express your dreams to. Maybe it was just as sad that he had only a virtual stranger by his side, but he didn't feel that way. He felt grateful.

How nice it was not to have to put on airs, not to have to be the earl or the war hero or the politician or anything other than just a man enjoying his morning. His shoulders relaxed and his face split into a wide smile of contentment.

"What?" she asked, a bemused smile riding her face.

"I was just thinking how nice it was to be with someone who wanted absolutely nothing from me but my friendship," he said, deciding on frankness. "You're a refreshing change, Liliana." He held her gaze and found himself saying, "One I could get used to."

Her smile froze, her eyes turning downward. Alarm clenched his gut. Damn. She didn't look comfortable with his admission. Indeed, she looked much like he imagined he did when cornered by marriage-minded debutantes. He'd need to guard his words better so as not to push her away.

They continued to the summit of the hill in silence, then rode along the ridgeline, where distinctive outcroppings of rocks marked a change in the landscape. Farther up the ridge, Geoffrey located what he was looking for. Wooden posts and steel chains dotted the ground where surveyors had marked the most appropriate and safest places to drop the mine shafts. Satisfaction stole over him at this tangible sign of his plan coming to pass.

When they came upon the site, he found a suitable place to tie off the horses and assisted Liliana to dismount.

"What is all this?" Liliana asked, reaching a hand out to run her fingers along links of chain. She looked over at him, her violet eyes wide and inquiring, curious and intelligent, sharp and incredibly sexy.

"That," Geoffrey said, "is the spot marking the first of three main vertical shafts of the new Fealty Lead Mine of Shropshire."

Liliana's brows furrowed together, but her lips curled. "You're digging a lead mine?"

Geoffrey laughed. "Not me personally, but yes." He pointed out several yards. "Shaft two will be there, and number three, off to the right there. This whole area is rich with lead ore. My men will use the shafts to reach mineral veins, then dig horizontal tunnels or levels between the shafts so they can cut the lead ore out and bring it to the surface for processing."

Liliana turned in a circle, looking all around. Her nose crinkled and she cocked her head. "Why would you deface your land with industry?" she asked, but her tone held no judgment. Just that curiosity she seemed to exhibit for most things.

"To put my money where my mouth is," he said. "To create jobs for as many ex-soldiers as I can." He explained much of what he'd told Joss last week, but telling Liliana seemed different. For one, an uncommonly vulnerable sensation settled around his heart. He hadn't cared what Joss thought of his intentions, yet he became aware of a keenness for Liliana's good opinion. His chest lightened with each thoughtful nod of her head as he laid out the situation. "So you see, I must lead by example," he said. "If I'm not willing to put my own fortune on the line, why should I expect others of my class to do any different? I hope to prove to my peers that it would be to their benefit to fund projects such as this."

"You mean monetarily beneficial?" she asked shrewdly.

He nodded. "I believe there is more benefit to be had for the country than that, but yes . . . profit is often the best motivation. My hope is to persuade a few to do what I intend to—take the profits and invest in other ventures that will create employment opportunities."

Liliana stared at him so long he thought he might actually squirm beneath her regard. He, who'd stared down armed combatants over a battlefield.

"You're not at all what I expected," she said finally.

Geoffrey huffed a breath, marveling at the tightness in his chest. "Is that a good or a bad thing?" he asked, because her expression wasn't clear.

A look Geoffrey could almost classify as sadness crossed Liliana's face, making his heart clinch. "I'm not sure," she murmured and turned away from him.

Geoffrey stood there, as still as stone, uncertain as to what, exactly, was passing between them. Something intense, something unspoken and something he desperately wished came out in his favor. Once again, he recognized that Liliana was a woman with walls built around her heart. He knew it because he had similar walls. He knew where his had come from but wondered what comprised the mortar of her own.

Liliana cleared her throat, and when she turned back to him, whatever she'd been feeling had been wiped from her face.

"So you plan to bring soldiers here to work the mine," she said. "Where will they live?"

Geoffrey watched her face for a moment but saw no opening to explore what had just happened. He adopted an easy tone and said, "We'll build a sort of barracks right there." He touched her shoulder, bidding her to turn where another area was marked out. "This will be better lodging than they ever had during the war, and many of the men are unattached, so they'll be happy to come. But eventually, my hope is for them to have families and homes of their own, so I plan to build a village."

She blinked up at him in surprise. "A village?"

"A small one, yes. I'd hoped to build the village before the mine opened, and then a smelting mill, but — " Geoffrey snapped his mouth shut. He'd almost just blurted out that his finances were uncertain and he couldn't justify the expense until he knew where he stood. Liliana was so easy to talk to, he'd nearly forgotten himself. "But that hasn't worked out," he said instead. "So I've had to adjust. For the first year or two, we'll cart the ore to the smelting mill at Ironbridge for processing. That will cut into our profit, but we'll use what little we have to build the village first, then a mill of our own. Once that's operating, we should quickly have enough to invest in other things."

Liliana's eyes softened, and the smile she gave him seemed filled with approval and admiration and something indefinable.

Geoffrey's lips lifted in response. The look in her eyes made him feel as light as air and filled him with a piercing happiness he hadn't felt in years.

"Where will you place your village?" she asked.

Geoffrey nearly grabbed her hand but stopped short. What had gotten into him? He offered his arm, as was proper, but a deep satisfaction filled him anyway as she laid her hand upon him. He led her to the crest of the hill, where a wide valley opened up. "There," he said, pointing to a green area that would make the perfect spot. "It's flat, the land is fertile and that creek that runs through it flows year round. Eventually, I hope to add a small church and a school and—"

Liliana stiffened beside him, and she gripped his forearm, drawing his full attention. "You can't place a village there."

Geoffrey frowned. "Whyever not? It's the perfect place—"

"It's the worst place possible," she interrupted.

"I disagree. The mine supervisor I've hired has much experience, and he says nearly all mines are laid out in such a fashion."

Liliana pulled her arm away from him and turned to face him, looking directly into his eyes. "That may be, but if you care for the health and well-being of your soldiers and their families, you will find a different spot."

Geoffrey crossed his arms, unaccustomed to being challenged. Yet he knew Liliana to be extremely intelligent and so was willing to listen to what she had to say. "Why should I take your advice when it flies in the face of years of practical experience?"

She faced him squarely, challenge burning in her eyes. "My father spent his life studying the effects of contaminated air and water on the human body. I have continued his work, albeit in a different discipline, and I am telling you that placing a village in that valley will slowly but surely kill its inhabitants."

Geoffrey sucked in a breath. Liliana's passion and conviction rang from every part of her being. But while he appreciated her stance, he wasn't about to change months' worth of planning without some proof of her claims. "Nonsense. My mine supervisor and I chose the valley precisely because it would be farther from the smoke of the mill. I don't see what else could be a problem."

Liliana scoffed. "Yes, well, neither you nor your mine supervisor know anything about chemistry." She grabbed his arm and dragged him over to an outcropping of rock. She ran a finger along it. "These mineral veins that make this area such a rich deposit of lead ore are precisely the problem. Lead ore, as well as other metals like copper or silver, are sulfides. Your men will be digging this out of the earth, bringing it to the surface, yes?"

"Of course."

Liliana gave one sharp nod. "Do you know what happens to sulfide when exposed to oxygen and water?"

"No, I do not."

"It becomes sulfuric acid," she said. "Which means every time it rains, the sulfides will react and turn to acid, which will then leach into the ground or will rush down the hill if the downpour is heavy enough, right into the very creek your villagers will bathe in and drink from. And it will soak into the soil they grow their food in, as well."

Geoffrey examined the innocent-looking rock in a different light. "You're certain? You can prove that?"

"I can create sulfuric acid from this rock quickly enough," she said. She took a deep breath. "But I can't prove a direct health consequence so easily. I can show you what acute exposure to sulfuric acid would do to a body, but a deluge of water would dilute the properties of the acid so much that it might take time for a cumulative effect to be directly discernable," she admitted.

Liliana impressed Geoffrey with her honesty. He knew from the timbre of her voice and the fire in her eyes that she felt strongly about this issue, yet she'd willingly given him the flaw in her argument. Her obvious integrity only increased his respect for her.

"But I can tell you that at normal concentrations, sulfuric acid burns skin and tissues and, if ingested, can perforate one's esophagus or gastric tract," she stated. "If inhaled, it damages one's lungs. It only stands to reason that even in small quantities, over a long period of time, exposure cannot be good for people."

Liliana grasped his hand, sending a shock of awareness through him. Through her, too, if her expression was any indication, yet she held on, squeezing him firmly.

"I know my theory is correct. It may take me some years to gather conclusive data, but I know it." Pink bloomed in her cheeks and she sighed, releasing him. "Forgive me. I've overstepped myself." She turned her face away.

"Oxygen and water, you say?"

Liliana nodded.

"I wonder if that's why my father closed that old well behind the folly a couple of years before he died," he mused. "The villagers complained but he said the water was dead."

"That certainly could be, if the well dug into the lead ore at any point," she said.

Geoffrey gazed out over the valley, where he'd envisioned his soldiers living happily with their families, their children. He had no wish to do anything that might harm the very people he was trying to help. And if there was even a chance . . . "I'll move the village."

Liliana snapped her head around. Her eyes widened, but a small smile curled her lips and her shoulders relaxed. "You will?"

He nodded, her obvious relief convincing him that he was making the right decision. "I'll have to clear some land behind us, but it can be done. I may even move the smelting mill down into the valley," he said, calculating what such a move would cost in efficiency, as well as pounds sterling. "It shall be more expensive to operate, but I don't wish the children to breathe the smoke it will generate."

Liliana's smile grew wider, even as her eyes took on a wondering look. "You *are* a good man," she whispered.

Something tilted within him, and Geoffrey gave in to the need that had been building for days.

He kissed her.

It was no sweet suitor's kiss, begun with a slow lean and fraught with anticipation. No, it was a hungry kiss, initiated first by his hands, which cupped Liliana's face in a firm grip, followed by his mouth, which enveloped hers with ravenous desire.

She moaned low in her throat, a velvety sound that shot fire through him. He half expected her to pull away, but instead, she leaned up on her toes, relaxing into his hold and pressing herself against him. She opened to his exploration, allowing his tongue access to her mouth. Her skin was soft beneath his hands, like satin as his finger brushed the tender underside of her earlobe. She shivered in reaction, sending a tremor through him as well. By damn, she was so responsive it would take only—

Geoffrey yanked himself back, gasping for breath. "I'm sorry," he said. "I should not have taken advantage." He dropped his hands to her shoulders, gently putting her away from him, lest he drag her into his arms and take real advantage . . . the kind that could not be undone.

Liliana, it seemed, was having just as much difficulty regaining her composure. Her chest rose and fell, and he could see the throbbing of her pulse against her neck, very near where his hand still rested. He released her, taking a step backward.

Her extraordinary eyes were wide but had darkened sensually into a deep amethyst. That incredible curiosity of hers gleamed in their depths as she watched him ... that quality that he knew would make her an exceptional lover. He groaned. Thoughts like that would not help him in his bid to be a gentleman. "Forgive me," he said, taking another step back.

Liliana remained, her chest rising in deeper, slower breaths. Her tongue darted out to moisten her lower lip, or perhaps to soothe it. His kiss hadn't been gentle. Yet Geoffrey couldn't regret it, even though he knew he should.

"I'll not forgive you."

Geoffrey grimaced. He straightened his shoulders and lowered his head, prepared to allow her to heap whatever well-deserved condemnation she wished upon him.

"There is nothing to forgive," she said softly.

He raised his head, focusing on her face. Her lips were swollen, had deepened a shade from his kisses. Yet they were smiling.

"I have something to say." Her voice didn't waver, yet her cheeks pinkened, alerting him that whatever was on her mind wasn't an easy thing to get out. "I'm going to be blunt, though it may cause you to think I am not a lady."

Geoffrey held very still, his attention rapt.

Liliana took a deep breath. "I've told you I have no intent to marry, but that does not mean I have no wish to ..."

He found he could no longer breathe.

"That is, I've been thinking since the night you kissed me in the library ..." She shook her head and started again. Her chin trembled, barely enough for him to notice, but notice he did. "I am four and twenty. I have studied science since I was a girl. I am well aware of how ... reproduction works."

She took a small step toward him, and prickles of sensations rolled in waves over his skin.

"But I am only now becoming aware of a . . ." She licked her lips again, seemingly unconsciously, but it was as if she'd licked his own instead, so real was the jolt of lust that took hold of him. "A desire to experience it for myself."

"Liliana," he whispered, his throat too dry to speak. She waited for his response as bravely as any young soldier he'd ever witnessed, yet her lips quivered just a touch with a vulnerability that moved him. Still, he needed to understand what she was asking just as much as he needed time to cool his ever-increasing need so that he could think clearly. He swallowed and tried again. "You must know that I want you. A man doesn't . . . kiss a woman with such fervency if he doesn't desire her greatly."

He waited for her nod before continuing. "So you understand that at this moment I would like to make love to you, more than anything else I think I've ever wanted?"

A shy, yet radiant smile accompanied the flaming blush that swept Liliana's face, and for a moment Geoffrey thought he would lose his resolve to remain, in practice at least, a gentleman. A plan was forming in his mind, but he could not act on it until he'd had time to consider it fully without the influence of lust that currently dominated his every thought.

"Yet, I cannot," he said as gently as he could. "I have too much respect for you to allow you to throw away your maidenhood, which by all rights should belong to your husband."

Liliana frowned, her eyes turning downward. "But I've already told you—"

He held up a hand. "I know, but you might yet change your mind. In fact—" Geoffrey stopped himself from saying the words aloud, but he could not halt them in his head. *In fact, I hope that you will.* He stepped forward, cupping his hand around her cheek. "I cannot do anything that will take that choice away from you. That would make me the worst sort of man," he whispered, staring deep into her eyes. "A dishonorable one."

She dropped her head, the weight of it resting in his hand. He caressed her cheek, drawing his thumb lightly over its surface before drawing it over her lips.

"But neither can I deny us both what we want," he murmured.

Liliana brought her head up, her eyes contracting with confusion, with shame and with something that looked suspiciously like hope.

"I will show you some of what you wish," Geoffrey said, knowing he shouldn't say it but unable to keep the words inside. "But only so far. I will not allow us to do anything irreparable." Yet even as the words left his mouth, Geoffrey was afraid that what they began was already irreversible. "And we will take it slowly."

In answer, Liliana turned her lips to his thumb, which was still absently caressing her, and kissed it. Geoffrey closed his eyes, unable to watch the incredibly erotic kiss.

"Do you agree?" he said.

"Yes," her voice reached his ears. He opened his eyes. Liliana looked as mesmerized as he felt.

"Good," he said roughly. "Because I'm going to kiss you now, properly, as I should have from the first."

He leaned toward her, gently pulling her to his lips. His heart leapt when she leaned in to meet him on her own.

The first touch of her lips on his nearly brought a moan from his still tight throat. It was as if the stricture was melting at her touch, allowing him to breathe in fully of her, her scent, her being.

Her lips were warm, tentative, as if she feared showing her passion lest he call a stop to her experimentation. He tightened his grip on the back of her neck, caressing, massaging as he moved his lips lightly from side to side.

Familiarizing hers to his touch, showing her that he could be gentle, too. He could feel the puffs of her breath on his face, becoming shorter, faster. Hell, at least she could breathe.

When he could stand it no longer, he tilted his head and fitted his mouth to hers. He brought his hand back to her face and put enough pressure on her chin with his thumb to get her to open her mouth. As his tongue swept inside, he returned his hand to her neck, holding her as close to him as he could.

She moaned, welcoming him, yet he sensed she still held herself back. That was fine with him. He didn't know if he could handle it if she didn't. He tried to keep the kiss light—tried to contain the force of his own passion that he struggled to keep leashed. He stroked her tongue with his, long strokes, short ones. Exploring her, savoring her as he hadn't had time to during their previous, heated kisses. He'd expected her to taste of lemon, but it was apples and honey that came to mind, tart yet sweet. Her taste was as contrary as the woman herself.

When she finally allowed her tongue to stroke his, the leash slipped. He gathered his arms around her, lowering them to the soft grass on their knees. He maneuvered to his backside, then brought his left hand around her back and slipped his right under her knees to gather her into his lap, never breaking the kiss. When he had her settled, he brought both hands to cup her face, deepening his kiss, ravenous for her.

He'd been so tempted to settle her astride him, as he'd imagined ever since seeing her galloping astride on horseback. Her cotton shirt and breeches would be a paltry barrier between them, and the urge to feel her breasts against his chest, her warmth pressed against his arousal with only the thin cotton between them, was almost irresistible. But then he would be breaking the very rules he'd just set.

Besides, there was always later.

Geoffrey admitted, the moment she touched her

tongue to his, there would be a later with this woman. She made him feel things ... His passion-charged mind couldn't fully comprehend it, but despite his claims to the contrary, he knew. Knew he would have to have her.

He broke the kiss, gasping for breath. He was still caressing the side of her neck when she lifted her chin, struggling for her own breath. His lips immediately found the pulse point at her neck, his tongue darting out to feel the beat of her heart against him. He ran his mouth down to the hollow of her throat as his hand trailed over her collarbone to her chest, cupping a full breast in his hand.

Her low moan brought his lips back up to hers in a drugging kiss—he didn't want her to surface from her sensual haze yet. He knew they couldn't remain in the open like this, yet he wasn't ready to let go. He gently squeezed her breast, sweeping his thumb across her nipple, feeling it tighten beneath the cotton of her shirt.

She moved restlessly in his lap. It was his turn to groan as the globes of her bottom brushed against his arousal. He was quickly losing control. He dragged his lips from hers. He could not, would not take her here, not now, after he'd just told her he wouldn't dishonor her. He had to think, get some perspective.

He tucked his face into the side of her neck, trying to calm his breathing. Her breast was still cupped in his hand, nipple straining against his palm. He slid his hand gently down her side to settle on her waist. It took supreme effort to remain still, not to touch her, to let her regain her composure.

Liliana lifted her head, her eyes direct. "Is it always like this?" she asked, her voice a breathy sound that stroked him as surely as if she'd touched him. "This ..." She pressed her lips together and her brows dipped, and Geoffrey knew her innocence struggled to find the words for how she was feeling. "This overwhelming, gnawing ache inside?" She smoothed her palm down her center, settling it low on her stomach.

Geoffrey shook his head. It had never been like this for him before. Ever. "No," he whispered. "This is something special."

She gave a slow nod of comprehension, never looking away from him.

She *was* something special. What she made him feel was something special. Something he'd never before even wanted to feel but now was beginning to suspect he didn't want to live without.

Geoffrey held her in his lap a moment longer, loath to lose the weight and warmth of her. Then he helped her to rise, to right herself. As they restored their appearances and gathered the horses, Geoffrey's mind was awhirl, and though it circled quickly, he didn't doubt what he was thinking. His instincts had proven to be solid throughout his life, and they were telling him one thing emphatically.

He wanted Liliana as his wife.

Honest, forthright, curious, unconventional, passionate, brilliant Liliana.

But she didn't want him. Not as a husband, anyway. She just wanted to experiment.

But he could change her mind. She'd given him the perfect opening, just the right ammunition—her nature. If experimentation was the way to a scientist's heart, he'd oblige her. And every step they took would bind her more and more to him.

Deep in his chest, Geoffrey felt a smile form and expand until it couldn't be contained. It built, rose in him until it burst forth on his face. He was more and more certain Liliana would be a good wife for him. She was one to keep herself closed, however, which gave him pause. She didn't seem the sort who succumbed to tender emotions. Even if he were slowly coming around to the idea that opening his heart would make for a better marriage, he feared caring for a wife more than she cared for him. It would give her all of the power in the marriage, a power she could use to devastate him, as his mother had his father.

But then, Liliana couldn't be any more different from his mother, could she? He couldn't see her ever lying to him, deceiving or manipulating him, and that was what was most important.

How ironic that he was now no different from everyone else here at Somerton Park.

He was planning to trap someone into marriage.

Chapter Eighteen

Liliana knew the moment they left the stables at a slow amble that something this morning was different. Since their glorious kisses at the mine two mornings past, each day had started with an exhilarating race to find the most far-flung spot on the grounds for another experiment in seduction. Yet when she'd arrived in Amira's stall moments ago, her own body already buzzing with anticipation for this morning's romp, Geoffrey had seemed in no hurry.

No, in fact, he moved slowly, and a mysterious expression that hovered between the hint of a smile and an arrogant grin flitted onto his face when he thought she wasn't looking.

What could he be up to?

A delicious thrill unfurled upward from her middle, twining around her nipples and taking root in her chest.

Whatever he had planned, she was certain she would like it.

She covertly glanced at Geoffrey as he rode beside her. How could he look so relaxed when she was a brimming jumble of eagerness and desire? A lock of his black hair lay across his forehead, and his chest peeked at her through the open V of his plain cotton shirt, giving him a particularly adventurous appeal. He'd dressed simply this morning, as had become his habit the past two days for their rides—easier access for her experiments, he'd told her with a wink. And indeed, yesterday he'd allowed her to remove his shirt and explore the planes of his chest and the hard ridges of his abdomen, the lines of his back, the strong, sinewy musculature of his shoulders and neck. And when it had seemed he could no longer stand her exploration, he'd dragged her to him and kissed her quite senseless.

Her own desires had taken Liliana by surprise. She could hardly credit her boldness, nor—for once in her life—did she allow herself to think on it, to analyze it. Guilt did its best to gnaw at her, but she shoved it aside. She didn't want to examine why she was acting thus, or how she'd not searched for clues since her foray into the village. Nor did she wish to contemplate that she might be able to use this connection growing between herself and Geoffrey to accomplish her goal—she didn't wish to tarnish the glorious way she was feeling. She now knew in her heart that Geoffrey had had nothing to do with whatever had happened to her father. He'd shown himself to be too honorable a man. Yes, his father may very well have, or perhaps even his mother, and Liliana promised herself she would rededicate herself to finding the truth as soon as this madness passed.

But not right now.

For now, she was too busy just being. Just being a woman—not an oddity, not an orphan, not a deceitful interloper—but a woman. A woman who was discovering herself.

Her first revelation was that she was quite wanton, though she suspected only where Geoffrey was concerned. For another, she'd found herself rather enjoying a bit of frivolous society, as long as Geoffrey was by her side. They'd formed a passable whist partnership and she'd learned she was quite good at charades, though she admitted with some chagrin that she was sometimes too literal. She'd need to relax a little if she truly wanted to acquire some finesse.

But the finesse she wished to develop this morning had nothing to do with parlor games and all to do with the man by her side. A man who moved entirely too slowly.

Liliana hitched her legs and pushed Amira ahead, forcing Geoffrey to speed up to take the lead, which she knew he would because he obviously had a destination in mind.

They circled the east side of the park until they came to the largest of Somerton Park's three lakes. Geoffrey slowed and Liliana followed suit, delighted when she realized where he was taking her.

The abandoned folly stood nestled in a grove of old-growth trees and overlooked the water from the farthest side of the lake. As they drew closer to the columned circular structure, with several of its massive foundation stones darkened with age and moss, Liliana couldn't contain her gasp of pleasure.

"This is lovely," she said, her gaze sweeping the view. The waking sun reflected in the lake, casting pink and orange shadows over the faded stone steps leading to the folly's entrance.

"Yes, it is," he murmured, yet his eyes stayed solely on her.

The vines of desire rooting beneath her breastbone stretched and tightened.

"The design was inspired by a Greek revival temple," he said, releasing her from the intensity of his gaze. "My great-grandfather, William Wentworth, commissioned it just before the end of the seventeenth century. I understand he was taken with ancient ruins while on his grand tour." Geoffrey led her to a marble mounting block and they tied the horses.

"He enjoyed a touch of whimsy, too, did he?" Liliana asked as they climbed the stairs. She pointed to the faded painted ceiling as they passed under the columns where caricaturized scenes from Greek mythology graced the domed panels.

Geoffrey laughed, a rich sound that echoed off of the stone. "No. Well, perhaps. William was quite a character if the stories I've heard are true—brash, adventurous, lucky in love but not at the card table—but the farcical ceiling was the work of my father," he said.

Liliana turned at the strained note she heard in his voice. A tightness had appeared around Geoffrey's eyes, but his smile seemed easy enough. Yet something tugged at Liliana that made her sad—an intimate understanding, perhaps. It was apparent that Geoffrey had loved his father, just as she had loved hers.

"This was our special place," Geoffrey said. "My father ..." He coughed, one short little burst. "My father painted those one summer, and we would sit out here for hours when I was a boy, lying on our backs, looking up and concocting ridiculous stories to accompany the scenes."

Looking up, Liliana noticed the faded scenes, and yet some of them were bright with fresh paint. Had Geoffrey been restoring the panels?

Geoffrey pushed open the wooden doors, which, to Liliana's surprise, opened easily, with no creaks and groans. As she stepped inside, she realized that this place had not been abandoned at all. It was clean and tidy, and while the furnishings were sparse—two overstuffed chairs, a daybed, a writing desk and a small table—they looked comfortable. She turned inquiring eyes to Geoffrey.

"It's now become my special place when I am home," he said. "My private place."

"Is that why you're repainting the ceiling? To keep your father's memory alive?" She swallowed, understanding. Isn't that why she'd fought so hard to be allowed to learn chemistry?

"Perhaps." His voice lowered and his eyes turned soft in that way that Liliana had come to recognize precluded, at the very least, a kiss guaranteed to curl her toes.

A sudden nervousness gripped her. Geoffrey had never before taken her somewhere so ... secluded. Which meant the opportunity existed for their intimacy to be taken to the next level. Her breasts grew heavy and her breath short.

"Your private place, eh?" she said, striving for lightness even as that peculiar yearning that had become a near constant companion these past days took hold. "Pity," she teased. "I'd thought the folly abandoned and had quite set my sights on a lovely laboratory. You wouldn't mind, would you?"

An indiscernible look crossed his features as he made a slow advance upon her. "Not at all," he said, his voice turned gruff with arousal. "There are many things I might be convinced to share with you, Liliana." He stopped directly before her. "The first of which is this."

He took her lips in a kiss that felt at once familiar and thrillingly different. A kiss with an intent unlike his kisses past. Her body responded to the urgency of his and she threw one arm around his neck, anxious to get closer, closer, now.

The trembling fingers of her other hand reached for his shirt, wanting his warm skin beneath hers like yesterday.

"Ah-ah-ah," he said, pulling away from the kiss and trapping her hand against his chest. "Not today, my little researcher." He tilted her face up. "Today, I turn the table. You, my dear will not be the experimenter, but the experimentee."

Liliana uttered a nervous laugh. "That's not even a word."

"No?" Geoffrey's mouth spread in a slow smile as he leaned in toward her again. "Well, it should be," he said, taking her lips for the second time. As their tongues entwined, Liliana had the vaguest sense of being moved, backed toward something. The cushioned cover of the daybed met the back of her knees a second before Geoffrey slowly lowered her onto it.

He settled her in the middle, his lips never leaving her. He arranged her body just so, his hands tender as they glided over arms and knees and breasts and face. Heat filled her, so much that her clothes seemed to burn her skin, and she moaned. Geoffrey seemed to understand, as he slipped the buttons of her shirt free, allowing cool air to kiss her heated chest.

"Today I intend to show you what your body can do," Geoffrey murmured.

"I understand"—Liliana gasped as Geoffrey slipped his hand inside the opening in her shirt and brushed a finger across her nipple, which hardened almost painfully—"understand how the female body works."

A low chuckle accompanied another flick of his finger. Then Geoffrey cupped her breast in his warm palm and squeezed it gently, dragging his rough thumb back and forth over her distended areola. "You may have knowledge of what I speak," he said, "but until you experience it, you won't *understand*."

Liliana nodded, closing her eyes. She'd agree with anything he said if he'd only keep doing that.

"For example," he murmured, bringing her eyes open to look at him again, "do you know what purpose women's breasts serve?"

"Of course." Heat scored Liliana's cheeks, but she answered. "Glands inside a female mammal's breasts produce milk to nurture her offspring."

Geoffrey nodded. "Mmm . . . that's correct, my smart darling." He flicked her nipple again with this thumb, and a sharp pang shot from Liliana's nipple to an answering nubbin far lower. Geoffrey slipped another button loose with his free hand, baring her breast to his sight. "But did you know that babes are not the only ones who might suckle from a woman's breasts?"

"Wh-what?" She could barely breathe as Geoffrey leaned in closer, as if to kiss her, but at the last moment he detoured and lowered his head to her chest instead.

"Let me demonstrate," he murmured, and then he opened his mouth upon her.

"Oh!" Liliana groaned. She couldn't tear her gaze from the sight of Geoffrey's dark head at her breast. His eyes were closed, yet his mouth worked, suckling her. She watched the curves of his cheek hollow as he drew more deeply of her, and then she had to close her eyes, so sharp were the sensations, a tugging that pierced her, stealing her breath and setting off a rhythmic throbbing below in time with Geoffrey's draws upon her breast.

Liliana's other breast felt horribly ignored. She moaned and Geoffrey seemed to understand. He broke from his task long enough to whip the shirt over Liliana's head. She hardly noticed, so intent was she on expressing her desire for him to treat her other breast to the same experience. She grasped his hand, pulling it to her neglected breast, and gasped in pleasure as he cupped her.

Geoffrey dropped his lips to her and opened his hot mouth. His hand tweaked and rolled her other nipple between his fingers at the same rhythm his mouth drew upon her.

Sir Isaac's ghost, she didn't know how much of this she could stand. Liliana writhed in pleasure. Who knew this was possible? No book she'd ever read had alluded to anything like this.

Geoffrey released her nipple from his mouth, then lapped at her one last time, which shot sensation straight through her. He raised his head and speared her with his gaze . . . His cobalt eyes burned hot, deep blue pools that simmered.

"Do you understand what else your breasts were made for, Liliana?" he asked, sensual challenge in his voice.

She shook her head, waiting for him to show her.

He'd cupped both of her breasts now and was gently squeezing, pumping, shaping them. "Caressing your breasts will help make you ready for . . . other things." He took each nipple between the thumbs and index fin-

gers of his hands and gave a sharp pinch at the same
time.

Liliana gasped.

"Do you feel that?" Geoffrey asked.

"Yes." She struggled with words. "It's like . . . like there
are invisible strings drawn between my breasts and
my . . . my mons. What is it?" Liliana could feel the heat
on her face, but her curiosity won out over her embarrassment, as it always did.

Rather than answer, Geoffrey said, "Observe how
tight the strings become the more stimulation your
breasts are given." He dropped his mouth again, suckling deeply while rolling her opposite nipple between
his fingers simultaneously.

Liliana clenched her fists as the sensation spiraled, the
string drew tighter and tighter and the throbbing pressure below built and built until she thought the strings
must surely snap. She didn't know what would happen if
they did, and she alternately yearned for and feared
finding out.

Finally Geoffrey ceased his torture, bringing his head
up to rest against the side of her neck. His hot breath
brushed against her and satisfaction swelled within her.
He was just as affected as she, and she'd yet to touch
him. How fascinating.

"Do you feel it now, Liliana?" Geoffrey rasped.

"Feel what?" She felt many things, mostly an urge for
more.

"The heat," he said, "between your thighs. Do you feel
moisture there?"

Mortified that he would mention such a thing, Liliana
nodded against him nonetheless. Just thinking about it
gave her an urge to press her thighs together. She gave
in to the idea and moaned at the sensation.

"Good," he said roughly. "That means you are becoming more and more ready for me." Geoffrey sounded as
if he could scarcely breathe. "Not only will caressing your
breasts prepare you, but indeed, so would caressing

many other places on your body. Your very skin is a con-
duit of sexual energy," he said. "If we had more time, I
could show you several spots that will excite you thus."

"Really?" Liliana blinked, even more fascinated. She
supposed she shouldn't be, but truly, the very idea of it
stimulated her senses.

Geoffrey laughed. "Yes, really." He placed an open
palm against her stomach, just above the waist of her
pants, and all laughter died. "But you don't need that
today, Liliana. You're more than ready for what comes
next."

Almost as if in answer, more moisture gathered between her legs and Liliana instinctively pressed her
thighs together again.

Geoffrey chuckled and placed his hands at the fasten-
ing of her trousers. "May I?" he asked, and as Liliana
looked into his face, she knew he was making her choose.
Choose whether she wished to learn more or whether
she wished to let things remain unknown.

"Yes," she said emphatically, knowing she wished to
experience anything this man would show her.

"Good." Geoffrey's smile was quick and his voice low,
sending warmth spreading through her. "Because I'm
about to show you what your wonderful body is truly
capable of."

Liliana's chest expanded, almost with a relief. He was
going to make love to her. She knew she should feel
ashamed, at the very least modest, but she did not. No,
rather, she felt nothing but burning excitement, and that
need that caused her mons to throb grew more insistent.

Geoffrey slipped her pants over her hips and she
kicked her legs, impatient to be rid of the hindrance.

"Patience, love," Geoffrey said, and then he cupped
his hand over her most private of places, pressing the
heel of his palm against the spot from which those invisible strings seemed to originate.

Goodness, it was as if every nerve ending in her body

were centered in that one spot. How was this possible? Surely her—

Geoffrey's fingers moved, dipping lower to her moist heat. He kept delicious pressure on his palm, on her, yet his long finger moved inside her gently. She couldn't help herself. She planted her heels and lifted her hips, pressing herself more into him.

"Relax, love," Geoffrey soothed. "I know what you need. Trust me to give it to you."

Liliana groaned but subsided. She did trust him. Now if only he would—

One finger drove deep, and Liliana felt herself clench around it. Geoffrey groaned and she wondered how he could be feeling pleasure when it was he touching her. Yet she remembered the satisfaction she'd gotten yesterday when she'd run her hands over his body, eliciting shivers and groans. This phenomenon would certainly need to be explored further. For posterity's sake, of course, but not right now. She was fast losing her ability to think objectively.

Geoffrey withdrew, drawing moisture from within her and bringing his finger up to circle that wondrous little spot. Liliana gasped, nearly coming off the daybed.

"What? What?" She couldn't get the question out.

Geoffrey circled her again, this time with all of his fingers. She delighted in the pressure, the movement, the swirling, the building . . .

"Geoffrey?" What was happening? She was losing control of her own body.

"It's all right," he murmured. "Perfectly natural . . . Just let it happen, Liliana."

"But—"

He cut her off with a kiss. Liliana latched onto his tongue, grateful for the anchor. Yet it did not hold her to the ground. Geoffrey's hand continued to work its magic, and it was as if her entire being lifted and contracted into that swirling mass.

She moaned, her body tight and strung for an endless moment.

And then she exploded. It was the only word her overwhelmed mind could come up with . . . She flew apart, into a million tingling pieces. She cried out against Geoffrey's mouth. She could hear little moans through her buzzing ears and knew they came from her.

"That's right, love. Just relax and let it take you."

Waves of pleasure rolled from her mound, cresting through to her fingers and toes. Just when she thought they'd subsided, another would set off and ripple, until at last she floated in a calm, pleasurable sea.

She opened her eyes, as heavy as they were, and blinked up at Geoffrey, who sat beside her on the edge of the daybed. A grin that could only be classified as male arrogance rode his face, bringing an answering smile from her.

"What was that?" she asked around a thick tongue.

"That's the pleasure that can come from a man and woman coupling," he answered.

Liliana blinked. She was innocent, but she'd read enough to know that they hadn't coupled at all. Why, she'd never even touched his— "Did you experience the same . . . release?"

A pained look crossed his face. "No. What did it feel like for you?" he countered.

She shook her head. How could he expect her to put magnificence like that into words? Surely he knew, unless . . . "Can only women feel this?"

Geoffrey barked a tight laugh. "Having never been a woman, I can't vouch for whether the experience is the same, but men do have a similar release," he said.

Liliana sat up, intrigued. "Even without actually coupling?"

"Yes."

She moved to her knees and evaluated him. Lines of tension showed around his lips and eyes. She dropped her eyes to his lap, where evidence of his arousal strained against his trousers. If he could bring her such wonderful feelings by merely touching her, maybe she could do the same for him. A purely feminine desire to please Geoffrey hardened her still bare nipples and she reached a hand out. "You mean I can touch you and—"

"Whoa!" Geoffrey leapt from the edge of the bed. "You're the experimentee, today, remember?"

Liliana frowned. "That's hardly fair."

"Be that as it may," he said, still backing away, "it's all we have time for."

Liliana looked to the windows of the folly. He was correct. The sun was fully in the sky. They'd be pressed to return undiscovered as it was. Still, Liliana didn't think she could wait until tomorrow to see the same bliss overcome Geoffrey as he'd given her.

She rose, unashamedly naked, and strode across the room to him. A small smile lifted the corner of her mouth as his chin dropped. She was only now beginning to appreciate the kind of power a woman could have over a man, and she had to admit, she liked it. She'd like to explore that further, too.

She wrapped her arms around Geoffrey's neck, pressing herself against him, pressing her mound against his hardness and relishing the moan that echoed from him. "Fine," she said. "We don't have time now, but I don't want to wait until morning to have my turn experimenting on you. So what do you propose we do?"

Geoffrey swallowed, the sound audible to her. "The library," he rasped. "Meet me in the library tonight after everyone goes to bed."

An ironic smile lifted her lips. "You like kissing women in the library, don't you?" she murmured, pressing her lips to his.

"Mmm," he said. "Only you."

Chapter Nineteen

Geoffrey rearranged a pillow on the chaise for the seventy-second time. He was smoothing the fringe when the clock struck one in the morning. The supper ball had come to an end and the guests had finally dispersed nearly an hour ago. He thanked the stars for early country hours, for he didn't know how much longer he could wait for Liliana to arrive.

He'd uttered the word *library* when she'd made her enticing demand because it had been the first thing to enter his mind. Yet it couldn't be a more perfect place for their rendezvous. He spent the majority of his nights amongst the stacks or in his study anyway, as sleep often eluded him due to the nagging ache of his injuries. The staff had long ago learned never to disturb him here.

"Setting the scene for your own seduction?"

Her voice reached across the darkness, the husky timbre caressing him like a lover.

"I suppose I *could* make use of a chaise," she said, locking the double doors behind her.

As she came into the light, Geoffrey noticed she'd donned the same dark day dress she'd worn that first night, probably to be less conspicuous sneaking through the halls. How thoughtless of him. He'd have to show her the secret passageway so she didn't risk being caught next time she came to him.

And there would be a next time, if he had anything to do with it. These past days had been sweet torture for him, but his plan was working. Liliana was becoming as addicted to him as he was her—he was certain of it. It should be only a matter of days before he convinced her to extend their rendezvous for a lifetime.

"The scenery hardly matters," he murmured. "You began your seduction of me long ago."

Liliana cocked her head in that way he found entirely enchanting. "I did?"

"Yes." *The moment I first saw you.* "I've been able to think of little else since this morning, imagining your hands upon my body as mine were upon yours. I've been strung tight all day."

"You have?" she whispered. "How horrible for you," she said, yet her smile was all female satisfaction.

Geoffrey tried for a stern frown, yet he felt the corners of his lips straining to lift. "Yes. And it was deuced disconcerting, I must say, politely greeting stodgy old guests whilst your sweet cries rang in my memory." Hell, he'd been stiff as stone all bloody day. He didn't know how he'd last a moment when she actually got around to touching him.

Liliana blushed, but she stepped closer. "Well, we shall have to remedy that, won't we?" She leaned up on her toes and fitted her lips to his.

Geoffrey moaned. He couldn't help himself, as her tongue boldly forayed into his mouth with no preamble. It seemed he wasn't the only one strung tight all day. Her hands went immediately to his shirt. He'd removed his cravat and untucked for easier access, and she unerringly found her way to the heated skin of his stomach. Her hands danced along his skin under the cotton, rising until she found his nipples. She brushed her fingers lightly over them, then pinched simultaneously.

Geoffrey gasped, breaking his lips from hers.

"Did you like that as I do?" she asked, avid curiosity gleaming in her purple gaze.

"Mmm . . . ," he said, trying to nod. "Back to being my little experimenter, are we?"

"Mmm . . . ," she repeated, before once again reclaiming his lips.

Geoffrey lost himself in her kiss, allowing her to explore at her leisure. She ran her tongue along both sides of his own, testing the texture, swirling and dueling, then dipping along the inside of his cheeks, his teeth. She suckled him into her mouth in a rhythm that brought to his mind other ways she could please him, ways she would have no way of knowing unless he showed her. Just the very thought of her lips wrapped around other parts of him brought him dangerously close to losing himself. He pulled away from her kiss, setting her back from him a bit.

"Hold a moment, love," he said. "A man can only take so much."

"Or what?" she asked.

"Or he spills his seed and the fun is over too soon."

She nodded her head thoughtfully. "I see."

She didn't, but she would before the night was through. A niggle of guilt worked its way into Geoffrey's mind at what he was about to let her do, but he chased it away. She would be his wife, after all. That made it only a matter of timing. He stepped back, removing his shirt, and sat upon the chaise.

Liliana followed and said, "Lie back," while she pulled an ottoman close.

Geoffrey obeyed, the brocade of the chaise rough against his skin.

"May I assume that since you liked it when I stimulated your chest, men and women are not so very different?" she asked, a chestnut brow cocked as she looked down upon him. "And that you might like the other things you did to me this morning?"

Good God, he didn't know if he could stand that. Still, he nodded. "That would be a safe assumption."

She sat on the ottoman and leaned in, brushing his lips with hers. Her hand returned to his chest, this time swirling around his nipple, tweaking, soothing. Her mouth moved down his neck, suckling at his racing pulse point as he'd done hers many times.

Geoffrey gasped for breath, closing his eyes and doing his best to hold still for her. Yet when her hot mouth closed around one of his nipples, he nearly came off the chaise. He'd never had a woman kiss him thus, had no idea how pleasurable it would be. A groan ripped from his throat as she drew deeply from him. "Liliana, please."

His plea started her hand moving again, downward over his stomach. His breaths became shorter—he couldn't get enough air as he waited for her to touch him.

Yet she hesitated, lifting her head.

His eyes popped open, and he tried to focus them on the lovely woman over him.

"I'll need your help . . ."

"Of course." He lifted his hips, dragging his trousers over them, a relief of sorts taking him as he sprang free.

"Oh my," she whispered, seemingly enthralled. How had he gotten so lucky to have been gifted such an intelligent, curious woman in his life and soon to be in his bed? She looked up at him. "May I touch it?"

"I think I might die if you don't."

Her lips curved into a smile before she turned to her task. She reached out, touching him lightly at first, just a tentative brush of her fingers, but Geoffrey felt it in his very bones. She glanced up, gauging his pleasure. He thought he nodded encouragement but couldn't be sure.

When she touched him again, it was with her entire hand, circling him, squeezing gently, then harder. "It's such a contradiction," she murmured. "So soft, yet so hard . . . like satin over steel. I've seen men naked before, of course, when I've treated them, but I never imagined . . ." She raised her head to him again. "Show me what to do."

Geoffrey encompassed her hand in his own, modeling how to stroke him, how to vary her speed and grip. He showed her how to run her thumb over his head, how to tickle the rim and how to cup him and give a little tug. Liliana tried each suggestion so enthusiastically, he knew he could not last. Indeed, the burning in the base of his spine intensified so quickly he jerked away from her, grabbing his shirt from the back of the chaise and covering himself only seconds before he spilled himself with a harsh groan.

"Did I hurt you?" she asked, concern marring her features.

"Hurt me?" he said when he could breathe again. "Not unless you count killing me with pleasure."

A relieved smile crossed her face, but then she asked, "So you just experienced what I did this morning?"

He nodded, still finding words difficult to muster.

"You were right," she said. "That was finished too soon." She reached for him. "Let's try it again."

Geoffrey sat up, holding his hands out. "Good Lord, woman!" He laughed. "My body doesn't work that way. Men aren't so lucky as women. We need some time to recover before we can *try it again*."

Liliana clasped her hands in her lap. "You mean women don't? We can . . . release more than once in a day?"

A wide smile stretched Geoffrey's face. What fun it was going to be, being married to this woman. He had a feeling his life would be one long discovery, in and out of the bedroom.

"You can release more than once in five minutes," he said, enjoying the way her eyes widened.

"I don't believe you," Liliana said, her lips firming.

He leaned in, taking those lips in a soft, happy kiss. "You will."

The moment Geoffrey's lips touched hers, Liliana's

entire being churned with a need that felt almost explosive. It had been building inside as she'd pleasured him, the rush of satisfaction when he'd lost control nearly bringing her to a similar peak. That sensation had banked, but now Geoffrey stoked it back into roaring flame.

More than once in five minutes . . . If Geoffrey were telling the truth, she didn't know how she would survive it, so intense was the feeling already.

In quick order, he'd divested her of her dress . . . She couldn't even say the moment it happened. She'd only felt the cool air on her puckering nipples and noticed the dress was gone. Liliana waited for the pleasure of his mouth upon her breast, but Geoffrey didn't oblige. Instead, his mouth moved to her neck, to the sensitive shell of her ear. His moist tongue swirled inside, followed by a nip of his teeth that shot gooseflesh down her body.

"This time, we have all night," he murmured, his breath warm against her. "We'll let your climax build slowly, string you so tightly that one release will not be enough to bring you back down to earth."

Oh my. He lathed her neck and shoulders with his tongue and teeth, sending shivers skittering over her as he tested her flesh with his mouth. Finally, his hands cupped her breasts, weighing them, plumping them. If he were trying to bring her along slowly, he was failing miserably.

"Please, Geoffrey." She writhed against him, trying to drag his hand down her body, anxious for his touch in the place that ached most for it.

"In due time," he murmured, resisting. But he moved his mouth to her breast. He sent his hands skimming over her. Liliana marveled how even the simplest touch reverberated in her core. It didn't matter where he touched—a spot on her hip, the place behind her knee, along her inner thigh—it all intensified her need to feel him *there*.

And finally, he touched her. Liliana couldn't control the urge to raise herself into his swirling touch. Maybe that made her wanton, but she didn't care. She cared for nothing but the release he promised her. Higher and higher she rose. Having experienced this ride only once, her instincts told her the leap was fast approaching nonetheless, and before she had time to fully prepare herself, she was flying.

She cried out, her own passion-grated voice echoing back to her ears. Shocking spasms enveloped her, and every muscle in her body went tense. Geoffrey whispered words to her, but she couldn't understand what he said, couldn't focus on anything but the sensations flowing through her.

When she at last emerged, she lay limp on the chaise, Geoffrey's hand still cupping her intimately. Heat touched her face, and Liliana ducked her head, a little embarrassed at how she'd lost control.

"Now I know you lie," she said. "There is no conceivable way my body could do that again so quickly."

A wicked grin spread over Geoffrey's face. "Care to wager, Miss Claremont?" he asked. "Last time, though I didn't know it then, I was at a disadvantage. This time, I am not."

Liliana pressed her lips together in a smile. He may know more about relations, but he couldn't feel how completely spent she was. And yet, she was intrigued. What if he were correct? She'd never get a chance again to test the theory. "What kind of wager, Major?"

He looked at her intently, his eyes narrowing slightly as if he wished to say something very difficult and very important. But the look passed and he said instead, "The winner chooses the time and place of our next tryst."

Something akin to disappointment touched Liliana. She wished he had said whatever had been on his mind. Still, she lifted her shoulders, and tension began coiling once again in her belly. "Done."

Geoffrey kissed her, but his lips did not remain on

hers long. She gasped as Geoffrey's tongue stroked her most intimate of places. Two thoughts came in quick succession. First, she had no idea such a thing was possible, and second, could she pleasure him in the same way? "What are you doing?"

"Winning my wager," he murmured before suckling her clitoris—she'd looked the word up this afternoon—into his mouth and stroking soft, soft and slow, then fast and rough, sending her senses upward like a shot.

As he had earlier, Geoffrey eased a finger into her. The long strokes teased, searched, until he found a spot that nearly brought her off the chaise.

She had no words . . . couldn't come up with a single word to describe what was happening to her. For once in her life, Liliana let her mind go silent and just allowed herself to feel.

She exploded with such intensity, she didn't know if she'd ever be put together again. It was as if her body, her mind, her heart, her very soul had been rent into several pieces, and she didn't even know if she had the energy to pick them up, let alone assemble them back into one.

"I believe that was well within five minutes, my dear." When she opened her eyes, Geoffrey grinned above her. "I would say I win."

She huffed an exhausted laugh. "I would say you did," she murmured, closing her eyes once more.

Geoffrey watched Liliana for a long moment, the rise and fall of her breasts, the sleepy relaxed expression on her face, and his chest filled with pride. Odd, but having brought her to completion gave him more satisfaction than when he'd received the same pleasure himself.

He let her rest, slipping on his trousers before gathering her clothes.

"Hero, saint and ladies' maid?" she said.

"What?" he asked, turning back to her.

"Mmm . . . nothing." She sat up, and once again, Geoffrey was struck by her comfort with her own nudity. Being a scientist, she was probably practical about such things, like him. Twelve years of war had divested him of modesty for certain.

Liliana twisted her knees to the side, scooting over to make room for him on the chaise. He sat beside her and breathed in her scent as she nestled into his shoulder.

"I have this need to be close to you," she said, her voice laced with bemusement, as if she could hardly countenance the feeling. He supposed an independent, intelligent woman like her might wonder at that.

"Most women have that inclination after lovemaking, if they've been well satisfied," he explained, knowing Liliana craved the knowledge.

"Do men feel the same?" she asked, snuggling in closer.

"Men have an inclination to go immediately to sleep."

She slapped him in the arm.

"I'm quite serious."

Liliana pulled away, eyeing him. "You don't look very tired to me."

Geoffrey smiled. Sitting here, enjoying her pleasure-sated features, he never wanted to close his eyes again. "How could I sleep knowing I would miss this moment of having you in my arms?" he asked, holding her gaze.

She looked away, blinking. Geoffrey wondered if she even understood her feelings for him. Yes, she was a curious creature, but no virgin could give herself in such an unabandoned fashion without having a care for her lover.

"It's not always like this, either, is it?" she asked, her voice solemn.

"No."

"Not even for husbands and wives?"

A harsh laugh escaped him, surprising him in its vehemence. "I would say rarely with husbands and wives, which is a damned travesty."

She nodded. "My parents were a love match," she said

after a moment. "I was too young when my mother died to remember much interaction between them, but I've been told stories of their great love for each other." She shifted, turning her head away. "And I was witness to what it does to a person to lose the one he loves." She pulled away from him and stood, reaching for her dress. As she pulled it efficiently over her head, Geoffrey mourned the loss of her closeness.

He also wondered at her words. Did fear of losing the ones she loved make up the bricks of the wall that surrounded her heart? She'd lost both parents at a young age. That would have to affect a person.

When she'd righted herself, she sat back down, albeit at a respectable distance from him. "Did your parents love each other?"

Geoffrey frowned, wondering at her question. What was going on in that brilliant mind of hers? By the way she looked at him, he was almost afraid to answer, thinking she might draw a conclusion that wouldn't be in his favor. Still, it was his nature to be honest.

"Hated would be a more appropriate word." Geoffrey sighed. Since he was going to marry Liliana, she'd find out the whole sordid tale eventually, so it might as well be now. "But he was an earl, and she the daughter of a rich, well-respected family, and they were married. They had nothing in common except, in the end, a complete disrespect for the other."

Geoffrey closed his eyes, memories assaulting him of his parents' screaming fights, of slamming doors and hateful words. "I think it made my father sad, though," he said, remembering the far-off looks his father would sometimes get. "He loved her, in the beginning. Even after he found out what she was truly like—a lying, deceitful, manipulative, cruel woman—he loved her anyway. And that is the real tragedy."

Liliana's hand covered his. He opened his eyes and saw not pity in her expression, but compassion, and the tightness around his chest cracked, letting warmth slip in. He brought her hand to his lips, then settled it into his lap, not letting her go.

"But whatever their feelings in the beginning, they disintegrated into nastiness. I was told many a time it was fortunate I took after my father in looks, else he'd have doubted I was his."

Liliana made a shocked sound. "You mean she took other men to her bed whilst married to your father?"

"I'd imagine she never went to my father's bed again after I was born," Geoffrey said, rubbing his eyes with his free hand. "She'd given him his heir and his spare and then she was done with him. Hated him so much, when he died she removed all vestiges of him, redecorated nearly every room and had all of his things boxed up and moved into one of bedrooms in the family wing, where they still sit, covered in dust."

Liliana stiffened beside him, her grip growing tight. Geoffrey sighed. He wasn't painting a very pretty picture of marriage to a Wentworth, was he? "But not all marriages are like that, Liliana," he said, reaching to take her other hand. "Some are based on respect. Some can be a true partnership, where husband and wife have similar goals and passions and can lift each other to achieve more than they could have alone. Some have . . ." *love*. As much as he realized he was coming to covet her love, he couldn't promise her the same, was unsure whether it would even matter to her, so he left the word unsaid. ". . . that something special you're feeling right now."

The chime of the clock rang out two baleful gongs in the silence.

Liliana pulled her hands away from Geoffrey and stood. "It's late, and dawn comes early." She had to leave this very moment, before the maelstrom of guilt and self-abhorrence rising in her chest overwhelmed her and she made a fool of herself. Oh, what had she done? And what was she *going* to do?

A crease formed between Geoffrey's brows. Her abrupt

change in attitude must have confused him. Liliana tried to school her features.

"You should sleep in tomorrow," he suggested, watching her closely, "as I can't ride with you. I'm meeting some of the more recently arrived gentlemen for an early hunt. Some political maneuvering to be done on horseback, it seems."

She nodded once, hard, and turned for the double doors, looking for escape.

"Don't go that way." He walked over to the bookshelf and flipped the hidden latch that she'd searched to find with no luck. "Let me escort you back through the passageway, where no one will see you."

Liliana moved to the darkened doorway, peering inside. She'd been trying to get into this very door for days, yet now the idea of exploring it sickened her because of how she'd gained access to it.

"Where does it lead?" she asked, her voice dry yet calm to her ears.

"Ultimately to the family bedrooms, but it's truly a labyrinth, passing nearly every room in the house at some point," he said. He lit a candle and ushered her inside.

As they passed a closed doorway, he said, "There is my study, for example, which is the only room that doesn't have its own exterior entrance, though it does open to the library via a hidden door."

Just as she'd expected. A little farther down, he pointed out more. "And here is the drawing room, the parlor next to it, and the dining room farther still. I have no idea what my ancestors must have been thinking when they had it built. Either they were a devious sort, or they were fond of secret trysts. I'm particularly fond of the trysting theory," he murmured as his arms snaked around her middle. Liliana stiffened, closing her eyes against the burning sting of tears as his lips brushed the back of her neck, shame scoring her. She was the devious sort in this pairing, and though Geoffrey hadn't said it in so many words, deceit was the one thing he abhorred. She'd seen it in his face when he'd spoken of his mother, and every word had been a dagger.

Geoffrey pulled away from her slowly, as if sensing that something was not right, but she couldn't see his expression in the dim light. She heard him take a deep breath, as if to say something, but then he steered her to the right and they ascended a narrow staircase to the second floor. "Here are the private family parlors down that wing and, farther past them, the family bedrooms," he said, indicating the left passage. "To the right is the guest room hallway. The tunnel doesn't lead directly into those rooms at any point . . . so perhaps my theory of secret trysts is wishful thinking."

He popped a door, which from the outside appeared as a hallway bookshelf. When they exited the passage, he shut the shelf behind them, then pulled down the fourth book from the right, exposing a keyhole.

Geoffrey touched her shoulder, turning her toward him, his cobalt eyes creased with concern. "Liliana, is everything all right? I . . . I didn't push you into something you were uncomfortable with, did I?"

His kindness brought the ache of tears higher in her throat. "No," she said. "You've done nothing wrong." *I have. And I'm sorry.*

He touched her face, running his thumb down her cheek. "You're certain?"

"Of course."

He nodded, reaching into his pocket. He removed his hand and held it out to her. "Take this," he said. A dull brass key rested in his palm. "As the winner of our wager, I shall set our next tryst as tomorrow night, same place, same time. I want you to use the passageway so as to preserve your reputation."

She reached her hand out, noticing it tremble. He handed her the means to complete her search, yet he offered it in trust. In friendship. Perhaps in something more.

But she closed her fist around the key anyway. She was the worst sort of person because she knew she would take advantage of his trust to find the truth. Because the truth was all-important. She'd been a fool to allow herself to pretend otherwise, even for a few blissful days.

"Liliana?" Geoffrey asked, bewilderment in his voice.

"Good night, my lord," she said, and turned away, hurrying to her door. She slipped inside without looking back, knowing that once she found her answers tomorrow, she would have to tell Geoffrey all. And she knew in her heart he would hate her because she'd deceived him all this time.

Chapter Twenty

Liliana pulled the bedroom door shut behind her and leaned into it. The straight, hard line of the wood against her shoulders seemed the only thing holding her up. She brought her head forward then let it fall back again, but the momentary sting did nothing to distract from the ache in her chest.

"It's about time you came to bed. I was worried." Penelope's voice reached her, coming from the sitting area. She'd apparently been waiting up.

Liliana brought a hand to her face, furiously swiping at the tears she'd been unable to hold in. Thank goodness for the dim light that kept her in shadow. She didn't think she could handle explaining any of this to Penelope tonight. Maybe ever.

"I'm sorry if I've kept you awake," Liliana said, making for the dressing screen. She could regain her composure while changing into her night rail.

She heard a rustling and hoped it meant Penelope had taken herself to bed. Instead, when Liliana emerged from behind the screen, the candelabras on either side of the bed and on the table splashed the room with light and Penelope was waiting for her, a stubborn set to her chin and her finger pointing.

"Now, don't think you are going to dodge me again, Lil—" Penelope's hand dropped. "What's wrong?"

To Liliana's mortification, the tears started up again and all of the roiling emotions she'd tried to hold in burst forth. "I'm a whore."

"What?" Penelope dropped onto the bed, likely as stunned as Liliana was at the words that had passed her lips. Yet she couldn't take them back. They were true. Even if she hadn't begun the physical side of her and Geoffrey's relationship with that specific intention, even if it hadn't crossed her mind these past days when she'd been so caught up in him, she couldn't deny that when the opportunity presented itself tonight to ask about his parents' relationship, she'd taken it. And had learned where Edmund Wentworth's private possessions were.

"I've used my . . . *charms*"—she spat the word—"to get the information I needed. That makes me a whore."

Penelope's face paled. "You've slept with Stratford?"

Liliana released a long breath. "Not exactly." She vowed to say nothing more specific. "But that's splitting hairs."

"Rather important hairs, I'd say." Penelope studied her for a moment. "But you say you found what you were after. Now you can solve the mystery of Uncle Charles' death and bring the truth to light. Isn't that what you wanted?"

"I thought it was, but . . ." Liliana paced the floor at the foot of the bed. Insecurity, confusion and regret swirled around in her like an elixir swishing along the glass sides of a beaker. The combination upset her, at once disconcerting and unfamiliar. She wasn't accustomed to any of these feelings. Since her father's death, she'd forcibly tamped down any emotions that didn't move her toward her goals. Years spent overcoming her aunt's attempts to change her bled into the years trying to prove herself worthy of recognition in the world of science. Had she ever allowed insecurity or indecision a foothold, she was positive she would have been lost.

Like she was now.

"I don't want to hurt him," she whispered.

"Then walk away," Pen suggested.

"I can't." She shook her head. "You know I can't. Besides, someone killed Geoffrey's father, too. Maybe the same person killed mine, and if that's true, he has a right to know just as much as I do."

"You've taken to calling Stratford Geoffrey? You *have* grown close."

Heat touched Liliana's cheeks. Penelope could never know how close. "We've become friends. He's not at all what I'd expected." Far from it. She hadn't expected his playful side, nor the grins that transformed his face into a carefree rogue's as they raced across the park. She hadn't expected that he would be truly interested in her work, yet he'd plied her with questions. And she certainly hadn't expected that when he would stop midsentence and stare at her mouth, she'd want to lean forward and fit her lips to his.

"You love him," Penelope said, wonder in her voice.

"What?" Liliana choked, coughing as she tried to catch her breath. "Are you mad?"

Pen sat up straight and squared herself to Liliana, raising her palm and extending her fingers as if to tick off the points. "I am perfectly sane. You, however, have been acting oddly for days now." She touched her index fingers together. "First, you're crying. I've never seen you cry, not even when Mama gave you her worst. Second"—her pointer moved to her middle finger—"there is that dreamy look upon your face. You just had it a moment ago. What were you thinking?"

Liliana wasn't about to say she'd been thinking of Geoffrey's kisses. She pressed her lips together, narrowing her eyes.

"Fine," Pen said. "Don't tell me. But you've arrived home for the last three days from your morning rides with that same look. And," she said, hooking her ring finger, "you've been happier, more peaceful than I think I've ever seen you, even in company. You should have seen Mother's jaw drop when Stratford cajoled you into that game of charades. She's commented on the change in you, too."

Liliana frowned, realizing that she *had* felt differently of late, comfortable in her own skin . . . or at least not hyperaware of how irregular she was. Could that be because of how Geoffrey looked at her? How he listened to her, sought her opinions?

Penelope waggled her pinkie. "And fourth, you've stopped talking about Stratford, nor have you shared any progress on your mission with me." Pen paused, and an expression—part hurt, part envy—passed over her face. "Perhaps because you've had him to share with."

"That's ridiculous," Liliana said, but was it? Her and Geoffrey's time alone, of course, had been spent mainly in each other's arms, yet many hours had been spent talking while they participated in various activities. Talking about what he hoped to achieve in his political career, discussions regarding future projects aimed at employing soldiers. Liliana had expanded the subject to the poor in general—employing them, certainly—but she'd brought up health and sanitation issues that would improve the quality of lives for all. Geoffrey had considered her ideas thoughtfully, tossing around possible scenarios he might present to Parliament in coming years, given the proper research. He'd even joked that they should partner up together and change the world.

"Would it be so bad, Lily?" Pen asked gently. "You've said you know in your heart he had nothing to do with whatever happened to Uncle Charles. Would it be so bad to love Stratford?"

"It would be awful," she whispered. Because when he came to despise her, as he surely would when she explained why she'd really come to Somerton Park, it would break her heart if she actually loved him.

"I think it would be wonderful," Pen countered. "I think it's fantastic that someone has finally breached that outer wall you keep around yourself. I'm just relieved Stratford has made you feel something. I feared perhaps . . ." She trailed off pensively.

"Perhaps what?"

Penelope regarded Liliana for a long moment before sighing. "I thought perhaps losing Uncle Charles had damaged you somehow. I know his death was shattering, but you've idealized him your entire life. I was afraid you might never let another man into your heart."

Liliana was taken aback. "When did you get so insightful? Perhaps you've missed your calling," she joked, trying to ease the tension. But Penelope just pressed her lips together in annoyance.

Liliana considered Pen's words. True, losing her father had been devastating, but that had nothing to do with her choice not to pursue a husband. A husband would have forced her to give up her dreams. Men wanted their women filling the nursery, not experimenting in the laboratory.

Yet, had she ever let a man into her life since Father's death? Liliana frowned in thought. No, she hadn't. She was close to no man—not even her uncle, Lord Belsham, who had made considerable efforts at a relationship over the years.

Why was that? Because it hurt too much to love? Perhaps, particularly if you lost that person. Look what it had done to her father to lose her mother. What losing her father had done to her. She never again wanted to open herself to such pain.

But she couldn't think about that now, and besides, Pen was looking at her expectantly. "I . . . care for Geoffrey. I think he's a good man, but that is all I will ever feel for him."

Penelope sat back, biting her lower lip as if she wished to say more. "If you say so," she finally relented.

"I do."

"So what are you going to do when you find what you are looking for?"

That blasted aching knot took up its place in her throat again. "What else can I do? I'm going to tell Geoffrey the truth."

Liliana let the drape fall closed, shutting out the steel blue light of daybreak. She'd just witnessed Geoffrey and several male guests depart for the morning's hunt. It was time to complete her search.

She'd been unable to sleep, mulling over what she thought she knew, what she hoped to find. What she hoped not to find. Her conversation with Penelope featured heavily in her thoughts, too, as did every moment of the past few days spent with Geoffrey.

Could she love him? She couldn't say if she even knew what love was. Her entire life she'd surrounded herself with cold science, never giving that softer emotion the slightest consideration. It was as foreign to her as the concept of electrochemical dualism would be to someone like Lady Jane.

Desire, Liliana understood. She may not have experienced it before now, but it was a natural phenomenon, a measurable physical response to stimuli.

But love?

She slipped out of her room carrying a lit candle and went to the hall bookshelf. She pulled the fourth book from the right and removed the key from her dress pocket. She inserted it and turned. A click later, the shelf opened and Liliana stepped inside.

The passageway was cool. Of course, this morning she didn't have Geoffrey pressed against her. Nor would she ever again.

Liliana crossed the first turn, where she would have gone left to the study, and instead carried on straight into the tunnel that led to the family rooms. Coming to the first door, she pressed her ear to listen. Of course, without knowing the thickness of the door, would she even be able to hear if someone were occupying the room? What she wouldn't give for a spy hole.

After hearing nothing for several moments, she inserted the key Geoffrey had given her, hoping it opened all of the doors. She turned it clockwise. "Yes," she whispered as the door opened.

Liliana stepped into a bold red room, trim gleaming white with gilded edges, the lines clean and cold. A portrait of Lady Stratford hung over the fireplace. This must be the countess' parlor—she seemed the type to hang a likeness of herself in her own space.

After what the old valet had told her of his suspicions, Liliana had to consider Lady Stratford a viable suspect. What had Geoffrey called her? Lying, manipulative and deceitful? Perhaps whatever activities had gotten her father killed may have been centered around the countess rather than the late earl.

It made some sense, really. No one ever suspected a woman, particularly not men. Liliana knew all too well that most men didn't think women capable of having a brain, though her father certainly wouldn't have been one of those. Still, if Lady Stratford was the guilty party, then killed her husband barely more than two weeks later, perhaps because he'd discovered what she'd done—well, that would wrap things up neatly.

Liliana moved to the desk. Opening a drawer, she found only writing implements and other sundries. She moved to the next, searching for a handwriting sample to compare. She found a packet of vellum and reached out for it, yet she hesitated before opening it, her mouth going dry. What would she do if the countess' handwriting matched?

She firmed her lips and flipped open the packet. A list of names marked the first sheet. Scanning them, she realized it was a prospective-brides list. Nineteen girls, including herself, listed in one handwriting, another three in a different scrawl that she recognized as Josslyn Wentworth's.

Lifting the page, she found copious notes about each of the girls. *Dowry of £50,000* or *Niece to the Duke of Clarendon* or *Atrocious table manners, but her mother bore five sons.* There were stars by Lady Jane's name, of course. Notes the countess would make, yet the handwriting was not the one Liliana was looking for. She released the breath she'd been holding. Another dead end.

She scanned to see what the countess had written about her. *Orphan, upstart, completely unsuitable!!!* Liliana smiled. All true.

She made a cursory search of the rest of the room but, as expected, found nothing. She placed everything back where she found it and let herself into the passage.

Now to find the room that housed the late earl's belongings. She'd just have to try each door until she reached the right one.

Placing her ear at the first, she heard murmurs of female conversation. Likely the countess' room, as it was next to her parlor. Liliana moved to the next. Hearing nothing, she entered.

The moment she stepped into the room, she knew it belonged to Geoffrey. It was as if he lingered in the air. His spicy scent, always overlaid with mint, tickled her nose, bringing a sensual memory of him on the chaise, of her bringing him pleasure. Her body flooded with warmth, the now familiar moisture gathering between her legs. My goodness, is that all it took to make her hunger for him, now that her body knew what to crave?

Liliana forced her focus on the room. The walls were covered in a rich tan silk, the large poster bed and furnishings simple but sturdy. Spartan, yet elegant, like the man who lived here.

The bed coverings were plush, a solid color that brought to mind steaming cups of chocolate. And rumpled. The counterpane was pulled back and the indention of a large body dimpled the sheets. It seemed Geoffrey had taken her advice and returned to sleeping in his bed rather than on the floor. Liliana couldn't resist bringing

her head close to the pillow and breathing in . . . Spice
and mint permeated the linen, filling her senses. What
would it be like to awaken with that scent in her nose
every day?

Fool. Why did she torture herself with things that
could never be?

Curious, she bent down on hand and knee to see if he
had reinforced the mattress with slats as she'd suggested.

A black leather volume caught her eye immediately.
Her heart sped up as she reached under the bed to retrieve it. Pulling it into the light, she realized it was the
same black book she'd nearly broken her neck to reach
that very first night. She'd scoured the place for it since
then, and it had been here in Geoffrey's room all along.

Had he been hiding something after all? She couldn't
fathom it, not after the way he'd kissed and stroked
her—Liliana rolled her eyes. She'd done all that to him
as well, and she'd been hiding much.

She brought the book up, laying it on the bed. Did the
evidence she'd been seeking lie here? She flipped the
cover open, anxious to finally discover what Geoffrey
had taken such pains for her not to see.

At first, Liliana did not believe her eyes. She flipped a
page, then another. Sir Isaac's ghost . . .

A bleating laugh gurgled from her lips. She was unable to control it. Really, how could she?

It was a book of etchings. Highly erotic etchings, quite
well-done in her limited opinion, of couples in flagrante
delecto.

No wonder Geoffrey had been so desperate to retrieve the book from her, given that he'd just accused
her of trying to trap him. He must have—

Liliana gasped as mortification swept over her, remembering how she'd tried to scoot out of the library, book in
tow. Did he think she'd known what was in it? He must
have thought her rather fast. A reluctant smile curved
her lips . . . She'd proven him right on that, she supposed.

Liliana closed the book, sliding it back where she

found it, then sat upon her bottom, pulling her knees up and resting her folded arms atop them.

Everything she'd suspected when she'd arrived at Somerton Park had turned out to be something else altogether. Maybe she'd been wrong. Maybe this absurd moment was a sign that she should end this and move on with her life.

If she gave up on her search, she'd never have to tell Geoffrey that she'd deceived him. Yes. She could let him remember her as a pleasant diversion, a lovely memory. She felt herself nodding. She must divulge what Witherspoon had shared about his father, of course—having lost a father to nefarious means, she couldn't leave Geoffrey in the dark about that. But Witherspoon had practically volunteered that information. Liliana wouldn't have to explain a thing, and then perhaps she and Geoffrey could—

Could what? Go on as they were now? She dropped her head down onto her folded arms. Of course not. No, in two more days this house party would be over. She would leave as she'd come, without answers and destined to a life alone. Geoffrey would likely go on to marry Lady Jane, or someone like her. Someone well connected, who would dedicate herself to being a perfect wife.

He would be happy, and he would do great things in the world. And so would she, albeit on a much lesser scale.

That's what she should do, she decided as she unfolded herself and rose.

After she looked at that one last place. She'd never be able to live with herself if she left the stone unturned. She'd find Edmund Wentworth's belongings, and if they, too, turned out to lead nowhere, she'd put the matter to rest for good and cherish her last two days in Geoffrey's arms.

Chapter Twenty-one

Geoffrey stepped past a group of men who'd stopped to chat after the early hunt. He was anxious to return to the manor and find Liliana. He couldn't wait to tell her how well the negotiations had gone with some of the more influential men in English politics. And he had her to thank for it, as he'd used several of her more persuasive arguments to sway them to his side.

"Enjoyable morning, Stratford," the Earl of Manchester called out.

Damn. Geoffrey stopped and turned back.

The older man waved him over and clapped him on the back as he joined them. "Though had I known that we were the fox and *you* the hunter, I may have kept to my bed."

A raucous laugh followed the earl's remark. Geoffrey stiffened. Perhaps things hadn't gone as well as he'd thought.

Manchester harrumphed, the wispy tips of his graying mustache moving upward on the exhalation. "That's not saying I don't respect your tactics. You military men and your strategies. Wellington is forever vexing me with his maneuverings."

"Indeed," answered another man, a viscount whom Geoffrey had been targeting for quite some time as a potential ally. "But there are many things about your plans that I, for one, approve of."

"Same here," said a third.

"But you know, of course, Northumb is the key, my boy," Manchester said, as the others murmured their agreement. "He and that brother-in-law of his in the Commons. If I were you, I'd cement his promise now while the arguments are fresh in his mind. Northumb isn't one to go back once he's given his word, but his attention can be fleeting." Manchester tipped his head toward Northumb and Wakefield, who were walking ahead, deep in conversation. "I understand Northumb is fond of brandy after an invigorating hunt. French, preferably. Missed it sorely during the war."

Bollocks. Seeing Liliana would have to wait until later. Geoffrey thanked Manchester and hurried after Northumb and Wakefield instead. Slowing his pace as he neared them, Geoffrey affected an easy smile. "Gentlemen," he acknowledged, coming along beside Northumb.

"Stratford." Northumb was a small man, given his great influence. Indeed, standing next to the man, Geoffrey estimated Northumb to be shorter than Liliana, who was admittedly tall for a woman. Yet his voice boomed, as many great orators' did. "Nice shooting this morning. Had my doubts, hearing like I did that you'd let a woman unman you on the practice field." Northumb chuckled. "Say it isn't so, man."

Geoffrey winced inwardly. He didn't need to give the notoriously fickle Lord Northumb anything to distract him from the important matters at hand. "In truth, it was Lord Aveline who outshot me, though Miss Claremont did certainly give the man an advantage."

Northumb humphed. "Never tangle with a headstrong woman, son. Better to surround yourself with well-behaved ones. Like my Jane."

"Yes," Geoffrey said. The hairs on the back of his neck prickled. Northumb had never before actually mentioned Lady's Jane's name in connection to him. He had always been more subtle than that. "Your daughter is a lovely girl, a great compliment to you."

Northumb eyed him, then nodded. "She is. Interesting ideas you presented this morning."

"I am gratified you found them so," Geoffrey said, relieved the conversation was moving to politics. Yet he had the feeling the subject of Northumb's daughter wasn't closed . . . He only hoped the two wouldn't prove to be entwined. "I'd value your further opinion. Yours, as well, Wakefield," Geoffrey added in deference to the beefy gentleman accompanying them. "Perhaps over a drink later? At your convenience, of course."

Northumb pushed out his lips, his eyes narrowing in contemplation. His expression brought to mind the image of a wizened old cod, one well accustomed to swimming through the rough waters of Parliament. Geoffrey knew firsthand that politics could be a vicious pond, full of big fish and small, most angling for their own inclinations with wicked hooks and barbs. The reforms this country so desperately needed, the ones Geoffrey was committed to seeing through, would not always endear him to his peers. He'd do well to learn what he could from Northumb on how to survive it all with most of his scales intact.

"Now's as good a time as any," Northumb said.

Minutes later, the men settled themselves in the library. When all three had cut-glass snifters of expensive liquor in their hands, Northumb went straight to the point.

"You could have a real future in the party," Northumb said, propping his ankle on the opposite knee and negligently resting his brandy on the arm of the chair. "I wasn't so certain last year, when you came up like a green pup, but I can see you learn from your mistakes. Liverpool was right to assign this task to you."

Geoffrey leaned forward, setting his glass on the side table. "It's not my future I'm concerned with, but Britain's. Yes, this bill starts with employing the men I care most about, but it extends beyond that. More jobs mean less criminals. More industry equates to stronger economic—"

"So you've said," Northumb interrupted. "I am unconvinced. And three quarters of a million pounds is a lot of money that could be used elsewhere. Don't you agree, Wakefield?"

"I do," came the matter-of-fact reply from Northumb's companion.

Geoffrey sat back in his chair smoothly, picking up his snifter along the way. He held Northumb's gaze as he took a sip, yet the tips of Geoffrey's ears burned with anger. He shouldn't be surprised that Liverpool had shared the details of the bill—Northumb was a powerful man. But Northumb would also then know that the prime minister supported the bill, which should have been enough to ensure Northumb's support as well. This hesitation was pure politics.

"I care about the country, too," Northumb said, "but do you know what I care more for?" Northumb glanced over at Wakefield. "Family. A man's family is what truly matters in this world. And the alliance between strong families is the pillar that holds our nation together."

He's trying to use my passion for the Poor Employment Act to force my hand in marriage to his daughter. Geoffrey kept his expression purposefully blank. Well, as blank as he could while clenching his teeth together. Hell and damnation, the man was no better than Geoffrey's own mother.

"I like you, Stratford. You're bright, you're forward thinking, you're loyal and you're a patriot." Northumb stood, downed the remainder of his brandy and set the glass on the wooden table with a clink. Wakefield rose as well, bringing Geoffrey to his feet. "Think about what I've said. Family sticks together." Northumb pinned Geoffrey with a cool gray stare. "Family votes together, too."

Geoffrey remained standing long after the other men departed, a sick feeling twisting his gut. Faces flashed before him, of his men, gaunt and hungry. Of Tom Richards, when Geoffrey had found him several months ago, begging on the street. Of women and children whom he knew would be helped if this bill passed.

Maybe he could get the bill passed without Northumb's support. The group of gentlemen he'd spoken with this morning had seemed convinced. Yet, only weeks remained before the vote. There might not be time to sway enough others, particularly if Northumb came out against it. And if the bill didn't pass, it would be at least another year before Geoffrey could try again. What would become of his soldiers and their families then?

Geoffrey rolled his neck, pushing back his shoulders to release the tension and lengthening his spine, as Liliana had shown him. He noticed only a twinge of discomfort. Normally, after such a jarring hunt, he'd be in agony.

In only a few days of listening to Liliana, the quality of his life had improved immensely, in more ways than one. And she was quickly becoming the only person truly on his side, the only person who wanted nothing from him but himself. He longed to talk to her, even about this unusual situation, certain that she would understand. When had she become his safe haven?

"Congratulations are in order, I hear."

Geoffrey's head snapped around to look over his shoulder. His mother stood in the entrance to his study, where she must have been concealing herself. If the bookshelf-door had been open even a crack, she'd have had no trouble hearing the entire conversation, and judging from the triumphant smile on her face, she had.

"You'll have to ask the girl, of course, but it's clear her father has already given his blessing. I know her mother has." The countess brought her hands together. "As do I, not that you care. Lady Jane is an excellent choice, everything you could hope for in a wife, and you'll be guaranteeing the passage of your bill, to boot."

Marry Lady Jane and achieve his goal. It seemed so simple. And so damned manipulative it turned his stomach. God, how he abhorred when people tried to force his hand.

And what of Liliana? This morning, when he should have been entirely focused on securing votes for the bill, instead he'd felt her absence like a deep well within him. He could no longer fail to acknowledge that when he was with her, he felt full. Whole.

He hadn't felt that way in years.

Nor did he wish to give that feeling up.

But could he sacrifice the well-being of so many others by refusing Northumb's "offer"?

Mother paced past him in short, quick strides. "Let's see . . . We've selected St. George's for the ceremony. I can have the London house ready for a proper wedding breakfast in only a few weeks. And—"

"We've?" Geoffrey's jaw tightened as Mother's face went pale. She wouldn't have . . . He closed his eyes. She would. "What did you have to do with this?" Geoffrey barked.

"What do you mean?"

"Mother," he growled.

The countess rolled her eyes with an exasperated huff. "I only gave Lady Northumb a bit of intelligence."

"Who then, in turn, told her husband how exactly to put me over a barrel," Geoffrey muttered.

"That was rather crass," Mother admonished. "All we did was help you to make the best decision for you, and now you will be—"

"I'll not marry Lady Jane," Geoffrey said, the weight of the past few minutes floating off of his chest and pulling the corners of his lips up as it rose past his face.

The countess whipped around, narrowing her sharp gaze. "What? Don't be a fool. What will you tell Lord Northumb?"

"I'll tell him that if he loves his country, as he says he does, then he'll support the bill on its merit alone, and that if he chooses not to, then he'll face me again next season." Geoffrey advanced upon the countess, actually taking glee in what he was about to say.

"And I'll tell him I've already chosen a wife."

"Who?" The countess' chin lowered and a perplexed frown crossed her face a moment before her eyes widened and her nostrils flared. "Geoffrey! You—you—can't be serious," his mother sputtered.

"Oh, but I am." It was probably a sin against God, how much satisfaction Geoffrey took saying those four little words, what with the whole "honor thy parents" dictate. Yet months of purgatory, perhaps even hell, would be worth it for the look upon his mother's face. It would certainly be worth it for the lifetime of heaven that awaited him in Liliana's arms. "Liliana Claremont is exactly what I want in a wife. She's intelligent, compassionate and completely honest. In fact, I'd wager she doesn't have a deceitful, manipulative bone in her body, and to me, that is the only qualification that matters."

Geoffrey left his mother standing in the library, his step light and relatively pain free. This afternoon, he'd seek out Lord Northumb and make his position clear.

Then tonight, when Liliana joined him in the library, he'd ask her to be his wife.

It was in here. She knew it. The connection between her father and the Wentworth family lay somewhere buried in these dingy, dust-covered trunks. She'd felt it when she'd entered the unused room—a tingle that danced down her spine like the fat brown spider gliding across its gossamer web in the unswept corner.

There was no doubt these were Edmund Wentworth's belongings. In addition to being precisely where Geoffrey had said they were, there was an ornate EW inscribed on the brass key plate of the largest trunk. Liliana traced her finger over the initials, much as she had the seal on the letters that had brought her to Somerton Park.

Rather than the excitement she'd expected to feel at

this moment, a great sadness weighed upon her. There was nothing to be done but to finish her search. Liliana pushed up her sleeves and surveyed the stacks of boxes and trunks. From the amount of dust and cobwebs covering them, she could well believe they had been up here for thirteen years. Liliana swiped her hand across the top of a nondescript wooden box, brushing clean a swath the width of her palm.

She used her hand to clear the rest of the lid and frowned. There were pry marks on the edges, and the lid lifted easily, the lock broken.

The box was stuffed with papers that were yellowed with age. They were also quite disarranged, as though they had been thrown in without care. Or, given the pry marks, searched through hastily. She pulled a handful. There were receipts, bills and descriptions for what seemed to be normal personal items. Liliana took a few moments to scan through them but saw nothing to draw her attention. She did the same through the rest of the box before placing the lid back on it and moving it to the side.

She chose a medium-sized trunk next. It came open with no effort, the lock also broken. Someone had definitely searched through Edmund Wentworth's things before her. Liliana peered inside, only to find more papers. She sorted through a few to sample their contents.

Her hand began to shake as she came upon a packet of folded vellum tied with a burgundy ribbon. She untied the knot, her fingers fumbling. When she opened the packet, letters written and signed by Edmund Wentworth, late Earl of Stratford, stared up at her. She closed her eyes. The handwriting on the pages was the same as that on the letters she'd found in her father's study.

Somehow, she'd always known it would be, but actually seeing it with her own two eyes pierced her. The same elaborate *E*'s, the same flourish on the *S*'s and *O*'s.

Liliana scanned the letter quickly, her heartbeat pounding in her ear. It was a missive written to the curator of the British Museum, agreeing to provide funds for the renovation of an exhibit. She was sure that had nothing to do with her father, who to her knowledge had no interest in antiquities, but that wasn't what made the letter valuable.

Tears burned her eyes, her nose, the back of her throat. She finally had a tangible, concrete link between the late Earl of Stratford and her father's death. She carefully folded the letter with the incriminating handwriting and placed it in the pocket of her dress.

Now all that was left was to see if her father's return correspondence might be somewhere in this dusty graveyard of papers, the last record of a man's life.

Liliana resumed delving through the trunks. She found Edmund Wentworth's certificate of membership into the Society of Antiquaries, dated 1782. She found more papers, journals detailing descriptions of architectural discoveries, all in the earl's hand. She found bills of lading for ships importing crates from Greece, Egypt and India, amongst other exotic places. It all looked quite aboveboard, as far as Liliana could tell. Nothing suspicious. Nothing that spoke of treason. Nothing that mentioned Charles Claremont directly or in passing. Nothing that told her anything more than what she already knew.

Finally, she came to the last trunk. It was filled with bric-a-brac, a letter opener, a magnifying glass, a polished stone . . . the odds and ends of a life that made no sense to someone who didn't know the owner. There was also a book, a hefty tome some four inches thick. Odd that it wouldn't be in the library with the rest of the books.

Liliana used both hands to lift it out of the box, nearly tossing it as it flew upward, much lighter than she'd expected. This wasn't a book at all, but something else. She ran her hands over it, marveling at the realistic page edging, the supple leather cover. Then she opened it.

It was a book, after all, but one cleverly sliced and converted to hold a secret cache, a cache of letters. Her father's familiar script leapt off the page and Liliana's vision blurred with tears.

Sorrow and outrage bubbled inside her, warring for supremacy. There was no doubt now that she'd been on the right trail all along, which brought a sweet stab of justification, yet profound regret tempered it.

As much as she'd been anticipating their upcoming rendezvous in the library tonight, she now dreaded it tenfold. She had no choice but to tell him the whole truth. Geoffrey would be devastated. And worse, there was no way to avoid his realizing that he had been used.

Chapter Twenty-two

Light filtered into the passageway from the open book-shelf. Geoffrey must have left it cracked for her and was likely waiting just beyond the door, anticipating a much different encounter than what lay in store.

Liliana's steps faltered and she hugged the wooden box to her chest. She tried for a deep breath, but her lungs refused to expand. That was all right. She could manage on minimal oxygen for a time—this would be over soon enough.

She needed to look at the next few moments as she would a festering wound. The more quickly she cut, allowing fresh blood to flow and cleanse, the faster healing could begin. For Geoffrey, that was, not for her. She would never be whole again. The infection ran too deep, and her immunity was spent. He had invaded her system and she feared she would forever bear the scars.

When she stepped through the opening, Geoffrey turned. He must have sensed her presence, as she'd made no sound. A slow smile spread over his face and lifted even the corners of his eyes. A particular warmth shown from his gaze—not the heat of passion, though a flicker of that banked emotion flashed in the blue depths—but something more tender.

Something that made her want to weep.

"You're here," he said, his shoulders relaxing as if he'd worried she might not come. He crossed the room toward her. "I thought this day would never end."

Geoffrey stopped before her. "I have much I wish to share with you, but first . . ." He opened his arms, reaching to embrace her.

She couldn't let him touch her. If she did, she'd be lost. Not knowing what else to do, she thrust the box out in front of her, blocking him.

Geoffrey pulled up short, blinking. His gaze darted to the box, then to her face, and he gave her a questioning look.

She shook the box, once, continuing to hold it out like a shield, but Geoffrey took it with both hands and, without giving it another glance, sat it on the table near her and stepped easily into the space he'd cleared.

"But *first*," he repeated, dropping his head as he simultaneously angled his mouth toward hers. She was prepared for the flash of fire in his kiss, so the gentle brush of his lips instead sent a piercing ache through Liliana's chest. His hands glided over her shoulders and back. His touch conveyed warmth, caring . . . beyond just the sexual. How had she missed that? And how much more would that hurt him when she confessed all?

Geoffrey tightened his embrace, breaking the kiss to nestle his cheek against her temple. The piercing ache sharpened at this display of affection, coming to a razor point when he breathed in deeply and released a contented sigh.

"I never used to care for the smell of apples, you know. The taste, either." He dropped his mouth to her neck, and Liliana shivered as his tongue tasted her. "Yet every morning for the past week, I've demanded apple tarts drizzled in honey for my breakfast," he murmured. "Cook thinks I've gone quite nutty, but I can hardly explain why I crave them so all of the sudden. Do you know why?"

Liliana shook her head, unable to utter a word as his

mouth returned to feasting upon her skin, just below the lobe of her ear this time.

He brought his lips up a fraction, his hot breath brushing her as he whispered, "Because I dream of you in the night. I awaken so hungry for the taste of you on my tongue that I am nearly mad for it. I cannot even wait until our morning ride, so desperate am I for you." He lifted his head, pulling his torso away from her while retaining his hold. Liliana opened her eyes to find his gaze intently upon her.

"Yet the substitute never truly satisfies." He let his words sink in before the corner of his mouth twitched. "I fear I shall become quite portly if this continues. The barrage of sweets cannot be good for my health. As I see it, there is only one cure, and that is to have you beside me every morning when I wake."

Liliana's stomach dipped wildly. What was Geoffrey saying? She must put a stop to this madness. She reached an arm toward her box of evidence. "Geoffrey, I've brought—"

His kiss cut her off, and she closed her eyes against the growing hunger she sensed in him. But it ended as abruptly as it had begun, leaving her spinning.

"I can't imagine what you've brought me." He let her go, walked to the hearth and fetched something from a shelf. He returned carrying a long, narrow box of his own, plain and undecorated. "But I insist you open my gift first."

He thought she'd brought him a gift. This couldn't be any more awful. Liliana shook her head forcefully. "No, I—"

"Indulge me," he said, almost a plea, as he held the offering out before her. An indefinable emotion lurked in his cobalt eyes, and Liliana reached for the box, unable to disappoint him.

She took it, turning it gingerly in her grasp. It was lighter than she'd expected and gave the impression of fragility. What could he possibly have gotten her and why?

"Open it."

A terrible idea, yet Liliana still lifted the lid from the box. She reached inside and felt the cool kiss of glass against her fingertips. Curious, she circled the neck of the object with her fingers, pulling it from its container.

She gasped. "Oh my." A thick glass matrass emerged. The vessel was well made and oval shaped, with a long neck for distilling. Chemical glassware was not inexpensive—or easy to obtain. He must have gone to some trouble, yet it was the key tied around the matrass' neck by a silken ribbon that drew her attention— another key, given to her in good faith. She glanced up at Geoffrey, who watched her avidly. "What is this?"

"It's the key to my folly," he said, "which I hope to convince you to convert to your laboratory when you agree to become my wife."

The matrass slipped from Liliana's fingers. The heavy glassware did not shatter but rather made a dull clank as it struck the Aubusson rug and rolled off onto the wooden floor.

Geoffrey's rich laughter joined the rotating rattle as he grasped both of her hands. "Not exactly the reaction I was hoping for, but as long as you say yes, it will do."

Liliana tried to tug her hands away, but she couldn't seem to muster the strength. Had Geoffrey just asked her to *marry* him?

A hysterical giggle slipped out before she could silence it, and all she could think of was how Aunt Eliza would finally be pleased by something she'd done.

But that ridiculous thought was quickly followed by a burst of pain behind her breastbone that brought tears to her eyes. Dear God. *Geoffrey had asked her to marry him.*

And, oh, how she wished she could forget everything else and say yes.

The realization shocked her to her toes and at the same time devastated her. Liliana succeeded in pulling her hands away and turned from him, crumpling onto the chaise like a moonflower when touched by the morning sun.

A rustling of fabric alerted her that Geoffrey had followed, but she couldn't turn to him. Couldn't face him.

"Liliana?" His warmth registered, seeping into her leg where he knelt beside her. "Sweet, look at me."

She took a deep breath and complied. His intense eyes contracted with concern, which only made her feel worse. How beautiful he was, this compassionate soul—an honest man who put others' needs before his own. She should have known, should have known by the way she'd opened herself to him, how she'd responded to him from the beginning. She should have known, but she hadn't.

And now, as he reached up to touch her face, she could no longer deny the glaring fact. She was in love with Geoffrey Wentworth.

"Tell me what is the matter." He ran his hand behind her neck, cupping it while skimming his thumb along her jaw. "I knew something was wrong last night. I shouldn't have let you go without . . ."

His voice faded away. Oh, he was still speaking, but she could not focus on what he was saying.

Dear God. She was in love with Geoffrey.

Liliana shook her head, words failing her. She was in love with him. And now that she was aware of it, it rose in her, like an experiment gone wrong, boiling over until it couldn't be contained—

"I love you." The declaration spilled from her lips.

Geoffrey stopped speaking midsentence, his mouth remaining open as if it hadn't quite gotten his brain's message.

She shouldn't have said it, but she wouldn't take it back. She'd never expected to say the words to any man. Yet they were the most honest words she'd ever spoken. When this was all over, at least she could console herself with that. Geoffrey, on the other hand, was certain not to believe anything she'd said or ever would say again.

He remained on bended knee, seemingly not breathing, apparently stunned.

This was her moment, her one moment to show him her heart. He might decide her words were all false, but maybe, just maybe, if she could make him believe her love was true by her actions, then he would forgive her when the rest came out. Maybe he would understand. Maybe they could have a future.

And if not, then she'd always have this night in his arms to remember.

She slipped off of the chaise, dropping to her knees as he was. His other hand came up, as if automatically, framing her face. Liliana rose as high as she could while kneeling and wrapped her arms around his neck in a similar fashion.

Please. Let him understand.

She pulled his head down and kissed him.

Geoffrey burned, his feelings a conflagration that seared through him, leaving nothing unscorched.

She loved him.

He hadn't dared hope. Certainly he'd suspected Liliana was coming around to the idea of a relationship, but he'd expected it would take months, possibly years, to break through the wall she kept around her heart.

And yet she'd said she loved him.

He squeezed her to him, tightening his hold as he deepened the kiss. Christ, he never wanted to let her go. There was only one way to ensure that, and she'd yet to answer him.

He broke the kiss, gasping for air. He reframed her face between his hands, waiting for her violet eyes to open. Purely male satisfaction stole through him at her dazed expression. "So your answer is yes?"

Liliana's slow blinks became more rapid. "Let's discuss that later," she murmured, arching herself toward him and brushing his manhood.

Geoffrey pulled back, though the effort cost him. His body screamed to conquer her, to take her here and now. Yet he would not let her get away. Call him a cad, but he wasn't above using her obvious desire to get his way. After all, she'd already admitted her love for him. He wouldn't let her retreat. He'd push his advantage now, knowing if she gave her word, it was golden. "No, now. I will not make love with you unless you agree to be my wife."

She shook her head, tugging at him, trying to bring him back to her.

"No, Liliana. Not until you say yes."

She closed her eyes with a frustrated moan.

What could she be thinking? He knew she'd never wanted to marry. He suspected she feared a husband would control her as her aunt had tried to do, would forbid her work. Most men would. But surely she knew by now that he would not, that he would encourage her and could indeed help her by using his influence. Surely she saw, as he did, what they could do together, how good they'd *be* together.

Liliana lifted her lids and looked him directly in the eyes. "I will marry you," she said.

"Thank the Lord," he muttered, struck by the balm of relief that soothed his suddenly overwhelming need to own her, to possess her, not as an object or a person to control, but so that she would never leave him. He moved in to seal her promise with a kiss, but Liliana's hand snaked up and she pressed four fingers against his lips.

"If," she whispered, and his heart stopped. "If you still wish me to in the morning."

He tugged at her arm, pulling her hand away as his mouth closed in on hers. For such an intelligent woman, she could be quite nonsensical. How could she possibly think he would change his mind once he'd bedded her? If anything, his need would only grow, expand, bind him to her eternally.

Liliana moaned against his lips, opening herself, trying to draw his tongue deeply. Yet now that he had her promise, Geoffrey wished to take this slowly. Just the knowledge that they had forever made him want to savor rather than conquer.

He considered moving them to his rooms. It wasn't ideal to take his future wife on the library floor, but as Liliana tore at his shirt, desire pounded through him, mocking his intentions. Who was he kidding? They'd never make it upstairs. Hell, at this rate, they wouldn't even make it to the chaise.

Instead, he decided to give in to an urge that he'd had since the first moment he'd seen Liliana astride his prize mare. He gathered her in his arms, twisting to bring his legs in front of him as he lowered from his knees to a sitting position. He ruched Liliana's skirts up her thighs with one smooth move, spreading her legs as he settled her astride him.

Her heat scalded him, separated from his by nothing more than the fabric of his trousers. A groan ripped from his throat as lust shot through him, hardening him impossibly more. Almost as if by instinct, Liliana ground down upon him. He clamped her hips, unable to stop himself from arching into the pressure.

"Sweet, we must slow down," he groaned.

In answer, Liliana rotated her hips against him. "I don't wish to."

Geoffrey barked a laugh. *She didn't wish to*. He clenched his eyes shut. He'd wanted to make this night perfect for her, but he was fast losing his ability to think properly in the face of her need.

Liliana's hands found his chest, and without warning she pinched his nipples hard.

Geoffrey gasped, his eyes flying open as the combination of pleasure and pain ricocheted to his cock.

"Now, Geoffrey," she commanded. "Please."

He quit fighting the need and reached for the fall of his trousers, his hands trembling like a green boy's as he pressed her skirts higher. "Do you wish me to come to you? Or would you like to mount me, much as you are now?"

Her eyes widened in surprise, but then her brows drew together, telling him he'd intrigued her. "That's possible?"

"More than possible," he said, realizing in this way he could show her that a union with him did not mean he would dominate her. "And it allows you most of the control."

He could tell by the seductive smile that crossed her lips as she considered the options that the idea appealed to her. Hell and damnation . . . for a smile like that, he'd give her control of anything she desired.

"How?" she asked, and he knew she'd made her decision.

"I'll show you."

Cool air brushed his heated skin as he freed himself from his drawers. "Raise up on your knees," he commanded. When she did, his hand cupped her and she moaned. He slipped his fingers along the slick outer folds of her mons, dipping inside to ensure she was ready for him. The hot moisture that greeted him nearly sent him spilling.

With one hand gripping her hip, Geoffrey guided himself to her entrance. The skin of his cock stretched impossibly tight, so ready was he to possess her. Yet he ceded control to Liliana. "Place your hands on my chest. When you are ready," he rasped, "lower yourself onto me." He wondered if he would be able to stand her slow descent as she adjusted to him, but he vowed not to take charge even if he had to bite through his lip to remain still.

Liliana braced herself on him and closed her eyes, and then she was surrounding him, an inch at first but steadily, inexorably she took more.

Geoffrey gritted his teeth against the pleasure of her body tightening spasmodically around him. And yet he did not move. All feeling centered squarely on where they were joined, all focus on the woman giving herself to him without fear or hesitation.

By God, she was the most beautiful thing he'd ever seen. Perspiration beaded her forehead as her face tightened in concentration. Her teeth tugged at her lower lip as she experienced his intimate invasion.

She took a deep breath as he came to her maidenhead. Her violet eyes opened, and the look as she gazed at him spoke of pure trust, of love. Gratitude burst within him. What had he done to deserve her? Whatever it had been, he would spend his life repaying fate for sending her to him.

She leaned forward, her chestnut hair cocooning his face, and she kissed him at the exact moment she lowered her body completely, giving herself to him.

"Oh God, Liliana," he groaned when he could once again breathe. The exquisiteness of being fully seated inside her was like nothing he'd ever known. He couldn't explain, couldn't think of anything other than the fact that he felt *right*. And responsible. Responsible for taking care of this precious gift of a woman, not only in this moment, but for all time.

"Let me," he whispered, taking her hips in his grasp. "Let me love you."

As he said the words, he realized he was unafraid. Liliana had erased the fear. He didn't know if he could love her in the way she deserved after spending a lifetime fighting that emotion, but he wanted to try.

She rose upright, arching her back as she pressed herself to him. "Yes."

Geoffrey surged upward, lifting her, yet he held her still at the crest as he withdrew. She bent her head, her eyes searching his, and then she cried out as he brought them together again, hard and fast.

"Yes, Geoffrey. Please." Liliana's breath came quickly as he pounded into her again, and each gasp whipped him.

Geoffrey groaned, knowing he couldn't last much longer in her heat. He had to make this good for her. She'd caught the rhythm well enough, so he released her hips. He moved one hand to her mons, his thumb finding the center of her pleasure. He brought his other around her neck, pulling her to him for a hot kiss.

His lips devoured her, pouring every bit of emotion he could into his kiss as his hips thrust up to meet hers in a frenzied, rotating flurry. His thumb circled her clitoris in counterpoint, and he could sense her tightening around him. *Hurry. Hurry, darling.*

It had never been this good, and he was quickly losing control. His only thought now was to take her with him.

He pressed her tightly, using every last bit of his effort to steady his thrusts. Then he released her clitoris from beneath his thumb and flicked it.

Liliana exploded around him, gripping, milking, moaning her release. He slammed upward one last time, and then Geoffrey knew nothing else other than what it felt like to empty his very soul into another person.

Chapter Twenty-three

Feeling came back slowly as Geoffrey emerged from a satiated fog enough to comprehend the sensations. The finest linen and wool money could buy abraded his overly sensitized skin like the coarsest broadcloth. Gooseflesh raised on his body as cool air traveled over places that had recently burned. Hot drips splashed against his neck where Liliana had buried her face after collapsing upon him—

Hot drips? It took some doing but Geoffrey opened his eyes and blinked. Liliana still lay astride him, but she was draped over him now with her head tucked into the crook of his shoulder. The tantalizing scent of apples and lemons wafted from her hair, filling him with a measure of peace, and yet . . .

A hitching, irregular movement registered. Liliana seemed unable to catch her breath. Geoffrey focused, and alarm raced through him as he put the clues together. The hot drips raining down upon his skin must be tears. Her tears.

He instinctively tightened his grip, smoothing his hands over her back and shoulders. Yes, now he could hear her soft sobs, and the sound ripped through his heart. Had he harmed her? He hadn't been gentle, but she'd seemed to have preferred him that way.

Bloody ass. She'd been the novice, he the experienced one. He should have maintained control, as she hadn't known any better what she'd been asking.

He brought a hand up, running it over her temple and through her cascading curls. "Liliana?" His voice croaked from his throat, which shouldn't surprise him given the raw shouts of pleasure he'd barely stifled. "Love, are you all right?"

She tensed atop him and held her breath, but a fresh wash of tears splashed against his neck. His chest tightened. "Sweetling," he murmured, wishing she would raise her head so that he could see her face. "Have I . . ." He swallowed, dreading the answer. "Have I hurt you?"

At that, she lifted her head, and Geoffrey ached at what he saw. Liliana's lips were flush, the lines of her face smooth and sated, yet the satisfied look of a woman well pleasured warred with one in abject misery.

She raised herself to a sitting position. The sliding movement shot pleasure through him even as he slipped from inside her, yet Liliana only wiped at what seemed to be an endless torrent of tears. Geoffrey's alarm increased. She wasn't the sort to cry. He'd known women who had wept tears of release after intense climax, but this was different, serious. Dread chased away Geoffrey's lingering afterglow.

"Oh, love," he said, his stomach twisting. "I'm so sorry—"

As she had just before accepting his proposal, Liliana stopped his words with her fingers upon his lips. Only this time, those fingers trembled. "No," she whispered. "If anyone should apologize—" She bit her lip, her head moving slowly from side to side. Moisture had deepened her irises to a violet pool. Her chest rose as she inhaled, and her eyes fluttered with rapid blinks as she composed herself. "It is I who am sorry, Geoffrey," she said, her voice once again strong, yet with a note of bravado that tweaked his heart. "More than you can know."

Geoffrey braced his hands on the floor at his sides and

pushed, raising his torso off the ground in a swift move that brought him to a semiseated position, one that left Liliana still straddling him.

Her eyes widened as his sudden shift rocked her position, sending her back against his thighs, which he'd brought up to support her, yet also to trap her.

Was she truly sorry she'd given herself to him? Anger battled with tenderness and an annoying insecurity. He'd never bedded a virgin before, and particularly not one with a curious mind like Liliana's. Perhaps he had not lived up to her expectations. A huff escaped him, remembering the blissful wonder on Liliana's face when she'd found her release. He knew, at least in that, she had been well pleased.

Then what was this about? What was currently swirling around in her head? Guilt? Confusion? Fear? Whatever it was, it was contrary to what she should be feeling at this moment, and by God, he would *not* let her waste one more second on regret.

He leaned forward, narrowing his eyes so as to convey his absolute conviction in what he was about to say. "You are going to be my wife, Liliana. There is nothing more right than making love with your husband." At the shake of her head, he said, "Certainly, there are those who say we should have waited until after the vows were spoken." Geoffrey softened his voice, bringing his arms around so that he could take both of Liliana's hands. "But in my heart, we were married the moment you agreed to be mine."

Her full bottom lip trembled.

"You have nothing to apologize for, nor anything to fear."

She dropped her head onto his chest, wracked with sobs that were now silent. Bewilderment and fear settled in Geoffrey's chest. There was something else the matter here, and he hadn't a clue what it could be. All he could do was hold her until she was ready to explain.

At long last, she leaned away and raised her face to

him, but what he saw twisted something within Geoffrey. Liliana's face had smoothed, and though she still trembled, she also looked strangely resigned. What had she gotten into her head? He tried to pull her back, but Liliana scooted away, the harsh rustling of fabric sounding as she rose from the floor to stand above him. She turned and walked over to the table near the still open passageway.

Geoffrey rose and adjusted his clothing, trying to remain calm. Yet the silence that descended upon the room took on an eerie, still quality that he recognized immediately. It was the calm before the storm, the reflective quiet he had experienced many times before a battle as he waited for the enemy to strike.

The familiar surge of adrenaline heightened his senses, and at the same time, tiny prickles needled the back of his neck, a sensation he'd only ever felt in times of danger. Geoffrey frowned, knowing the feeling to be completely out of place. He swallowed and rolled his neck to dispel the irritating reaction and made to follow Liliana.

She turned just before he reached her, that box she'd brought held tightly in both hands.

"I think it's time you open this," she said. The solemness of her tone combined with her tear-ravaged face brought a sick feeling to his stomach.

Geoffrey stared at the nondescript box and immediately backed away. He couldn't explain why. He only knew that if he never saw what it contained, he would be a happier man for it.

But Liliana persisted, pushing it into his hands until he had no choice but to take it. The hard lines of the wood scratched his fingers as a splinter pierced his skin.

Geoffrey moved to the chaise and sat, ignoring the sting of pain, the drip of blood that smeared the surface. He removed the lid and placed it on the seat beside him before peering inside the box.

Three bundles of letters wrapped in aged ribbon lay on the bottom, along with some miscellaneous papers.

Geoffrey glanced up at Liliana, who stood before him, perhaps four feet away. She looked as if she weren't breathing. Tension marred every part of her being, and the edge of her bottom lip was caught between her teeth. "What is this?" he asked.

"Proof that your father was responsible for the death of mine."

"What?"

She'd said the words so unemotionally, so matter-of-factly, so soberly, that for a moment Geoffrey didn't grasp them. Yet the breath caught in his throat and his mouth went dry as his body comprehended her meaning, even if his mind was slow to follow.

Liliana clasped her hands together in front of her, as if in prayer or perhaps supplication. But Geoffrey could see the strain in her forearms. "I told you my father was murdered."

"Yes, by street thugs," he said.

Liliana dipped her head. "That was the official ruling. What I failed to tell you is that he'd received a letter in the days before his death. A letter that lured him to the place where he was attacked."

Geoffrey's eyes darted back to the box, drawn to a faded scrap of vellum, marked with a broken seal . . . a familiar seal.

"A letter written by your father," Liliana finished, saying the words he'd known would come next.

Shock, like a swift kick, exploded through him and radiated to his temples. Anger followed quickly. "My father would never do such a thing," he growled, and yet he reached into the box and snatched up the missive. He easily recognized his father's scrawl.

We have been compromised. Meet me two days hence. Same time and location.

"Where did you get this?" he demanded, not looking up, his mind awhirl. And how long had she had it?

He heard Liliana draw a breath, as if she were having as much difficulty with that simple body process as he.

"In my father's library, in a secret cache hidden behind his bookshelves."

He jerked his head up, pinning her with his gaze. That meant she'd brought the note with her and had had it *the entire time she'd been at Somerton Park.* An image of her falling into his arms that very first night in the library flashed before him. She'd been . . . what? Dressed all in dark clothes, he remembered. Searching? An ache formed in his chest, but he willed it away. First, he needed to figure out exactly what Liliana was saying.

"What else was in the cache?"

She nodded her head toward the box on his lap. "Two of those three bundles of letters."

Geoffrey picked up the packets, setting the box aside. His movements were slow and sure, and part of him recognized that the soldier in him had taken over, had shut down emotion. The paper felt brittle beneath his fingers as he raised the first bundle. The words were in French, the handwriting unknown. The second bore the script of his father. Geoffrey closed his eyes. He couldn't believe his father would have anything to do with murder, but clearly, a connection to Liliana's father was certain. And if Liliana was to be believed, her father was murdered shortly after he received this final note.

Bloody hell. Could *this* be what the blackmailer had alluded to in his threat? Or *her* threat? He eyed Liliana suspiciously, thinking once again about her behavior the first night she was here. Could she possibly be the one who'd sent the note? No. The idea of her as blackmailer made no sense. Why would she bring the evidence to him if she were the one trying to extort him? But clearly she had knowledge that could harm his family, and if she breathed even a word of it, his political reputation and all that he'd worked for would be in shambles.

"The letters in French and the ones from your father were together," Liliana said, interrupting his thoughts. "The others, the ones from my own father, I found here."

Geoffrey glanced at the third packet but untied the

ribbon around his father's notes and skimmed through them instead, trying to ascertain what could possibly be fodder for a blackmailer. Yet, the letters spoke of nothing in particular, just paragraphs of narrative that made no sense. What was their importance and why had Liliana's father possessed them? "These letters are completely innocuous," Geoffrey said.

"Yes," Liliana acknowledged. She came forward hesitantly and her clean scent tantalized his nose. Despite the situation, desire rose in him and he found it a challenge to focus on her words. "You'll find the ones from my father match in tone and content. The ones in French are devoid of real meaning as well, appearing to be nothing of consequence."

"Yet you believe otherwise. Why?" The question floated from his mouth, an automatic reply that sounded odd and hollow to his ears. It was the proper question, the appropriate response in this conversation, and yet Geoffrey couldn't seem to wrap his mind around the topic at all. Only moments ago, he'd been making love with this woman, had actually asked her to *marry* him, and now he was calmly asking why she thought his father had killed her own and trying to ascertain how much of a threat she might be to his future.

She sat on the chaise beside him, as tentative as a bird ready to take wing at the first sign of danger, yet the look in her eyes almost begged for something. Forgiveness? Understanding?

Geoffrey did his best to shield himself from the pain threatening to skewer him.

"The fact that both of our fathers not only kept the letters but secreted them away, for one," she said.

Geoffrey nodded. He'd come to the same conclusion, but he wanted to hear her thoughts. He couldn't think about all of the implications now, yet a dull throbbing ache filled his chest. Liliana might be duplicitous and cunning, but she was also a brilliant woman. He'd be a fool to discount whatever theories she might have, but he'd need to use caution. He'd give her nothing until he sorted out this situation himself. Alone.

How it hurt to realize he was the only person he could trust after all.

"But also because of this." Liliana reached into the box and drew out another paper and unfolded it. Her arm brushed against his in the process, and the ache he felt intensified.

Liliana held the paper where he could see it, too. Her efficient handwriting had marked several letters in different succession, with interspersed blanks, almost as if she were trying to break a code. He raised his eyes to hers.

"You believe there's a code?" he asked.

She nodded. "Yes. In the months before my father was killed, he grew obsessed with codes. Since it was just he and I, he usually included me in whatever he was working on, and this was no different. He began to leave me notes in code all of the time. Now I can see it was likely a way to keep me distracted and out from underfoot while he . . ." A frown crumpled her features before she cleared her throat. "He would shift the alphabet, matching the letter *A* to a letter of his choice."

A Caesar shift. Geoffrey was familiar with the common cipher, once used by the Roman army, but it wasn't very sophisticated. It could be broken easily, which was why it was rarely used anymore.

"And I would try various patterns until I found the one that deciphered his message." A sad smile flitted across her face. "He said it taught me to use my mind and to learn persistence."

It seemed she'd learned that lesson well, since she'd been searching since she'd arrived at Somerton Park— A sick feeling grabbed him. Had her persistence led her to pursue him so that she could glean information when she'd run out of clues?

Liliana sighed. "But I've tried all twenty-six variations to no avail," she said, confirming the worst of it.

Geoffrey's anger burst through the dam he'd hastily erected at her very first accusation. *That's* why she'd finally brought this to him. Because she could go no further on her own and she needed his help.

The realizations he'd been trying to hold back came rushing through the breach. Liliana had been deceiving him from the first moment they'd met. She *had* been rifling through his library when he'd accused her of trying to trap him into marriage. He thought back to how she'd tried to avoid him in the days that had followed. It made sense, now that he knew she'd been sneaking behind his back from the very beginning.

Had she learned his habit of morning rides and arranged their meeting in the meadow? Damn it all. And he'd fallen for it like a fool, telling himself she was different. What else had she manipulated? Pain burst within him, stealing his breath, but he couldn't let her see. He couldn't think about the breadth of her betrayal right now.

Geoffrey forced calm. He had to focus on the problem at hand. A code. A Caesar shift. What could he remember about those? *There had to be a key.* Yes, to make a Caesar shift more difficult to crack, the parties would often choose a specific word. They'd start the alphabet with that word, skipping any letters already used, until the key was spelled out. Then it was only a matter of filling in the rest. Without the key, the code would be nearly impossible to break.

But both men who might know the key had been dead for fourteen years.

He looked back at the box, his eyes drawn to the third packet, the letters from Liliana's father. "You said you found your father's letters here at Somerton Park? Where?" Father had always been a bit absentminded. He would have likely stored the letters in a place that would remind him of the key.

Liliana's entire body seemed to lower. Her shoulders drooped, her head dropped, her eyes fell. "Amongst your father's stored things in the family wing."

"How the hell did you—" It hit him like a punch to the solar plexus. She'd used the secret passage. And he'd given her the access himself so as to preserve her reputation during their trysts. Bile rose in Geoffrey's throat. Everything had been a lie. Every sweet kiss, every stolen moment a scheme to find what she was after.

His skin crawled as he thought of how he'd felt moments ago, when she'd sweetly given herself to him. How his heart had swelled with joy, when all she was doing was using him. And her declaration of love, her tears of remorse. Weren't they just another ploy to win his sympathies when she was forced to come to him for help?

He wanted to hurl the accusation at her feet, but he couldn't. Not until he got what he needed from her.

"Where specifically?" he asked, glad his voice remained calm while his insides were raging. "Were they hidden inside anything?"

Liliana nodded, her expression sad and open. Geoffrey could hardly stand to look at her, but he held her gaze. "Yes. They were in a book safe."

"Did the book have a title?"

The corners of Liliana's eyes turned down and tiny lines formed around her mouth. "It was a biography of Marc Antony," she said. "Why?"

Geoffrey made his face as blank as an erased school board. His father had always been fascinated by history and antiquity, particularly Egypt—which had naturally led to an interest in Antony, who was so wrapped up in both. Geoffrey had never cared for the Roman general, whom he'd thought weak for letting a woman completely ruin his life.

And now he was no better.

He narrowed his eyes. "Just curious. Having been in the dark all this time, can you blame me now for wanting every detail?"

Liliana's cheeks fired red. Good. Perhaps she'd be focused more on her shame, if that was what she was feeling, and less on why he'd asked that particular question. Still, Liliana was smart. It mightn't take her long to figure it out.

Well, she'd given the letters to him. He wouldn't give them back and allow her a chance to crack the code without him. Indeed, when he cracked it himself, he wouldn't share what he learned with her at all. It would serve her right, to have whored herself for nothing.

"I never meant to hurt you," Liliana whispered, her amazing violet eyes brimming with tears, and for a horrid moment, Geoffrey longed to engulf her in his arms and soothe her.

"Don't." Whether he said these words to her or to himself, he was not sure. The harshness in his voice betrayed more than Geoffrey would have liked. But he could hear no more of her lies. How many times early in his parents' marriage had he watched his father give in to Mother's tears and manipulations? How long had his father been made miserable because of his feelings for a deceitful woman?

"But, Geoffrey, I need—"

"I've heard enough of your lies," he bit off. He could no longer contain his rage. She looked so beautiful there beside him, tears glistening off of her lashes just like the moisture clinging to the tips of that extraordinary plant they'd picked in the bog. Indeed, wasn't she just like the majestic sundew, a carnivorous trap of a flower, luring creatures to their demise? Well, he'd made a close escape. But he wouldn't allow her to devour his heart.

He gathered the contents of the box and stood, tucking it beneath his arm in possessive challenge. He raised his chin and pressed his shoulders back in a rigid stance. "I want you out of my sight."

A lone tear slipped down Liliana's cheek, and Geoffrey felt it like hot acid stripping a trail down his soul. She stood, a bit shakily, but only nodded and turned to leave.

A sick panic gripped him. "Liliana?"

Wide eyes turned back to him, a wealth of emotion churning in them.

He steeled himself against it. "Don't you dare leave Somerton Park until I say you may go."

She flinched, keeping her eyes downcast as if unable to meet his.

Part of him wished she would look up—whether to plead with him or so that he could rail at her, he did not know—but she left without another word.

Geoffrey told himself that he'd given that command only so that she would be nearby if he needed more information from her. But as he watched her walk away, he could no longer deny the painful truth he'd been holding at bay. Cursed love bloomed inside him with rough petals that scraped and stung no matter how hard he tried to stem it.

Just like his father, he'd fallen in love with a cunning, untrustworthy female.

Chapter Twenty-four

Gringolet's stall stood empty when Liliana arrived at the stable an hour before dawn. Whatever bravado held her shoulders high escaped like hydrogen leaking from one of Jacques Charles' gas-filled balloons. She slumped against the wall.

If only she could float away on the breeze like one of those famed contraptions. Yet her desire to leave her heartbreak behind was tethered by a sad combination of her love for Geoffrey and her ever-present need to finally know the truth. She couldn't leave Somerton Park without closure on both fronts.

Where had Geoffrey gone? Should she remain here at the stable until he returned? She hadn't really expected he'd be here to meet her for their morning ride, but she'd run out of options. She'd already looked for him in his rooms and his study using the key he'd neglected to take back. The image of his face when he'd realized she'd used that key to search the family wing had haunted Liliana all night. Remorse ached inside of her, sharp and poignant, not blunted even by the conviction that she hadn't set out to hurt Geoffrey specifically. She'd only been seeking justice.

She had to see him. Though her chances to convince him of the veracity of her feelings were slim, she feared how painful the regret would grow if she didn't at least try. She also needed to tell him of the old valet's suspicions regarding his father's death. He deserved to know everything she did.

Her heart constricted. Geoffrey mustn't feel the same, however. He was keeping something from her. Something important. Something that strangely enough had to do with where her father's letters had been found, but she couldn't fathom what it could be.

An impatient whinny and the irregular prancing clop of hooves drew Liliana's attention to the neighboring stall. Amira must have sensed her presence and been anxious to run the countryside. Liliana's turbulent emotions ceded a bit at the thought. A good hard ride might be just what she needed, and there was always the chance she'd come across Geoffrey on the grounds.

Liliana entered Amira's stall and stroked the mare's nose. In short time, she saddled the horse and galloped off toward the eastern sunrise with no destination in mind. This morning, of all mornings, she craved thoughtless escape.

Shortly after the sun broke the horizon, Liliana spotted Geoffrey's stallion in the distance. Relief and trepidation rose in her. The beast was tied to a post outside the folly—the folly Geoffrey had offered for her laboratory as an inducement to marry him.

Liliana tried to picture that moment, the tender look upon Geoffrey's face when he'd made his sweet proposal. But all she could dredge up was the pained betrayal in his eyes when he'd tossed her out of the library. She squeezed her eyes shut on her wretched emotions. They'd get her nowhere.

She slowed Amira as they came around the lake, bringing the mare to a halt next to Gringolet. The horses nickered in greeting. Liliana dismounted, secured Amira to the post and walked over to stroke Grin's flank. Cool and smooth. He hadn't been run in some time and had clearly been brushed down after arriving. Had Geoffrey spent the night out here, then?

She glanced at the shuttered folly, which looked empty and lifeless. Had she not seen Grin, she would have ridden right past ...

Deciding on a plan, she untied the horses and led them around the back of the structure, where they were hidden from view, and found a tree sturdy enough to secure them to. The morning had handed her the perfect opportunity to hash things out with Geoffrey away from the prying eyes and ears of the manor.

As Liliana mounted the front steps, she was grateful it had been hours since she'd eaten. Certainly nothing would have stayed in her stomach with this nervous churning. But she vowed she wouldn't leave the folly until she discovered what Geoffrey was keeping from her. And until he heard her apology. She couldn't force him to accept it, nor did she expect him to. She could only hope saying it would be enough to release her from this gnawing guilt.

She didn't knock, simply tested the handle, which turned easily. She pressed the heavy wooden door just wide enough to slip through, blinking as her eyes adjusted to the relative darkness. Dim slivers of light cut the shadow through the ancient slatted shutters but did little to illuminate the interior of the folly. The air seemed still. Yet Liliana's body tingled with awareness. Geoffrey was definitely here.

She felt her way toward the daybed, trying vainly to shut out the memories that assaulted her. Geoffrey, smiling wickedly as he'd teased her to the breaking point in this very spot. The glorious bursting release of her very first orgasm. The swelling of tenderness she'd felt afterward that she only now recognized as love ...

The daybed was empty. If her memory served, there was a chair and writing desk off to the left in the "corner" of the round space. She moved silently that direction.

The soft snippet of a snore broke the silence, and Liliana tensed, coming to a halt. Then she relaxed her stance. He was asleep.

By the time she reached him, her eyes had fully adjusted to the dimness. Liliana easily made out Geoffrey's sleeping form, lithe even in repose. She shook her head. His back would be killing him when he woke. One shoulder was scrunched down and wedged between the back and side of the wingback chair, one leg was propped with the ankle resting on the opposite knee, and his head lolled back and to the right. Yet his hand still gripped a pencil, as if he'd leaned back to contemplate something he was writing and had nodded off before he could complete the thought.

Scraps of vellum littered the desktop. Off to the side, open bundles of letters, the ones from their fathers, lay spread out by date. Had Geoffrey been trying to break the code? Did he not think she'd properly checked all variations?

She leaned over the desk to see what he'd been writing.

MARCNTOYBDEFGHIJKLPQSUVWXZ
ABCDEFGHIJKLMNOPQRSTUVWXYZ

Warm, strong fingers clamped around her wrist, and Liliana jumped with a startled gasp.

"What are you doing here?" Geoffrey demanded, his voice gravelly and raw. It also brooked no dissemblance.

She nearly blurted out that she'd been looking for him, but then indignation burned through her. "What are *you* doing here?"

"Last time I checked, this folly belonged to me," he said drily, releasing her wrist and scrubbing a hand over his eyes.

"That's not what I meant," Liliana snapped, glancing down at his masculine scrawl. She slammed a finger down on the cipher. *MARCNTOY . . . Could that mean*

Marc Antony? "Is there a password? Is that what you're thinking?"

Geoffrey's face went blank, but his eyes sharpened and his lips pressed together tightly.

Her burst of anger turned, and Liliana experienced the sting of betrayal herself. She swallowed, and her voice sounded very small when she said, "You've figured it out and you weren't going to tell me."

Geoffrey exhaled a resigned sigh accompanied by the rustle of wool as he straightened in his chair.

Liliana withdrew her finger and drew her hands together, clasping them in front of her. She brought her shoulders in, too, lowering her head. She'd given him all of the evidence she had, hoping he would see, as she did, that their best chance to learn the truth would be to work together. Even if he hated her. But obviously he'd intended to shut her out.

Geoffrey rose and walked away without a word.

Could she blame him? Liliana fought the sting of tears—hurt tears, but also ones of frustration. Yes, she *could* blame him. Certainly she'd shocked him with her admission. Even wounded him. But did he have no care for her feelings? For her situation? Could he not understand that her father had been *murdered*, for goodness' sake?

Geoffrey returned bearing an oil lamp and a wooden chair and arranged them so that two people could work side by side at the desk. He seated himself in the primitive chair, indicating she should sit in the more comfortable cushioned one.

She did—before he could change his mind—and tried not to squirm beneath his scrutiny.

After a long moment, he said, "I thought I had, but I was mistaken." Liliana listened carefully as he explained his theory about a key and told her that he'd thought he'd found it in the name of the book his father had kept the secret letters in.

"But nothing I tried worked," Geoffrey concluded, his voice flat and impersonal, businesslike. His tone scraped her heart, but she was glad that he was sharing the problem with her. That was something. Perhaps even enough to build a future on when all of this was over? She tried not to hope, yet it stole into her heart all the same. "And with both men having been dead so many years, I have no expectation that we will be able to break the code."

Liliana took in a deep breath. Hope mingled with despair as she considered the possibilities. Focusing on a problem had always been her escape, her saving grace from troublesome emotion. She tried to reason out what she knew. Knowing her father, the password could be any manner of things, yet *not* knowing Edmund Wentworth, she was at a loss as to a word the two men might agree upon. But . . . if what Geoffrey said was true, that his father had been absentminded and would have left himself a clue . . .

"What if you weren't wrong?" she asked suddenly, the tingling excitement of discovery pushing out the feelings she couldn't deal with right now.

Geoffrey frowned. "I told you, I've—"

"Tell me how the password is supposed to work again," Liliana said, grabbing a scrap of vellum and his discarded pencil.

"Take the key word and write it out, omitting letters you've already used. Then fill in the rest of the alphabet," he said.

Liliana started writing.

MARCUSNTOIBDEFGHJKLPQVWXYZ
ABCDEFGHIJKLMNOPQRSTUVWXYZ

She wrote the cipher out again on a different scrap of paper. "Here," she said, thrusting it toward him as she reached for one of the letters. "Try this."

Geoffrey took the cipher, glancing down. "What is this?" he asked, a winged brow rising—not in challenge, she thought, but in curiosity.

"My father was a scientist," she answered. "He would have insisted on Latin. *Marcus Antonius.*"

A corner of Geoffrey's mouth rose a fraction as his head bobbed a sharp nod. "Of course," he muttered, and grabbed a letter of his own.

Liliana gauged the length of the letter she held. The words flowed in narrative, which would be terribly difficult to construct if each word was used in the message. "Try the first letter of the first word of each sentence," she suggested, and bent her head to her task.

A trucelike silence swelled between them, broken only by the scratchings of lead on vellum. Given all that had happened in the last twelve hours, Liliana was amazed by the feeling of comfortable camaraderie that settled over her. Being married to Geoffrey would have been like this, she knew, both of them passionately working together toward common goals . . .

A terrible ache formed in her heart and she shook her head to disabuse the notion. She couldn't think of what she'd tossed away by foolishly keeping the truth from him for so long. Instead, she jotted letters by rote, not paying attention to any patterns until she reached the end. As she finished the last mark, she sat back in the chair and held the message before her eyes.

FRMTYESPRICEARRMIDOCTWTHPCEFORXCHNGE

Liliana straightened. Not perfectly formed, but definite words stood out. This was the right password, she was certain. *FR.* Father? No, that didn't feel right. *FRM.* Farm? Firm? No. From? That could be. She looked at it again. *From 'T,' yes price. ARR* . . . arrive?

Arrive mid Oct with piece for exchange.

Heaviness descended, covering Liliana like a shroud. Price? And it said "piece." That sounded like more than just information. What *had* her father gotten involved in? It couldn't be good, given the secrecy surrounding it and how it turned out—for both men. She glanced up at Geoffrey.

He, too, had finished his letter and was contemplating a message of his own. That there was one was clear, given the grimace lining his mouth and the tired, sad downturn of his eyes.

Liliana's heart ached for them both.

"What does yours say?" she asked quietly.

His eyes snapped to hers and Liliana tried not to recoil from the pain in them. She suspected he saw similar hurt in her own, as his mouth softened.

"As best I can make out, it says, 'Authentic corselet, belonged to Cleopatra, emeralds in gold. Exchange for asylum and funds for life. Advise offer.'"

Liliana read her message aloud as well, which seemed to follow his. She scrunched her face, her mind reeling. Whatever she'd been expecting, it certainly wasn't this. "Treasure?"

"Egyptian treasure," Geoffrey clarified. "It fits my father, at least."

"But not mine," Liliana said. "He never showed any interest in such things." She looked back at her message, staring at the initial *T*. *T* would be neither Edmund Wentworth nor Charles Claremont. So who could it be? These letters were the ones her father had written, the ones she'd found amongst Edmund Wentworth's things. So that meant *T* was known to her own father, as it seemed he was the one brokering whatever exchange was meant to happen. But her father associated only with other scientists.

Liliana gasped. "When Napoleon invaded Egypt, he took with him one hundred and fifty French scientists. They were called the savants. Napoleon ordered them to catalogue and classify every aspect of the country."

Geoffrey nodded. "I remember," he said. With his mind distracted by the mystery, it was as if he forgot his anger with her, and his tone was one of easy intimacy. It caressed Liliana's battered heart like a lover. "When things got hairy, the coward abandoned them there. They were stranded in Egypt until British troops 'rescued' them in 1801. Of course, we relieved them of all of their findings and treasures, including the Rosetta stone, and sent them home empty-handed."

"Exactly," Liliana said, excitement and hope finally bubbling through her gloom. "After my mother died, my father stayed in England with me, but before that he traveled extensively throughout the continent, studying and lecturing. He could have easily met and befriended one of those scientists who would later become a savant and . . . Oh!" she exclaimed, a memory surfacing. "Triste. My father shared rooms with a French scientist named Triste at university. He used to talk of his old friend, when I was little. The *T* must stand for him." Without thinking, she grasped Geoffrey's hand and a bolt of current shot through her, raising gooseflesh.

Geoffrey stiffened at her touch, his face once again going blank. He pulled his hand away and stood, the wooden chair scraping against the stone floor.

Liliana's throat tightened, tears once again stinging her eyes. Her hand still burned where she'd touched him, but Geoffrey had gone cold. He paced beside the desk, one hand gripping the vellum he still held and the one she'd touched balled into a fist.

"So what if Triste was a savant," he said, his voice equally cool, "and was able to retain this . . . corselet? He'd have returned to France in an upheaval, with Napoleon about to declare himself emperor and gathering all wealth to himself."

Liliana stood as well, unable to keep her seat. She tried to make her voice sound as impersonal as his so he wouldn't see how his rebuff stung. "Yes, and Triste would no doubt be bitter over being abandoned in Egypt for those long years and might think the treasure should be his alone—"

"So he gets in touch with his old friend." Geoffrey stopped before her.

"My father." Liliana nodded.

"And asks him to find someone in England who would be willing to purchase the piece so he can start a new life here," Geoffrey finished. He raked his fingers through his black hair and blew out a breath. "It's thin."

"It's reasonable, given what we know," Liliana countered. She pulled one of the bundles of letters to her. "Now we need to decode the rest and see if we're right."

Geoffrey narrowed his eyes and Liliana held her breath. She resumed her seat, determined to remain until the mystery was solved. She wouldn't leave, even if he ordered her to. Even if he tried to physically toss her out on her bottom. But she prayed he wouldn't.

He dropped into the chair next to her. "Fine." He snatched the letters she held but thrust another stack forward. "However, *I* will decode the ones from your father, and you, mine. That way, *neither* of us is able to hide anything from the other."

Liliana swallowed, knowing by *neither* he meant her. She accepted it, knowing he didn't trust her. Might never trust her again. She was only grateful he hadn't fought her staying, because she'd known very well when she'd given him all of her evidence that he could have her tossed off of the estate. It had been a risk she'd been willing to take, showing her trust in him. Whether he would ever see it that way was yet to be determined. She nodded her head and set to work.

Long minutes passed, each of them scribbling furiously. An odd peace stole over Liliana. Their savant theory grew more and more feasible with every message she decoded, and while she still was unsure what had gone so terribly wrong that it had ended with her father's death and possibly Geoffrey's father's, too, just knowing she'd been right to pursue her instinct acted as a balm on her ragged, conflicted feelings.

There was no clue as to how Charles Claremont and

Edmund Wentworth met, as by the time they started using coded letters to communicate, it was clear their
scheme was already afoot. As Liliana read on, bits and
pieces of the story unfolded. A price agreed to, a plan for
T to bring the piece to England himself. A date set. Then,
a snag. *T* being watched, unable to escape France. Scrambling for another plan. Agreement to pay a bribe to one
of Napoleon's government officials for safe passage of
the piece to a university in Belgium, where it would be
sent on to her father, hidden amongst scientific papers,
with *T* to follow at a later date.

And then . . .

Liliana's breath caught as she stared at the next decoded message.

HVARRNGDFORSONTODLVRPKGASHEPASSESBRDR

*Have arranged for son to deliver package as he
passes border.*

She put the letter down, her hand shaking. When she
glanced over at Geoffrey, he watched her intently, likely
drawn by her gasp. Yet his usual robust coloring had
washed pale, and she knew he must be reading similar
messages from her father's side of the communication.

"Did you know you were paying a bribe?" she whispered.

Black lashes dropped, even as Geoffrey shook his
head in a slow denial. He looked as if he were going to
be sick. "Father asked me deliver a vase, told me it was a
priceless antique he wished a friend of his in France to
have, but because of the war, he couldn't send it through
normal channels. The bribe money must have been inside, but I never knew it."

Liliana searched Geoffrey's face. Lines of sorrowful
anger marked his features. She believed him. At the
same time, she longed to reach out to him, to pull him

into her arms and give him comfort. In only a few hours, everything he thought he knew had been turned on its head. He must be reeling.

When he raised his eyes to her, Liliana's breath caught at the anguish in them. "Do you know what this means?" he rasped.

Liliana shook her head, yet the hairs on the back of her neck tingled to life.

"It means I committed treason."

Chapter Twenty-five

"That's ridiculous. Of course you didn't commit treason," Liliana insisted, a deep V forming between her chestnut brows. She sounded almost offended for him, and yet the expression on her face spoke of concern, of compassion. She looked rather as if she wished to reach for him, and Geoffrey felt an almost undeniable pull to let her, to lean on her.

He placed his hands on the edge of the desk and shoved, pushing himself away and gaining his feet. These last hours had thrown him more than he wanted to handle, and as far as his feelings for Liliana were concerned . . . well, they vacillated like the pendulum of human nature, from good to evil, love to hate . . . hope to regret. He couldn't trust anything he was feeling at the moment.

What he could do was focus on how to handle the most recent blow.

"Intentionally, no. But do you think that will matter to my political opponents? Or to the men I've been working all year to convince to invest in employment opportunities?" His face tightened as he clenched his jaw. The weight of every ex-soldier he'd seen starving, suffering, slowly dying before his eyes seemed to bear down on him. He gritted his teeth against the crushing burden.

"Christ, all it would take is a whiff of scandal and everything I've worked for will be for naught."

He turned his glare upon Liliana and she flinched. He closed his eyes, marshaling his emotion. This wasn't her fault. Hell, she'd been a child when all of this had happened. He'd been barely a man himself. Yes, she'd brought it to his door, had ripped his heart out by the way she'd chosen to go about her investigation, but really, hadn't she done him a favor? At least now he knew what the blackmailer must have against his family. However, *that* was none of her business. As far as she was concerned, they were the only two people who knew of this sordid affair.

When he looked upon her once more, Liliana hadn't moved. She looked so achingly beautiful as she sat there with her face open and imploring. His heart twisted. No, it wasn't her fault, but damn, how he wished he'd never laid eyes upon her. Had never kissed her satiny skin, never ran his fingers through her silken tresses, never breathed in her crisp, clean scent.

But he had—and much more. That alone obligated him to do what was right by her. The fact that he had inadvertently been involved in the death of her father only compounded his duty. By marrying her, he'd make up for her loss in some way.

Liliana stood, her moves graceful and slow, never breaking eye contact. "Then no one ever has to know."

He scoffed. If only it were that simple, but someone else already knew. Worse, *he* knew. Knew how she'd been wronged. Knew how she'd used him. Knew how his father had used him, had duped him, had potentially made him party to murder.

"I know you don't believe me, Geoffrey, and I don't blame you, but I would never do anything to hurt you." Liliana winced and looked away. Then she straightened her shoulders and took a step toward him. She reached out to her left and snatched one of the decoded letters from the desk and held it out before her. "I plan to stay until we discover the truth. I need to know what went wrong, what really happened to my father, but then"—she crumpled the letter in her hand—"I'll disappear. You'll never hear from me again, if that's what you want, and I'll never tell a soul. You can trust me on that. I lo—"

She clamped her mouth shut and cleared her throat.

Geoffrey narrowed his eyes. She'd almost claimed to love him again. At least she'd stopped herself from uttering the lie. But then, she didn't need to pretend to love him anymore, did she? Still, the truth and magnitude of her deceit knifed through him anew.

Liliana began again. "I ..." Her eyes suddenly widened, her face taking on a look of horror. "Oh no, Geoffrey. Someone else *does* know. A man—he tore apart my father's library. Everyone thought it a robbery at the time, but he could have been after the treasure."

"When was this?"

"A few weeks ago."

Damn. Another person? Or was this the blackmailer, searching either for the treasure or for more evidence against him? Was there even a chance to keep all of this quiet?

"We can't worry about that until we've solved the rest of the mystery." Geoffrey reached for her closed fist, which still held the crumpled note. He gently pried her fingers open and took the letter, detesting that the mere touch sent a sweet ache through him. He let her go and smoothed the vellum out. "How many more letters have you to decode?"

Her lip trembled and dropped, but she gamely said, "Three."

He had only one left. He nodded to her chair and sat himself. "Then, let's finish this."

The last message from Claremont indicated that the piece had arrived from the university in Belgium, and he inquired about making the exchange. Geoffrey sat back in his seat and steepled his hands, touching his index fingers to his lips. It should have been simple, so what had gone wrong? As angry as he was with his father for lying to him—for duping him into committing an act of treason, for God's sake—he didn't see the man as greedy, willing or even able to kill for money—

"Here," Liliana's voice broke through his thoughts. "Your father has set up a meeting with mine, for December twenty-third. Father was to bring the treasure and exchange it for the money, which he would then hold for Triste." She stood and paced beside his chair. Apples and lemons wafted to him as she passed, and despite everything, desire poured into his veins. "Yet the meet was moved up two days, and my father was killed. Why?"

A cold chill slithered over Geoffrey. "Your father was killed on the twenty-first of December of aught-three?" He swiftly calculated. That was little more than a fortnight before his own father died, an awful coincidence. Or was it? What if his father hadn't died of natural causes?

Liliana watched him, empathy etching her features ... not surprise, as if ... "You knew our fathers died less than three weeks apart?" he cried as he leapt to his feet, outrage boiling in his gut that she would keep something like this from him. "Since when?"

"Since we visited Witherspoon in the village," she said quietly. "Your father's valet told me he suspected your father was poisoned. He smelled almonds on the body ... which speaks to cyanide."

"And you said nothing?" Christ. Too many things hit Geoffrey, and he backed away.

"I tried to yesterday, but you wouldn't let me—"

"You've known for days!" He narrowed his eyes, seeing Liliana as if for the first time. "Did you even care for that old man's health? Or did you just use him for information like you did me?"

Liliana winced and looked down.

Geoffrey tunneled his fingers through his hair. She was nothing he'd thought she was. Everything she'd done, everything he'd loved about her was a lie, and yet his heart still ached, still yearned. Why couldn't he hate her instead?

He turned his back on her, striving for control in the silence.

"If I could go back and do things differently," she said softly, "I would. But I can't. All I can do is see this through. We're so close. I know it."

He faced her, his emotions once again tightly laced. "You're right."

Liliana's shoulders relaxed and she briefly closed her eyes, and then, like the pragmatic scientist she was—or the cold, calculating one—she returned to the problem at hand. "I can't figure out why, when they'd gone to all of this trouble to send unsigned coded messages, the last note from your father was in plain English and bore his seal, where the other ones didn't. Do you think perhaps he didn't send it?"

Geoffrey frowned and reached down to the desktop. He raised the letter in question and examined it closely. "No, it's definitely my father's handwriting."

"But it makes no sense. Could the letter have been forged?" Liliana tapped a finger against her mouth, her brow furrowing in thought. She stopped before the desk and tossed the last of the letters she'd been decoding down, blowing out a frustrated breath. "And what happened to the treasure? These papers can't tell me, and the only people who can have been dead for fourteen years."

"Perhaps not." The words slipped out without thought, and yet as Geoffrey uttered them he accepted that Liliana had the right to know everything. He might abhor her tactics, but he understood her motives, now more than ever, with the very real possibility that his father might have been killed as part of this sordid mess as well. He regained his seat and gestured toward her chair. "Please, sit."

Liliana obeyed and he told her of the blackmail attempt. She listened, eyes widening, as he explained everything from the missing money to the current threat to his attempts to uncover the man's identity. Oddly, sharing the story with Liliana felt natural, like a relief, like telling a friend or a ... lover. But he knew the feelings not to be real. Damn her for taking that away from him.

"So the man who broke into my home—he could have been the blackmailer?" she asked.

"Yes, or more likely working for him. I've been wondering why his threat was so vague. He must not have solid proof or only have part of the story and is hoping that my desire to preserve my political reputation will be enough for me to roll over."

Liliana's curved fingers tapped the desk. "Yes, but perhaps the part of the story he has is the part that we are missing." Her voice rose with hope. "Are you close to discovering who he is? I can describe my intruder for you, though I don't know how much help it will be if he was only the blackmailer's accomplice."

Geoffrey straightened. Perhaps it would give him at least something to go on. "You saw him?"

Her lips flattened into a grimace. "Not well. I was sort of ... grappling with him at the time."

Geoffrey lost eight years off his life as Liliana related the tale. She could have been killed! There was one good thing about their marrying ... at least she'd be under the protection of a man, as she should be, not fending off dastardly henchmen on her own. A mirthless smile raised the corner of his mouth. "You know, for a brief moment last night, I thought perhaps you were in league with the blackmailer, searching my library for substantiation. Little did I know you were, only not for a villain but for yourself."

Liliana colored. "Well, I suppose that can be forgiven, considering I originally suspected you must have been involved in this scheme. While you *were*, you didn't know it." She crossed her arms in front of her as if hugging herself and exhaled a sighing breath. "What a pair we are. We were both right about each other, yet so very wrong."

Geoffrey considered her words. Was he wrong about her now? Just the possibility that someone had killed his father, too, had sent such rage through him that he could understand Liliana's motives. But did that make her different from his mother?

He let his eyes slide over her. Exhaustion rimmed her features but made her no less beautiful. But beauty was only skin deep. Liliana still had used and hurt people to get what she wanted.

Still, he couldn't deny the sexual energy that hummed through the room now and had since he'd first opened his eyes and saw her standing over him. He was just so confused, had been hit with too much too fast.

I'll disappear. You'll never hear from me again, if that's what you want . . .

Was that what he wanted? Or could he forgive her deceit? Could he trust that her lies were a onetime occurrence, caused by special circumstance, and make a life with her? He knew he had to marry her—it was his duty, his obligation, given that she'd been a virgin daughter of the ton. The right thing to do. But with this between them, could their marriage still work as a partnership or would it never be more than an empty shell?

He longed to reach out for her, to cup her chin, look into her eyes and just ask her. But he wouldn't. The fact that he wanted to so badly even while so emotionally raw only illustrated the power she held over him.

What the hell was he thinking? He clamped down on his feelings, wishing he'd never even considered the idea of love. If he opened himself to her as he'd been on the path to doing before she'd revealed her deception, it was only a matter of time before she realized that power. It would be only natural to wield it when she wanted something, even if she did it in a way completely unlike his mother.

He would reset the terms of a union between them to protect himself, and only—

Liliana slapped her hand down on the desk. "Aveline."

"What?"

She stood, gesturing with both hands as if her mind were running faster than her tongue. "The day of the musicale, the day he departed, I saw Aveline sneaking out of the library. I thought it odd then. Remember? I asked you about him later, but I didn't know about the blackmailer so I wouldn't have made the connection. What if *he* were searching your home for evidence, too?"

"Bloody hell," Geoffrey muttered. Aveline had never been a friend, per se, but they'd been neighbors their whole lives. *Could* Aveline be the blackmailer? Those years the man had been detained in France at the start of the war were a mystery. What if he'd caught wind of part of these doings while he was over there and capitalized upon it when he returned home? It was possible.

Geoffrey would need to compare the dates of when money started disappearing to when Aveline returned from the continent. He'd also need to discreetly look into his neighbor's finances. And his current whereabouts.

A terrible thought struck. Did Aveline also know about the treasure? Was that why he'd attached himself to Liliana? Geoffrey's stomach balled as ice doused his veins when he thought of how easily Aveline could have harmed Liliana if he'd thought she had any knowledge of the treasure's whereabouts. If anything ever happened to her . . .

Geoffrey stood, taking Liliana by the shoulders. "Think back to every conversation you had with the man. Did he ask any probing questions, anything else that struck you wrong?"

Liliana's mouth shifted to the side and she tugged upon her lower lip in that way she did when she was thinking. "No. Nothing."

"Did he ever try to get you alone?"

Liliana squinted her eyes at him. "No. He was ever the gentleman. He did mention in his note that he'd like to see me again in London, but—"

"You're not going back to London," Geoffrey said. "Or Chelmsford, either. You'll be staying here." Now was as good a time as any to tell her what he'd decided.

Liliana stiffened and pulled away from him. He let her. "That's ridiculous, Geoffrey. The house party ends tomorrow, and guests will be departing. I can't very well stay at Somerton Park."

"You can if we're to be married."

Liliana's delicate chin dropped, her pink tongue flashing through her open mouth. "I hardly think—"

"You agreed last night, before we made love. Or were you lying to me then, too?"

"N-no. Of course not." Her head whipped from side to side. "I said, 'If you still—'"

"Wanted you to in the morning." He strode over to the shuttered window and threw one wide. A blast of sunshine streaked through the room. "It's morning, and I still want you as my wife."

Her face went slack, but Geoffrey could see her mind racing behind those intelligent violet eyes.

"But why?" she finally whispered. "Have you forgiven me, then?"

"No. Nor do I expect to," he said, even if he could understand why she'd lied. Still, it wouldn't do to let her know that. Better to set clear boundaries now. He'd lost his way before, but he vowed not to let her under his skin again. This would be a marriage where he maintained the upper hand. One that didn't involve his heart—once he figured out how to *un*involve it. "But the fact of the matter is, we have made love. You very well may be carrying the next Earl of Stratford as we speak."

A streak of satisfaction shot through him as Liliana dropped her hand protectively to her stomach, eyes widening as if she hadn't even considered the possibility. A picture of a laughing babe, with his black hair and her violet eyes, pierced him and he realized he hoped it were so . . . a sick testament to his muddled feelings where Liliana was concerned.

"We will read the banns this Sunday and be married in three weeks' time." Once she was his wife, he could protect her, could watch over her, could keep her near. And though he might tell her he married her for honor's sake, even after everything that had happened, he realized he still wanted her in his life and in his bed.

"But you don't trust me?" she asked in a small voice that twinged his heart.

"No. I don't have to trust you. As my wife, it will be in your best interest to protect my reputation."

He purposely misinterpreted her meaning, and he could tell by the way she stiffened that his words stung. He steeled himself against her pain. It was for the best.

She stood up straight and looked him in the eyes. "Without trust, there can be no love."

A sharp pain burst in the vicinity of his heart. There already was love, but he'd be damned before he ever told her that and gave her the power to manipulate or control his feelings again. And he'd be double damned if he let his love grow any more. He would quash it, viciously. Love did nothing but hurt, especially if you were the one who loved. Watching his father had taught him that.

He'd been a fool to ever think otherwise.

"Love isn't necessary."

Chapter Twenty-six

Liliana stared at her left hand where it rested on the table, a large amethyst betrothal ring encircling her third finger. She twisted her wrist and followed the shards of colorful candlelight reflecting through the cut jewel onto her white table napkin.

Low murmurs of subdued conversation hovered over the dinner table, punctuated by envious glances and curious stares. Once again, Liliana was seated to Geoffrey's right, this time not to honor her victory on the tournament field, but as his affianced.

She touched her fingertips to her temples, where the low throb of a headache had taken root and now grew, fertilized by the blatant scrutiny of the assembled diners. She supposed many, like Aunt Eliza, considered Liliana's enviable position as Geoffrey's betrothed to be the ultimate victory.

But beside her Geoffrey sat stiffly, a cool smile riding his face. Her chest swelled with a heavy sadness.

Love isn't necessary.

If marrying Geoffrey was a victory, it was hollow and dead, like a once majestic oak felled and left to rot in the bog.

"Smile, Liliana," Geoffrey murmured, not looking at her, "lest people think this is not a happy occasion."

She complied, but the expression felt dusty and brittle on her face.

She supposed *occasion* was one word to describe this mess. The day had been a whirlwind, and Geoffrey a force of nature who had allowed nothing to alter his course. Upon their return from the folly this morning, he'd wasted no time in announcing his intentions, not giving Liliana a chance to protest.

First he'd told his mother—whose howls of dissent were said to have been heard clear down to the servants' quarters. Then he'd paid a visit to Aunt Eliza, who'd had the opposite reaction, of course. She'd been only too happy to halt the packing of their belongings for tomorrow's departure and instead make arrangements to stay for the three weeks until the wedding. Oh, Aunt had fussed a bit about the rushed nuptials, but then wisely ceased her complaining, murmuring something about not looking a gift horse in the mouth.

Geoffrey had then closeted himself in the billiards room with the other gentlemen, ostensibly to talk politics, giving Liliana no opportunity to speak her mind.

She pushed her plate away and looked around the table. A room full of people was not the ideal place for the discussion she planned to have, but he'd left her no choice. This was the last night of the house party, and he'd already told her the Town gentlemen planned to wrap up their political discussions over cards late into the evening. Yet she couldn't go to sleep with her feelings so unresolved.

"And you would say a loveless marriage is cause for happiness, my lord?" Liliana asked, keeping her voice low.

Geoffrey did turn to her then, and a shimmer of emotion rippled over his face before it smoothed back into coolness. "Of course, when it's between two people who complement each other as we do."

Liliana's breath caught. He masked it well, but she'd seen something in his expression, some feeling. If only she knew what it was and if it could ever go back to how he'd felt about her yesterday, before her awful revelations. She decided to probe for more. She needed to know what drove him to insist upon a wedding to someone he didn't trust or love. Perhaps there was something there she could cling to, something with the potential to grow. "While I agree that in many ways we'd be a good match, I, as I said from the moment we met, haven't the need for a husband."

Fire flashed in his eyes, yet his voice remained cold and detached. "Don't be a fool. You've been compromised, albeit at your own instigation." A tic appeared in his jaw. "We'll get on well, and we'll accomplish great things between us. I will require some conventionality of you as my wife, but you needn't fear I will curb your work overmuch. I doubt many husbands would offer the same concession."

"I daresay you are right on that count," she ceded, but her hopes died. "However, that's not a basis for marriage."

Beneath the table, his hand slid up her thigh. Heat radiated from his palm through the satin of her skirts, strangling the breath from her chest as he leaned close. His scent overwhelmed her, and like a flash fire she boiled over with desire.

"Perhaps not." His hand rose higher, fingers skimming over her through the layer of fabric. "But this is."

Liliana looked away, trying not to betray herself. His touch still aroused, still burned with passion, but beneath it lay a leashed anger, so different from the tenderness with which he'd caressed her just last night. If only she could be certain that warmth and affection toward her would return, maybe she'd have the courage to go through with a marriage.

But how could she take the chance that it would not? How could she live with Geoffrey, loving him so, knowing he might never love her?

His hand slid away, and he turned to converse with a gentleman on his left who'd asked him a question. Liliana returned her gaze to Geoffrey, envisioning life between them. Polite. Perhaps passionate at first, but growing apart as the novelty wore off. Long, distant years, her heart breaking a little more each day.

No.

She'd come to Somerton Park with a purpose. Romance had been the furthest thing from her mind, not part of her formula at all. In fact, she'd never thought herself capable of love. But now, having tasted it, the idea of being in a marriage without love seemed as sour as the acetic acid that made vinegar so pungent.

The only thing keeping her here was the unknown still surrounding her father's death. But didn't she know enough? Her father had willingly involved himself in dangerous activities, albeit to help a friend—the best of intentions. She'd been relieved to discover nothing nefarious on her father's part, yet he'd been an adult who'd made the choices that led to his death.

And even if she could prove that Geoffrey's father had dealt the killing blows himself, which she doubted given the suspicious nature of the man's own death, she would never breathe a word of it to anyone. She couldn't destroy what Geoffrey was working so hard for. She couldn't do anything to harm him.

Liliana twisted her napkin in her lap, coiling it ever tighter. Who was she kidding? She'd already hurt him, badly. Whether she'd intended to or not, she'd pursued this delicate situation as a scientist, not as a woman. Not as a person with feelings who cared for other people's feelings, too. As a scientist, she always sought the truth with precision, pursuing theories to the end regardless of what was upset in the process, like a horse with blinders seeking only the finish line.

But what she'd done to Geoffrey was wrong. She couldn't take it back, but she could put an end to it before any more damage was done. He, and how the truth would affect him and his work, was more important than the truth.

An uncommon peace stole over her at a startling revelation. For once in her life, she was okay with leaving things unknown. She had enough to satisfy and she was going to move on.

But to what?

She cast one final glance at Geoffrey, the ache of tears lodged in her throat. Not to a life as Lady Stratford. That was certain.

She'd return to Chelmsford and resume her work. It would be a lonely existence, even more lonely now that she knew what she'd been missing. And yet, no matter how miserable that prospect seemed, it had to be better than a life where she'd be forced to face the love she could have had but didn't, every day across the breakfast table.

She let her eyes linger on Geoffrey's noble chin, his bold features, the lips that had brought her such pleasure and joy and pain.

Good-bye, sweet love.

She'd leave first thing in the morning.

"Well done, Stratford!" Geoffrey's partner chortled as he raked in yet another purse of winnings. Geoffrey nodded absently. The smile he'd held all night with some effort now seemed frozen on his face as the fingers of dawn approached.

He should be quite satisfied. It had been a fruitful night all around. He'd sent the countess into a fit of vapors with his choice of bride, his negotiations with several prominent gentlemen had gone better than he'd hoped and he had verbal agreements from four of them to fund various industrial projects, and he'd made peace with the Earl of Northumb. The older man had slapped him on the back, admonishing Geoffrey for keeping his "romance" with Liliana a secret and insisting he would have never pressured him into marrying his daughter had he known Geoffrey's heart was already engaged. He also pledged his support for the Poor Employment

Act, which all but guaranteed it would pass later this summer.

All of that, along with the realization that in three short weeks he'd have Liliana in his bed every night, should have made him a happy man. Yet he couldn't shake the stricken look upon her face at dinner.

Well, she'd adjust. He'd had time to cool throughout the day, though he knew his anger was merely banked beneath the surface. But perhaps eventually it would fade entirely. After a few months together, he hoped they might fall into a comfortable partnership. And if he ever sensed further manipulations on her part, he would set her straight immediately about the kind of man she married.

"I must say, I was sure when I drew you as partner that we would lose our shirts." Lord Goddard, the neighbor Geoffrey would forever think of as a wizened old turtle after seeing him in armor on the tournament field, raised his glass. "But you're a sight better card player than I expected. I'll take you as partner anytime."

"Many a night was passed playing one game or another with my fellow soldiers," Geoffrey said, "but why would you think I'd be so awful?"

Goddard shrugged, counting his winnings. "Just figured you took after some of the other men in your family when it came to luck. Or skill."

Geoffrey huffed. What a strange old buzzard. "I don't recall cards ever interesting my father, and you're certainly too young to have been at the tables when my great-grandfather haunted them. Did you play with my brother, then? I hear he took some heavy losses in his day."

Lord Goddard guffawed. "No, no. That young buck ran with a different crowd than I. I meant your uncle."

"Joss?" Geoffrey glanced around at the other players, but as usual, his uncle wasn't amongst them. "I've never seen him so much as look at a deck of playing cards," Geoffrey said, thinking perhaps Lord Goddard had had one too many sips of the cognac.

"Well, he probably hasn't in your lifetime. At least not in polite circles, but when we were young men, he took after old William Wentworth. You couldn't drag him away from the tables." The older man's eyes clouded with a faraway look. "Was a terrible player, most times. Got into trouble more than once. But then his luck changed . . . at least until he was caught cheating."

Geoffrey frowned. He'd never heard anything of the sort. "Cheating?"

Lord Goddard's gaze cleared and snapped back to Geoffrey. "Well, not exactly cheating. Worse, in my opinion. Your uncle had a habit of picking on men who were well into their cups."

That sounded nothing like the Uncle Joss he knew. The man he knew lived a benign existence. Nice enough, but without ambition or real backbone, easily led by forces like the countess. And yet, as he thought about it, Geoffrey wondered if that wasn't the kind of personality that could easily be lured into addictions as well. Still . . . "While that's not exactly honorable, men shouldn't play if their faculties are impaired."

Lord Goddard's wrinkled face drooped into a scowl. "Oh, he didn't take their money on the table. He waited until they were so foregone they wouldn't remember their own mothers, then forged notes claiming winnings due. He was deuced good at it, too. Men couldn't tell his forgeries from their own handwriting to save their lives. He'd wait a few days to call in the notes and the poor sots would hand over the blunt, figuring they'd just played too long into their cups. No telling how many men he fleeced before he was finally caught."

Hackles rose on Geoffrey's neck. *Forged notes?* He leaned toward Goddard. "How can that be? Why wouldn't he have been run out of town if that were true?"

Goddard didn't draw back an inch. "You don't remember your grandfather, o' course, but the man carried a lot of weight here and in Town. He made recompense to every man known to have been taken by your uncle, and probably some who weren't. Then he used his influence to quash any rumors. Your uncle disappeared for a time, and 'tweren't long before other scandals churned the gossip mill a new direction. He only returned after your father had become the earl." The old man finished the amber liquid in his snifter with a smacking sound that could be made only by missing teeth. "But some of us haven't forgotten."

Geoffrey shot to his feet, impossible notions ricocheting through him. What if Liliana had been right and the final note to her father had been forged?

More disturbing was that if his uncle had known enough to forge a letter to Charles Claremont, then Joss had been involved from the beginning. Uncle Joss had been his father's confidant, which was why Geoffrey had trusted him with the sensitive information about the Poor Employment Act, which Joss had run and told the countess.

What if his father had confided his dealings with Charles Claremont to Joss? If Joss had been in trouble at the tables, would he have tried to appropriate either the treasure or the money for himself?

He *was* the only man left alive. Could he have killed both Liliana's father and Geoffrey's own for the corselet?

Geoffrey clamped a hand over his mouth to stifle the bile rising in his throat.

"Is everything all right, Stratford?" Lord Goddard's face turned up, his tortoiselike eyes blinking.

Geoffrey swallowed. "Of course," he answered. "I just realized it's time I found my bed."

And my duplicitous uncle.

Chapter Twenty-seven

"Could you please personally make certain the mare is returned to the Earl of Stratford's stables?" Liliana pressed a coin into the young groom's hand. "But not until late this afternoon. Be sure to tell Mr. Richards you were promised another coin when the horse arrives safely." She'd lowered her voice and pulled her hat down to obscure her face. She was fairly certain no one at the coaching inn was wise to the fact that she was female.

The boy nodded his agreement and dashed off to fetch the horse she'd rented to carry her to the next stopping point.

Liliana hadn't intended to take Amira, but when she'd arrived at the stables, Richards had been mucking out the stalls and assumed Liliana was going out for her customary morning ride. He'd saddled Amira for her and she'd reluctantly ridden off on the prize mare. To refuse would have raised too many questions. She'd also been forced to stash her bag with food and a change of clothes behind the stable.

Liliana stroked Amira's long nose. "Farewell, Princess. I'm certain the boy will take good care of you." Promising him double pay should ensure Amira was well treated, even though it was coin Liliana could scarcely spare.

The boy returned, leading a tired-looking bonesetter in his wake. Liliana accepted the horse and watched as Amira was led across the yard. She turned away, tears clogging her throat. Not over saying good-bye to the horse, but because Amira was the last tie she had to Geoffrey.

Her hand dove into her pocket. Not the last tie, precisely. Amongst precious few coins and her decorative tinderbox, Liliana closed her fingers around an old metal key. Though she'd left his betrothal ring behind, she hadn't been able to part with the key to the folly. That was how she'd choose to remember Geoffrey, as a creative and thoughtful lover who'd once wanted her enough to offer her his most special place.

But there would be no more tenderness. No more races through the morning dew or exhilarating conversations with a man who truly listened to her ideas and didn't dismiss them as less simply because they came from a woman. No more stolen kisses or moments of bliss in Geoffrey's arms.

Liliana led the nag to the mounting block, determined not to wallow or second-guess. There was no guarantee there'd ever be any of those things again if she'd stayed, either. When he'd insisted they still marry, she'd been shocked, but a part of her had rejoiced. She'd agreed, if only because she so desperately loved him. She'd thought maybe, given time, they'd be able to put the past behind them and start anew.

But Geoffrey had turned cold, angry, and she didn't blame him. As he saw it, her actions had been a deliberate breach of trust . . . one he had no intention of forgiving. When she looked into his eyes, she saw no love, only distrust. And that was her fault.

Her heart tripped when she considered how he'd react when he realized she'd gone. Would his feelings of betrayal deepen and his anger toward her grow even more entrenched?

Liliana wiped a tear from her cheek, ducking her face. She had to quit sniffling like a ninny lest she give her disguise away.

It hardly mattered how he'd react. She couldn't live like this. And neither should he. In the long run, no matter how much it tore her soul, leaving was for the best. She wouldn't allow him to throw away his chance to find someone he could trust, and therefore love, for a sham marriage to assuage his misplaced sense of honor. When she was certain she was not carrying his child, she would send him a note to ease his mind. And if she was? Well, she'd deal with that wh—

"Miss Claremont?"

Liliana whirled at the sound of Geoffrey's voice, missing her step and nearly stumbling as her foot slipped off of the block in her surprise.

The bright sun filtering around him made her squint, and Liliana saw the figure before her only as a silhouette against the light. Her chest constricted for the briefest of moments. Hope, love and joy sprang up inside of her before her mind could quash it. The illusion faded as the man broke through the blinding light and drew nearer.

Not Geoffrey, she realized as her heart stopped forcing so much blood to her brain, but his uncle. Sir Isaac's ghost, for a moment she could have sworn . . .

"I barely recognized you, dressed as you are. Are you going somewhere?" Joss Wentworth inquired, his slightly graying black hair glinting in the sun. The polite smile he always wore was firmly in place, but in this blend of light and shadow, it made her uncomfortable. Maybe *because* it was so similar to Geoffrey's.

And yet so different. She'd never compared the two before, but having just mistaken the two men, she couldn't help but see the differences. Geoffrey's smiles always touched his eyes, the kindness in them coming from his heart. She looked hard at Wentworth. His smile seemed only face deep. False, almost like a mask . . .

She shook off the thought, certain she merely reacted to being caught running away by one of Geoffrey's relatives.

"I—" What could she say? She supposed the truth would be known soon enough. "Yes. I have decided a marriage to Lord Stratford will not suit and am returning home to Chelmsford."

Geoffrey's uncle's brows furrowed much as his nephew's did. "Does Geoffrey know this?"

Heat crept up Liliana's face, but she set her jaw. "Not as of yet, but he will soon enough." When—*if*—he cared to seek her out and discover she'd gone.

Wentworth frowned, his countenance again eerily similar to the expression his nephew made and yet different, more . . . irritated? "I'm not certain this is a good idea."

"I appreciate your concern," Liliana said, "but it's truly for the best." She turned back to her horse and lifted her foot to the block.

"I can't stand by and let a lady ride off on a rented nag."

Liliana suppressed a sigh. Misplaced honor apparently ran in the family. But this was hardly the time for chivalry. She faced him and opened her mouth to refuse.

"Please," he interrupted. "I won't say I understand why you're leaving, though my nephew can be trying, I'm sure." He smiled, taking her horse's lead and tying it to the post.

Liliana frowned at his presumption, but then he took her arm and placed it on his and started across the courtyard.

"While I'm of the opinion that you should stay and try to work out whatever lies between you and my nephew, I admit it is not my business. However, I insist you at least let me give you a ride to your destination."

Liliana considered tugging her arm from his, but she didn't wish to be rude. Wentworth was only doing what he thought best. "That is truly unnecessary. I am accustomed to traveling alone and will be perfectly fine."

He kept walking, ushering her through a stone archway to where a nondescript black carriage waited. Odd—nothing marked it as a Wentworth carriage.

"It is the only way I can assure Geoffrey that his intended made it home safely," Wentworth insisted.

She'd had enough. She'd made up her mind, but the man refused to listen to reason. She tugged at her arm, but he caught it, clenching her forearm in a bruising grip.

What in the world? "Sir, please. Unhand me."

They'd reached the carriage door, which Wentworth flicked open. "You're coming with me."

A chill shot up Liliana's spine at his tone, and the tiny hairs on her arms rose despite the warm morning sunshine. "I am not."

He yanked so fiercely, pain exploded in her shoulder, as if he'd pulled it from its socket. Liliana gasped in shock and agony.

"Oh, I think you are. Quietly."

Her gaze flew to the driver, a great hulk of a man, but he ignored her plight, keeping his face deliberately turned away.

Wentworth shoved her inside, following behind. He tossed her into the seat and settled in beside her, blocking her exit. He banged a hand on the ceiling of the carriage, which rocked into motion.

Dear God, what was happening here? Was Geoffrey's uncle really kidnapping her? Why? Certainly not to return his nephew's errant bride to him.

"Where are we going?" she asked.

"Where is the corselet?" Wentworth demanded.

"The what?" Shock melted her to her seat. How did Wentworth know of the treasure? Had he overheard while following her and Geoffrey about?

"Don't toy with me," he growled. "The treasure. Where did your father hide it?"

Where did your father hide it? A wave of nausea rolled

over Liliana, sucking the breath from her as her mind tried to process his words. They smacked of intimate knowledge, more than could be gleaned by eavesdropping.

She looked at Wentworth, with his fake smile that had turned to a snarl. Could *he* be the blackmailer?

The old valet's story popped into her mind, a tale of murder and poison. She nearly gasped, barely suppressing the urge in time. Could Wentworth be the killer?

Thoughts, memories and scenarios swirled around in her brain. What if she'd been right that the note that lured her father to his death had been a forgery?

Where did your father hide it? Anger boiled through Liliana. How would Wentworth know whether her father had hidden the treasure unless *he* had tried to get it from her father and failed. Maybe killed him in the attempt.

And then killed his own brother to cover up his deed? Or for the exchange money.

And now she was trapped in a carriage with him. Dear God, what did he intend to do with her? She glanced at the door, then at the man blocking her path. There would be no escape, at least not until they stopped. Her only choice was to play along, buy some time.

"I don't know anything about a treasure," she said, hoping to sound confused rather than horrified, as she actually was.

Wentworth reached a hand into his vest, withdrew a pistol and pointed it at her chest.

Liliana stopped breathing. He *was* the killer, and if she didn't do something, she might be his next victim.

"You're lying," he said. He pushed the gun forward and metal prodded her rib cage. Her bluff wasn't working.

"Okay, I know about the corselet, but I don't have it," she blurted.

Wentworth's eyes narrowed, and in their blue depths, Liliana recognized desperation. Desperate men did rash things. Wentworth's grip tightened on the pistol and Liliana's insides went all watery. She had to say something, anything, or he very well might dispatch her and no one would ever know what had become of her.

"But I know where it is."

Uncle Joss was nowhere to be found. In the chaos that surrounded the packing of carriages and guests hurrying to breakfast early before starting back to London, no one could remember seeing the man. Geoffrey had looked in the family wing, the common areas, even the servants' quarters. All he learned was that Uncle Joss' longtime valet was missing, too.

Mother, who'd blessedly given him the silent treatment since he'd announced his intention to marry Liliana, had broken it long enough to tell him she hadn't seen Joss since last night's dinner.

Geoffrey bounded up the stairs to the guest hallway. Before he left to search the grounds, he needed to warn Liliana to stay inside. If he was right about Joss suspecting she had knowledge of the treasure's whereabouts, she could be in danger.

He reached her rooms and knocked on the door. He had no desire to besmirch Liliana's reputation by his unorthodox visit, but it was imperative that he fill her in. Besides, they'd be married in three weeks, and any breach of etiquette would be forgiven.

Geoffrey checked his timepiece and banged harder on the door.

The door opened a crack and Liliana's cousin's face appeared. Her eyes widened as she registered him.

"I must speak with Liliana," he demanded without preamble.

Miss Belsham blinked rapidly, but her mouth firmed. Geoffrey realized she was stalling. Something was wrong. Air filled his lungs as adrenaline spiked through him. He rose to his full height.

"Miss Belsham, I demand to know—"

"She's gone." Liliana's cousin said, pinning him with surprisingly hostile blue eyes. She narrowed them, showing uncommon fortitude for a slip of a girl.

"What do you mean *gone*?"

The girl's shoulders slumped and she opened the door wider, inviting him inside. She turned her back and walked over to the nightstand on the far side of the bed. The tiny wooden drawer opened with a creak and she retrieved something. When she returned, she thrust out her hand and opened her palm.

Amethysts and gold winked up at him, the ring a mockery of the excitement he'd felt when he'd chosen it to match Liliana's stunning eyes. When he'd chosen it for the woman he loved . . .

"I mean *gone*. She's left, run away, departed the premises." Miss Belsham glared at him with accusation, as though she was certain it was entirely his fault.

Geoffrey took the delicate betrothal ring from Miss Belsham, stunned. The jeweled band felt heavy in his palm . . . and cold, like a blade of steel poised to stab him through the heart. "Did she say anything to you?"

Miss Belsham sighed. "No. When I awoke this morning, her side of the bed was empty."

Rejection sliced through him. She'd left him without a word, after she'd agreed to marry him. Certainly she hadn't seemed happy about it, but she'd said yes, damn her.

"But she was miserable last night," Miss Belsham said, her voice angry. "I've known Liliana my entire life, and before she met you, I'd never seen her cry. Yet she was a virtual watering pot the whole night through."

Geoffrey winced, remembering a choice few of the awful things he'd said in the last couple of days, the cool way he'd treated her. Was that why Liliana had left? Had he driven her away with his harsh tongue and cold demeanor?

But damn it, that was the only way he knew to protect himself. Still, that didn't make him feel less of a cad.

He looked down at her cousin, afraid of the answer but unable not to ask the question. "Did she say why?"

"Not in particular. But I'm worried. She was unhappy, yes, but also very anxious. And cryptic." The girl frowned, an expression that seemed entirely out of place on her normally open face. "She said that whatever happened, she hoped people would understand why she did it and not judge her harshly." Miss Belsham shook her head. "I can only assume she meant walking out on the betrothal, but that makes no sense."

She hoped people would understand why she did it? Did what? Left the man she was to marry? Unless . . . had her agreement been just another ploy to placate him until she could recover her evidence and avenge her father?

The blood left his face in a dizzying swoop. *Son of a bitch.* What if she'd returned to the folly and took the letters? It wouldn't have taken her long to find them, smart girl that she was. And now she intended to do . . . what? Make his family pay for what they'd done to hers?

Geoffrey let his forehead drop into his hands. He should have known. Liliana came here to solve her father's murder and get justice. She'd risked much, and he'd thwarted her plans. He should have known she wouldn't just let it go. Wouldn't let herself just marry him and sweep it under the rug.

Yet he understood. He wasn't even certain his father *had* been killed, and he was ready to tear into his uncle, his last remaining male family member, to get at the truth.

But damn it all. That didn't make him feel any less a fool. Christ, if only he hadn't opened his heart to her . . . but it was like a door that, once opened, he couldn't slam shut. Geoffrey closed his eyes and let out a pained exhalation. After years of watching his own father suffer the sting of love unrequited, how had he come to this? And how had he underestimated how badly it would hurt?

Still, there was too much at stake. Liliana had to understand that she was sacrificing more than just one life for her family's honor. If his reputation was harmed, and his Poor Employment Act failed, the welfare of too many innocents was at risk. He had to find Liliana and stop her, which meant finding Uncle Joss would have to wait.

Geoffrey gave Miss Belsham a curt nod and turned on his heel, heading for the stables.

"You must think me a great fool, as only a dimwit would take you back to Somerton Park." Wentworth eyed her skeptically, his gaze narrowed.

Liliana tried to keep an indifferent expression on her face, but inside, her heart thumped a frantic beat and her mouth felt like she'd swallowed a drying agent.

"You followed me this morning," she said, certain she was right. "You know I don't have any treasure with me."

Wentworth huffed. "I was certain you'd finally found the treasure and were making off with it, planning to keep it all for yourself."

"Well, you were wrong," she said, quite proud that her voice didn't warble when she spoke. "But you were also right. I did discover the key to finding the treasure, but I knew I wouldn't be able to get it without drawing notice." Her only hope was to keep him convinced that she alone could get the treasure for him. But first she had to get him to take her back to Somerton Park.

"So, I left," she said. "When I departed, I left with nothing. I also left behind an insulting note guaranteed to prick Stratford's pride," she lied. She *had* left the betrothal ring, but she'd been too upset to put any of her feelings into words, deciding instead to make a clean break. "And that's the beauty of my plan. I told him I was returning home and demanded he not follow me. You know how he is . . . all full of duty and honor. He expects people to do what they say they will. He will be so angry at my defection, he won't be able *not* to give chase. He'll be halfway to Chelmsford, never suspecting that I circled back and recovered the treasure on my own. I plan to be long gone before he realizes he's been duped."

One of Wentworth's winged brows rose and his lips thinned into an ugly line. Liliana jutted out her chin just a bit, challenging him to refute her ludicrous explanation.

But she could see his mind working, debating whether she could be believed. *Please, please . . .*

Liliana knew she had only one chance. Geoffrey didn't trust her. Once he discovered her gone, he'd probably suspect she'd double-crossed him and went to the folly to find their fathers' letters. If luck were on her side, he'd arrive at the folly after she and Wentworth, and she'd be rescued. She'd say whatever it took to convince Wentworth the key to finding the treasure was there.

"So I was right about you . . . you were using him to find the treasure," Wentworth said.

"Of course," Liliana answered as loftily as she could manage. "You don't think I actually planned to marry into the family I hold responsible for my father's death, do you?" She scoffed, hoping to come off as greedy as him. Greed understood greed. Maybe, if she sounded convincing enough, he'd believe her. "The treasure should belong to me for all that your family took from me." She looked down at the pistol still lodged against her ribs. "However, I can be persuaded to share, I suppose . . ."

Wentworth laughed, a hollow sound, but better than the agitated desperation he'd exhibited earlier. He called out to the driver to turn the carriage toward Somerton Park, and Liliana nearly wept with relief.

"I'm afraid my debts will devour most of the treasure's worth, my dear, and I'll need the rest to make my escape from England, so there won't be any left for you. However"—he nudged her with the pistol—"since I will be long gone from these shores, I suppose it won't matter if I let you live. If you find the treasure for me and hand it over without a fuss, that is."

Liliana didn't believe that for a moment, but she pretended to contemplate her situation. She let out a forced sigh. "You leave me no choice."

Chapter Twenty-eight

iliana gripped the seat, holding on to avoid being pitched to the floor. She could see little but uneven mounds of wildflower-covered ground through the thin sliver of carriage window beneath the shade.

"Stop the carriage here," Wentworth called out, rapping on the ceiling. The conveyance lurched to a stop.

Liliana released her hold and tried to quell her churning stomach from the wild ride.

The door cracked open and she squinted against the harsh rays of sunlight that illuminated the carriage's interior. She cast her gaze beyond the opening, trying to ascertain where on the property Wentworth had taken her. Panic buzzed in her chest. She didn't recognize anything, not a landmark, not a copse of trees. He could have taken her anywhere.

"Let's go," he ordered, waving the pistol at the door. She moved slowly, inching her way off the seat and toward the opening, scanning the landscape. She'd need to keep her wits about her, look for an opportunity to escape. If she could just discover where she was, perhaps she could run.

Liliana kept her head down, faking submission or at least resignation. Hopefully, Wentworth would consider her less than a threat, giving her time to formulate a

plan. She was glad she'd dressed in boys' togs thi:
morning ... She wouldn't be hampered by skirts if she
chose to flee. She was younger than Wentworth by a
least thirty years, so she might be able to outrun him.

Her eyes flitted to the weapon he kept trained upon her
as she analyzed her chances. A standard flintlock pisto
wasn't known for accuracy, particularly at a moving tar
get. If she could just get ahead of him far enough, he'c
have to stop chasing her in order to aim, and maybe —

"Stay here with the carriage," Wentworth said to the
man on the box. "Keep it at the ready. I'll want to leave
quickly when I return."

When I return. Liliana's stomach dropped despite the
tight reign she kept on her emotions. Either Wentworth
intended to let her go when she gave him the treasure, o
he planned to dispose of her before escaping himself
Neither option boded well, for she hadn't a treasure to
give.

She wondered if she had any chance of appealing to
the driver's humanity to save her, but then he turned hi
face and shock ran through her — it was the man who'c
searched her library. Wentworth must have sent him af
ter the treasure. He would be of no help. She clenched
her fist, drawing a breath meant to calm. She could only
pray that she'd be able to string Wentworth along unti
she found a way out of this mess or until —

Wentworth stepped to her, taking her above the el
bow. "Shall we?"

Liliana nodded, pretending a meekness she didn't feel
Her muscles tensed with adrenaline. She tried to will he
body not to waste the energy before she could use it, bu
it wouldn't listen. Blood pumped through her and he
skin tingled with the anticipation of flight.

Wentworth led her to the edge of the tree line. He wa
taking her into the woods? She could feel the thumpin;
of her heart in her ears as breath became harder and
harder to catch. Had he seen through her ruse? Was h

planning to cut his losses now that she knew him to be a villain?

"Where are you taking me?" she asked, unable to control the fear in her voice.

"You didn't think we'd just enter the front gates and stroll to the folly, did you?" Wentworth scoffed.

Her chest eased. He still planned to take her as far as the folly at least. The rest was up to fate.

Or to Geoffrey. She gambled on his distrust of her, a sorry state of affairs that just might save her life but would ultimately shatter her heart.

As she and Wentworth approached the edge of the forest, the markings of an old footpath became visible. It was well grown over now, but there was a definite, albeit tiny, break in the trees.

They walked in relative silence for several minutes, the noises of nature echoing around them. Wind blew through the trees, birds chirped as they flitted about feeding their young, twigs rustled as small creatures went about whatever business they had. Life in the forest carried on, oblivious to the drama unfolding within it.

A profound regret settled upon Liliana as realization became devastatingly clear. Her time with Geoffrey had shown that she had *stopped* living that long-ago December night when her father had been taken from her. Oh, she'd carried on outwardly, had made plans, had achieved successes, had imposed purpose to her existence. But she hadn't lived where it mattered. She hadn't lived in her heart. She had closed out those around her. She'd never really given people a chance. Not her aunt and uncle, who in their own way had wanted what they thought best for her. Not other girls who had tried to befriend her over the years. Not even men who had expressed interest. She'd never let any of them in, fearing to allow anyone close lest she lose them, too.

Until Geoffrey. He'd broken through her resistance with his gentle prodding, with his sense of humor, with his ability to nettle and challenge her yet his willingness to listen and affirm her. And what had she done? Broken his trust. Broken any chance that he could love her.

She should have told him everything the moment she realized he didn't know about her father. She should have trusted him as the honorable man she knew him to be. But she'd selfishly wanted the magical time with him to never end, and because of that, she'd lost him, too.

And if a miracle didn't happen, she'd never get the chance to tell him that he'd changed her, that he'd unlocked a part of her that maybe, someday, would heal. Though she'd lost his love, she wanted to thank him for opening her heart.

The footpath ended at a small stone circle. The rocks appeared ancient, and weathered boards covered the top. Liliana could now see that the footpath curved around it, heading off to the right.

"What's this?" Liliana asked as they passed.

"A dead well," Wentworth said.

The well Geoffrey had mentioned, which meant they were in the grove of trees behind the folly.

"It used to supply some of the manor's water, but my brother had it closed off when a man from Town told him the water was bad."

Liliana's head came up. Could *that* be how her father had met Geoffrey's?

"Here we are," Wentworth said as they turned another corner. The folly's dome stuck up over the tree line now.

The adrenaline that had been flowing through her now settled like a sickness in her belly. Soon Wentworth would know that she'd lied to him, and who knew what he'd do then? *Please, Geoffrey. Be there.*

And yet part of her prayed he would not be. Geoffrey couldn't be expecting an armed man, much less his uncle. He'd be taken completely by surprise. If Wentworth were as desperate as she suspected, he might not blink at harming Geoffrey, too. Whatever she had to do, she couldn't let that happen.

Wentworth led her to the back entrance. He reached out and tried the door, jiggling the latch when it wouldn't give. "Damn it," he said, kicking the door.

Here was her opportunity to enforce his misconception that she was after the treasure for herself. She pulled the key Geoffrey had given her from her pocket. "Here. I filched the key before I left Somerton Park."

Wentworth turned and looked at her over his shoulder, his eyes narrowing in a speculative gaze.

Liliana tried for a smarmy smile.

He snatched the key from her outstretched hand and turned to open the lock. "You know, Miss Claremont, you're craftier than I'd thought," he said, the words sounding much like a compliment, but to Liliana, they rolled over her like slime. "I knew you were clever, of course. And I was quite impressed by the way you cozied up to my nephew, but going so far as agreeing to marry him publicly and then running off only to double back and double-cross him? Sheer genius." He chuckled as the lock clicked open.

His words evoked dueling emotions. On the one hand, relief that for now, at least, Wentworth seemed to buy her story. On the other, anguish at the thought that Geoffrey might take her actions the same way.

Once Wentworth ushered her inside, he reengaged the double-sided lock and pocketed the key, killing any chance she might have to run. He directed her to open some shutters for light. "Only the ones in the back that can't be seen by passersby."

As the room lightened, Liliana knew she'd run out of time. She'd need to be convincing, stall as long as she could. She decided to be aggressive.

"Now," she said, whirling around as if to convey a great hurry, "we need to find where Geoffrey hid the letters."

"Letters?" Wentworth asked, his face screwing up in confusion.

"Yes," Liliana snapped. "The coded letters your

brother and my father exchanged. My father divulged
where he hid the corselet in his last missive, but before I
could decipher it, Geoffrey took the letters and hid them
here in the folly. That's why I agreed to marry him. To
buy more time at Somerton Park until I could figure out
where he stashed them. When we find the letters, we find
the treasure." Hopefully the search would take some
time, giving either Geoffrey a chance to get there if he
was coming, or her a chance to think of another plan.

Liliana turned her back on Wentworth and pretended
to search the shelf in front of her. He didn't move for
some time, and Liliana held her breath, certain he'd finally seen through her. But then she heard a shuffling
gait followed by the sounds of Wentworth rifling through
Geoffrey's desk.

She prayed she wasn't simply delaying her own demise.

Outside the back window of the folly, Geoffrey froze,
the words floating from the open sash kicking him in the
gut.

*That's why I agreed to marry him. To buy more time at
Somerton Park until I could figure out where he stashed
them. When we find the letters, we find the treasure.*

And yet . . .

In his heart, he knew they weren't true. Not entirely, at
any rate. Though he wasn't certain why Liliana had
agreed to marry him—was afraid indeed that she'd
agreed only so she could stay long enough to retrieve
her evidence—he was the one who'd decoded Liliana's
father's letters, and he knew very well there was nothing
about the location of the treasure in them. Liliana was
shamming someone in there, and he'd wager it was his
uncle. Which meant Liliana could be in danger.

Geoffrey fought to keep panic at bay. He'd need a
clear head if he were to be any help to her. Instincts
honed over a dozen years in the military took over. He
edged closer to the window, hoping to get the lay of the
battlefield before him.

He caught sight of Liliana, only feet from him, and anger threatened to burst through his tight control. Damn his uncle for putting her through this. Liliana's face was pale, and her hand shook as she moved books around on a shelf. She was trying to hide it, but Geoffrey could see her fear growing.

Movement drew his eye to the right, and Joss came into view, pulling items out of Geoffrey's desk drawer and piling them on the surface.

A glint of metal caught the light, buried beneath the papers Joss was haphazardly tossing onto the desk. Could that be a gun? Had Joss threatened Liliana with the weapon? Rage fired his brain, but Geoffrey tamped it down. Knowing Liliana was in immediate danger changed his battle plan entirely. He gauged the shuttered window. Could he get the tip of his own pistol through the slat and fire, killing Joss or even just wounding him enough that he was no longer a threat to Liliana?

He considered the angle of the slat and knew it would be impossible. The shot would have to be fired up and would be well over Joss' head, giving Joss ample opportunity to pull his own weapon and either fire back at Geoffrey or fire at Liliana.

There was no time to return to the house for reinforcements, either.

He'd have to take the man by surprise, then. If he kicked in the back door, Joss' attention would be on him, giving Liliana the chance to run or at least hide. She didn't deserve to be caught up in this. She never should have been. His uncle had done her a horrid disservice, and so had he. He'd apologize a thousand times when this was all over. For now, he needed to save her life and end this thing with his uncle.

Geoffrey slowly ducked below the window and crept toward the back door.

Gooseflesh rose on Liliana's arm. *Geoffrey.* He was near. Though she couldn't see him, her body told her it was so. *He'd come.*

A shadow caught her eye from the left. She glimpsed dark hair moving toward the back door just beneath the window. He was going to try to come through the back door, but it was locked. Even if he'd brought a key, the sound of it clicking the mechanism would give him away.

Liliana's heart kicked into a fluttery rhythm. Geoffrey couldn't know his uncle was armed. He would be shot for sure, and it would be her fault. She was the one who'd run away, who'd allowed herself to be lured into Wentworth's carriage. She'd led the villain here, counting on Geoffrey to save her, knowing it was her only chance.

But she would not be responsible for Geoffrey's death. She'd have to create a distraction when he came into the room. If he were quick thinking, he could take advantage of Wentworth's distraction and get to safety.

She looked around her, scrambling for an idea. She thought about just yelling that she'd found the letters, but that would bring Wentworth to her, making her easily captured and used as a hostage. That would put Geoffrey at a disadvantage, because no matter how angry he was with her, she knew him to be too honorable to just let her be killed. He would try to negotiate for her life, thus endangering his own.

Her eyes lit upon Geoffrey's paint supplies. Oils, rags, brushes . . .

Turpentine—highly flammable, with possible explosive tendencies. That might work. She reached into her pocket, her hand closing around the decorative tinderbox with her experimental accelerant inside. If she could get it lit and drop it inside the container of turpentine, she should have time to move to a safe distance. But even if she couldn't, it wouldn't matter as long as Geoffrey got away.

The door burst open with a loud crash that sent Liliana a foot into the air. Geoffrey must have kicked the door in, aiming for the element of surprise.

Wentworth shrieked like an old woman but quickly swiped his gun from the desk and pointed it at Geoffrey.

Liliana's world stopped moving.

Geoffrey kept his eyes on his uncle's face and tried not to focus on the pistol aimed right at him. His own pistol was cocked and tucked in the waistband of his breeches, behind his back where his uncle wouldn't notice it. He raised his hands slowly. He had to make no sudden movements, had to keep Joss focused solely on him so that Liliana could make it to the door.

As much as he wanted to look upon her, to ensure himself she was fine, he kept his gaze trained on Joss. Geoffrey's chest eased a bit as he glimpsed Liliana inching toward the entrance.

"Are you planning to kill me, Uncle, as you did my father?"

Uncle Joss flinched, but the gun did not. "I hadn't planned to," he finally answered. "I've lived with the guilt of your father's death for years, although things were good for me when your brother was earl. It was easy to divert money when I needed it from beneath his unwatchful eye. But you aren't the fool Henry was. I had hoped to blackmail you long enough to cover my gambling losses—and then I was going to quit. I swear it. But then *she* showed up." Joss bobbed his head in Liliana's direction, but to Geoffrey's relief, he didn't turn to see her inching away. "I recognized her surname, of course, so I knew why she must have come. I figured if I could follow her, figure out where she was searching and get to the corselet first, I could break it up and sell the jewels. I could have paid my debts with no need to involve you, but without it, I may have to kill you after all. Then I will be earl and I can pay what I owe."

Liliana stopped moving toward the door and bent down. Why didn't the foolish woman run? Damn it. If she would just get clear, he could finish this. He needed to keep his uncle talking until she got the hell out of the way.

"Who would loan you so much money you fear for your life?" Geoffrey asked.

"Percenters, a nasty lot of them," Joss answered.

What in the blazes was Liliana doing? Geoffrey couldn't tell, as she was simply a blur in his peripheral vision. He daren't take his eyes off Joss, but he wanted to shout with frustration. She was crouched too close to Uncle Joss, only two arms' lengths away.

"Let me pay your debt," Geoffrey offered, straining for a soothing tone. "Let me get you help for your problem." Though it galled him to say the next, he said it anyway. "You're my family."

Joss' gaze wavered, and it seemed as though he wanted to accept. But then his face hardened. "As if you would help me now that you know I killed your father."

It seemed his uncle wasn't a fool, after all.

"Of course, I'll have to kill Miss Claremont, too," Joss said. He took a quick step back and snatched Liliana up to him, turning the gun on her.

Geoffrey stopped breathing. It took everything in him not to reach for his own weapon. But he'd never be able to kill Joss before the man pulled the trigger, and he couldn't risk Liliana. He dropped to his knees. "Please, Uncle, don't harm her."

Liliana forced herself to hold perfectly still, even though every nerve in her body screamed to get as far away as possible from the explosive she'd just lit. *Four . . . five . . . six . . .* She had no idea how long it would take for the turpentine to ignite, but as contained as it was, when mixed with the ingredients in her tinderbox, she expected at least a flash explosion sometime soo—

The force of the blast knocked Liliana to her stomach. Pain exploded in her head as it came in contact with the floor, and heat licked up her legs, but she paid it no heed, rising to her hands and knees and looking frantically for Wentworth. Screams rent the air behind her, and she whipped around.

Flames ate their way up Wentworth's breeches. He'd dropped to his knees but hadn't lost control of his weapon, which he now aimed at Geoffrey. Liliana turned her head to where Geoffrey was still on his knees. Why hadn't he run, blast it? He reached behind his back, pulling his own weapon, but from the corner of her eye, Liliana saw the flex of Wentworth's hand as he pulled his trigger.

"Geoffrey," she screamed, fear and painful heat overwhelming her.

Two reports filled the room, one slightly before the other. She didn't get a chance to see anything more before she was tackled by a blur and she was being rolled, patted, smothered, and rolled some more before being dragged across the floor.

When she stopped moving, she became aware of a vicious stinging pain encompassing her lower legs. She also realized she was being cradled in Geoffrey's arms. *He's alive.* Her heart soared and tears burned the backs of her eyes. She breathed in, craving his scent of man and mint, but all she could smell was smoke and chemical fumes and something she was distinctly afraid was burned flesh. The pain in her legs grew so much that she didn't think she could bear it, and her head throbbed mercilessly.

"Your uncle?" she croaked.

"Dead." Geoffrey's voice was hoarse.

"How? His weapon was aimed before yours was completely pulled."

Geoffrey hugged her to him, and Liliana moaned against the shift in position. He immediately stilled and pulled back, brushing her hair tenderly from her face as he looked down at her.

"A spoonful of sugar in my powder," he said. "A trick a brilliant chemist once taught me."

"You fool," she said, meaning to tell him that under improper conditions, that trick could have backfired, but before she could get the words out, everything went dark.

Chapter Twenty-nine

Liliana struggled to open her eyes. A sharp sting in her legs and a deep throbbing in her head stole her breath, and her eyelids clamped tight as if her body refused to surface from painless sleep.

Why do I hurt so badly?

She gasped, memories flooding in. The explosion. Wentworth firing his pistol at Geoffrey. Geoffrey cradling her in his arms, stroking her tenderly, almost as if he loved her ...

She jerked to a sitting position, her orbital muscles finally accepting her consciousness and allowing her eyes to open, but she couldn't contain a cry as her legs shifted in the bed.

"You're awake."

Penelope? Blinking as her eyes adjusted, Liliana located Pen sitting in a chair near the head of the bed. She noted the set of Pen's brow, the worried twist of her lips.

"I'll call the doctor." Concern colored her cousin's voice, but not fear. So she'd live, then. "He can give you something more for the pain."

Liliana glanced around her. The celadon draperies and counterpane told her she was back in her room at Somerton Park. She squinted against the light, bringing her hand up to press at the tender knot near her temple. So that was why she felt so muzzy.

"No, no doctor," Liliana rasped, taken aback by the rawness of her throat. She wanted only one thing. "Geoffrey."

Penelope's mouth drooped and she squinted, as though she knew something she didn't want to say.

Liliana's throat closed and her chest tightened as her heart picked up. "Pen?" Liliana didn't even try to disguise her fear. Geoffrey had been fine, hadn't he? Had he been hit and she hadn't noticed because of her own injuries? "What's wrong?"

Penelope twisted in her chair, taking Liliana's hand. Pen's hand seemed overly hot, telling Liliana her own was freezing. "He's fine, Lily, but he's been taken into custody."

"For what? He killed his uncle in self-defense." She shook her head, shifting to a more seated position. "Surely the local magistr—"

"Not for murder," Penelope cut in. "And not by the magistrate."

"Then what?" Liliana asked.

"He was arrested for treason," Penelope said, squeezing Liliana's hand.

Oh God. Liliana's stomach curdled.

"Lord Aveline and some men were waiting for him when he came rushing into the house, carrying you in his arms and shouting for a doctor. They let him settle you in this room, but then they took him away."

"Aveline?"

Penelope nodded. "Yes. Apparently, Aveline is a government agent with the War Department."

And somehow he'd found out that Geoffrey had paid off a government official during wartime and had likely assumed the worst. "Oh no, no," Liliana said, shaking her head as if her denial could make it not so. If Geoffrey were arrested for treason, all that he'd worked for would crumble. He'd lose everything, perhaps even his life. "But he did nothing wrong!" she exclaimed. *Not knowingly, anyway.* But she knew some wouldn't see the difference.

"I know nothing more than I've told you," Penelope said. "Mother is closeted with the countess, insisting you be released from your betrothal and—"

Liliana flung the spread off of her, grimacing as she shifted her legs to the side of the bed.

"What are you doing?" Pen asked, putting a staying hand on Liliana's chest.

"I'm going to find Geoffrey." She shrugged her cousin off. She couldn't allow this to happen. Surely Aveline and whoever was with him would listen to reason. "I'm going to clear this up." And if they wouldn't listen . . . well, she'd think of something.

She gritted her teeth as she stood. She wobbled a bit and looked down. Beneath her night shift, angry red marks covered by a sheen of ointment marred her legs. While her skin was blistered, she could see nothing life threatening. None of the marks looked as if they'd even leave a scar. It just hurt like the very devil.

She took a tentative step, grateful when she felt no additional pain in her feet. The boys' boots she'd worn must have protected them from the flames.

She strode straight for the door and down the hallway. Perhaps she was acting a fool, but she couldn't let this happen. Not that she was certain what she could do to stop it, but Geoffrey shouldn't stand alone, accused, when he was truly the only honorable player in this sad tale.

"You . . . you can't go out in your nightdress," Pen sputtered, following her.

Liliana stopped. Pen was right, of course, and besides, if she had to depart immediately for London, she would need to be properly attired. She turned around and walked back to the room. "Fine. Choose something suitable for travel, but hurry."

While Pen selected a conservative blue riding habit, Liliana cleansed the ointment from her legs. She delved into one of her trunks and selected a concoction of her own making—a combination of aloe and lavender oil, amongst other herbs, with a touch of camphor for pain. Relief was nearly immediate, not only from the sting but also from the realization of how fortunate she'd been—the burns were shallow and confined to mainly her outer calves. She took a tincture of willow bark for her headache, as well, since she knew she'd need to be able to think clearly.

She eschewed Pen's attempts to right her hair and hurriedly dressed, dashing for the staircase the moment the last lace was pulled. Reaching the bottom, she started across the central hall, determined to discover where Geoffrey had been taken and then get there by whatever means necessary.

The butler stood near the closed library doors, facing away from her.

"Where is Lord Stratford?" she demanded.

The man jumped at her barked question, his eyes widening. She imagined she must look a fright with her hair so unkempt and out of breath from her dash, but she didn't care. All that mattered was seeing Geoffrey and convincing Aveline of his innocence.

"Where have they taken him?"

The butler pursed his lips. "Lords Stratford and Aveline are inside, miss, along with their"—he cleared his throat—"guests," he said, indicating the library door.

Liliana moved to open the door, but the butler stepped between her and the knob.

"I'm not to allow anyone in," he said, rather officiously.

Liliana raised herself, looking down her nose as she'd seen her aunt do many times. She lowered her voice and leaned in closer to the man. "You do realize that I am going to be mistress of this house very soon," she said. Though she still had no intention of entering into a loveless marriage with Geoffrey, she wasn't above bending the truth in order to get to him. "I daresay the transition will go easier for you if *step aside right this moment*."

He blinked. His jaw didn't drop, but Liliana could see that he held his placid expression with effort. He stared at her, probably debating how much of a threat she truly was. She added a scowl and hoped it was nearly as fierce as the ones Geoffrey had turned on her in the past days.

Without a word, the butler moved away from the door.

Liliana took a deep breath, finger combing hair that felt like straw beneath her hands. She had one last theory to test, and for Geoffrey's sake, she hoped she was right.

"Just a few more questions, Stratford, and then you can check on your lady love," the Duke of Wellington said with a chuckle.

Geoffrey brought his gaze back to his guests from where it had strayed toward the door yet again. Only the fact that the doctor had promised to fetch him if there was any change had kept him from Liliana's side this long, respect for his former commander be damned.

"Yes," said another white-haired gentleman seated near the fireplace, legs crossed, cravat neatly tied. "We must be absolutely certain that no one outside of this house gets wind of this story, else all we've worked for will be for naught."

Geoffrey turned to the man. "No need to worry, Robert. My uncle admitted to being the blackmailer before he died and we have his valet in custody, so we should have no worries in that quarter. As for—"

The door burst open with a startling bang as the ancient wood knocked against the shelf behind it. All four men in the room automatically turned to the door, three tensing as if for battle like the ex-soldiers they were.

"Liliana?" Geoffrey shot to his feet. Surprise turned quickly to relief, lifting his heart and the corners of his lips as he saw with his own eyes that she was well. Then he registered the pale hue of her skin and her obvious upset. His face settled into a frown. "Sweet, you shouldn't be out of bed," he murmured, crossing to her.

She stormed right past him, making a beeline for Aveline, whose typically blasé expression turned quite comical at her aggressive approach. Even when they had been boys, Geoffrey had never seen the man back away from anything in his life, and yet Aveline took a step away from Liliana.

"I demand you release him," she commanded, causing Aveline's black brows to shoot even higher. "He's done nothing wrong."

"Miss Claremont," Aveline said, "We know Stratford paid the bribe—"

"Because his father asked him to without telling him what it was!"

Geoffrey took a step toward Liliana. After what she'd been through today, she shouldn't tax herself so on his behalf. He opened his mouth to tell her so, but she stayed him with a hand.

"Listen, Aveline," she said, her voice softening. "You've known Geoffrey for years. I've known him for only a couple of weeks, but we both know that regardless of what evidence you have, he would never do anything to betray his country. He is an honorable man, who has much to offer the world."

Aveline looked over at Geoffrey, clearly uncomfortable.

"Whereas my father is dead," Liliana continued, and for a moment, her voice warbled. But then she took a breath. "He made the decision to involve himself in this mess. Geoffrey didn't. If you must have someone to blame, I can give you the perfect means to tie up this mess, placing the fault entirely with my father and leaving Geoffrey and his family out of it."

Geoffrey swallowed. Was Liliana trying to save him? He should tell her that—

"What means?" Wellington asked. Geoffrey started

at the booming voice, having forgotten there were others in the room, so intent had he been on the exchange between Liliana and Aveline. He shot his friend and ex-commander a scowl for dragging things out unnecessarily.

Liliana flinched as well but turned to Wellington and squared her shoulders. "In all of your questioning, has Geoffrey told you where the treasure is?"

Three men answered in the negative.

Liliana nodded. "Nor will he, because he doesn't know, and neither did his father."

She finally darted her gaze at him, but Geoffrey's stomach clenched with uncertainty at what her enigmatic look could mean.

She turned her face back to Wellington. "But *my* father did," she said. "And so do I."

Geoffrey's heart stuttered. "What?" He couldn't help the question that slipped through his lips. That made no sense. She'd have told him—or at least told his uncle, to save her own life. She *couldn't* have known all this time.

Liliana didn't look back at him, however. She kept her gaze trained on Wellington. "And I will lead you to it on one condition—that whatever story you choose to bandy about regarding its discovery places the blame solely on my father, and in no way taints the earldom or Geoffrey's reputation. You know as well as I that Geoffrey will do great things for his fellow man. My father would have, too, had he lived. In this small way," she said, a tear slipping silently down her cheek, "he still can."

Further questions died on his lips, and yet Geoffrey's heart beat back to life. Whatever else was going on here, Liliana loved him. Why would she sacrifice her father's honor for his unless it was so? That the point was moot mattered not. It still took everything in him not to pull her to him and kiss her senseless, regardless of who else was in the room.

"You realize, young lady," Wellington said, "that you

would be forever known as the daughter of a traitor. You would be willing to live with that?"

Geoffrey frowned. No one was going to be branded a traitor. "I hardly th—"

"I am," Liliana said, "if it means that Geoffrey's name remains clear."

Geoffrey's mouth snapped shut, stunned at the gravity of Liliana's words.

Robert stood, inserting himself into the conversation. "That's very admirable, my dear, but quite unnecessary. Come, Wellington, Aveline." He motioned for the men to follow him. "We'll give you two a few moments alone, before Miss Claremont takes us to this treasure. Shall we meet outside, then, in, say, ten minutes?"

Geoffrey nodded absently, his gaze fixed on Liliana.

Robert clapped him on the shoulder as he walked past. "And you said she didn't love you," he murmured as the three men departed.

"Wellington?" Liliana finally said, her eyes wide. "As in, the Duke of?"

Geoffrey nodded. "Yes."

"Then who was the man—?"

"Liverpool," Geoffrey answered.

"The prime minister?" She touched her hair, patting it as her cheeks bloomed with color. "I look a fright. What must they have been thinking?" Liliana muttered, covering her face with her hands.

Geoffrey stood in silence, his throat stinging, forcing him to swallow. "They were thinking how damned lucky I am to be marrying you."

Her head snapped up. Then she began to shake it. "I don't understand what just happened."

"But I do," Geoffrey said. She'd risen from her sickbed in certain pain, charged downstairs and challenged three very important men on his behalf. Liliana, whose goal it had been to find justice for her father at all costs, had just tossed the man under the carriage in order to save him, Geoffrey.

A selfish, deceitful woman would never do such a thing. His mother would never do such a thing. But Liliana was not his mother.

He stepped to her, reaching to take her in his arms. All of the love and hope he'd bottled up burst into his chest and threatened to bubble over.

But Liliana backed away. "Then explain. Penelope told me Aveline had arrested you for treason."

Geoffrey sighed, knowing she deserved enlightenment, and he wanted some explanations of his own. His apologies would have to wait. "Aveline did come to Somerton Park to arrest me for treason. He'd been working in France and had heard that an influential Briton had been involved in paying off an official of Napoleon's, though it was unclear for what. Naturally, the War Department was very interested, so Aveline was assigned to delve into the matter. He came to the house party for the same reason as you—to investigate."

"Then why did he leave so suddenly?"

"He got a tip that took him back to France, where he uncovered part of Triste's story. Unfortunately, nothing about the treasure, only that Triste had been executed for treason, which, ironically, made my connection to him seem more nefarious."

"So Aveline thought you were a traitor, too," Liliana concluded.

Geoffrey nodded. "Yes, and he was sent to arrest me Quietly. Wellington and Liverpool insisted upon accompanying him, however, determined to hear the explanation for themselves. Wellington, in particular, didn't believe it."

"But he does now?"

"No. Thanks to our fathers' letters, they have all the evidence they need to prove the true nature of the endeavor, and while what I did could technically be considered treason, none of the men wished to pursue it further."

"Oh God." Liliana closed her eyes, her charcoal lashes

fanning against the faint purple circles below. She looked exhausted as well as embarrassed. "I just made a fool of myself, then."

Tears pricked the back of Geoffrey's eyes as he considered what Liliana had thought she was giving up for him. "No, love. Never a fool." Indeed, he'd been the fool, and he'd do everything he could for the next fifty years to make it up to her. However, first he needed to ask, "Were you bluffing about the treasure?"

Liliana slowly shook her head. "No. At least not intentionally. I'm pretty certain I know where it is."

"Where?" Geoffrey couldn't help the tightness in his voice. Until this moment, the treasure had been an afterthought, a chimera—not a tangible thing that at least three men had been killed for, including his father.

"I'd wager it is in the old well behind the folly," Liliana said.

"The well?" He searched his memory. "The one my father had closed?"

"Yes," Liliana said. "This morning, your uncle mentioned as we passed it that a 'man from Town' had advised your father that it was dangerous."

What was it Liliana had said that day at the mine? *My father spent his life studying the effects of contaminated air and water on the human body.* And at once, it clicked. It must have been Charles Claremont who had advised his father to close the well. *That* was how the two men had become acquainted.

"I don't know why I didn't think of it before," Liliana said. "All of the notes between our fathers had been coded, *except* the last one your uncle forged. Father *must* have been suspicious when he received it. It only makes sense that he would suspect something was not right, and hide the treasure."

"So you think he might have brought the treasure here and lowered it into the dead well he'd sealed off two years earlier?"

"Yes. Then, if the meeting was legitimate, he could tell

your father its location, and if not, the treasure would remain safe."

"Undisturbed all of these years . . . And right under my uncle's nose the entire time," Geoffrey murmured. Indeed, if Liliana were correct, it had been here even before his own father had been killed for it. A long-familiar ache squeezed his chest . . . Senseless death, all of it.

A discreet tapping interrupted his thoughts. Barnes' balding pate appeared in the doorway. "My lord, Lords Liverpool, Wellington and Aveline await you in the entry."

"Of course." Geoffrey turned back to Liliana and offered her his arm, as much to draw from her strength in this surreal moment as it was an offer of his own. "Come, let us finish this. We must lay our past to rest before we can look to our future."

Our future.

Twenty minutes later, Liliana dismounted, tying Amira next to the other four horses at the post near the folly.

She glanced at Geoffrey, so achingly handsome in the waning afternoon sun as he hefted the hastily assembled bag of supplies they'd brought with them—a length of rope, mallets, strips of clean cloth, an old spyglass.

Our future.

What had he meant? This moment *was* their future, and once it was over, so were they. She'd be forever grateful to Geoffrey for bringing her heart back to life, but she still had no intention of dooming them both to a marriage without love on both sides.

Liverpool and Wellington carried lanterns. Though light still cascaded through the treetops, it would fade quickly. And the interior of the well would be dark, at best.

"It's not far," Liliana said, leading the group to the overgrown footpath through the woods. "Only a dozen yards or so." Several feet in, a bramble caught at her skirt, and Liliana bent to tug it free.

"May I help?" Geoffrey's low voice caused a shiver as he knelt beside her.

"No, thank you," she said, giving her skirt a yank. She winced as a thorn bit at the back of her ankle.

"Do your burns pain you?" Geoffrey asked, his features colored with concern.

Liliana glanced up to tell him she felt fine but was quickly drawn into his intense cobalt gaze. How nice it would be to simply stay there for an eternity, lost in his eyes. She blinked, breaking the spell. *Concern is not love,* she reminded herself. Both of them had been through a horrible scare today. Geoffrey was too honorable and decent a man *not* to be concerned about her well-being, just as he would any person's. But she mustn't forget that he was able to rescue her at the folly today only because he'd gone there thinking she'd betrayed him. How long before his natural concern faded and the cold, distrustful Geoffrey returned? No matter how much she longed to seek shelter in his arms now, she couldn't marry him. It would be unfair to them both. "No. I am fine."

Geoffrey rose as she did and they continued their trek into the forest.

Moments later, the well came into view. The small structure was crafted from ancient stone, its mortar crumbling in places but still strong. Nails had been driven through weathered boards, barring the well from use.

Liliana stepped up to the stones, reaching her hand out and running it across the boards. The rough, striated wood was hard beneath her fingertips, the iron nail heads cold. Had her father driven these nails himself? When he'd said to find *them* at summer, had he meant the jewels rather than the letters?

"Step back, Miss Claremont," Aveline instructed.

Harsh strikes of mallet on wood and the wrenching

crack of old boards giving way filled the forest as Geoffrey and Aveline set to breaking them free. Liverpool and Wellington held the lanterns, letting the younger men do the physical work.

As a gaping black circle appeared, the musty aroma of damp moss permeated the air—neither pleasant nor unpleasant, simply overwhelming.

As the last of the boards were cleared, Geoffrey ran a hand along the inside rim. "I feel nothing, not even a rope from which anything could dangle."

Liliana peered over the side but saw only blackness. She bent to gather a small stone, then tossed it over the side and waited . . . and waited . . . *splash*. The distant echo of stone hitting water drifted back up. Newton's apple, it was a long way to the bottom—too far for them to search tonight, certainly.

Still, she didn't think her father would just toss the treasure into an open hole without giving himself a way to retrieve it. She supposed if he had dangled it from a rope, fourteen years of musty air might have weakened it enough to snap, but likely not.

"Tie a rope to one of the lanterns," she suggested. "Let us lower it in and see if we spot anything."

Geoffrey complied, and Liliana bounced on her toes, anticipation racing through her as a glowing ring of light slowly spread the darkness. Though finding the treasure had no bearing on Geoffrey's freedom, as she'd first thought, she realized she wanted desperately to discover it. Geoffrey was right about one thing . . . *she* needed to lay the past to rest, so she could look to *her* future. She scanned the stone walls as the lantern dipped lower, and lower still.

"There!" she cried, spotting a roughly hewn spike protruding from the wall of the well, a length of rope knotted around it. She reached her arm back, snapping her fingers while keeping her eyes fixed on the spot. "The spyglass."

A heavy coolness filled her hand, and she whipped the

spyglass around, holding it to her eye and squinting to focus. Tiny unraveled strands came into view, standing from the thick rope like the tiny hairs on the back of her neck. "Keep lowering," she commanded.

She trained the spyglass to follow the rope in time with the shaft of light until— "I see a bundle." She tightened her grip. There it was, a cloth-wrapped package tied to the rope in a simple square knot she'd seen her father tie a hundred times, yet the end was completely out of reach.

She turned away from the well, stomach churning with a cheerless excitement, and walked over to the sack of supplies. She replaced the spyglass and pulled out another length of rope, tying it around her waist.

"What are you doing?" Geoffrey asked, his voice low and incredulous rather than curious.

Liliana looked over her shoulder as Geoffrey handed the rope bearing the lantern to Aveline and started toward her. She frowned at him. "I'm securing the rope so that you may lower me into the well."

Four male voices erupted in protest around her, Geoffrey's loudest of all.

"*I* will be going in," he insisted, his hands snaking around her waist to work at the knot she'd already gotten cinched tight.

Cursed awareness burned through her at his nearness, and at the deft fingers moving against her, albeit through her clothing, as he worked the knot loose. "That's— that's ridiculous." She cleared her throat. "I am the lightest, and the least valuable should a slip occur. Every one of you is, or will be"—she glanced at Aveline—"a Peer of the Realm, and besides that, it is my father who placed the treasure here. It is only right that I should be the one to retrieve it."

Nonetheless, Geoffrey tugged the rope from around her waist, bringing his lips close to her ear. "You are the *most* valuable one here. To me," he murmured, then turned away, leaving Liliana in stunned silence.

Geoffrey looped the rope around himself, tossing the other end to Wellington, who walked it around a young tree trunk. Aveline handed off the lantern rope to Liverpool and braced himself against the outer stone of the well to help Geoffrey ease over the side and begin his descent.

You are the most valuable one here. To me. Liliana blinked to clear her head. She hadn't time to dwell on Geoffrey's odd words. She rushed over to the well, peering over the side. Lantern light glistened against the blackness of Geoffrey's hair as he carefully picked his way down. Wellington had joined Aveline in lowering Geoffrey's weight, but their faces grimaced with the strain.

"Here," Liliana said, taking the rope bearing the lantern from Liverpool's hands. He nodded in understanding and joined the other men.

Several tense but silent moments later, Geoffrey's voice erupted from the well.

"I have it."

Chapter Thirty

Barnes exited the library after delivering the hot water and rags Geoffrey had requested, and had been tasked, once again, with keeping any and all others from entering the room. Geoffrey had to give the butler credit. The man had colored and shot a look at Liliana, probably embarrassed at having failed to keep *her* out earlier, but otherwise hadn't blinked an eye, even given the fact that Geoffrey was covered in dust and dirt and the others, including the prime minister of the bloody country, were rather disheveled.

Liliana stood apart from the men, still clutching the bundled treasure to her chest, much as she had done since he'd handed it to her at the well.

At least she no longer had that stricken look upon her face, the one that mirrored how he was feeling inside, how he had been feeling since the moment he'd touched the cursed treasure both of their fathers had given their lives for.

Still, her shoulders slumped and she wouldn't lift her gaze from the floor. Unease spread through Geoffrey. Yes, she was no doubt exhausted, and might very well be dealing with the reality of her father's last actions, but something else was wrong. He was certain.

She hadn't looked at him—really looked at him—

since this afternoon in the folly . . . well, except for that moment when he'd knelt next to her as she'd tried to free herself from the thorn bush. But then only because he'd startled her, and she'd looked away as quickly as she could.

Even when he'd handed the bundle up to her from the well . . . Call him mad, but it was as if she'd gone out of her way to make sure her hands didn't touch his.

His disquiet multiplied. Despite her actions earlier in this very room, she wasn't acting like a woman in love.

What if the reality of today's discoveries had been too much for her? She'd learned for certain that his uncle, a member of his family, had murdered her father. Bloody hell, she was holding the proof in her hands this very moment. Or worse, Geoffrey knew he closely resembled his uncle. What if Liliana couldn't bear to look at him, much as he'd been unable to countenance being in a room alone with Joss, who'd reminded him so much of his own father? What if she couldn't reconcile her feelings? What if he lost her?

"Let's have a look." Liverpool's words drew his attention back to the task at hand. Still, as much as Geoffrey wanted to see what the bundle contained, he was more anxious to have this over with so he could get Liliana alone and figure out what troubled her.

Liliana brought the treasure over to the spindly table Geoffrey and Aveline had dragged near the fireplace as an impromptu staging area and placed it in the center. He and the other men gathered round, and only then did Liliana lift her gaze to him. He knew what she was asking. He gave her a nod.

Her capable hands trembled only a little as she untied the rope and unfolded the fabric. The treasure appeared to also be wrapped in protective leather, which Liliana deftly disposed of.

Geoffrey leaned forward, not breathing as a flash of green caught his eye.

Liliana lifted the corselet, slowly unfolding the

golden ... *garment*, he supposed would be the appropriate word. Maybe *vest*—if one could use such a word to describe something of such splendor.

"Good God." That from Wellington, who'd seen much in his days but certainly nothing like this.

The others, Geoffrey himself included, seemed at a loss for words as Liliana lifted the magnificent piece of royal jewelry. Gold chain strung together dozens of square emeralds as a collar, glittering in the firelight. Another cluster of hundreds of the green gems joined together in a band, nearly the width of a Hindi cummerbund, which would circle the wearer and was attached to the collar by gold chain mail. And strung at the chest and back were two of the largest square-cut emeralds Geoffrey could even imagine, much less had ever seen.

"This could only have belonged to a queen," Liverpool murmured.

"I remember my father saying that Cleopatra prized emeralds over all other stones and was responsible for bringing the gem to such fashion in the world," Geoffrey remarked. "It must have belonged to her."

"I can't even begin to fathom its worth," said Aveline.

Geoffrey couldn't, either, but he could see why his uncle had wanted it so badly. Even if the man had never touched the larger stones, the hundreds of smaller ones could have been sold off and kept him well for years to come.

"Whatever its value, it's not that of three men's lives," Liliana said, tears glistening in her eyes even as she held the corselet reverently.

Geoffrey turned the Bramah lock on the parlor safe in his study, securing the corselet until Liliana decided what she wanted to do with it. He slanted his eyes to her now, where she paced in front of his desk. The others had long departed, claiming reports to write and such. He'd been glad to see them go, but now that he had Liliana alone, fear kept him from asking her what was truly in her heart. Instead, he asked the easy question. "Have you any idea what you'd like to do with the corselet?"

She stopped and looked up, seemingly startled by his voice. Her eyes strayed to the safe and her brows dipped, giving Geoffrey the impression that the treasure was the furthest thing from her mind. Which led him to think that her troubled expression did, indeed, have something to do with him. His throat tightened.

"I can't keep it," she said. Despite her protests, the consensus of the men was that the treasure should belong to her. Aveline reported that Triste had no heirs, and Liverpool decreed that since Triste had given the corselet over to Liliana's father, it should by rights go to his daughter. He only asked that Liliana be discreet, should questions arise.

Geoffrey considered urging Liliana to take to her bed, to get some rest and look at things with fresh eyes tomorrow. But he knew that wasn't in her nature, and besides, the idea of passing the night not knowing what Liliana was thinking made him shudder. He couldn't risk waking up in the morning only to find she'd run off again.

"You could sell it, I suppose," he said. "I'm certain your father would have liked for you to have the security that kind of wealth would offer." But the conversation felt lame upon his tongue. It was time he quit acting the coward and broach the subject that really mattered. "Of course, you have no need of any more security than you'll have as my wife."

Liliana looked down, almost as if in shame, and something inside Geoffrey withered.

"I will not be your wife."

Even though he'd known in his gut that was what she'd say, her words still pierced him. "I know today's revelations have been a shock," he said, not even minding the desperation in his voice. Good God, he'd nearly lost her before his very eyes today, and just that glimpse had shown him he couldn't bear not having her in his life.

"But, Liliana, please, given some time I pray you can forgive my unfortunate family connection—"

"It's not that, Geoffrey." She tilted her head. "Do you think I would hold you responsible for your uncle's actions?"

Panic squeezed his chest. If that wasn't the reason . . . "Then why?"

Liliana's face crumpled and she turned away from him, taking with her his very heart. "Do you know why I convinced your uncle to take me to the folly today?"

Geoffrey gave a slow shake of his head, as sound would simply not squeeze past the constriction in his throat.

"Because I knew that was my best chance to be rescued. I knew once you discovered I was gone you would immediately assume I'd betrayed you again and doubled back to get those letters." Everything in her posture, from the defensive way she wrapped her arms around her torso to how she slunk back from him, cried out her hurt.

Geoffrey closed his eyes so she wouldn't see his shame.

"There can never be love without trust, Geoffrey, and you don't trust me." Her voice broke. "Therefore, you will never love me." He heard a rustle of fabric and then her hand slipped into his, and she gave him a gentle squeeze.

He opened his eyes, staring down into shimmering violet pools.

"And life is too short to live without love," she said. "For both of us." She sighed, and a watery smile crossed her face. "I never knew I wanted love in my life until I met you. And I thank you for teaching me that." She took a shuddering breath. "And I'm sorry I lied to you. My intention was never to hurt you, but I did and I was wrong. You deserve better."

Liliana let go of his hand. "I hope one day, a woman comes along who earns your trust *and* your love." She moved to walk away from him.

Geoffrey couldn't catch his breath. He couldn't just let her leave.

He dropped to his knees, snagging her hand as she brushed by.

She stopped and turned her head, doubt and hope mingling in her face.

And that hope gave him hope. Dear God, *she did love him*, he knew it. And yet she was just as certain he didn't love her. Simple words of love would never suffice after the things he'd said to her. What *could* he say to make her believe him?

"I lied to you, too," he said.

The corners of her kissable lips turned down in confusion.

"When I told you that love didn't matter." Geoffrey knew that nothing short of baring himself to Liliana would make her understand, would make her trust his love. He swallowed the emotion clogging his throat, desperate for his words to come through strong and clear. "When I told you that I'd never love you—that I didn't love you—it wasn't true." He drew in a deep breath. "I didn't *want* to love you, but I couldn't help myself."

Liliana didn't move, only stared, her eyes glassy and disbelieving.

"I told myself you were selfish and manipulative like my mother, but I could feel regret radiating off of you. My mother doesn't have a remorseful bone in her body. I was a fool to think you were anything like her," he murmured. "Some things can be faked, but not the core part of a person, not who they are underneath. And your intelligence, your spirit, your passion for the well-being of others—all of the things I *love* about you—I knew to be real. But in my anger and my hurt, I didn't want to see it."

Geoffrey reached out and took her other hand, and his hopes leapt at her tight grip, as if at least some part of her didn't want to let him go. If he could convince her of the truth of his feelings for her, maybe she wouldn't feel she had to.

"Later in life, my father admitted he'd known who the countess was on the inside. He'd just foolishly hoped his love could change her. But I don't want to change anything about you. Certainly, I'd like to change the circumstances that brought us together. I wish you hadn't felt the need to lie to me, but I understand why you did. And I forgive you."

A tremble ran through Liliana, and a single tear slipped from her eye, but she didn't release her grip on his hands. "You say you love me, but by you going immediately to the folly, your actions show me differently. There can be no love without—"

"Trust?" He blew out a breath, knowing he was on shaky ground. "I won't lie—the thought did cross my mind. So much has happened in the past few days, so many pillars of my life upended. But I think you've got it backward. With love, there can be trust. It will grow. It's already started."

She said nothing.

Geoffrey's chest squeezed. Had he been too late in declaring his feelings? Had he lost her?

He pulled her hands to his lips, brushing her petal-soft skin against his mouth. "Dear God, Liliana," he whispered, "I love you so much." His voice caught, as if it alone understood that by admitting his love, his vulnerability, she could use it to push him around like so many pieces on a chessboard. But he no longer cared. It was more important to show her that he trusted her to do with his love as she pleased. "I *love* you. And I'm sorry, more than I can say. Please, forgive me. Marry me." A hot tear slipped down his cheek. "Love me."

And he gave her a little tug. Nothing that would upend her if she didn't wish to come, but enough to let her know that she was wanted, needed. Another tear followed the first when she dropped to her knees along with him.

"I do," she whispered. "Oh, Geoffrey, I do."

He moaned, clasping her to him with all of his strength. A part of him registered that she held him equally tight. "Liliana," he said, pulling back so that he could see her eyes, but he couldn't long resist the need to kiss her, nor to run his hands over her hair, her face, anywhere he could touch to assure himself she was real, was here, had chosen to stay with him. She tasted of apples and honey and salty tears . . . and of happiness and promise and love.

Her tongue delved past his lips and desire flooded him, raging through his body nearly as fiercely as his love. Yet he reined it in. After the events of the day, Liliana must be exhausted. And they had their whole lives . . . "Sweet, you need your rest—"

His bold little scientist cut him off with a voracious kiss of her own, her hand trailing down his stomach and caressing him. "I need you more than I need rest," she said, breaking her kiss. "I need this—to make love with you knowing that there is nothing between us. No lies, no secrets, just need."

"Just need," he whispered. Dear God, there was that. He let his reins go, setting his hands free to roam over her. His lips trailed to her cheek, which had flushed with heat. He could feel her excitement, smell it radiating from her skin, and it spurred his own.

"One day," he gasped, pulling at her skirts as her own hands tore at the fall of his trousers, "I'd like to actually make love to you in a bed."

Her throaty chuckle sent a shiver racing down his spine, and the touch of her hand on his bare cock sent it racing back up again. He shifted from his knees to a sitting position, spreading Liliana across his lap.

"Don't you think a bed would be rather conventional for your lady chemist wife?" she teased.

Geoffrey's only answer was a harsh groan as he slid inside her wet heat. He held her tight to him, fully seated, fully surrounded by her for as long as he could stand it.

Then he lifted her hips and started the rhythm he knew would bring them both to fiery completion.

"My lady chemist wife," he said when he could breathe, and hugged her tighter to him. Liliana certainly filled his life with chemistry of the very best kind.

And he would do his very best to fill hers with love.

Epilogue

June 16, 1817

"Quite a day it's been, hasn't it, my love?" Geoffrey wrapped his arms around his wife's soon-to-be-expanding waistline, discreetly caressing the life that lay within.

Liliana pushed at him. "Not in front of all of these people," she whispered, blushing to the roots of her chestnut locks, which glowed with the sheen of impending motherhood. Or happiness. He liked to think both. "What if someone should guess?"

He chuckled, moving his hands away from her middle. He knew she intended to keep her condition secret for a few weeks longer—at least until after they traveled to Penelope's surprise wedding.

Just this morning, Liliana had been by his side as the Poor Employment Act of 1817 was signed into law and commissioners were appointed who had the authority to loan money for up to three years to those who could demonstrate they would use it to create employment opportunities.

And now here they were, surrounded by their family. Liliana and her aunt had made both amends and apologies and seemed to be settling into a comfortable relationship. As for he and his mother—well, she'd attended the wedding and, to his surprise, had even come along this morning. Though he couldn't ever foresee great warmth between them, perhaps there was hope for peace.

"I wish they could be here to see this," Liliana said, and Geoffrey knew she meant their fathers.

He looked out at the assemblage—scholars, scientists, philanthropists and the curious alike—eagerly awaiting a glimpse of Cleopatra's corselet, which had been the talk of the town when Liliana had worn it in their wedding, and which had then been generously donated to the British Museum by Lord and Lady Stratford.

As the director of the museum began his speech, filled with half-truths about how the corselet came to be in British hands, and dedicating the donation to Lord Edmund Wentworth and Sir Charles Claremont, Geoffrey watched his wife.

He sent up silent thanks to their fathers. Without their having met, he'd never have found Liliana. Geoffrey kissed the top of her head, hugging her to him.

"Your father would have been very proud of you," he said.

She turned in his arms. "And yours would have loved to see the man you've become."

Geoffrey smiled, content. Yes, his father would have been happy, for his son had finally learned what it meant to love and be loved.

Author's Note

I hope you enjoyed reading *Sweet Enemy*. The spark of idea for this story came from my visit to the Linda Hall Library of Science, Engineering and Technology in Kansas City, Missouri, which was hosting an exhibition on Napoleon's scientific expedition to Egypt. While perusing the fascinating display, I learned that Napoleon abandoned his scientists there and that the British, while rescuing them, also confiscated their findings. I started to wonder, *What if? What if a French scientist had been able to sneak out a valuable treasure*... Then I had to decide who that French scientist would try to enlist to help him fence said treasure, which led me to an English scientist—Liliana's father—and a story, and his daughter was born.

Of course, while creating the character of Liliana, I had to delve into the chemistry of the time, to really discover what made her who she was. The late eighteenth and nineteenth centuries were exciting times in the world of chemistry. Arguably the two best-known "fathers of modern chemistry" were the English scientist Joseph Priestly and his French counterpart Antoine Lavoisier. Lavoisier, however, distinguished himself above all others and is credited with starting the Chemical Revolution in 1789 with the publication of his paper "Elements of Chemistry." Moreover, he encouraged modern chemists to begin investigating and disproving the long-held hypothesis of the ancient Greeks, and he conducted some of the first truly quantitative chemical experiments, a crucial jump that would lead to the rapid advancement of chemistry in his age. Tragically, his life was cut short upon the guillotine in a political move during the Reign of Terror. A year and a half later, Lavoisier was exonerated as wrongly convicted as a traitor, but the world had lost a true genius.

It was during this time that Liliana's father would have been working as a chemist. Charles Claremont started out in the fields of eudiometry and pneumatic medicine, philosophies that believed that there were "bad airs," which were detrimental to the health and safety of the public and could be measured around marshes, sewers, cemeteries and the like, and "good airs," which could heal a body through their inhalation. Claremont would have naturally carried his studies into the quality of water, as well.

By the time Liliana would have come into her own as a scientist, the field of eudiometry had been mostly debunked. However, she took her father's dreams to better the health of humankind a step further, trying to isolate the chemicals within living things so that they might be re-created and reproduced medicinally. She would have been just a little ahead of her time... Between 1826 and 1828, a German chemist, Johann Andreas Buchner, and a French chemist, Henri Leroux, did just what Liliana was attempting to do—isolated salicin from willow bark. Salicylic acid would later become the main ingredient of aspirin.

I chose to use the modern names for some of the chemical substances you read in the story. While sodium chloride and sodium sulfate, for example, were well-known, experimented with and easily produced, they would have been called by different names you mightn't have recognized. Therefore, for the ease of the modern reader, I put the more familiar names in the book.

Margaret Cavendish, the Duchess of Newcastle, was indeed the first woman allowed to attend a meeting of the Royal Society—and only once, in May of 1667. The first paper written by a woman to be presented at the Royal Society was by an astronomer named Caroline Herschel in 1798. Another wouldn't be presented until Mary Somerville's paper on magnetism in 1826. Of course, neither woman was allowed to present the papers herself—they were read to the Society by Herschel's brother and Somerville's husband, respectively, as women were not allowed to attend meetings of the Royal Society.

As for Liliana's hope to become the first woman member of the Royal Society? Sadly, she wouldn't have lived to see it. The first woman was not admitted until 1945, though Queen Victoria was made an "honorary member."

Don't miss the next novel in the
Veiled Seduction series,

SWEET DECEPTION

Available in August 2012
from Signet Eclipse

Derbyshire, August 1817

The medieval tower rose high and proud above the bilberry heath covering the castle's grounds, its vibrant red bricks proclaiming it a foreigner among a plateau of white limestone. Derick Aveline, Viscount Scarsdale, exhaled with a snort—he certainly knew what *that* felt like.

If there was one place on earth he'd hoped never to set eyes upon again, his northernmost family estate was certainly it. He supposed that would surprise most people, given the dangerous and often unpleasant spots he'd been to over the years. But these lush rolling hills and deep, narrow valleys of his childhood boded ominously and more treacherously for his well-being than even the filthiest of French prisons that had once held him.

With a sharp tap of his heel, Derick directed his steed down the knoll and onto the lane as a wealth of memories he'd thought long locked away assailed him. The restless boy he'd been, roaming the hills and dales of White Peak, with endless summer days stretching out before him. His mother's red-rimmed eyes, looking at him with alternating sadness and indifference. The last day he'd seen this patch of England, the day his identity had crumbled away like the ancient limestone the area was named for.

Gravel crunched beneath his stallion's hooves as they entered the stable yard, shaking Derick from his thoughts. He'd been a fool to come back. If not for this last mission for the Crown, he would have never returned. But he always did what must be done for love of country.

Even when it wasn't his country to love.

"Boy!" Derick called out, throwing his leg over his saddle and dismounting. He rolled his shoulders, stretching knotted muscle. He'd had to race to stay ahead of the weather and felt every rough mile bone deep. If God were merciful, a hot meal, a warm fire, and a clean bed waited within. He scanned the yard for a stable hand.

The lane leading up to Aveline Castle was in clear view of both the stables and the main hall. It was inexcusable that no one waited to greet him, particularly as he'd sent word well ahead to expect him.

Several moments passed, yet no one appeared.

"Damnation," Derick grumbled, turning up his collar against the chilly wind. The clime this far north had yet to recover from last summer's unimaginable cold, and with dusk fast on Derick's heels, there was little sun left for warmth. He'd only managed to beat the coming storm by minutes, he guessed. He led his horse to the deserted stable, secured the mount, and promised the animal he'd send a groom straightaway to brush him down.

Derick strode along the north side of the fifteenth-century castle, his gait far from the languid, leisurely manner he usually affected. He would slip into his ne'er-do-well persona once there was someone about who might observe him.

He climbed the front steps two at a time. When he reached the stoop, he found the massive door half-open. Had the staff lost all discipline since his mother had died? The place was drafty enough without them carelessly leaving the door unlatched. He pushed it wide, the ancient carved English oak giving way with a groan.

No candlelight greeted him. Indeed, it was as if the place were deserted. Derick frowned, his steps echoing as he walked into the stone foyer. The hairs on the back of his neck rose. His trunks, which had been sent ahead and should have long been unpacked, sat stacked at the base of the grand staircase. No fire burned in the grate. No lamps had been lit.

Where the devil was everyone?

"—take this area, from the bend in the creek to the waterfall—"

A female voice, full of authority, drifted to him from the back of the house.

Curious, Derick started in that direction.

"—and Thomas, you and John Coachman take from here to Felman's Hill."

Derick furrowed his brow. There was something eerily familiar about that voice, which was ridiculous given the only woman he'd known in Derbyshire was his mother, and she'd been dead two years. As he turned into the long hallway leading toward the kitchen, light spilled from the dining hall and a low murmuring of voices reached his ears.

He slipped unnoticed into the room, melting into the shadows along the far wall. It wasn't even a challenge, as no one paid him a bit of mind. His eyes took in the whole room at once, a skill honed through years in the espionage game.

A dozen and a half people of mixed age and company hovered around the table—all servants from their dress. Aveline Castle only employed a skeleton staff now that his mother was gone. So who were all these people whispering quietly, their faces grim?

The room smelled crisp, filled with the tang of the outdoors carried in on the clothing of people. And indeed, most of the room's inhabitants were dressed for the elements, garbed in coats and hats or scarves. Several noses were red, as if they'd been long out in the wind, and many boots were dirty, covered with mud.

The group seemed to be waiting for something or someone. Derick shifted more into the corner until he found a break in the wall of people large enough to see through.

Ah, the source of the mysterious voice, he'd wager. The woman stood at the head of the table, but he could not see her face, as she was leaning over a large square of paper that was rolled out across the polished mahogany. Her position made it difficult to gauge her height as well, but there was no mistaking the ample curves her simple muslin dress couldn't hide.

Her well-tailored frock was a vibrant green, the dye not faded as a castoff would be. A lady of quality, then. One slender hand braced her as she marked furiously upon the paper. The tilt of her head and the way she held herself in determined focus niggled at his memory. Derick tried to place her, but locks of chestnut hair had slipped her coiffure, obscuring even her profile from him.

He turned his attention to the paper and squinted in the low light. That looked suspiciously like— A discarded frame propped up against the wall caught his attention then. His eyes snapped back to the table, to the blotchy-inked areas the mystery woman was currently drawing lines through.

She was scribbling all over an irreplaceable Burnett map of the countryside that his grandfather had commissioned over a half century ago.

He should have been appalled. But Derick had long ago shed any care for the trappings of the viscountcy. Instead he eyed the scene with detached curiosity, angling for the best way to use it to his purposes. *Hmmm.* Outrage would be precisely what people would expect of the pampered aristocrat persona he typically used for these missions. And Little Miss Map Despoiler had given him the perfect opening. All he had to do was take to the stage she'd inadvertently set for him.

"What the devil are you doing?" he barked as he pushed off from the wall. His exclamation had the desired effect. A chorus of gasps registered, but Derick ignored them as he reached the head of the table in three long strides and snatched the priceless map from atop it.

He rolled the map with deceptive casualness, the dry paper making a hissing sound against his palms in the now otherwise silent room. He raised a brow and injected a supercilious tone into his voice as he turned to the woman standing frozen before him.

"Do you mind telling me just who you are"—his gaze traveled up her body in an intentionally arrogant perusal—"and why you are vandalizing *my* property?"

The last word caught in his throat as his eyes finally reached hers.

A flash of memory came, of a scrawny blond pest who'd trailed behind him every summer like an unwanted hound, a little hoyden with unforgettably wide amber eyes.

No longer a blonde, he noted.

And no longer a girl, his baser side chimed in. Derick pressed his lips together, hard. Damnation. The neighbor girl, Miss Wallingford.

Anna? Ella? No, *Emma.* Derick was surprised he recalled her Christian name. He'd always just called her Pygmy. She'd hated the nickname, thinking he poked fun at her tiny stature. There *was* that, but he'd really given her the moniker because her golden eyes and tenacious nature had reminded him of the pygmy owlets who hunted these hills at twilight.

She was apparently still a pest—and one who was already interfering with his plans, even if she couldn't possibly know it.

Miss Wallingford's wide gaze narrowed, and her mouth flattened in what was certainly pique.

Derick waited for her answer, tapping the rolled-up map against the highly polished mahogany tabletop in feigned irritation.

Well, mostly feigned. This wasn't quite the foot he'd hoped to get off on with Miss Wallingford. As sister of the local magistrate, she could prove integral to his mission. He'd intended to call on her at her home, play on their childhood friendship—if one could call it that—to gain better access to her brother. Not snap her head off in front of a room full of witnesses.

But what was done was done. Derick had learned long ago that the key to a good deception was to always go on as one had begun. He'd brazen through, play his part, and find a way to sweeten Miss Wallingford later.

Emma Wallingford had never felt so riveted to one spot in her entire life. It was as if she were carved out of marble, much like the statues of the Greek scholars she'd so admired on her only trip to London. *Move Emma, you ninny!*

What was this abominable awareness? It was only Derick. Her stomach fluttered and Emma amended that thought. Yes, it was Derick, but he was also . . . *more.* His hair was still black as night, thick and unruly, yet the lines of his face were more angular now, more chiseled. His shoulders seemed wider, his hips more narrow. His eyes hadn't changed, though. They still glittered like fiery emeralds and still gazed at her as if she were the bane of his existence, sent by Hades himself with the express purpose of bedeviling him.

"My—my Lord." Billingsly, Aveline Castle's aged butler, brushed past her, his stooped form cutting through her line of sight, rescuing her from Derick's hard green gaze. Emma dropped her eyes to the floor, grateful for the moment to collect herself as the chaos of stammered excuses erupted around her.

His arrival shouldn't be such a shock to her—the entire village knew he was due today. Only she hadn't intended to come anywhere near Aveline Castle while he was in residence, but then Billingsly's note had arrived and—

Emma gasped. How could she have forgotten?

Taking advantage of the continued distraction, she stepped forward and plucked the map from Derick's oosened grasp, berating herself for her loss of focus. She spread it out on the table and resumed drawing the border she'd started. With dusk coming, time had become critical.

The voices around her stilled abruptly, and Emma swore she could feel Derick's gaze boring into her more surely than Archimedes' famed screw. Which was impossible, of course, as a mere gaze had no actual physical properties.

She didn't look up from her task as she said, "I'm certain Lord Scarsdale will agree that explanations can wait until *after* we find his missing upstairs maid."

Crack!

The sharp, sizzling pop of lightning served as harsh punctuation to her pronouncement. A low rumble of thunder followed quickly behind. Emma glanced over her shoulder at the window in time to see the first fat drops of a summer storm splash against the panes. *Fig.* If Molly were outside and injured . . . Emma mentally kicked herself for the bit of time she'd squandered mooning over a man who obviously didn't even remember her. She returned her eyes to the table and scanned the map again.

"My missing upstairs maid?" Derick repeated, sounding dubious.

"Yes." Without raising her gaze to him, Emma held up a hand to forestall any more questions. She ran her finger over the map. If her calculations were correct, the only feasible place Molly could be that they hadn't already searched was this area to the east of—

"*Miss* Wallingford," Derick growled in a voice that demanded her attention.

So he did remember her.

"As these are *my* resources you seem to be marshaling," he said, "I expect an explanation."

She looked up at him then, annoyed. Had he just referred to his staff, and some of hers for that matter, as *his resources*? Emma narrowed her eyes, considering the possible ramifications of ignoring him completely. She had more important things to do than appease his "lord of the manor" sensibilities, particularly when this lord hadn't bothered to grace this manor with his presence in more than a dozen years.

But Derick had risen to his full formidable height, taller even than she remembered. His glittering eyes had taken on a look of arrogant command. Emma gritted her teeth.

"Molly Simms," she explained. "The gardener's daughter. No one's seen her since she retired last evening."

His shoulder rose in a half shrug. "That's not even twenty-four hours," he said. "I'd hardly consider that *missing*."

Emma pursed her lips. What did he know of anything? "Well, the rest of us disagree," she said. "We feel Molly did not leave of her own volition, and fear her situation may be dire."

She'd given him as much of an explanation as he was going to get. Emma dismissed him and returned her gaze to the map.

"Yes, but *why* do you disagree?" he asked, plopping his hand down in the center of the map to block her view. "Do people in this village routinely find themselves in dire circumstances? Have you had a rash of dastardly events?"

Emma pinched the bridge of her nose. The Derick she remembered hadn't been so tiresome. But then, she'd only known the boy. He'd been seventeen when she'd seen him last, a whole lifetime of changes ago.

"Of course not," she said. Being situated at the south end of the Peak District, they'd had a bit more crime than perhaps was normal due to the number of strangers that passed through. Even a few suspicious deaths but nothing like that for at least two years.

"Were there signs of a struggle?" he persisted.

"No," Emma admitted.

"And yet you suspect foul play ..." Derick lifted his hand and crossed his arms with a slow negligence that set her teeth on edge. "The girl is young. She's probably visiting with a . . . *friend* and has lost track of the time."

The tips of Emma's ears burned with indignation.

"Or perhaps she eloped with the lucky git," he offered.

Emma nearly gasped at his cheek. Could Derick truly have become such an insensitive boor? A lifetime of changes or not, people didn't usually transform into someone completely unrecognizable.

Regardless, she'd heard enough. She raised herself to her full five feet two inches, which unfortunately only put her at his chest. Her cheeks warmed as she remembered that horrid nickname he used to call her as a child. Still, she gave Derick her fiercest glare. He was *going* to take her seriously and get out of her way, so help her.

"I suppose that in the realm of possibilities, these are all reasonable questions. However, if I may point out"—she emphasized the point with a poke of her finger right to his breastbone—"that you don't know Molly from Eve. You can credit those of us who do for having considered all likely scenarios and having exhausted them."

Another rolling boom of thunder sounded, ever closer. A quick glance confirmed that the sunlight was fading fast.

She turned her gaze back to Derick and narrowed it on him. "Molly is out there, somewhere, and the more time we waste chatting about it, the less chance we have of finding her before dark."

Derick regarded her. He still looked as though he doubted her conclusions, but gone was the arrogant tilt to his nose, the pinched lines around his mouth, the bored ease of his stance. "I su—"

"She t'weren't anywhere, Miss Emma." Two footmen came through the door then, cutting off whatever Derick had been about to say. The taller one spoke for them. "We searched the whole spot ye told us."

Emma grimaced. The men stood in the doorway, taking great gulps of air and wiping moisture from their faces. Her frown deepened at their rain-sodden coats.

She waved them toward the kitchen, not caring if Derick took issue with her directing *his resources*. "Thank you. Go on and get a hot drink, then hurry right back. We'll need you both as soon as you're able."

She turned back to the map, bracing herself on the table with her left hand and using her right to draw lines through the section the men had been assigned—another search area combed through without success. Emma scanned the darkening sky through the window, mentally calculating how much daylight remained. She factored in how much area a man could cover on foot in that time, divided by the number of servants available.

Rain pelted the glass in an ever-increasing tattoo.

She'd better account for that variable in her time estimations. She was doing just that when a large bronzed hand planted itself to the outside of her smaller pale one. Emma sucked in a breath, startled by the long, blunt-tipped fingers, the knuckles and skin dusted with a hint of black hair. Her entire body warmed as Derick leaned over her back to see what she was doing.

"You're mapping search areas," he said, his voice sliding past her right ear in a hot breath.

"Y-yes," Emma answered, damning herself for the catch in her throat. What in the heavens was wrong with—

She shuddered as the inside of his jacketed arm brushed the outside of her pelisse. His right hand reached out to run a finger down the eastern border she'd recently traced, and she almost swore she could feel the light touch as if it were she he stroked rather than the vellum.

"And this unshaded portion is what you have left to search?"

Emma gave a jerky nod. "Those two footmen just finished searching here." She pointed to a marked area to the northeast, abashed to see her finger tremble just a bit. "Since their greatcoats were soaked, I can only assume it's been pouring east of here for some time, which you may remember—"

"Is prone to sudden flooding," Derick said. He straightened, pulling away from her so quickly that gooseflesh prickled her skin at the sudden absence of his heat. "Don't let me interrupt further, then."

She nodded, relieved, but whether more from the fact that he'd capitulated or that he'd moved away from her she wasn't certain. At least he would no longer interfere. Emma quickly divvied up the eastern boundary into manageable sections.

"Right." She addressed the tired servants, her middle tightening with unease. "We haven't daylight left to search the remaining area in pairs," she said, suppressing her discomfort as she always did—with action. "We'll all have to take our own section."

As each man or woman came forward, Emma assigned them a small, defined boundary until only she, Billingsly, and Derick remained in the room.

"Billingsly." Emma motioned the butler to follow as she exited the dining hall and made her way toward the front entrance. The old servant was too frail to be out searching in the rain, but she knew he'd want to be useful. "As the searchers return, you and Cook do what you can to get them warmed, dry, and fed. God forbid we need to continue the search tomorrow," she muttered, shoving her arms into a coat and struggling to pull it on.

The coat lifted from her shoulders, as if by unseen hands, before the heavy wool settled around her. She whirled around in surprise, her elbow coming into solid contact with a hard wall—

"Ooof," Derick grunted, his black brows dipping as he winced.

—of abdomen, as it were.

"Oh! Oh, pardon me . . . ," Emma mumbled, though truthfully she didn't regret the accidental jab. But how had he appeared behind her? She looked down at his heavy black boots. Certainly she should have heard a man of his size clomping down the hall after her.

Derick rubbed at the spot where Emma's elbow had

speared him. The spot she'd poked on his chest still smarted, too. She was quite strong for such a compact little thing. And as bright as he remembered, given what he'd seen of her tactical mind, even if she were overreacting. Emma always had been one to take things too seriously and infect those around her with her imaginings. He guessed she was making a mountain out of the proverbial molehill.

She was also adept at giving orders and accustomed to being obeyed. Oh yes, little Pygmy had grown into just the kind of woman he'd thought she would.

Emma turned her back on him—again. Derick shook his head as he watched her struggle with the heavy oak door.

She still had more intelligence than common sense, however, since she was apparently planning to run out into a dangerous storm alone.

He reached around her and grasped the handle, stopping the door from opening. "You neglected to give *me* an assignment."

Emma turned, effectively caged by his arm and the door at her back. Those large amber eyes widened as he loomed over her. Which heightened his own awareness of how close his body was to hers, nearly touching. How fragile she seemed . . . how diminutive, and yet he'd already been the recipient of her tart tongue and sharp appendages. Besides, he knew her to be tough. As a girl, Emma had always kept up with him, no matter how he'd tried to lose her.

As if to demonstrate that her stubbornness still remained, Emma lifted her chin in challenge. "I hadn't thought you would—"

"Wish to help?" Derick returned her challenge, raising a brow. Damn. Her assumption irked. And the fact that he'd been stung by it irked more. He'd long grown accustomed to not caring what anyone thought. "Feel responsible for a member of my household?"

Emma blinked. "Your household?" she sputtered. "You haven't been to Derbyshire in fourteen—"

"No, but I *am* human, Miss Wallingford." Derick stepped closer, bringing his other arm around and planting it on the door behind her, trapping her. Only so that she would listen to him, of course. Not at all because of her tantalizing scent, a heady mix of lavender and ... something he couldn't quite place. "I may not agree with your assumptions, but it is clear you strongly believe the maid is in danger. If there is a chance you are correct, I would like to do what I can."

A huff of exasperation escaped her lips, a gesture Derick took to mean she didn't think too highly of him or his offer. He allowed a half-cynical smile to curve his lips. What did he care if Miss Emma Wallingford disapproved of one of his many alter egos? It wasn't *him*, after all.

Besides, he doubted she'd like him any better if she knew his *true* purpose in Derbyshire.

To investigate her brother for treason.

Ashley March

Romancing the Countess

Sebastian Madinger, the Earl of Wriothesly, thought he'd married the perfect woman—until a fatal accident revealed her betrayal with his best friend. After their deaths, Sebastian is determined to avoid a scandal for the sake of his son. But his best friend's widow is just as determined to cast her mourning veil aside by hosting a party that will surely destroy both their reputations and expose all of his carefully kept secrets...

Leah George has carried the painful knowledge of her husband affair for almost a year. All she wants now is to enjoy her independence and make a new life for herself—even if that means being ostracized by the Society whose rules she was raised to obey. Now that the rumors are flying, there's only one thing left for Sebastian to do: silence the scandal by enticing the improper widow into becoming a proper wife. But when it comes to matters of the heart, neither Sebastian nor Leah is prepared for the passion they discover in each other's arms....

"A glorious new voice in romance."
—Elizabeth Hoyt